Later, when Connor tried to pu he would say it felt as if the air ..... gone out of the room.

Blinding pain struck his temples, as if an iron pick had been shoved through his eye, and he fell to his knees, clutching his head. Dimly, he was aware of groans and cries, and of thudding noises that suggested at least some of the men at the Council table had fallen to the floor.

Connor struggled for breath. His heart pounded, its beat deafening. The air had become thick as nectar, making it difficult for his chest to rise and fall. It felt as if everything around him shifted. He curled into a ball, shielding himself with his arms, prepared for tremors that would send glass and statuary crashing from the shelves around the room, but there was only silence. Nothing fell. After a moment, the pain receded, and Connor warily stretched out, climbing to his feet.

"My lords, are you injured?" Connor, much younger than the others at the Council table, ran toward where the men slumped in their chairs. Radenou had been thrown to the floor, as had Merrill. They were surrounded by their stewards, who helped them to their seats.

"What in the realms of the gods was that?" Radenou's voice was angry, but beneath the rage, Connor heard fear.

"The magic," Merrill said, and his voice was not quite steady. "For a moment, it disappeared."

BOOKS BY GAIL Z. MARTIN

ICE FORGED

BOOK ONE OF THE ASCENDANT KINGDOMS SAGA

GAIL Z. MARTIN

www.orbitbooks.net

Orbit
Hachette Book Group
1290 Avenue of the Americas, New York, NY 10104
www.HachetteBookGroup.com

First Edition: January 2013

Orbit is an imprint of Hachette Book Group, Inc. The Orbit name and logo are trademarks of Little, Brown Book Group Limited.

The Hachette Speakers Bureau provides a wide range of authors for speaking events. To find out more, go to www.hachettespeakersbureau.com or call (866) 376-6591.

The publisher is not responsible for websites (or their content) that are not owned by the publisher.

The characters and events in this book are fictitious. Any similarity to real persons, living or dead, is coincidental and not intended by the author.

Library of Congress Cataloging-in-Publication Data
Martin, Gail.
    Ice forged / Gail Z. Martin. — 1st ed.
        p. cm. — (Ascendant Kingdoms saga ; bk. 1)
    ISBN 978-0-316-09358-3
    1. Penal colonies—Fiction.   I. Title.
    PS3613.A77865I27 2013
    813'.6—dc23
                                                    2012016167

10 9 8 7 6 5 4 3

RRD-C

Printed in the United States of America

Thanks first of all to my husband, Larry, and my children Kyrie, Chandler, and Cody, who are (very) patient about living with a writer. Thanks also to my con and Rennie friends, who ease the stress of travel, to my Meetup group and social media friends who help keep me sorta sane, to John for being a great beta reader, and to all the wonderful bookstores, Renaissance festivals, and conventions that have welcomed me and my books. Thanks to the great folks at Orbit and to my agent, Ethan Ellenberg, for believing in me. And thanks especially to my readers, who make all this possible.

PROLOGUE

"THIS HAS TO END." BLAINE McFADDEN LOOKED at his sister Mari huddled in the bed, covers drawn up to her chin. She was sobbing hard enough that it nearly robbed her of breath and was leaning against Aunt Judith, who murmured consolations. Just sixteen, Mari looked small and lost. A vivid bruise marked one cheek. She struggled to hold her nightgown together where it had been ripped down the front.

"You're upsetting her more." Judith cast a reproving glance his way.

"I'm upsetting her? Father's the one to blame for this. That drunken son of a bitch..." Blaine's right hand opened and closed, itching for the pommel of his sword.

"Blaine..." Judith's voice warned him off.

"After what he did...you stand up for him?"

Judith McFadden Ainsworth raised her head to meet his gaze. She was a thin, handsome woman in her middle years; and when she dressed for court, it was still possible to see a glimpse of the beauty she had been in her youth. Tonight, she looked worn. "Of course not."

"I'm sick of his rages. Sick of being beaten when he's on one of his binges…"

Judith's lips quirked. "You've been too tall for him to beat for years now."

At twenty years old and a few inches over six feet tall, Blaine stood a hand's breadth taller than Lord McFadden. While he had his mother's dark chestnut hair, his blue eyes were a match in color and determination to his father's. Blaine had always been secretly pleased that while he resembled his father enough to avoid questions of paternity, in build and features he took after his mother's side of the family. Where his father was short and round, Blaine was tall and rangy. Ian McFadden's features had the smashed look of a brawler; Blaine's were more regular, and if not quite handsome, better than passable. He was honest enough to know that though he might not be the first man in a room to catch a lady's eye, he was pleasant enough in face and manner to attract the attention of at least one female by the end of the evening. The work he did around the manor and its lands had filled out his chest and arms. He was no longer the small, thin boy his father caned for the slightest infraction.

"He killed our mother when she got between him and me. He took his temper out on my hide until I was tall enough to fight back. He started beating Carr when I got too big to thrash. I had to put his horse down after he'd beaten it and broken its legs. Now this… it has to stop!"

"Blaine, please." Judith turned, and Blaine could see tears in her eyes. "Anything you do will only make it worse. I know my brother's tempers better than anyone." Absently, she stroked Mari's hair.

"By the gods… did he…" But the shamed look on Judith's face as she turned away answered Blaine's question.

"I'll kill that son of a bitch," Blaine muttered, turning away and sprinting down the hall.

"Blaine, don't. Blaine—"

He took the stairs at a run. Above the fireplace in the parlor hung two broadswords, weapons that had once belonged to his grandfather. Blaine snatched down the lowest broadsword. Its grip felt heavy and familiar in his hand.

"Master Blaine..." Edward followed him into the room. The elderly man was alarmed as his gaze fell from Blaine's face to the weapon in his hand. Edward had been Glenreith's seneschal for longer than Blaine had been alive. Edward: the expert manager, the budget master, and the family's secret-keeper.

"Where is he?"

"Who, m'lord?"

Blaine caught Edward by the arm and Edward shrank back from his gaze. "My whore-spawned father, that's who. Where is he?"

"Master Blaine, I beg you..."

"Where is he?"

"He headed for the gardens. He had his pipe with him."

Blaine headed for the manor's front entrance at a dead run. Judith was halfway down the stairs. "Blaine, think about this. Blaine—"

He flung open the door so hard that it crashed against the wall. Blaine ran down the manor's sweeping stone steps. A full moon lit the sloping lawn well enough for Blaine to make out the figure of a man in the distance, strolling down the carriage lane. The smell of his father's pipe smoke wafted back to him, as hated as the odor of camphor that always clung to Lord McFadden's clothing.

The older man turned at the sound of Blaine's running footsteps. "You bastard! You bloody bastard!" Blaine shouted.

Lord Ian McFadden's eyes narrowed as he saw the sword in Blaine's hand. Dropping his pipe, the man grabbed a rake that leaned against the stone fence edging the carriageway. He held its thick oak handle across his body like a staff. Lord McFadden might be well into his fifth decade, but in his youth he had been an officer in the king's army, where he had earned King Merrill's notice and his gratitude. "Go back inside, boy. Don't make me hurt you."

Blaine did not slow down or lower his sword. "Why? Why Mari? There's no shortage of court whores. Why Mari?"

Lord McFadden's face reddened. "Because I can. Now drop that sword if you know what's good for you."

Blaine's blood thundered in his ears. In the distance, he could hear Judith screaming his name.

"I guess this cur needs to be taught a lesson." Lord McFadden swung at Blaine with enough force to have shattered his skull if Blaine had not ducked the heavy rake. McFadden gave a roar and swung again, but Blaine lurched forward, taking the blow on his shoulder to get inside McFadden's guard. The broadsword sank hilt-deep into the man's chest, slicing through his waistcoat.

Lord McFadden's body shuddered, and he dropped the rake. He met Blaine's gaze, his eyes wide with surprise. "Didn't think you had it in you," he gasped.

Behind him, Blaine could hear footsteps pounding on the cobblestones; he heard panicked shouts and Judith's scream. Nothing mattered to him, nothing at all except for the ashen face of his father. Blood soaked Lord McFadden's clothing, and gobbets of it splashed Blaine's hand and shirt. He gasped for breath, his mouth working like a hooked fish out of water. Blaine let him slide from the sword, watched numbly as his father fell backward onto the carriageway in a spreading pool of blood.

"Master Blaine, what have you done?" Selden, the grounds-keeper, was the first to reach the scene. He gazed in horror at Lord McFadden, who lay twitching on the ground, breathing in labored, slow gasps.

Blaine's grip tightened on the sword in his hand. "Something someone should have done years ago."

A crowd of servants was gathering; Blaine could hear their whispers and the sound of their steps on the cobblestones. "Blaine! Blaine!" He barely recognized Judith's voice. Raw from screaming, choked with tears, his aunt must have gathered her skirts like a milkmaid to run from the house this quickly. "Let me through!"

Heaving for breath, Judith pushed past Selden and grabbed Blaine's left arm to steady herself. "Oh, by the gods, Blaine, what will become of us now?"

Lord McFadden wheezed painfully and went still.

Shock replaced numbness as the rage drained from Blaine's body. *It's actually over. He's finally dead.*

"Blaine, can you hear me?" Judith was shaking his left arm. Her tone had regained control, alarmed but no longer panicked.

"He swung first," Blaine replied distantly. "I don't think he realized, until the end, that I actually meant to do it."

"When the king hears—"

Blaine snapped back to himself and turned toward Judith. "Say nothing about Mari to anyone," he growled in a voice low enough that only she could hear. "I'll pay the consequences. But it's for naught if she's shamed. I've thrown my life away for nothing if she's dishonored." He dropped the bloody sword, gripping Judith by the forearm. "Swear to it."

Judith's eyes were wide, but Blaine could see she was calm. "I swear."

Selden and several of the other servants moved around them, giving Blaine a wary glance as they bent to carry Lord McFadden's body back to the manor.

"The king will find out. He'll take your title...Oh, Blaine, you'll hang for this."

Blaine swallowed hard. A knot of fear tightened in his stomach as he stared at the blood on his hand and the darkening stain on the cobblestones. *Better to die avenged than crouch like a beaten dog.* He met Judith's eyes and a wave of cold resignation washed over him.

"He won't hurt Mari or Carr again. Ever. Carr will inherit when he's old enough. Odds are the king will name you guardian until then. Nothing will change—"

"Except that you'll hang for murder," Judith said miserably.

"Yes," Blaine replied, folding his aunt against his chest as she sobbed. "Except for that."

"You have been charged with murder. Murder of a lord, and murder of your own father." King Merrill's voice thundered through the judgment hall. "How do you plead?" A muted buzz of whispered conversation hummed from the packed audience in the galleries. Blaine McFadden knelt where the guards had forced him down, shackled at the wrists and ankles, his long brown hair hanging loose around his face. Unshaven and filthy from more than a week in the king's dungeon, he lifted his head to look at the king defiantly.

"Guilty as charged, Your Majesty. He was a murdering son of a bitch—"

"Silence!"

The guard at Blaine's right shoulder cuffed him hard. Blaine straightened, and lifted his head once more. *I'm not sorry and I'll be damned if I'll apologize, even to the king. Let's get this over with.* He avoided the curious stares of the courtiers and nobles in the gallery, those for whom death and punishment were nothing more than gossip and entertainment.

Only two faces caught his eye. Judith sat stiffly, her face unreadable although her eyes glinted angrily. Beside her sat Carensa, daughter of the Earl of Rhystorp. He and Carensa had been betrothed to wed later that spring. Carensa was dressed in mourning clothes; her face was ashen and her eyes were red-rimmed. Blaine could not meet her gaze. Of all that his actions cost him—title, lands, fortune, and life—losing Carensa was the only loss that mattered.

The king turned his attention back to Blaine. "The penalty for common murder is hanging. For killing a noble—not to mention your own father—the penalty is beheading."

A gasp went up from the crowd. Carensa swayed in her seat as if she might faint, and Judith reached out to steady her.

"Lord Ian McFadden was a loyal member of my Council. I valued his presence beside me whether we rode to war or in the hunt." The king's voice dropped, and Blaine doubted that few aside from the guards could hear his next words. "Yet I was not blind to his faults.

"For that reason," the king said, raising his voice once more, "I will show mercy."

It seemed as if the entire crowd held its breath. Blaine steeled himself, willing his expression to show nothing of his fear.

"Blaine McFadden, I strip from you the title of Lord of Glenreith, and give that title in trust to your brother, Carr, when he reaches his majority. Your lands and your holdings are likewise no longer your own. For your crime, I sentence you to transportation to the penal colony on Velant, where you will live out the rest of your days. So be it."

The king rose and swept from the room in a blur of crimson and ermine, followed by a brace of guards. A stunned silence hung over the crowd, broken only by Carensa's sobbing. As the guards wrestled Blaine to his feet, he dared to look back. Judith's face was drawn and her eyes held a hopelessness that made Blaine wince. Carensa's face was buried in her hands, and although Judith placed an arm around her, Carensa would not be comforted.

The soldiers shoved him hard enough that he stumbled, and the gallery crowd awoke from its momentary silence. Jeers and catcalls followed him until the huge mahogany doors of the judgment chamber slammed shut.

Blaine sat on the floor of his cell, head back and eyes closed. Not too far away, he heard the squeal of a rat. His cell had a small barred window too high for him to peer out, barely enough to allow for a dim shaft of light to enter. The floor was covered with filthy straw. The far corner of the room had a small drain for him to relieve himself. Like the rest of the dungeon, it stank. Near the iron-bound door was a bucket of brackish water and an empty tin tray that had held a heel of stale bread and chunk of spoiled cheese.

For lesser crimes, noble-born prisoners were accorded the dignity of confinement in one of the rooms in the tower, away from the filth of the dungeon and its common criminals. Blaine guessed that his crime had caused scandal enough that Merrill felt the need to make an example, after the leniency of Blaine's sentencing.

I'd much prefer death to banishment. If the executioner's blade is sharp, it would be over in a moment. I've heard tales of Velant. A frozen wasteland at the top of the world. Guards that are the dregs of His Majesty's service, sent to Velant because no one else will have them. Forced labor in the mines, or the chance to drown on board one of the fishing boats. How long will it take to die there? Will I freeze in my sleep or starve, or will one of my fellow inmates do me a real mercy and slip a shiv between my ribs?

The clatter of the key in the heavy iron lock made Blaine open his eyes, though he did not stir from where he sat. *Are the guards come early to take me to the ship? I didn't think we sailed until tomorrow.* Another, darker possibility occurred to him. *Perhaps Merrill's "mercy" was for show. If the guards were to take me to the wharves by night, who would ever know if I didn't make it onto the ship? Merrill would be blameless, and no one would be the wiser.* Blaine let out a long breath. *Let it come. I did what I had to do.*

The door squealed on its hinges to frame a guard whose broad shoulders barely fit between the doorposts. To Blaine's astonishment, the guard did not move to come into the room. "I can only give you a few minutes. Even for another coin, I don't dare do more. Say what you must and leave."

The guard stood back, and a hooded figure in a gray cloak rushed into the room. Edward, Glenreith's seneschal, entered behind the figure, but stayed just inside the doorway, shaking his head to prevent Blaine from saying anything. The hooded visitor slipped across the small cell to kneel beside Blaine. The hood fell back, revealing Carensa's face.

"How did you get in?" Blaine whispered. "You shouldn't have come. Bad enough that I've shamed you—"

Carensa grasped him by the shoulders and kissed him hard on the lips. He could taste the salt of her tears. She let go, moving away just far enough that he got a good look at her face.

Her eyes were red and puffy, with dark circles. Though barely twenty summers old, she looked careworn and haggard. She was a shadow of the vibrant, glowing girl who had led all the young men at court on a merry chase before accepting Blaine's proposal, as everyone knew she had intended all along.

"Oh, Blaine," she whispered. "Your father deserved what he got. I don't know what he did to push you this far." Her voice caught.

"Carensa," Blaine said softly, savoring the sound of her name, knowing it was the last time they would be together. "It'll be worse for you if someone finds you here."

Carensa straightened her shoulders and swallowed back her tears. "I bribed the guards. But I had to come."

Blaine shifted, trying to minimize the noise as his heavy wrist shackles clinked with the movement. He took her hand in both of his. "Forget me. I release you. No one ever comes back from Velant. Give me the comfort of knowing that you'll find someone else who'll take good care of you."

"And will you forget me?" She lifted her chin, and her blue eyes sparked in challenge.

Blaine looked down. "No. But I'm a dead man. If the voyage doesn't kill me, the winter will. Say a prayer to the gods for me and light a candle for my soul. Please, Carensa, just because I'm going to die doesn't mean that you can't live."

Carensa's long red hair veiled her face as she looked down, trying to collect herself. "I can't promise that, Blaine. Please, don't make me. Not now. Maybe not ever." She looked up again. "I'll be there at the wharf when your ship leaves. You may not see me, but I'll be there."

Blaine reached up to stroke her cheek. "Save your reputation. Renounce me. I won't mind."

Carensa's eyes took on a determined glint. "As if no one

knew we were betrothed? As if the whole court didn't guess that we were lovers? No, the only thing I'm sorry about is that we didn't make a handfasting before the guards took you. I don't regret a single thing, Blaine McFadden. I love you and I always will."

Blaine squeezed his eyes shut, willing himself to maintain control. He pulled her gently to him for another kiss, long and lingering, in lieu of everything he could not find the words to say.

The footsteps of the guard in the doorway made Carensa draw back and pull up her hood. She gave his hand one last squeeze and then walked to the door. She looked back, just for a moment, but neither one of them spoke. She followed the guard out the door.

Edward paused, and sadly shook his head. "Gods be with you, Master Blaine. I'll pray that your ship sails safely."

"Pray it sinks, Edward. If you ever cared at all for me, pray it sinks."

Edward nodded. "As you wish, Master Blaine." He turned and followed Carensa, leaving the guard to pull the door shut behind them.

"Get on your feet. Time to go."

The guard's voice woke Blaine from uneasy sleep. He staggered to his feet, hobbled by the ankle chains, and managed to make it to the door without falling. Outside, it was barely dawn. Several hundred men and a few dozen women, all shackled at the wrists and ankles, stood nervously as the guards rounded up the group for the walk to the wharves where the transport ship waited.

Early as it was, jeers greeted them as they stumbled down the narrow lanes. Blaine was glad to be in the center of the group.

More than once, women in the upper floors of the hard-used buildings that crowded the twisting streets laughed as they poured out their chamber pots on the prisoners below. Young boys pelted them from the alleyways with rotting produce. Once in a while, the boys' aim went astray, hitting a guard, who gave chase for a block or two, shouting curses.

Blaine knew that the distance from the castle to the wharves was less than a mile, but the walk seemed to take forever. He kept his head down, intent on trying to walk without stumbling as the manacles bit into his ankles and the short chain hobbled his stride. They walked five abreast with guards every few rows, shoulder to shoulder.

"There it is—your new home for the next forty days," one of the guards announced as they reached the end of the street at the waterfront. A large carrack sat in the harbor with sails furled. In groups of ten, the prisoners queued up to be loaded into flat-bottomed rowboats and taken out to the waiting ship.

"Rather a dead man in Donderath's ocean than a slave on Velant's ice!" One of the prisoners in the front wrested free from the guard who was attempting to load him onto the boat. He twisted, needing only a few inches to gain his freedom, falling from the dock into the water where his heavy chains dragged him under.

"It's all the same to me whether you drown or get aboard the boat," shouted the captain of the guards, breaking the silence as the prisoners stared into the water where the man had disappeared. "If you're of a mind to do it, there'll be more food for the rest."

"Bloody bastard!" A big man threw his weight against the nearest guard, shoving him out of the way, and hurtled toward the captain. "Let's see how well you swim!" He bent over and butted the captain in the gut, and the momentum took them both over the side. The captain flailed, trying to keep his head above water while the prisoner's manacled hands closed around his neck, forcing him under. Two soldiers aboard the rowboat beat with their oars at the spot where the burly man had gone down. Four soldiers, cursing under their breath, jumped in after the captain.

After considerable splashing, the captain was hauled onto the deck, sputtering water and coughing. Two of the other soldiers had a grip on the big man by the shoulders, keeping his head above the water. One of the soldiers held a knife under the man's chin. The captain dragged himself to his feet and stood on the dock for a moment, looking down at them.

"What do we do with him, sir?"

The captain's expression hardened. "Give him gills, lad, to help him on his way."

The soldier's knife made a swift slash, cutting the big man's throat from ear to ear. Blood tinged the water crimson as the soldiers let go of the man's body, and it sank beneath the waves. When the soldiers had been dragged onto the deck, the captain glared at the prisoners.

"Any further disturbances and I'll see to it that you're all put on half rations for the duration." His smile was unpleasant. "And I assure you, full rations are little enough." He turned to his second in command. "Load the boats, and be quick about it."

The group fell silent as the guards prodded them into boats. From the other wharf, Blaine could hear women's voices and the muffled sobbing of children. He looked to the edge of the wharf crowded with women. Most had the look of scullery maids, with tattered dresses, and shawls pulled tight around their shoulders. A few wore the garish colors and low-cut gowns of seaport whores. They shouted a babble of names, calling to the men who crawled into the boats.

One figure stood apart from the others, near the end of the wharf. A gray cloak fluttered in the wind, and as Blaine watched, the hood fell back, freeing long red hair to tangle on the cold breeze. Carensa did not shout to him. She did not move at all, but he felt her gaze, as if she could pick him out of the crowded mass of prisoners. Not a word, not a gesture, just a mute witness to his banishment. Blaine never took his eyes off her as he stumbled into the boat, earning a cuff on the ear for his clumsiness from the guard. He twisted as far as he dared in his seat to keep her in sight as the boat rowed toward the transport ship.

When they reached the side of the *Cutlass*, rope ladders hung from its deck.

"Climb," ordered the soldier behind Blaine, giving him a poke in the ribs for good measure. A few of the prisoners lost their footing, screaming as they fell into the black water of the bay. The guards glanced at each other and shrugged. Blaine began to climb, and only the knowledge that Carensa would be witness to his suicide kept him from letting himself fall backward into the waves.

Shoved and prodded by the guards' batons, Blaine and the other prisoners shambled down the narrow steps into the hold of the ship. It stank of cabbage and bilgewater. Hammocks were strung side by side, three high, nearly floor to ceiling. A row of portholes, too small for a man to crawl through, provided the only light, save for the wooden ceiling grates that opened to the deck above. Some of the prisoners collapsed onto hammocks or sank to the floor in despair. Blaine shouldered his way to a porthole on the side facing the wharves. In the distance, he could see figures crowded there, though it was too far away to know whether Carensa was among them.

"How long you figure they'll stay?" a thin man asked as

Blaine stood on tiptoe to see out. The man had dirty blond hair that stuck out at angles like straw on a scarecrow.

"Until we set sail, I guess," Blaine answered.

"One of them yours?"

"Used to be," Blaine replied.

"I told my sister not to come, told her it wouldn't make it any easier on her," the thin man said. "Didn't want her to see me, chained like this." He sighed. "She came anyhow." He looked Blaine over from head to toe. "What'd they send you away for?"

Blaine turned so that the seeping new brand of an "M" on his forearm showed. "Murder. You?"`

The thin man shrugged. "I could say it was for singing off-key, or for the coins I pinched from the last inn where I played for my supper. But the truth is I slept with the wrong man's wife, and he accused me of stealing his silver." He gave a wan smile, exposing gapped teeth. "Verran Danning's my name. Petty thief and wandering minstrel. How 'bout you?"

Blaine looked back at the distant figures on the wharf. Stripped of his title, lands, and position, lost to Carensa, he felt as dead inside as if the executioner had done his work. *Blaine McFadden is dead*, he thought. "Mick," he replied. "Just call me Mick."

"I'll make you a deal, Mick. You watch my back, and I'll watch yours," Verran said with a sly grin. "I'll make sure you get more than your share of food, and as much of the grog as I can pinch. In return," he said, dropping his voice, "I'd like to count on some protection, to spare my so-called virtue, in case any of our bunkmates get too friendly." He held out a hand, manacles clinking. "Deal?"

With a sigh, Blaine forced himself to turn away from the porthole. He shook Verran's outstretched hand. "Deal."

Velant Penal Colony, Six Years Later

CHAPTER
ONE

"PUT YOUR BACKS INTO IT! WE NEED THOSE FISH."
Blaine bent forward, grabbed the rough rope net, and leaned back, working in time with the line of other men who helped to draw the catch on board. The fishing ship *Pathi* was a herring buss, a fat-bodied vessel good enough to weather the squalls of the Ecardine Sea but not well suited for escape.

"Good work. That'll keep the gibbers busy, I warrant." The overseer stood behind them, chuckling at the size of the catch. "Empty them onto the deck and get the nets out again. Move. Move."

"I'm frozen to the bones," groused the man next to Blaine. Broad-shouldered with muscular arms, the man had eyes as cold and blue as the sea.

"Would you rather be gibbing?" Blaine asked, with a nod toward the men who scrambled into position to cut the gills and gullet from the fish before salting them and packing them into the barrels that filled the *Pathi*'s hold.

"What's the difference? They're just as wet as we are," the man replied, shaking his oilcloth slicker to rid himself of some of the water that had doused them as the net came on board.

"I figure we're warmer dragging in nets than sitting still gutting fish—and we might be able to get the fish stink off us once we get back to port," Blaine replied. "C'mon, Piran, you know it's true. The last time we got stuck gibbing, I smelled like a herring for a month after I got off the boat."

Piran Rowse chuckled. "You're assuming that you don't actually smell like that all the time." Piran had the build and temperament of a fighter, with a muscular frame, a neck like an ox, and a head of thinning light-brown hair, which he preferred to keep shaved, even in the Edgeland cold. Both his face and his body carried the scars of too many fights for Piran to remember, although one jagged scar beneath his eye was a memento from a broken bottle in a bar brawl. His nose was flatter than it should have been and a little off-center, but his blue eyes could glint with merriment for good music and passable ale. Piran's broad smile had no trouble winning him female companionship, an effect Blaine likened to the appeal of a friendly, but ugly, stray dog.

From what little Blaine had been able to get out of his friend, Piran had been a mercenary, a onetime soldier, and a bodyguard. Which of those jobs had gone wrong enough to land him in Velant, Piran was cagey about saying. Blaine had met Piran three years ago, when they both were transferred from the miserable ruby mines to the equally miserable herring fleet. Since then, they had become fast friends.

A high wave splashed over the ship's side, dousing them. Blaine cursed, getting a face full of seawater. The oilcloth slicker, gloves, and pants could only afford so much protection against the cold northern sea. Even with thick woolen clothing beneath the oilcloth, there was no escaping a dampness that chilled to the bone. Blaine stamped his feet, wishing his heavy leather boots were more waterproof. "At least the catch is good today."

Piran grinned. "Good enough to earn us a full measure of grog tonight, I wager."

The ever-present smell of fish grew sharper as the gibbers did their work. Blaine and the others continued to haul the heavy nets in with their catch. Other men sealed the barrels of salted fish and carried them below. Shouting to be heard over the wind and the waves, the overseer called out directions and cursed those who moved too slowly.

"Think the catch is good enough to keep us through the winter?" Piran asked as they shouldered into the next haul.

"Don't know. Why?"

Piran glanced both ways over his shoulder before replying. "Just some of the talk I've heard among the guards. Said that the last couple supply ships weren't as full as usual."

Blaine grimaced, standing back as the net cleared the railing and the deck shuddered with the weight of the catch. "If that's the case, we'll be living on herring and turnips before the winter's through."

Piran made a sour face. "Not the first time I'll have done with tight rations, but I'd rather have my belly full while I freeze."

A good day's catch meant backbreaking work. This far north, the sun never completely set, making the six-month "white nights" season the time when convicts and guards alike pitched in to provision the colony for the half year of darkness to come. Blaine shivered. Even after six years, he hadn't grown accustomed to the long subarctic nights. Donderath, half a world away, had a temperate climate, with four seasons and a winter that, while sometimes harsh, was nothing like Velant's brutal cold and howling winds.

After a twelve-candlemark shift at the nets, the "night" haulers came clomping up from the bunk rooms below with their heavy boots, growling and cursing at the cold wind. Weary and numb with cold, Blaine and Piran lined up to go below. Since it never got dark, the buss could fish day and night, and by alternating crew, give the men slightly more room in the cramped quarters belowdecks.

In the cramped area of the hold set aside for crew, hammocks swung with the motion of the boat. It was cold enough that Blaine kept his oilskin coat on until the hold grew warm from the press of bodies. Piran had wandered off to find someone who was still willing to play him at cards or dice.

"Give it up, Piran. I've already lost two measures of grog and my ration of smoke weed to you," complained a raw-boned, red-haired man.

Wide-eyed with feigned innocence, but barely suppressing a grin, Piran turned to the man's companions and held out his hand with three dice on his open palm. They all groaned loudly. "Not since I lost my best socks to you, dammit," complained one of the men.

Piran's smile widened. "I haven't worn them yet. You might win them back."

Indecision clouded the man's face for a moment before he nodded. "All right. For the socks."

Blaine turned away, chuckling. The longer the boat was at sea, the larger the number of fishermen who realized that Piran was uncannily fortunate when it came to games of chance. His luck stopped just shy of being so good as to raise accusations of cheating, though Blaine had known Piran long enough to suspect that sleight of hand, not magic, helped his chances considerably. Blaine had not played his friend for anything more valuable than a few measures of snuff since they had been in the mines together. On occasion Piran let him win.

Later, when most of the men lay snoring in their hammocks,

Blaine awoke as the ship rose and then fell so sharply that he was nearly thrown from his bed.

"By the gods! A few more like that, and it'll send us all to Raka," Blaine muttered, hanging on to his hammock and hoping that his supper ration remained in his stomach despite the way the ship lurched and pitched.

"If Raka is warmer than Velant, I'll go willingly," Piran replied, holding fast to one of the support beams, but to Blaine's eye, Piran's face had taken on a green tint.

"Velant is where the gods send the men Raka turns away," said the red-haired man, who had given up trying to stay in his hammock and braced himself between the hull and the support post.

Water flooded down the stairs from the deck, and the hold erupted with curses. Bad as it was below, Blaine knew it was worse on deck. Storms arose swiftly on the Ecardine Sea, with gale-force winds and sleet that could cut skin. It was not unusual to lose three or four men overboard each trip due to storms. Blaine had no love for Velant, but the idea of dying in the cold northern waters, his body and soul forever prisoner to Yadin, god of the dark water, seemed an even worse alternative.

That fate had obviously occurred to some of their fellow fishermen, because Blaine heard voices muttering prayers to both major gods and household deities alike, begging safe passage. Then a loud laugh cut across the hold, and Blaine looked at Piran.

"Tell Yadin and his ice demons that he's better off with the herring than the likes of us. The herring have more meat on their bones," Piran said. "As for the other gods, while you're at it, see if they can magic up better grog. What we've got tastes like sheep piss."

The red-haired man scowled at Piran. "You mock the gods?"

Piran laughed again. "I can't mock what isn't real."

The red-haired man looked as if he might take a swing at Piran, but the boat rose and fell again, sending him sliding across the hold to land hard against the other hull. Piran looked up at the deck above them as if it were the sky. "Is that the best you can do?"

"Shut up, Piran," Blaine muttered.

Piran looked at him and raised an eyebrow. "When did you get devout?"

Blaine shook his head. "I'm not. But I'd rather not clean you up after our bunkmates are done kicking your sorry ass."

Piran grinned. Two missing teeth were testament to just how much he relished a good brawl. "Let them try."

The ship canted hard to starboard, and several men lost their grip, slamming across the hold. Above their heads, they heard a crack like thunder, and the shouts and screams of men.

"We've lost a mast," Blaine muttered.

Piran let go of his hold on the support post and gave Blaine a shove. "Get up the steps. Now!" All joking was gone from his face. In its place was a cold reckoning that Blaine guessed had gotten Piran through the wars he had survived, battles he would only talk about when drunk.

Lurching like drunkards, Blaine and Piran stumbled across the hold. A few of the others struggled to their feet, realizing that if the ship were to go over, their odds of surviving were far better on deck than below. Many of the men remained frozen where they were, clinging white-knuckled to their hammocks or to the posts, eyes closed and heads down, praying.

"Stay below!" a guard shouted as they reached the top of the stairs, and belatedly tried to shut the door against them. Piran and Blaine threw their weight against the door, sending the guard sprawling. When the man attempted to grab at Piran's legs, Piran kicked him away.

"Maybe the gods were listening," Blaine murmured as they reached the deck. The main mast of the buss had splintered, leaving only the mizzen standing. The deck was awash with seawater, and the fishermen and sailors alike had lashed themselves to the rails. Piran and Blaine managed to do the same, ducking to avoid the worst of another wave that broke over the bow. Blaine came up sputtering.

"We'll drown by inches at this rate," Piran said, holding tight as the ship pitched.

"Can you see any of the other ships?" The *Pathi* had been one of thirty ships in Velant's fleet of herring boats. When Blaine had been on deck before the storm, he had spotted many of the other ships spread out across the water.

"I can barely see my hand at the end of my own damn arm," Piran replied. "Clouds above, rain between, and the sea below. I can't see worth shit."

If we founder, would the other ships bother to look for survivors? Or would they just gather the herring barrels they could find and head back to port? On one hand, Velant wouldn't care if two dozen convicts drowned. But even Commander Prokief might count the loss of an experienced crew, given the colony's dependence on fish for both food and trade with Donderath. And while the fishermen aboard the *Pathi* were convicts, they had fished long enough to be valuable.

Gradually, the storm lost its fury. Blaine dragged himself to his feet, gripping the rail hard enough that he thought his fingers might make indentations in the wood. The deck smelled of vomit and seawater, and every man aboard the *Pathi* was ashen-faced.

"Stared Yadin in the face and spit in his eye, we did." Piran chuckled.

"Shut up, Piran." Blaine was sore all over. He had long ago grown used to the hard work of hauling in nets. Last night's battle with the sea had left him battered and numb with cold. Storm crests had broken across the deck with the force of body blows. Blaine's shoulders, knees, and elbows ached after bracing himself all night long. From how stiffly his shipmates moved, Blaine guessed that they felt much the same. Many men were bruised and bleeding where the waves had thrown them into the railings or slammed them against the deck. And yet, despite the worst the storm had to offer, they were still alive and afloat.

Captain Darden came around the ship's wheel, where he had lashed himself through the storm. His dark, heavy brows and full beard made his scowling face look as ominous as the thunderheads that had just cleared from the sky.

"Muster on deck! I need a head count."

In the end, only two of the *Pathi*'s crew were missing, and miraculously, the ship had taken no damage other than the loss of its main mast. That alone was enough to present problems. The *Pathi* had been at sea for four weeks, nearly at the end of its six-week voyage. They were at the edge of their range, far out from the coastline, and even farther from any other ports.

Blaine and the others waited as the captain took out his sun board and calculated their position. Captain Darden's expression braced Blaine for bad news even before the man spoke.

"The storm took us off course and farther out to sea than our usual fishing sites," Darden said. "If we're lucky, maybe one of our sister ships will find us and tow us back to port. If not—" He shrugged, but they did not need him to finish the sentence.

Far from home without their mast, the sea would finish what it started.

"It's his fault!" the red-haired man, Isdane, shouted. He pointed at Piran. "He mocked the gods. Mocked Yadin himself. Dared the Sea God to take us."

Piran's face was pure innocence. He spread his hands and shrugged. "Just a figure of speech."

Isdane launched himself at Piran, a massive bull at full charge. Piran was faster, and sidestepped the big man, narrowly eluding his grasp.

"Piran!" Blaine spotted two of Isdane's friends just as they bent to rush Piran. Blaine stepped up beside Piran as the crowded deck erupted in shouts. One of the men threw a punch that connected hard with Piran's jaw, but Piran returned a sharp jab that sent the man sprawling. Blaine intercepted the second man, landing his fist squarely in the center of the man's face, breaking his nose.

Before the fight could go further, strong hands seized Piran, Blaine, and Isdane and hauled them back. Captain Darden stepped in between Piran and Isdane.

"That's entirely enough." Darden fixed them with an icy glare. "We've got all the problems we need without this."

"But I heard him. He mocked the gods!"

Darden looked at Isdane wearily. "I suspect the Sea God has more sense than to take offense from the likes of Piran Rowse." He turned back to Blaine and Piran. "Get below, and stay there. Any more trouble and I'll have you whipped."

Blaine and Piran followed Isdane and his friends down the narrow stairs in silence. But when they reached the hold, Isdane started toward Piran again. "It's your fault we're going to die out here."

Blaine shouldered his way between the two men, and shoved

Isdane backward into his friends, hard enough to make them step back a pace. "Shut up, fool. Dying's not certain, but whipping is, and I've got a mind to hang on to my skin."

Isdane glared at Piran, and Blaine stood his ground between them, hands on hips. "We've got water enough for at least another week, and herring enough for the rest of our lives. There's no reason for the other ships not to come looking for us; Commander Prokief'll have their hides if they cost him a boat and a cargo of fish. He won't be satisfied unless they bring us back or show wreckage to prove we sank. And in the meantime, mark my words, Captain Darden will have us fishing. I've got no desire to haul in nets with a striped back, or to have a bath of seawater after a flogging."

Behind him, he heard Piran open his mouth to comment, and turned. "Your mouth started this. Drop it."

Blaine could feel the heat from both men's gaze, but he did not back down. Finally, Piran gave a creative curse and walked away. Isdane shot Piran a murderous look, then turned to his friends. "Let it go, boys. We can always jump the sorry son of a bitch when we get back to port."

Isdane and the others retreated to one side of the hold. Blaine found Piran leaning against one of the support poles that held their hammocks. "On the whole, that went rather well," Piran observed.

Blaine swung a punch that caught Piran on the side of his jaw.

Piran's eyes went wide. "Hey, what was that for?"

"You could have gotten both of us thrown overboard to appease Yadin."

"You don't believe in the gods."

"No," Blaine replied, "but sailors are as superstitious as they come, and if anyone other than Isdane starts thinking you're a *jyng,* the captain's likely to toss you over you just to keep the peace."

Piran's mouth set in a hard line, but he made no retort and Blaine relaxed. "Hey, it could be worse," Blaine said. "Darden could have decided to split you open and read your entrails for omens."

"Don't give him any ideas. He doesn't like me."

"I wonder why."

Piran fell silent for a moment. "Do you think we'll really die out here?"

Blaine shrugged. "Velant's a death sentence. The only real question is what . . . or who . . . carries it out."

Piran raised an eyebrow and looked at him. "You really don't care, do you?"

Blaine turned away, tugging at the knots of his hammock. "No, I really don't."

CHAPTER TWO

G ET ON YOUR FEET, YOU LAZY ASS. WE'RE BEING rescued." Piran rocked Blaine's hammock hard enough that he nearly fell to the floor. Blaine struggled to clear his head. "The captain spotted a couple of *ventjers* on the horizon this morning. They must have been looking for us." *Ventjers* were smaller boats sent out from Velant to offload the gibbed herring and resupply the herring busses. With the *ventjers*, the busses could remain at sea for weeks at a time before returning to port.

"A whole team of *ventjers* aren't going to be able to tow us back to port," Blaine replied.

"There are three more busses with them. I wager they'll figure out a way to get us back."

Blaine grimaced. "You'll wager just about anything, with anyone."

"Can't help it; I'm a betting man."

It took three days to make it back to Skalgerston Bay, Edgeland's main port. Since both the port city and the port itself shared the same name, colonists often referred to the village as Bay-town, though none of the maps reflected that name. Blaine stood on deck as the *Pathi* was towed in. Along the waterfront were a collection of low log buildings. Some were warehouses to store gibbed and fresh-caught fish on ice. A few were taverns and brothels for the sailors who found their way to Velant's gods-forsaken port. Skalgerston Bay had a short row of shops where soldiers and convicts could purchase crockery, farming tools, and a few other necessities and luxuries from Donderath.

Behind the buildings of Skalgerston Bay lay the rest of Edge-land, the island at the top of the world. Blaine had heard the rumors that a few hardy trappers had found more remote shores, even farther to the north, but it was difficult to imagine that anything could be farther from civilization. Most of Edge-land was miles-thick ice and jagged rocky peaks. A narrow fringe of stony soil bordered the sea. On that fringe, guards and convicts scratched out their survival in the prison colony.

From the deck, Blaine could see some of the homestead farms in the distance. Edgeland's poor soil could still yield potatoes, turnips, and carrots, along with a few bitter native fruits and enough rye, barley, and hops to fuel a profitable—and illegal—trade in home-brewed ale and strong whiskey. Small herds of sheep, goats, and dairy cows, along with chick-ens and pigs, all sent from Donderath, augmented the fish served at every meal. Prokief's warden-mages, when not using their magic to keep the convicts in line, used their power and the heat of Edgeland's underground hot springs to grow more succulent plants, specialties reserved for the commander and his chosen favorites.

Blaine hoisted his sack of clothing and personal items onto his back and lifted the small barrel of gibbed fish he and every other fisherman had earned as part of their pay for the fishing run. Piran was right behind him, juggling his own sack and barrel, as they made their way down the gangplank.

"Show your Tickets, if you have them," the guard said in a monotone as Blaine and Piran reached the bottom. Blaine dug his Ticket of Leave out of the oilskin pouch that he wore on a leather strap around his neck. New convicts in Velant were housed in the sprawling barracks inside the stockade, under the constant eye of Commander Prokief's motley soldiers. Those that survived three years in the harsh conditions could earn both a meager stipend for their labor and the coveted Ticket of Leave. For the male convicts, "surviving" meant living through time in the brutal labor gangs of the ruby and copper mines. For the female prisoners, it was enduring the attention of the guards and the backbreaking work of the laundry.

With a Ticket of Leave, a "seasoned" convict could live outside the stockade. Ticket-holders became colonists, able to engage in a trade, offer merchandise for sale, and go about their business. It was a cruel illusion of freedom. Every Ticket-bearer could lay claim to a three-acre homestead. The promise of the offer paled once the homesteader tried to plow the frozen, rocky ground. Those looking to earn coin could sign on with the herring fleet or find work with a trapper or merchant.

"Looking forward to getting home?" Piran asked as he and Blaine paid a coin to the wagon master who would take them out of Skalgerston Bay and out to the homesteads.

Blaine shrugged. "I'm looking forward to drying out, and eating something other than that godsdamned fish."

By the time they reached the homesteads, it should have been night, though the winter sun remained low on the horizon. At the first rise in the road, the plume of smoke coming from a cabin's chimney was visible.

"Home sweet home," Piran said, slapping Blaine on the back. They climbed down from the wagon, shouldering their barrels of fish and their sacks of clothing.

A tall, lanky man was splitting wood in front of the cabin. He stopped when he made out two figures headed his way, and weighed the ax in his hands until Blaine and Piran were close enough to recognize. Then he sank the ax into the stump he was using as a chopping block and grinned broadly.

"Mick! Piran! Welcome back!" Dawe Killick pushed a strand of dark hair out of his eyes. Killick had a hawk-like nose and piercing blue eyes. His long-fingered hands, now calloused from hard work in Velant, retained the nimbleness of his original craft of silversmithing. He smiled broadly as Blaine and Piran approached, and he welcomed them with a handshake and a slap on the back. "You brought fish?"

Blaine groaned. "Of course. And this time out, we nearly became fish food." He and Piran set down their barrels. "The stories can wait until we've had something to eat."

"Food should be ready inside. I'll help you move the barrels into the shed." He looked skeptically at Blaine. "Rough seas?"

"Happy to be back on dry land, that's for sure," Blaine replied. "Is everyone well?"

Killick opened his mouth to reply, but the door to the cabin burst open and a woman stood framed in the doorway. "Mick and Piran! Thank the gods you're home." A petite red-haired woman bounded down the stairs. Kestel Falke wore the same homespun woolen garb as most of the other Ticketed prisoners, but as Blaine saw her stride toward them, the sashay in her walk betrayed her former occupation as a sought-after courtesan. She had green eyes that sparkled with wit and humor, and a figure that stood out even under her nondescript woolen dress. At the moment, someone might think her pretty but unremarkable. Her cheek had a smudge of cinders and her face was flushed from the hot stove. Yet Blaine had seen Kestel when she bothered to dress up for one of the local festivals, and even with the rough clothing and homemade cosmetics available in Edgeland, she could transform herself into a head-turning beauty. He could only guess just how beautiful she had been at court, clad in silks and velvets and adorned with diamonds and gold from her wealthy paramours.

Kestel greeted both Blaine and Piran with hugs, then linked her arms through theirs and walked them into the cabin with Dawe behind them.

"Did you miss us?" Blaine teased.

Kestel tossed her hair with mock seductiveness. "Not in the least," she joked. "Dawe and Verran don't make as much mess as the two of you."

Blaine gave Kestel a good-natured squeeze. "Ah, but everyone thinks we're the luckiest four men in Edgeland, sharing a house with you."

Kestel leveled a half-joking glare his way. "Let them *assume* all they want. After all, a courtesan's reputation is her biggest asset."

Blaine gave her an exaggerated glance from head to toe. "I wouldn't exactly say that," he drawled, and she smacked him on the shoulder. "But I'm still in awe of how you managed to arrange this. Everyone assumes that the four of us are your paramours. Meanwhile we four luckless, loveless bastards suffer in silence without relief and you know we can't set the record straight without making a mockery of our manhood."

Kestel grinned. "Damned right. No one needs to know that I've 'retired' from the courtesan business. And there's nothing stopping any of you from meeting your needs with one of our fine convict wenches or the strumpets down in Bay-town."

"You're lucky your other courtly skills include cooking and spying."

Kestel snorted. "You're lucky I was willing to lay my virtue on the line with Prokief to get you your Ticket, or you'd still be in the mines."

Blaine planted a brotherly kiss on the top of her head. "Right you are on that one, luv. I'll owe you eternally."

"Yes, you will." She shuddered. "I slept with more disgusting men at court, but at least they were rich."

Blaine chuckled. When the five of them had earned their Tickets, Blaine had offered Kestel his protection, no strings attached. A place like Edgeland presented a different set of dangers than the royal court. Kestel's renown as a courtesan had made her especially vulnerable to Velant's guards, until two of the first to force themselves on her had mysteriously turned up dead. No one had been able to say just what had killed them, but the others took note. It was then Blaine realized that Kestel could name "assassin" among her talents, along with sex and intrigue, and that while she valued his friendship, she scarcely needed anyone's protection.

"Has anyone mentioned that you two carry on like an old married couple?" Piran laughed.

Kestel crinkled her nose in mock disgust. "You do. Frequently. So far, I've been willing to overlook it."

She paused at the bottom of the steps and made a shallow bow. Next to the entrance was a small shrine to Charrot, Donderath's high god. Both male and female, one head with two faces, Charrot embodied both creation and destruction. A small hutch housed a ceramic figure of the god, next to which sat a dozen smooth pebbles, the offering of those who wished a favor or protection. Beside Charrot were several small carved wooden figures, the household and family gods Kestel insisted they honor. Blaine noticed that Kestel had placed a figure of Yadin, god of the dark water, in the hutch to ask for protection for the fishing fleet. He shivered, recalling what a close thing that had been. Though Blaine usually left it to Kestel to appease the gods, this time he inclined his head in thanks as he entered the cabin.

By Donderath standards the cabin was primitive. By Velant standards, it was very comfortable. Blaine, Piran, Dawe, and Kestel had met as new convicts in the hated dormitories, along with Verran Danning, who had befriended Blaine on the ship to Velant. A bond born of hardship had endured, and when they earned their Tickets of Leave and their acres of land, they had decided to pool their resources by building a shared house.

"Take your coats off and have a seat. I've got a pot of cabbage and mutton on the stove," Kestel announced, though the aroma that filled the cabin already had Blaine's stomach growling. "Dawe and I got some bread baked yesterday on the chance you'd be along. Once you're fed and rested, you've got your choice of digging turnips or gutting and smoking the rabbits Dawe caught this morning."

"Where's Verran?" Blaine asked as he set his sack to the side and sat down at the rough-hewn table. Piran followed suit.

Kestel was ladling out generous portions of the stew into wooden bowls. She placed the bowls on the table in front of Blaine and Piran, followed by a hunk of bread. Dawe brought them each a wooden tankard full of home-brewed ale. "Verran's been playing his music in some of the taverns in Skalgerston Bay. He'll stay a few nights each week, and come home with coins in his pocket and some wine or ale for the house." She sighed and pulled up a chair on the other side of the table. "The money he's bringing in bought some new sheep and it's gone a ways toward making sure we've got food enough put up for the winter."

"I'm surprised you didn't go with him," Piran said, breaking off a hunk of the bread.

Kestel snorted. "I've got no desire to go back to the courtesan business, especially with the likes of what wanders into a Bay-town tavern."

Blaine and Piran exchanged mock-offended glances. "I think we've just been insulted," Blaine said.

"Of course you have," Dawe replied from where he leaned against the wall, arms crossed over his chest. "Did you forget how our Sour Rose loves to whittle you down to size?"

Blaine swallowed his stew. "It's Kestel's other profession I was thinking of, when Piran suggested going into the Bay. Hard to be much of a spy out here in the wilderness."

Kestel grinned. "Spying always paid far more than being a courtesan. And for that matter, who says I haven't been to town? It's just that Bay-town is a small place. I hear more when I wait a little while between visits. That way, my friends have a chance to miss me, and they can't wait to catch me up on the news," she said with a wink.

Blaine finished his food and leaned back in his chair. "And what news have you heard since we've been out to sea?"

"Plenty," Kestel said, leaning forward conspiratorially. "And I want to hear what you learned out on the boats. Nothing like cards and grog to loosen men's tongues. I'm hoping you've got some tales to tell of your own."

"You first," Blaine said with a grin.

Kestel's green eyes glittered as she looked from Blaine to Piran. "Word has it that Prokief's warden-mages aren't doing quite the job they used to do. According to my sources, there was an escape a few weeks back. Man went over the stockade and it took them a day to realize he was gone."

Blaine frowned. "That's unusual. The mages made it their business to know who sneezed."

"Prokief was plenty mad about it. But I always thought he was scared of his own mages. Hard to do much to someone who can magick you with boils or snap your bones with a thought."

"Anything else?"

Kestel nodded. "The supply ships from Donderath still haven't come."

Piran shrugged. "So? They're always late."

Kestel shook her head. "This time, it's over three months. One of the merchants was beside himself about it. After all, without goods to sell from Donderath, the shopkeepers in Baytown have little to offer that people can't make themselves."

"Had he heard anything about why the ships are late?" Piran asked.

"Everyone's got ideas. But in one of the taverns, I turned the head of Prokief's supply sergeant." She lifted her shoulder and batted her eyes. "The barkeeper kept the ale flowing and the sergeant was so thrilled to have my full attention that he had to show off how much he knew."

"And?" Blaine prodded.

"One of Prokief's lieutenants told him there was a letter on the last ship from General Olvarth. Donderath can't spare supply ships on the schedule they'd been coming. Said we might see three or four a year, instead of one each month."

"Why so few?" Piran asked, frowning in alarm. "I don't like the sound of that."

Kestel shrugged. "That sergeant didn't know. But one of the guards I danced with at another tavern told me he'd heard the war with Meroven was going badly."

Blaine and Piran exchanged glances. "Oh?" Blaine leaned forward.

"The war's pulled in the other two kingdoms, and from what I hear, it's a bloodbath no one knows how to end," Dawe said, kicking away from the wall. "I overheard a couple of soldiers down at the tavern. Said they're almost glad they're here in Velant, because they didn't like the look of things back home." His gaze was thoughtful as he looked away, trying to remember the conversation. "Food shortages. Conscription is so bad, there weren't enough men to work the last harvest." He shrugged. "That was the news they got with the last convict delivery and supply ship three months ago. Could be worse by now."

Blaine frowned and sat back, crossing his arms. "All because Meroven made a grab for some of Donderath's borderlands."

"So the 'official' story goes," Dawe replied. "Word has it that Meroven is equally convinced that King Merrill made a grab for *their* borderlands. But from what I've heard, Edgar of Meroven is insane; I'd put my money on him having made the first move. The two countries have been fighting over some of the same godsforsaken land for generations. Of course, the real reasons for the war aren't likely to trickle down to any of Prokief's foot soldiers."

"Anything else?" Piran asked.

Kestel shook her head. "Just one soldier's observation that the men were never very fond of Prokief, and if food and pay began to run short..."

"No one's going to mutiny as long as Prokief has his warden-mages," Piran said with a snort.

"We might get more news soon," Kestel said. "I heard there are some convicts earning their Tickets. They might have heard something from the newest prisoners about what's happening back home." She grimaced. "I'll go down to the camp gates with some of the other Ticketed women. We'll help the lasses find their footing. A proper brothel for the ones who want to resume business and a sponsor and a job for the ones who don't." Her tone had grown bitter. "Sad, but it's better than some of them had before they were sent to Velant."

Kestel's voice had lost its bantering tone. It didn't take much for Blaine to guess the reason for her anger. Prokief's guards enjoyed bragging to the male convicts about the liberties they'd taken with every new group of female prisoners. Prokief and his guards used each new group of female prisoners as their own private bordello until a shipment with fresh victims arrived. For some of the women, the mistreatment was not far different from what they had experienced back in Donderath. For others, those sent away for minor crimes and petty infractions, the abuse was enough to drive them to hang themselves within a few weeks of arriving at Velant. And for the male convicts, who were likely to settle down with those women, the memory lingered as a constant reminder of Prokief's power over their lives.

Kestel's last announcement dimmed the high spirits of the homecoming, and the group scattered to their tasks. Blaine and Piran went to put their sacks away in the room they shared with Dawe and Verran, while Kestel cleaned up what was left of the meal.

Blaine put his few personal possessions away and headed outside to store the barrels of fish in the shed behind the cabin. When he finished, he pulled his cloak more tightly around him and headed down a path toward a stand of pine trees on a ridge behind the cabin. The snow crunched under his boots and as he climbed, the wind grew stronger, so that he raised his hood and had to hold its edge with both hands to keep the wind from blowing it off his head.

He followed the path to where it ended by a mound in the snow. Beneath the mound was a stone cairn, built two springs before. From the foot of the cairn, Blaine could see in one direction out over a wide expanse of pristine ice that stretched to the horizon. In the other direction, he looked down over the slope that led to Skalgerston Bay to the sea. But from this spot,

Velant's prison stockade was not visible. It was why Blaine had chosen the place, and one of the reasons why it had always given him a measure of comfort.

Blaine reached into a small pouch at his belt and withdrew a small piece of wood carved in the shape of a bird, no larger than his index finger. He bent over to lay the carving atop the cairn. "Brought you something, Selane," he murmured.

Blaine sighed, and his breath clouded around his face. "Ship just got in last night. Bad run of it with the weather. Just as well you couldn't worry. With the long dark coming, the fleet may not go out again before winter. I wouldn't mind that." He paused. "I know you can't hear me, but it was so much better coming home when you were here." His throat grew tight, and for a moment, he stood in silence.

Behind him, he heard the crunch of footsteps and turned. Kestel was making her way up, struggling in the snow, her cloak drawn around her, its edges fluttering in the wind. She finally made it to the top and stood beside him. He could see that the wind stung her eyes and reddened her cheeks. "I thought I'd find you up here."

Blaine shrugged but said nothing.

"I miss her too, Mick. We all do." She laid a hand on his shoulder.

"I should be happy for her. She's free. If the stories the Temple Guardians told about the Valley of the Gods have any truth, she's in a place where she won't be cold or hungry or imprisoned ever again. No damn fever to hurt her." He shook his head. He'd finally accepted the fact that he would never go back to Donderath, never see Carensa again. Selane had made it bearable. Together, they had something that Velant and Prokief couldn't take. Then the fever took her.

"I'm sorry, Mick."

Blaine turned to look at Kestel. "I don't think you followed me up here to rehash the past. Not in this cold."

Kestel used the edge of her hood to shield her face against the wind so that it was easier to breathe. "You and I are the only ones in Velant who knew the court of King Merrill. What do you really think about the news from the tavern? Do you think Merrill will lose the war with Meroven?"

"Do you?"

Blaine watched Kestel intently. While it was true that before running afoul of Donderath's law, both of them had access to the king's court, Blaine had not known Kestel. She, however, had recognized him on sight, and knew the court gossip that surrounded his banishment. It had counted for something that Kestel claimed that many in the court secretly sympathized with Blaine, and that his father's reputation had not gone completely unnoticed.

"Merrill's not a bad king," Kestel said, thinking as she chose her words. "He can be clever, and the generals respect him."

"Just how well did you know him?"

Kestel smiled enigmatically. "Personally? Not at all. However, for a time I was Lord Janoron's courtesan and I had the pleasure of attending balls and private dinners in the presence of His Majesty. To him, I'm sure I was invisible. I prefer that. When I'm invisible, I can observe better."

"My father spent more time with the king than I did," Blaine replied. "They enjoyed the hunt, and father had done Merrill great service in the war against the Cerroden Rebellion. On the few occasions father insisted I accompany him to court, I was rarely included in any meetings with the king. Other than when he banished me, I can only remember being in private company with Merrill twice. But I agree: From what little I saw of him as a man, Merrill seemed even-tempered and fair."

Blaine's voice took on a bitter edge. "Even when he banished me, he let me know that he understood—and possibly sympathized—with my reasons."

"But he had to make an example."

"It would have set a dangerous precedent not to." Blaine looked down the slope toward the sea. "What worries me about the news isn't that Donderath and Meroven are at war, but that whatever's happened is bad enough that it affects something as minor as the supply ships to Velant. Under normal circumstances, what they send on a ship for the colony is trivial compared to the rubies they take back. A war with Meroven shouldn't disrupt sea trade. If it's true that Merrill can't send more ships, then I'm afraid something has gone horribly wrong."

"My thoughts exactly." Kestel met his eyes. "Without shipments of food and money to pay the soldiers, I don't know how long Prokief can hold the camp, even with the mages. He relies on the ships to send him fresh guards, and he holds the hope of earning a spot on a ship back to Donderath over the heads of the others. If Donderath were to suddenly withdraw its support, Prokief might face a rebellion by his own men."

"If anyone but the boys in the cabin were to hear us talking like this—" Blaine said in a warning tone.

Kestel's eyes took on a serious glint. "That's why we're talking up here. If Prokief is afraid, he's going to be more dangerous than ever before. The warden-mages will clamp down. That's a situation ripe for a coup—"

"Or for a slaughter," Blaine replied. "Be careful. The news that reaches us here is part rumor and part wishful thinking. If the prisoners were to rise against Prokief and Velant isn't cut off from Donderath—"

"There'll be troop ships headed this way to put down the rebellion within a month or two and we all hang."

"We've got to be careful, Kestel. Until we know, we don't dare make a move in either direction." Blaine sighed. "Since we're having this little exercise in treason, here's another thought.

"Suppose that for some reason, Velant is cut off from Donderath. How long would that last? Suppose that Prokief mucks it up completely with his soldiers and they riot. Gods, the soldiers assigned up here had a choice of Velant or the noose. They're not the best of the lot. Sooner or later, Donderath will remember we exist. They'll miss the rubies or the copper or the fish. They'll get around to sending new ships. It's one thing if the soldiers have rebelled. But if the convicts revolt, they'll pin the whole sorry mess on us and crush us." He shook his head.

"It won't work. I hate Prokief as much as anyone, but there's no way to cut ourselves free of him—"

"Unless Donderath itself falls." Kestel met Blaine's gaze and for a moment no one spoke.

"And if that happens, it'll be the freedom of the damned," Blaine said quietly. "Because without ships from Donderath, I'm not sure that Edgeland can survive."

CHAPTER THREE

THIS WAR IS MADNESS." LORD GARNOC THUMPED the tip of his walking stick against the wooden floor for emphasis.

"Perhaps," replied King Merrill. Donderath's War Council met in an upstairs chamber of Quillarth Castle, in a room as somber as its purpose. "But it seems unavoidable." The king's voice was weary. "Meroven shows no sign of backing down, no matter how many troops we send against them. Vellanaj has thrown in their lot with Meroven. I've just received envoys from Tarrant with word that their king will honor his alliance with Donderath against Meroven." King Merrill shook his head. "Mad it may be, but we have no choice except to stand against Meroven, unless we want to be ruled by Edgar."

Bevin Connor stood in the shadows against the wall behind his master, Lord Garnoc. He had been there long enough that his knees ached and his back cramped, but he kept his post in silence and resisted the urge to stretch. He brushed a lock of dark blond hair back from where it had strayed.

At twenty-two, he had been in the employ of Lord Garnoc for nearly ten years, since his fostering. His responsibilities had steadily increased as he grew older and as Garnoc's age took a toll on the old man's mobility. Connor was grateful for the position, since as the youngest son, he had no inheritance possibilities other than the possession of an old and middlingly well-known noble name. "Middling" was a word Connor thought suited him in many ways: average height and build, unremarkable features, and eyes that couldn't decide whether they were blue or green. Garnoc said that Connor was a perfect spy because he was good-looking enough to be welcome anywhere and unremarkable enough to be easily forgotten.

Now, Connor's alarm at the king's latest news was enough to drive all wish for sleep from his mind. *By the faces of Charrot! What except destruction can come from a war that engages all four of the Continent's great powers?*

Connor had been a silent and largely invisible witness to the debates of Donderath's War Council since the first skirmishes along Donderath's border almost three years before. Each time the Council convened, he hoped for better news from the front lines. Donderath had a long and successful history navigating the Continent's politics, and an equally illustrious record during the skirmishes and wars that had occurred when the major and minor powers had clashed. He had expected the conflict with Meroven to be quickly met and done, a bit of battlefield politics. For it to have burgeoned into a war set to consume all of the Continent's four major powers was as frightening as it was previously unthinkable.

"You're certain that Tarrant is sincere?" Lord Radenou's scratchy voice reminded Connor of the sound of a chair scraping along the floor. "Perhaps they mean for us to overextend ourselves. They have a long history of trade with Meroven. Why should they favor us now?"

"By the gods, man! Think of what you say," Lord Corrender

exploded. "If Tarrant is against us, that would put us three against one. Meroven's victory would be assured. Be grateful for such an ally—Meroven, I think, does worse. We should be glad it is Tarrant that wishes to fight on our behalf and not Vellanaj." Corrender, like Lord Garnoc, was a former military man, though more than a generation separated the two. Corrender's hair was still full and dark, though it was gray at the temples. He had lost half a leg in battle, and Merrill had requested that he serve in Council rather than on the field.

Garnoc, too, had once been known for his valor in battle, though it had been in the service of the father of Donderath's present king. As the men at the Council table glowered at each other, Connor took advantage of the pause to step forward and fill Garnoc's cup with the watered wine his master preferred when in company with the king. Garnoc gave him a nod of thanks and Connor withdrew once more to the shadows.

"The die is cast," Merrill said, taking a sip from his goblet of brandy. "In this, Tarrant has common cause with us. Our spies have reported messengers between Vellanaj and Meroven for some time now, even before Meroven attempted to seize land across our border. Tarrant realizes that if Meroven and Vellanaj succeed in their attack on Donderath, they will surely fall next."

"Yet the king of Tarrant wed the daughter of Jeroq of Vellanaj. Is that not an alliance with the enemy?" Lord Radenou demanded.

"And by all accounts, Jeroq was well rid of the harridan," Garnoc replied. His voice was gravelly with age, and his hair required no powder to be white as snow. Yet his blue eyes snapped with fire, and from the set of his jaw, Connor had no difficulty imagining his master as a firebrand in his younger days. He was still, even in his seventh decade, the most outspoken of the nobles, and the one to whom Merrill most often turned for private counsel. "One need not have spies to hear the report of how ill matched Zhon of Tarrant is to Jeroq's daughter. Any courtier who has traveled among Tarrant's nobility can verify that."

Radenou shrugged. "An arranged marriage is not for the happiness of the man and wife, but a business deal between the husband and the bride's father," he countered. Radenou had the silky manner of a courtier, and the instincts of an assassin. Connor had been privy more than once to his master's opinions of the recalcitrant lord.

"Such marriages are hardly unknown in Donderath, or do you forget that Queen Loana is the youngest of Edgar of Meroven's daughters?" Merrill countered. Connor thought he looked much older than he had just a few months earlier. "I'm afraid such brides are mere hostages, and if they commit their affection to their husbands, they are then torn between loyalties."

I'm betting the king knows a thing or two about that personally, Connor thought. The marriage between Merrill and Loana of Meroven had been brokered through all of the proper channels, yet it was widely rumored to have been a love match as well. Whether the bride and groom had discovered their affection before or after the vows, Connor did not know, but there was a warmth between them even in their public appearances that he did not believe was mere pretense.

"With Tarrant's help, can we push back both Meroven and Vellanaj?" Garnoc leaned forward, catching Merrill's eye with a question Connor was sure his master had timed to help the king out of an embarrassing thread of conversation. A flicker of gratitude flashed in Merrill's eyes as he nodded.

"I believe so. Vellanaj is not a particularly strong ally, though its navy is sizable. Already, there are reports that they have moved to blockade us."

"And the Cross-Sea powers? Will they take sides in this?" Correnders gaze fell to the map of the world powers that stretched across the table. The Sarnian Ocean stretched a vast distance between the Continent and the Peninsula, its nearest neighbor. "Nearest" was a relative term, Connor knew, since the sea voyage took several months, even with good weather.

Merrill shook his head. "No, thank the gods. They have officially declared their neutrality. This is not their fight, and they want nothing of it." A weary, cynical smile touched the king's lips. "Or rather, they desire to trade with both sides, and to have no hard feelings with whoever is proven to be the winner."

Tiredly, Merrill stood. "Gentlemen. I will take tonight's comments under consideration. When I receive messengers from the front, we will reconvene. Until then, we are adjourned."

The others remained seated until the king left the chamber.

"Mark my words, this war will not come to a good end," Radenou muttered as he pushed back his chair.

Correnders rounded on him. "Is that your prediction—or your hope?"

Radenou shrugged. "Merely my observation. It cannot be good for business or personal accounts when the four major powers on the Continent align against one another. The minor powers will scurry like rats dodging among the horses' hooves, playing both sides for fools. And when we have all beggared ourselves for want of a few acres of ground, we may find the world more changed than we would like."

"Much as it pains me to agree with Radenou, I think in this case, he may be right." They turned to look at Lord Onseler, who had remained silent throughout most of the night's discussion. Onseler was one of the Council's younger members, though he was well into his fifth decade. Like the others, he had served his time in battle for King Merrill or the king's father. Now the vast connections of his shipping business made him the perfect spymaster for the king. Lord Onseler had never lost the bearing of a career military officer, and his eyes were cold and cunning.

Well aware that everyone's eyes were on him, Onseler took his time rising from his chair. "I do not like the omens I see. Always before, when the four powers have clashed, it has been over token issues: a strip of long-contested and otherwise useless land, a trade concession, or an imagined diplomatic affront." Onseler shook his head. "Edgar of Meroven is a very different king from his father—and from King Merrill. Edgar is headstrong and vain, and by all accounts, he's surrounded himself with ambitious men. Vellanaj's king is weak and easily led. No doubt he basks in Edgar's supposed glory," he said with disdain. "I don't think this war will be as easily ended as the last skirmishes. I fear this war will redraw the map of the Continent—and we may not like the results."

Lord Garnoc said nothing until he and Connor were within their private rooms. It was so apparent that he was bursting to speak that Connor barely suppressed a smile, though the subject was no laughing matter.

"By Torven's horns!" Garnoc swore, and went on to curse in increasingly creative ways until Connor had poured him a liberal shot of brandy. "Radenou makes me wish I were twenty years younger. I'd like nothing more than to put my sword through that wagging tongue of his!"

Connor chuckled. "I daresay you'd find the rest of the Council offering to be your second in that duel, m'lord. Your opinion appears to be shared by all."

Garnoc settled into a chair by the fire. "All but the king,

though I think I know why Merrill puts up with him. It's better to keep your enemy close enough to watch."

"You're sure Radenou is truly the king's enemy?"

Garnoc gave a growl as he settled into the chair and thrust a pillow behind his lower back, giving Connor to know that part of his master's ill temper had less to do with the Council than it did with his aching muscles. "If you mean, do I think Radenou would take up arms for Meroven, no. But the man delights in being a gadfly, and his contrariness wears on me. His sour disposition affects those in his circle, who go off to poison others with their cynicism." His brows knitted together in a scowl. "Such cynicism can undermine a king, whether it's meant as treason or not."

Connor hurried to bring Garnoc his dinner from the covered plate a servant brought to the door. With a flourish meant to lighten Garnoc's mood, Connor set out the dinner on the table, making a show of laying out the rolls, napkin, tureen of soup with its crust of baked cheese and ramekin of fruit compote, with a perfectly roasted game hen plated with radishes and caramelized parsnips. "Dinner is served, m'lord."

Garnoc got slowly to his feet, but he waved off assistance. "I don't need you hovering over me, Bevin!"

"Yes, m'lord," Connor said with a deep bow that hid his smile. Garnoc was not always a congenial master, but he was a good and fair man who did not believe in beating either his servants or his horses. Unlike much of the nobility. Garnoc had also raised sons to maturity who willingly spoke well of their father.

"Show Millicent to the table," Garnoc said.

Connor went to the mantle and took down the small oil painting that traveled everywhere with Lord Garnoc. The oval painting showed a dark-haired beauty with tempestuous eyes and a full-lipped smile. Lady Garnoc was rumored to have had a force of personality equal to that of her husband, and the older servants still fondly remembered rows between the two that resulted in broken crockery. Yet their disagreements, however heated, had never gone beyond a few trampled trinkets, and from all recollections seemed to have been as much entertainment for the two as they had been about any subject of meaning.

Even now, twenty years after Lady Garnoc's passing and long after she had aged to be a respected matron in the court, the elderly chambermaids still blushed when they whispered about the trysts between Lord and Lady Garnoc. The passion that had bound them together had not cooled for Lord Garnoc after his wife's death, and he made it clear that he would never want anyone but Millicent.

Respectfully, Connor placed Millicent's portrait opposite where Lord Garnoc sat, and withdrew.

"I did not want to say so in front of the others," Garnoc said, "because I did not wish to appear to agree with anything Radenou says, but I, too, am worried." Whether he was speaking to Millicent or to Connor, Connor did not know, but such conversations were common, and Connor accepted them as part of his role as Garnoc's personal steward. "I have had dark dreams about this war. I don't think Merrill has considered the impact if Vellanaj's blockade succeeds, and I have told him as much in private."

Garnoc shook his head. "Merrill is worried. He won't show it, but I've known him since he was a lad, and I can tell this war wears on him. Merrill is a man of reason. He weighs his options and their cost before acting. Edgar of Meroven is hot-tempered and vain. Edgar must know his grab for land can't go without reply, but he's willing to risk everything, and for what?"

He glanced at Connor, who hurried to refill his brandy.

"What of the king's mages, m'lord? Do they give counsel?" Connor asked.

Garnoc sighed. "They speak in riddles, as always. But of late, even those riddles are dark. I was with Merrill the last time his visioner cast the cards. Dark omens of wild seas and fire raining down from a mountain and of an early, killing frost." He fell silent for a few moments as he finished his meal. "I don't always hold with the findings of the king's visioner, so I asked my astrologer, Atriella, to scry the stars for me."

"And what was revealed?" Connor was skeptical when it came to the proclamations of most of the soothsayers, smokereaders, and diviners who hung about every court and noble house like weevils in a granary. Yet Atriella was different. She did not affect the swoons and vapors that so many of the visioners used to announce their readings. When she searched the skies for signs of what would be, she was rarely wrong, despite her lack of showy ritual. Her accuracy had made many enemies among the lesser astrologers, who already held her common birth against her.

"You know that Charrot's figure in the night sky remains visible all year long, dipping and rising but always in view."

"Yes, m'lord. I've seen it when the sky is clear." Connor had indeed seen the pattern of stars that was named for the two-natured, diune god. He glanced toward a large tapestry on the wall that illustrated a scene from the epic poems that recounted the stories of the gods. One of the tapestries depicted three figures against the constellations of the night sky: Charrot, the Source, and the god's two consorts, Torven and Esthrane. Beneath them lay land, sea, and the realms of the dead and undead.

Charrot, the Source, ruled both the realm of gods and the realm of men. On one side of his body, Charrot had the form of a perfect warrior: broad-shouldered, with rippling muscles in his arms and thighs and exceptionally well-endowed manhood. His skin was a dusky yellow, and his chiseled, masculine face was always depicted by the artists as handsome. But Charrot was both male and female, and the figure in the tapestry was turned slightly so that both sides showed. Viewed from the other side, Charrot was a woman of surpassing beauty, with heavy, full breasts and thighs that promised both fertility and fecundity. With skin the color of twilight and hair the shade of a midnight sky, Charrot was the epitome of feminine beauty.

In the tapestry, the god held out its hands to its two consorts. Torven, the god of illusion, was a blue-skinned man whose beauty equaled that of Charrot himself. Torven and his progeny ruled the air and sea, water and ice, darkness and twilight, metals and gems, and the Sea of Souls.

Esthrane, the second consort, also equaled Charrot's feminine sensuality. With yellow-hued skin and a wide-eyed and sorrowfully knowing gaze, Esthrane and the gods of her offspring commanded fertility from the ground and from crops and herds, working their power in birth and fire. And it was Esthrane who kept watch over the Unseen realm, the wandering place of incomplete souls.

Beneath the feet of the figures in the tapestries were the artist's imaginings of the hundreds of household gods, patron deities, and place-gods who were revered and worshipped. Temperamental and fickle, these lesser gods figured much more in the lives of ordinary citizens than the sons and daughters of Charrot's consorts. From spoiled milk to turned ankles, the lesser gods influenced the daily routines of life, and a wise person knew how to beseech them for their favor.

Garnoc cleared his throat, pulling Connor back from his thoughts. "As I was saying—"

Connor nodded. "Atriella's reading of the stars," he said, embarrassed to be caught daydreaming.

"Aye. We're coming on toward winter, and Esthrane's constellation, Woman in Childbirth, dips below the horizon until summer, when life begins again. Torven's constellation, the Conjuror, rises for the winter." Garnoc sipped his brandy and cast a glance at Conner to assure his attention.

"You know of the planets in their courses?'

"Yes, m'lord. They move about our sun, like bees in a hive."

Garnoc nodded, pleased at Connor's answer. "You've been paying attention."

"Aye, m'lord."

"Atriella says that once every seventy years, the outermost planets, Veo and Iderban, form a perfect line. If they align when Esthrane's constellation is high, it augurs for prosperity and good harvest. But if they align when Torven's stars are ascendant, it is a dark omen, full of changes and of things not being what they seem."

Connor nodded, though he was unsure that he trusted in the star-seers as much as his lord. "Veo, the Thief. And Iderban, the Assassin," he mused. Garnoc had told him once that the most remote planets were so named because they were faint to the eye without a spying glass, with shadowy, elusive shapes.

"Atriella believes that the omen bodes badly for the war, and for Donderath's part in the fighting." Lord Garnoc shook his head. "Given the news that we're privy to, I fear she is right. If Vellanaj is able to maintain its blockade, we'll be forced to feed our people and provision our army without the benefit of trade from abroad." He paused for a moment, lost in thought.

"It's a bad business, with winter coming. Likely to stir up all kinds of unrest. Hungry people at home make it difficult for a king to focus on the warfront." He met Connor's gaze. "It's likely to create other problems as well if the folks in the ginnels start looking for someone to blame. I believe Lanyon will want to know what we've learned."

Connor nodded. "When do you want me to take the message?"

"Go now. It'll be a few days before the king has more news. This has potential to affect Lanyon and his people. He needs to be warned."

"Shall I wait until after you're finished with your meal?"

Garnoc smiled. "You can take care of the table when you get back. Millicent and I have some catching up to do."

CHAPTER
FOUR

CONNOR MADE SURE NO ONE SAW HIM LEAVING Lord Garnoc's rooms. He took the servants' stairs down to the first floor, pausing only long enough to retrieve his cloak from his own room. Quillarth Castle had dozens of back stairways and at this hour, long after supper, the passageways were quiet.

Even the stables were empty of groomsmen and hired hands as Connor saddled his horse and led it from its stall. He encountered no one until he reached the gate, when a bored guard asked only if he intended to return that night.

Connor had not gone far beyond the walls of Quillarth Castle before he turned from the main road. There was a full moon, and it lit the way as he urged his horse along the meandering streets that would lead him out of the city and into the countryside.

He had been careful to hide his feelings when Garnoc sent him on the errand, but inside, Connor felt his stomach twist. *How long until Garnoc realizes I may have betrayed him?* Connor wondered. The question was rarely far from his mind. Garnoc had already noticed something was wrong. He had admonished

Connor more than once for allowing his attention to stray. But the fact that Garnoc still kept Connor in his service told him that he had not yet been found out.

I should confess, Connor thought for the hundredth time. *Even though I don't quite know what I'm confessing about.* He had been down this line of reasoning before, and it always led him in circles. *What do I tell him? That twice I've been waylaid on the way back from carrying a message, but that I've got no clue about who attacked me? That they left me unconscious in a ditch, and I awoke with no memory of where I'd been for the past few candlemarks?*

Connor shook his head. *Who would believe me? I hadn't been drinking, but that's what they'll assume. Nothing was taken. And yet, I've lost candlemarks of my life. I don't know what I did or said. Gods help me! What if I've broken confidence, betrayed my master—and the king?*

Another possibility loomed, equally frightening. *Or perhaps,* Connor thought, *I'm going mad. I've heard that men can go into a frenzy and remember nothing. Gods! What if I've killed someone, done something awful, and don't remember? Either way, I've shamed my master, betrayed my vows, maybe even compromised the king.*

Always the thoughts circled to the same conclusion. *Confess my fears, and Garnoc will disown me. No one else will want an unreliable assistant. I'll starve. Or worse, Merrill will lock me up for treason. I can't bear that, especially when I don't even know what I've done.*

Stay, and it could happen again. He groaned, looking quickly from side to side to assure himself that he was alone on the road. *Gods forgive me! I don't have the courage to confess to a crime I can't remember. I could run away, but whoever's done this to me might find me—before I starve as a beggar. The king might fear I was a spy and send his men for me. What a choice! Run away and starve or stay and make it worse, and I can't even remember what I've done!*

In less than a candlemark, Connor had left the city of Castle Reach behind him. He paused for a moment and looked up at the sky. It was a clear night in late summer. He searched the sky for the constellations and found the lightning-like pattern of Charrot's stars, chosen by those who thought it represented the Source God's twin nature. Esthrane's constellation, a row of five stars for the body of the mother and emerging child and four other stars at the corners of a square for the goddess's hands and feet, were also visible. Connor guessed that the ancients who had named the stars had far more imagination than he did to envision such detailed images from a few points of light.

Autumn would come soon, and Esthrane's constellation would dip below the horizon as Torven's K-shaped pattern of stars—a conjuror with his arm outstretched holding a staff— would rise. Connor hoped that autumn brought with it milder temperatures and cooler tempers.

With a sigh, Connor urged his horse forward. Lanyon Penhallow's current home was a two-candlemark ride from Castle Reach. He shook his head to ward off sleep and nudged his horse with his heels. The night was already far spent and he knew that he must reach Penhallow's manor before dawn.

Finally, the lights of Rodestead House came into view. Connor slowed his horse so as not to alarm Lord Penhallow's guardsmen at the large stone gate. The manor was surrounded by an iron fence of unsurpassed workmanship, both sturdy and beautiful, wrought with symbols and scenes like a metal tapestry. Connor brought his horse to a walk as he approached the gate.

"State your name and business."

"Bevin Connor. I bear a message for your master from Lord Garnoc."

After a moment, the huge iron gate swung open. "You may enter the grounds," the unseen guard replied. "Wait at the manor door to be admitted."

By now, Connor was familiar with the ritual. He dismounted, and led his horse up the carriageway. As he approached the house, he felt the scrutiny of unseen watchers. He was careful to keep his hand well away from the sword at his side. Connor looped his horse's reins over the hitching post at the end of the carriageway and walked slowly up the broad granite steps to the manor's imposingly carved front door. Before he could knock, the double doors swung open. Framed in the large doorway was a thin man of indeterminate age.

"Welcome, Master Connor. Please come in." Hannes, Lord Penhallow's steward, stepped aside to allow Connor to enter. That he was met by the steward and not by one of the other servants gave Connor to guess that somehow, Lord Penhallow expected his arrival. Though he did not understand it, Connor had grown used to Penhallow's unusual prescience, on both trivial issues and matters of greater importance.

"I bear greetings—and a message—from Lord Garnoc," Connor replied.

Hannes nodded. "Lord Penhallow will be pleased. Follow me."

Rodestead House was eerily silent, though it was lit with candles as if for a ball. The huge iron chandelier in the entry hall glittered with dozens of candles, and sconces along the walls lit their way as Connor followed Hannes up the sweeping front stairway. Halfway up, Connor shivered, suddenly chilled to the bone though the night was mild. He caught just the barest glimpse of a shimmer in the air before the apparition was gone.

"Did one of our haunts give you a quiver?" Hannes asked with a chuckle. "Pay them no mind. There are many spirits here, some recent and many quite old. You're in no danger. Lord Penhallow has let it be known that you are under his protection."

Hannes's words, meant to be reassuring, sent another chill down Connor's spine. He did not doubt that it was an enviable honor to be under the watch of Rodestead House's formidable lord. Yet he had learned from his years at court with his master that all convenient arrangements had their price.

"You may wait in here," Hannes said, stopping in front of mahogany double doors. He opened them and made a shallow bow, gesturing for Connor to precede him. "The lord will be with you shortly." Hannes closed the door, leaving Connor alone.

Inside was a well-appointed library. The large fireplace was tall enough for a man to be able to stand without needing to duck his head. A fire burned brightly, warming the room. Hundreds of leather-bound volumes were arranged on beautifully carved shelves, and the scent of their leather and parchment filled the room.

Connor took in his surroundings without venturing farther, unsure of where his host would have him stand. In the years he had carried messages for Garnoc, Connor had rarely been ushered into the same room twice. Over the years, he had made a game of looking for clues about his taciturn host. This new room provided more pieces of the puzzle to help him decipher the man for whom Rodestead House was home.

In addition to books, a curious assortment of objects lined the shelves. Astrolabes and armillary spheres sat on a table at one side of the room. Trinkets of silver, jade, and glass were arranged on the bookshelves and on side tables. On the mantle, several small marble statues looked warm and lifelike by the glow of the fire. Many of the objects looked to be of a great age, and some Connor could not place as being from anywhere within Donderath or the Continent's kingdoms. Three large leather chairs faced the fireplace. Next to one of the chairs was a small table with a glass of dark liquid and a plate of sausage, dried fruits, and small pastries. A second partially filled goblet sat nearby, as if its owner had just stepped away.

Above the mantle was an oil painting. It showed a prosperous family dressed in the manner of several centuries past: husband, wife, son, and daughter. The young daughter toyed with a small dog, while her brother seemed to be making an effort to look older than the seven years Connor guessed him to be. The woman had a gracious look, seated with her hands in her lap, wearing a modest gown as befitted a gentlewoman. Her blue eyes were startling, even at a distance, and her long hair fell in ringlets around her face.

The man stood behind the woman's chair. His right hand rested possessively on his wife's shoulder, while his left hand lay proudly on the shoulder of his son. He had the look about him of a man who understood that he was born to rule, with high cheekbones and a stern, thin-lipped mouth that did not quite smile although everything about his manner said that he was satisfied with his lot in life. Confident, but not arrogant, with keen intelligence in his blue eyes. His brown hair hung loose to his shoulders, and his clothing spoke of money and position. Connor guessed that the painting was at least two hundred years old, and he also knew without a shadow of a doubt that the man in the painting was the same Lanyon Penhallow whose arrival he awaited.

"Do you like my library?" The voice startled Connor enough that he jumped and he heard his host chuckle.

"Yes, very much, m'lord," Connor replied, wishing his heart would stop thudding. He turned to see Penhallow standing behind him and searched the apparently seamless wall for signs of a hidden doorway.

Lanyon Penhallow stood framed against his books. His dark hair was caught back in a queue. He appeared to be a few years older than the man in the painting, perhaps in his late third decade. Tonight, he wore a simple, claret-colored silk shirt with a brocade doublet in muted tones over dark close-fit leggings. Against the rich colors of his clothes, Penhallow's skin seemed pale.

"Is Garnoc well?"

Connor nodded. "Yes, quite."

"And Millicent?" Penhallow's mouth quirked upward, just slightly, at the private joke. Endearment and forbearance colored his tone, without a hint of mockery.

Connor smiled, despite the apprehension he always felt in Penhallow's presence. "Milady Millicent is, as ever, looking splendid."

Penhallow walked closer. Connor did his best to look nonchalant, though his heart was beating at twice its normal rate once more. "Come now, my dear Bevin. Do I still make you nervous after all this time?"

Connor sighed. "Reflex, m'lord, or instinct. I know you are a man of your word."

Penhallow nodded. "And a man of few words. You and Garnoc are among only a handful to be granted my protection in these perilous times. It will not keep you from all harm, but it will reduce the number of people willing to interfere with our business." He paused. "You have a message for me?"

Connor unfastened his right cuff and turned his sleeve up until it exposed the whole of his inner elbow and forearm. "See for yourself, m'lord," he said, extending his arm, palm up, as he steeled himself, inadvertently making a fist.

Penhallow took the proffered arm and lowered his head. Connor barely felt Penhallow's sharp teeth sink into the throbbing vein in the hollow of his elbow, but he gasped seconds later at the by-now-familiar vertigo that accompanied Penhallow's feeding. He forced himself to stand still, though his most primal instincts urged him to run, knowing that his stillness would yield the least bruising and the cleanest wounds. The creases of both elbows were dotted with small, round white scars, badges of his role as witness and messenger.

Penhallow can read my memories. Can he see the gaps? Will he find me out? Another possibility occurred to Connor. *Did Penhallow send someone after me to take my memories? Oh, gods! Can he read my thoughts? Maybe I've given myself away. I don't know who to trust.*

Both he and Penhallow gained from the exchange. Undoubtedly, Penhallow gained the most, seeing through Connor's eyes all that had transpired in the War Council, and in his later discussion with Garnoc. Yet while Penhallow gleaned information, the feeding was part of the mysterious magic that granted Connor the vampire lord's protection. Though the scars were well hidden beneath Connor's sleeve, something of Penhallow's magic lingered. More than once, a common cutpurse bent on robbing Connor had drawn back at the last moment, as if warded off by an intangible presence. He did not know what other dangers Penhallow's magic had spared him, and he did not want to know.

Only a few moments passed, and Penhallow raised his head. No hint of blood colored his lips, and the wound on Connor's arm was clean, already healing rapidly. "How interesting,"

Penhallow said, his expression introspective as if he replayed Connor's memories in his mind.

Connor's heart was thudding, afraid that Penhallow had indeed realized his fears.

"You're more tense than usual," Penhallow said. "I forget how demanding travel is for a mortal. Please, have a seat and some refreshment," Penhallow said, snapping out of his thoughts and gesturing for Connor to move with him to a chair near the fire. Penhallow was a gracious host and was always quite solicitous toward Connor after the conveyance of the message, as if he guessed that Connor endured these meetings despite his mortal fear.

"When does Merrill hear next from his commanders?"

"A few days, m'lord. Garnoc does not expect a good report."

"Neither do I." Penhallow reached for the goblet beside his chair and swirled the dark liquid. It was as red and rich as cabernet, but it clung to the glass differently, so that Connor knew it to be blood. Connor looked away and availed himself of the repast Penhallow had set out for him, glad his own glass held brandy.

"I have my watchers at the front," Penhallow said, his voice as darkly lustrous as the liquid in his glass. "In fact, I'd like you to meet one of my main sources of information." He paused to sip his drink. "He should be joining us any minute."

As if on cue, the door to the study opened. A portly man came into the room rubbing his hands together. His clothing was dark blue, cut in the fashion of a military uniform, though it bore no rank or insignia. The newcomer was in his middle years, balding with a fringe of gray hair. He moved with surprising alacrity for his bulk, and while his manner was jovial, his dark eyes hinted at shrewd intelligence.

"Good evening, Traher," Penhallow said. "Please join us. You know where I keep the brandy."

Voss grinned. He gave a nod in Connor's direction, and then went to the sideboard to pour himself a generous slug of brandy before joining them near the fire. "This is the pup you mentioned, Lanyon?" he said with an appraising glance at Connor, who felt himself bristle. "Doesn't look like much, if you'll pardon my saying so."

Penhallow took on a bemused expression. "I believe the term 'pup' is yours, Traher, not mine. I beg to differ. I believe Lord Garnoc's attaché has more to him than we know," he said. "Bevin Connor, meet Traher Voss. Voss is a man of many talents, one of them being channeling information."

Connor's heart beat faster at Penhallow's introduction, unsure just what the vampire meant by his comment. *Could he tell from my blood that I might have betrayed him?* Connor wondered. He looked up to see Voss watching him, and felt his temper rise.

"You look to be a military man, yet you're not at the front," Connor said. "But men with your skills are needed badly."

Voss guffawed. "The pup can bark," he said, grinning. "Well, well." He knocked back the brandy in his glass. "My 'skills,' as you put it, go beyond bashing heads together, although I'll admit to being good at that." Connor glanced at the sword that hung by the man's side, a warrior's broadsword, not a nobleman's rapier. "I'm also pretty good at things like finding out secrets, which pays much better than being a target."

"Connor will bear our warning back to Garnoc, and through him, to the king," Penhallow said.

"I don't envy you repeating what I've got to say at court," Voss said, setting his empty glass aside. "Donderath is losing the war, and it is likely to lose even with Tarrant's help." He held up a hand to forestall Connor's protest.

"Meroven and Vellanaj have set a trap for Donderath, and Merrill has taken the bait. Meroven's mages are behind their army's success, and we believe that once Meroven's army has made sure that Donderath can't turn the tide, King Edgar's mages will attempt to strike a killing blow."

"You expect them to try to assassinate King Merrill?" Connor asked, looking from Voss to Penhallow, hoping the vampire would disagree.

Penhallow shrugged. "Perhaps, but only as part of a wider attack. No, my sources tell me that Meroven has held back its strongest battle sorcerers until the end, but that they are well equipped to turn the tide of the war—unless Merrill counters them with mages of equal power."

"How can you be sure?"

"I've got a spy among the mages at the front, and one among the mage-scholars at the university," Voss replied. "Our man at the university, Treven Lowrey, has found some sensitive information that may have bearing on the war."

Connor shifted uncomfortably. Although he had been a messenger for Penhallow and Garnoc for several years, he often wrestled with just how much of his own opinions—rather than observations—to share.

Penhallow watched him with a look that made Connor wonder if the rumors were true that claimed the undead could read minds. "I have the feeling there's a comment you'd like to make, but aren't sure you should."

Connor sighed. "It's just that—I get the feeling King Merrill doesn't like using mages in battle."

Penhallow's expression was resigned. "You're correct. King

Merrill is, in many ways, a very good king. I have existed long enough to know, and seen many monarchs who were unworthy of their crowns. Merrill's virtue, in this instance, is his undoing. He doesn't consider it 'sporting' to use mages in battle unless there's no other choice, and even then it's distasteful to him."

"Edgar of Meroven has no such hesitation, I gather?"

Penhallow nodded. "Edgar has no such hesitation about anything that he wants," he said, and his voice mirrored his disdain. "I've heard quite a bit about Edgar through my sources and none of it is good."

"Did your sources warn you of war?" Connor looked up sharply, not for the first time wondering whose side Penhallow was really on.

A faint smile touched Penhallow's lips, but it did not reach his eyes. "Did you think you and Garnoc were my only sources? I haven't survived for centuries without very good information." He paused. "I received no warnings of war that I did not pass on to the king through my various connections. But what Merrill does not realize is just how far Edgar will go to get what he wants."

"Is Edgar a madman?"

Voss laughed out loud. Penhallow's brow furrowed. "You mean, does he bay at the moon? No," Penhallow replied. "But he is quite without regard for what his ambitions cost others and utterly without feeling for the unfortunates who get in his way. Merrill doesn't yet realize, I fear, that to Edgar, all of Donderath—and Tarrant—are in his way."

"But what does Edgar covet so badly that Meroven doesn't already have? Their seaports are as favorable, their farmland as good by all accounts, their climate as pleasant."

"He doesn't have it all. He doesn't rule the Continent," Voss answered in a voice that made his contempt clear.

Connor blanched. "And Vellanaj, are they party to his madness? If Edgar wants to rule the entire Continent, then surely he'll turn on Vellanaj as soon as Donderath and Tarrant are swept aside, and the smaller states will be swallowed whole."

Penhallow nodded. "Yes, he will. Either Vellanaj isn't willing to see Edgar's ambitions for what they are, or they've convinced themselves that they are so valuable that he'll make an exception for them. They may be the last to be swallowed, but Edgar will want them as part of his empire sooner or later."

"I've been beside Lord Garnoc at the War Council. Merrill's reports are grim, casualties are high, but there's been no suggestion that we were about to be overrun—especially with Tarrant entering the war on our side."

"Merrill's being fed lies by his generals," Voss said, adding a creatively embellished curse for good measure. "They don't have the balls to tell him the truth."

Penhallow met Connor's gaze. "Merrill is not hearing the whole truth from his commanders. The war goes badly for Donderath, worse than the generals wish to admit. Edgar has been assembling an army of conquest for a long time. He'll sacrifice Vellanaj's troops first, then send in wave after wave of his own. Merrill's generals are only now seeing glimpses of Edgar's true power, and they refuse to admit the meaning of what they see."

"Where do the mages figure in this?"

Penhallow sat forward in his chair and watched the fire long enough that Connor was not sure he meant to answer. The firelight warmed the pallor of Penhallow's skin, and the flickering of the flame tricked the eye to give the appearance that Penhallow's chest rose and fell with breath. Connor's gaze rose to the oil painting over the fireplace. Centuries had passed and Penhallow himself looked no different.

No, Connor thought, *that wasn't correct. There's a sadness, a jadedness in his expression that the man in the portrait didn't have. Not so surprising, if one survives several lifetimes of disappointment and sorrows.*

"When Merrill was a young man, he fought in the war against Vellanaj. Merrill's father, King Landor, had no compunction against using mages and neither did the king of Vellanaj." Penhallow paused again and Connor wondered whether Penhallow had been a witness to that war.

"Neither side used their most powerful mages, but they made free use of lesser magic. Sheets of flame descending from the sky, incinerating everything in their path. Walls of water rising from placid lakes and rivers to sweep away armies and towns. Pestilence that had the opposing army coughing blood and writhing in pain in the few agonizing minutes before they died." Penhallow's voice grew quieter.

"Merrill saw how quickly magic could destroy and how vast its potential was for destruction, and I think he decided that the damage mortal soldiers inflicted was bad enough, without the help of mages."

"But if Edgar is willing to use his mages, his strongest mages—"

Penhallow nodded. "Merrill will have no choice. I've watched the war play out over the last few years hoping that my fears would not be realized, but I believe Edgar intended this outcome from the start."

Connor felt a knot of fear settle into his stomach. "If the magic Merrill witnessed wasn't what the strongest mages are capable of doing..." He let his sentence trail off, and found himself hoping Penhallow would correct him.

Penhallow's gaze did not leave the crackling flames in the fire. Voss answered. "Edgar's been 'collecting' mages for his service for some time now. Merrill hasn't. That means any mage with ambition—and without scruples—finds his way to Edgar."

Connor cleared his throat uncomfortably. "If mages are capable of such destruction, why hasn't it happened more often?"

"It has happened before," Penhallow said quietly. "Several times. The ashes of the empires that nurtured such ambition lie buried with their dead beneath our feet and across the lands of the Far Shores. Search your memory for the tales you've taken for legends. Have you never heard the stories about the 'wars of the gods'?"

Connor frowned. "Yes, of course."

"How the rivers ran red with blood and the land swallowed men and animals and the corpses of the dead were so poisoned that even the flies and the vultures died from eating them?"

A growing coldness stole through Connor, a chill that the fire could not warm. "Yes, I've heard."

"How many times have the gods remade this world? What do the legends say?"

Connor felt his heartbeat begin to quicken as the old tales became far too real. "Four times, the surface of the world was scoured clean by the sword of the gods, creating it anew for the remnant who were worthy."

Penhallow's glance was cynical. "I don't pretend to know what the gods do with their time, but neither the scouring nor the remaking was their work. Nor was the 'whole world' affected as the bards would tell you, just large enough swaths of territory that it seemed like the whole world to the wretches that survived." Connor saw an unfathomable sadness in Penhallow's eyes.

"And were you among those survivors?"

Penhallow regarded him for a moment without speaking.

"Once. On a far continent, beyond the West horizon. I 'survived' because I was already dead, though magic of that strength takes a toll even on us Elders, on all creatures who sustain their existence beyond the fringe of the mortal world."

Connor swallowed hard. "Was it as the bards tell? I always thought perhaps they embellished—"

Penhallow's gaze silenced him. "The bards did not tell half the horror. They dared not, or no one could hear the stories without despair. In a few candlemarks, I have seen a thriving empire leveled, most of its inhabitants killed. And while the bards sing of war, they say nothing of what happened afterward, of the madness and the starvation, of men living like animals and acting worse than beasts."

"Isn't there some way to warn Merrill? We can't permit Edgar to create that kind of catastrophe."

"Don't you think I've tried?" Penhallow's voice was raw. "We Elders have made sure that information reached the king, information he was not receiving from his generals. We dared not approach him directly. Merrill doesn't hunt us, but his forbearance is more from oversight than by design. We couldn't reveal ourselves, but our emissaries were well placed."

"And he refused to listen?"

Voss made a dismissive gesture. "The king hears what he wants to hear," he muttered.

"He trusts too much in the word of his generals," Penhallow replied. "His generals fear for their reputations. All great tragedies turn on small emotions—pride, greed, and an inability to see a harsh truth until it's too late."

In Penhallow's voice Connor heard anger, frustration, and resignation. The last, a concession to the inevitable, chilled him further. "Is there nothing we can do?"

Penhallow nodded to Voss. Voss crossed to the shelves that

were built into the walls on either side of the fireplace and stood on tiptoe to take down a chest that he unlocked with a key that hung from a cord around his neck. He withdrew a velvet-wrapped object from the chest and carefully laid back the wrapping to reveal an obsidian disk. The disk had several small decorative holes cut through its thin surface, and as Voss handed the disk to Connor, the fine carving on the disk's mirrorlike surface caught the light in a design Connor could not identify.

"Treven Lowrey was able to get his hands on this and bring it to me. I brought it to Penhallow," Voss said. "I've got Lowrey out looking for anything else that relates to this damned disk, but for now, this is what we've got. Take this to Garnoc. Remind him of an astrologer named Nadoren, a man who was in King Landor's service many years ago. When Landor was very old, Nadoren left court suddenly, under suspicious circumstances. It was rumored that he had stolen from the king's library. He disappeared and took with him several important maps that were never found."

Connor frowned. "What can that possibly have to do with the war? And what's so important about this pendant?"

Penhallow shifted in his chair, taking up the story. "The pendant is a key to a series of maps created several hundred years ago by a very powerful mage named Valtyr. Valtyr had traveled throughout the world, beyond the Continent and the Far Shores, to Edgeland and to lands our ships have only just begun to rediscover. Everywhere Valtyr traveled, he made maps of the places of power, places regarded as sacred or cursed, places where magic was strongest—or null. When Valtyr died, the maps fell into diverse hands. No one is quite sure how many there were, but at least four were known to be in the possession of King Landor."

"Until Nadoren stole them."

Voss nodded. "When Nadoren disappeared, so did three of the maps. It was thought that one of Landor's mages might have been studying the other map, or that it was stored separately and Nadoren didn't have the time to find it. Needless to say, once Nadoren made off with the others, the remaining map was more closely safeguarded." He grimaced. "That's why I've got Treven out looking for more information, but it's dicey. We're not the only ones interested in these things."

Connor looked to Penhallow. "Someone else knows?"

Penhallow gave a shrug. "So we suspect. You've heard Garnoc speak of Pentreath Reese?"

Connor nodded. He didn't add that whenever Garnoc had spoken of Reese, what was said hadn't been good. "I've heard."

"Reese and I have...bad blood between us," Penhallow said. "Reese is obsessed with the histories of the thirteen original lords of Donderath, the Lords of the Blood. Why he's interested, we're not yet sure. But I've found it wise to be suspect of anything Reese pursues."

"Reese works through Lord Pollard," Voss added. "Vedran Pollard. Name ring a bell?"

Connor nodded. Garnoc held Pollard in nearly as low regard as he did Reese. Voss chuckled. "Don't be so discreet. I know for a fact Garnoc hates Pollard. With good reason. Pollard is slime. Conscripted his liege men to serve in his place at the front, while Pollard stays behind to do Reese's dirty work." He paused, glancing at Penhallow, who gave a nod for him to continue.

"We think Pollard—and therefore, Reese—is behind robberies at the university library, and he might have had something to do with attacks on some of the scholars. We don't know exactly what he's up to, but we think it's got something to do with that," he said, nodding toward the disk in Connor's hand.

"The pendant?" Connor asked. Voss nodded.

Penhallow smiled, but it was an unpleasant expression that showed the tips of his long eyeteeth. "Nadoren knew about the maps, but not about the pendant key. Valtyr was a very clever man. His maps included coded information that can only be deciphered with the key. Nadoren was a simpleton, for all that he could read the stars. He was convinced, they say, that the maps hid a treasure. But Valtyr's only treasure was knowledge. And knowledge is what is needed."

Penhallow's long fingers stroked the smooth surface of the pendant's velvet case as he spoke. "The map that Nadoren didn't steal was of Donderath. I believe it is secured in the king's library. If Edgar unleashes his mages against us, Merrill needs to know where the places of power are located, because the effects will be worse there. Magic shouldn't be able to hurt the null places—it's where I'd send as many refugees as possible."

"Refugees," Connor repeated, his head spinning.

"Let's say the odds of survival will be higher in the null places," Voss answered.

"Is that where you'll be?" Connor's fear made his question sound like an accusation. He drew back as soon as he had said it. Neither Lanyon Penhallow nor Traher Voss were men he wanted to anger. To his relief, they ignored the slight.

"Quillarth Castle is a place of power. Many castles, forts, and even manor houses were built on places of strong magic, as well as temples and shrines. My advice would be to evacuate the castle and the city around it. Send people close to the null places, and away from the shrines."

"If Meroven breaks through the army's line and begins attacks inside Donderath, people are most likely to flee to temples and shrines to beg the mercy of the gods," Connor said in a hushed voice.

Voss nodded. "If I were Edgar, I'd count on it."

"Edgar's mages know about the places of power, don't they?"

"I believe so," Penhallow replied. "Most are obvious to anyone with a hint of magic. What was valuable about Valtyr's maps was that they located many places that weren't crowned with a palace or a shrine. And the null places tend to be overlooked completely because they are either too unremarkable to remember or have something about them that compels people to avoid them altogether."

"Is Rodestead House safe?" Connor asked.

Penhallow gave Connor the velvet cloth to wrap the pendant and replaced the empty chest on its shelf. "Having survived such a war once, I've taken precautions. My retainers and I will be leaving Rodestead House tomorrow night. Traher has made his own preparations." He turned back to Connor. "Tell Garnoc what you've learned tonight. As your blood gave me access to your memories, so my bite enables you to remember my words precisely."

And while he's never come out and said it, I wouldn't be surprised if it also carried a compulsion to do his will, Connor thought.

"If Garnoc can convince Merrill of the true danger, find the map and use it to protect as many people as you can. And if you can't convince the king, I'd advise you and Garnoc to leave the city and take the map and pendant with you." Penhallow had turned back to the fire that danced in the hearth. As their conversation had turned to darker predictions, Connor found that the flames no longer cheered him.

"If the worst happens, if Donderath falls, look for a man named Vigus Quintrel. He's a mage, and much more powerful

than anyone gives him credit for being. His abilities are...
unusual...which is what's enabled him to stay free of service to
the crown. You can trust Vigus. Show him the map and pendant. He'll know what use to make of them."

"Why haven't you given him the pendant yourself?"

"That's part of the reason why I believe we are running out
of time. Vigus Quintrel has disappeared."

The road back to the city was deserted. Connor gripped his
reins white-knuckled. His heart pounded, though not for fear
of the darkness. *Will it happen again? Did Penhallow know?
Have I betrayed all of us?*

The night was quiet, save for the hoofbeats of Connor's
horse. Connor looked from side to side, barely controlling his
desire to spur his horse into a full gallop and ride as hard as he
could for home. *That won't do*, he told himself. *There might be
guards around. It would be suspicious, riding like that. They
might take me for a brigand.*

In the thicket to the side of the road, a twig snapped. Connor
startled, but he could make out nothing in the darkness.

A black shape rose up in front of him, and his horse reared,
bucking Connor into the air. He braced himself to hit the road
hard, but felt himself borne up as if by invisible hands. That
same force kept him pinned as the dark form loomed over him.
He could make out a black cloak and cowl, but whether the
figure had a face beneath, Connor could not see.

"Sleep now," a deep voice said. "Sleep, and remember
nothing."

CHAPTER FIVE

BLAINE AND DAWE LEANED AGAINST ONE OF THE wagons that had been drawn up to the edge of the festival space. Across the broad, flat common area, a wonderland of sculptures glittered, lit from inside with candles or lanterns. They were made from Edgeland's most bountiful commodity—ice—and shaped into everything from statues of the gods to fanciful castles and mythical beasts.

"Nights like this almost make you forget where you are." Dawe Killick stretched his lanky form and tipped back his tankard of home-brewed ale.

"With this cold, it's hard to *ever* forget where we are," Blaine replied, sipping from his own tankard as they watched the festivities.

For those who had survived long enough to go from inmates to convict settlers, the end of the white nights was a time to celebrate before the long dark. Here on the back acres of the homesteads, as far away from Velant's prison as possible, the settlers did their best to enjoy both the feast days they brought with them from Donderath and events like the coming of the long dark that were unique to their new home.

Verran Danning and his fellow musicians kept up a lively series of tunes, fueled no doubt, Blaine thought, by the potent liquor that the minstrels' female admirers kept bringing to quench their thirst. The tune Verran and the others were playing was one that had been popular back in Donderath, and for a moment, Blaine let himself hum along, tapping his toe with the music. In the center of the gathering, a lively circle dance wove its participants back and forth as they changed partners.

Blaine didn't have to check that Kestel was among the dancers. He smiled. Even bundled up against the cold, Kestel was easy to spot in the crowd. She was shorter by a head than many of the women, tiny-boned and quick on her feet and such a good dancer that she made all of her partners look competent. Blaine doubted that the petty thieves and cutpurses who enjoyed a dance with Kestel would ever dream that she had once danced among the royal and noble. The song ended and Kestel sank, laughing, into the arms of her partner before twirling away from him with a peck on the cheek that seemed to leave the man as out of breath as the dance itself.

"A coin for your thoughts," Dawe prodded. "You're quiet tonight."

Blaine shrugged. "Can't stop thinking about the supply ships. If it's true they won't be back as often, we've got to make sure we have enough food put up to get through the winter." He raised his face to the wind. "Once the dark comes and the shallows of the bay start to freeze, they won't be able to take the fishing boats out as far. It'll make for a lean winter."

Dawe nodded. "We've been busy while you and Piran were out on the ships. Verran's not the only one who can earn a living. I've taken in some smithing—small things like fixing locks and making hoops for the cooper." He flexed his long fingers. "Not exactly silver work, but the idea is the same." He stretched, and Blaine caught a glimpse of the branded "M" on Dawe's arm. They'd both been sent to Velant for murder, but unlike Blaine, Dawe was innocent, framed by a rival silversmith. "I've also been toying with bits of copper. I've made some simple rings and such, to appeal to the ladies." He grinned. "So long as there are lasses in town, there'll be men trying to win their favor or claim their hand."

"We won't be able to spend coin if the merchants don't see supply ships for months."

"I'm ahead of you on this one, Mick. Verran and I have been buying chickens and rabbits to fill the hutches out back. Kestel's been drying the fruit and vegetables we raised, as well as everything we could buy. We set aside some extra sacks of wheat and flour as well, and paid a hedge witch to spell them against mice. Made some good homemade wine as well. With the gibbed fish you and Piran brought home, we should be able to go a while, perhaps most of the winter."

Blaine nodded. "Good to hear. Piran was going to set some traps for fox and wild rabbits." He gave a wan grin. "And let me guess, Kestel's been making extra offerings to the gods."

Dawe smiled. "How did you guess? The last sheep we slaughtered, Kestel made tallow candles, and offered the first two to Esthrane and Torven. She told me she was counting on favor from Esthrane for the last of the crops and for healthy herds this winter, and to Torven for mild storms."

Blaine snorted. "After the storm Piran and I just saw, maybe Kestel needs to leave better offerings."

Esthrane, one of Charrot's two consorts, was honored at handfastings and at both planting and harvest. Esthrane was revered among Edgeland's colonists during the unending days of the white nights. Torven, Charrot's other consort, ruled the long dark.

Dawe's expression turned serious. "The mood around here has changed since you and Piran went out with the fleet." He nodded toward the laughing and clapping revelers. "You can't tell by tonight, but there's something on the wind. Prokief's nervous, and cracking down."

Blaine drained the rest of his ale. "I plan to stay out of it."

Dawe met his gaze. "That might not be possible."

The music changed tempo and the dancers drifted back to the edges of the festival area. Light's End, the festival at the end of Edgeland's six months of daylight, was also the customary time for handfastings before the long months of darkness. As the music took on a more processional tone, three young women, each accompanied by an older woman, walked into the center of the festival area. Each of the young women wore a crown woven of straw and dried flowers and each carried a small bough of fir. As the crowd watched, three nervous men walked to stand alone in front of their intended brides.

"As I recall," Dawe drawled, "you looked about that scared yourself when you made your handfasting with Selane."

Blaine could not resist a chuckle. "I was just thinking the same thing."

The men did as they had been instructed, and each withdrew a hunting knife in a scabbard wrapped in a length of dyed rope or braided cloth, and presented the blade laid across their open palms to their brides. Back in Donderath, the ceremony would have involved a presentation of a sword-gift, but under Prokief's rule, swords were reserved solely for the prison guards and the city patrols.

The brides accepted the gift and passed the knives to the older women who accompanied them, who handed each of the brides a knife-gift for the grooms. On the pommel of each knife was a ring, and as the crowd cheered, the women who had accompanied the brides ceremoniously presented the bride and groom with their rings, then held their hands together and loosely bound their wrists with the lengths of rope. As the couples raised their twined hands, the crowd cheered once more, and Verran and the musicians began to play a familiar song. The crowd began to clap and sing, and the newly wedded couples danced one pass around the open area before the onlookers crowded toward them, joining in the dance.

The crunch of snow under running feet caught Blaine's attention. A dark figure barreled past the wagon where Blaine and Dawe stood, hurtling into the crowd.

"Get your hands off her!" A tall young man with a shock of dark hair hurled himself at one of the new grooms and knocked him to the ground. The groom, a man who looked to be several years older than his bride, struggled to his feet as the girl screamed. Well-wishers stepped back and the dark-haired man swung a solid punch that knocked the groom back several steps, but the groom came back swinging and connected solidly with his attacker's chin.

Friends of the bride went after the attacker, while the groom's friends came running. Across the clearing, Blaine could see Piran turn away from his card game to take note of the altercation.

"Come on," Blaine muttered to Dawe. "We'd better stop this before we end up with the guards called."

Blaine and Dawe waded into the fray from one side, as Piran shouldered his way in from the other. What had begun as a fight between two men had rapidly escalated into a free-for-all. The groom was holding his own, backed up by a handful of friends. The dark-haired young man who began the fight seemed to have taken the worst of the damage, as his eye was swelling and he had a growing bruise on his cheek, but he was still on his feet and surrounded by four angry—and more muscular—friends.

Blaine tackled the dark-haired man, while Piran lunged at the groom. The dark-haired man struggled and twisted, but Blaine held him fast. Piran's man was taller and heavier, but no match to Piran's experience as a soldier and bodyguard. With the help of Dawe and some of the other men who waded into the fray, the altercation came to an abrupt halt.

Blaine let go of the dark-haired man, who had stopped struggling, but Blaine drew his hunting knife from the sheath at his belt, and held it up as a warning. He turned to the groom, still restrained in Piran's iron hold, and then looked back at the attacker.

"What in the name of the gods were you doing?" Blaine asked the sullen man.

The dark-haired man glared at Blaine. "Essie was supposed to be betrothed to me," he spat. "She's been pressured into this," he said with a glare toward the would-be groom. "She doesn't want to marry him."

"Von," the bride begged, "don't do this. Please. Let it go. I'll...I'll be all right," she said with a nervous glance toward the groom. The groom had stopped struggling, but he was glaring at Von with a look that told Blaine the matter was far from settled.

One of the women stepped up. She was old enough to be the bride's mother, and wore the somber-hued clothing favored by the more mature women of the colony. In a place where none of the convicts had blood relatives, the older women banded together to look out for the youngest of the colonists, and to care for any of the colonists' orphaned or abandoned children. It was the "wise women" who negotiated the bride prices for young women, who saw to the births and made funeral arrangements for the dead. Regardless of what infraction had landed them in Velant's icy grip, the wise women had become the keepers of civilization beyond the prison's walls.

"The bride price was fair," the woman said, squaring her shoulders and meeting the dark-haired man's gaze defiantly. She had the raw-boned build of a farmwife, with hardship and sorrow etched in the lines of her angular face. Blaine guessed her to be somewhere in her third decade, which placed her among the elders. Few in Edgeland lived much beyond four decades.

"It's not about the damned coins," Von said, anger and frustration clear in his voice. "Dilan's a brawler and a drunkard," Von said with a contemptuous look at the groom, who had emerged from the fight unscathed but had inflicted serious damage to Von. "She's afraid of him, afraid to turn him down. You've got to stop this," he said, looking to Blaine and then to the wise women in appeal.

Essie, the young bride, stood between the two men. "It'll be all right, Von," she said, an edge of desperation in her voice. She cast a worried look back toward Dilan, who glowered in response. Essie dropped her voice and moved closer to Von. "You can't protect me from him, Von. He'll get what he wants, marriage or no marriage."

Blaine and Piran exchanged a glance at her words. Blaine stepped in front of Dilan, his hunting knife still in his hand. "I killed the man who took advantage of my sister," Blaine said in a low voice. He fixed Dilan with a cold gaze. "I don't much like men who don't treat their women well. I can make sure the problem doesn't go any further."

Dilan's gaze flickered between the knife in Blaine's hand and the hard set to Blaine's jaw. Piran still stood behind Dilan.

"I wouldn't push your luck, laddie," Piran muttered to Dilan.

"What's one more dead man when he's done time in Velant for murder already?"

Dilan glared at Blaine. "What I do in my own household is my own business."

Blaine shrugged. "Maybe. But out here in the wilderness, 'accidents' can happen very easily. Might be me, might be someone else, but we've all got warning now what you're up to. If Essie turns up hurt, Von won't have to come after you by himself. Do you understand?"

One of the wise women came forward. She gave Essie a shrewd look. "Bad enough to have been Prokief's prisoner, without being forced into another prison," she said. "Say now if you want no part of this."

Essie was trembling, but she shook her head. "No. I don't want to do this." She looked at Dilan. "He told me—"

"Shut your mouth!" Dilan commanded. Blaine moved forward to thrust the knife under Dilan's chin.

"I'd like to hear what the lady has to say," Blaine drawled, meeting Dilan's eyes. Dilan glared, but said nothing.

Essie straightened and collected her courage. "He told me that if I didn't marry him, he'd find me and kill me," she said, looking defiantly at Dilan.

The wise woman took out a small pouch of coins from her apron, and forced it into Dilan's hands. "Here's your bride price. The marriage is undone."

Dilan scowled at the wise woman. There was a killing glint in his eyes. "This isn't over," Dilan muttered.

Piran laid a hand on Dilan's shoulder, poking the point of his blade into the man's back. "Oh, yes it is," Piran said quietly. "The guards don't go looking for missing colonists. If you know what's good for you, you'll leave the young lady alone and go about your business."

Dilan jerked free of Piran's hold. His friends had already melted away in the crowd, but more men had come to stand behind Von. With a curse, Dilan turned away and strode off into the night.

Blaine did not sheath his knife until Dilan was gone. Piran and Dawe came to stand beside Blaine as the onlookers drifted back to the festival and Verran's musicians struck up a lively tune.

"How in Raka do I always end up in the middle of these things?" Blaine muttered to no one in particular.

"You've earned a reputation for a cool head and a hard fist," Dawe said with a shrug. "And surviving six winters up here is no small feat."

"I could use another drink," Blaine said, heading off with Piran and Dawe behind him. A small crowd gathered around the wagon where the tavern master had his barrels. Blaine glanced back toward the newlyweds, who were dancing in the center of the clearing with their friends, but Dilan had withdrawn to the edges of the crowd.

"Been no word of them at all," a man dressed in the skins and furs of an Edgeland trapper was saying as the tavern master poured him an ale. "They should have been back by now, since they left before my party went out onto the ice."

"Missing some hunters?" Blaine asked as he waited for his drink.

"It's more than that," the trapper said indignantly. His skin was rough and reddened by the harsh winds, and his dark hair was greasy, held down under a fur hat. "The lead trapper on one of those teams is married to a friend of mine. Amren is a good man, and a fine tracker. He knows the ice out there like a fox. So when he didn't meet up with us like he promised, we went looking for him." The trapper leaned forward. "We found their tracks. They went so far and just ended."

Piran frowned. "Fall into a crack in the ice?"

The trapper shook his head. "No cracks to be seen. No animal tracks, either. I've seen the great bears wandering the ice. They come across the sea on the ice floes, and leave the same way. But that's what I'm telling you—there were no tracks at all."

"That's not possible," Blaine said as he accepted a full tankard of ale from the tavern master.

"Aye, that's what we said. But it's grown strange out on the ice. I've been hunting here for five years now and I thought I had seen all that the wilds of Edgeland had to show me," the hunter said. His eyes had grown wide, and real fear tinged the man's voice. "We camped near where Amren and the others had disappeared. We thought they might come back, or that we'd get some idea what happened to them. That night it was as if the world went wild around us."

Blaine leaned forward. Something about the man's tale prickled at the back of his mind.

"The lights in the sky were red that night. Gods bless me, I've never seen the like of it. Looked as if all the world was aflame. And it wasn't just the lights. It was the magic."

"Magic?"

The trapper nodded. "I've got no more than a hedge witch. I have a bit of tracking magic that helps me find the animals and a wee bit that can stop a fox or a rabbit in its tracks to get off a shot. But that night, Yadin strike me if I lie, I could feel so much magic around me I thought I'd suffocate. Truly, I couldn't draw breath. I don't know what the others felt, but I could feel the air crackle and the ground under me shake.

"We gathered our things and ran," the trapper said, taking a large gulp of his ale. "I've never run like that from anything, not even the guards who sent me to this godsforsaken rock. But we all ran—and that's when we found out what became of the other ones."

"How?"

The trapper looked from face to face before he spoke. "The lights took them."

Blaine leaned back, skeptical. "The lights took them?"

The trapper nodded. "There were eight of us who went looking for Amren. All eight of us made camp at the place where we saw the lights. But only six made it out."

"What happened to the others?"

The trapper's face was tense, and his jaw tightened. "We don't know. Sure as the gods are my witness, we were all together when the lights started and the magic thickened around us. I saw all of my men when we began running. But when we reached a point where the magic felt like it lifted, two of the men were gone."

"No shouts, no calls for help?"

The trapper shook his head. "Nothing. But I couldn't help wondering, since the magic went away at the same time that they disappeared, whether it got what it wanted."

"The magic?" Blaine pressed.

"Aye." The trapper nodded. "The magic. It took the slowest of our group, the two who fell behind the others. And then it disappeared, just like they did. Just like Amren's group."

The crowd around the ale wagon peppered the trapper with questions, but Blaine turned away. Dawe and Piran caught up to him. "Some story," Piran observed. "Any truth to it, you reckon?"

Blaine shrugged. "Could be."

"Prokief would love to get his hands on magic that could make people disappear," Dawe muttered. "I wonder if the warden-mages have felt anything strange."

"Not that we're likely to hear about it," Piran added.

Blaine grimaced. "True. But Prokief would know about it. He already imagined that everyone was out to get him—"

"We were," Piran muttered.

"So if he finds out there's strange magic afoot, or worse, if people begin disappearing..." Blaine said.

"He'll blame it on the colonists," Dawe finished. "He won't care how it happened, he'll be looking for someone to take it out on and he'll figure it's a plot to unseat him."

"Then we'd better have a plan," Piran said. "Because I have a feeling this is going to get worse before it gets better."

CHAPTER SIX

"THINGS ARE GETTING WORSE INSIDE VELANT."
Verran Danning put his case with his pennywhistle and his flute down on the table. "I heard the guards talking down at the tavern. The warden-mages haven't been keeping the new convicts in line, so the guards have had to crack down."

"Is it just Prokief's mages?" Blaine mused. "I'd love to know if something's affecting all the magic, or just the warden-mages."

Verran shrugged. "I use a small amount of magic when I play. It's not much of a talent, but I can put the crowd at ease and give them a pleasant feeling toward me." He grinned. "You'd be surprised how much of a difference a little thing like that can make in the coin I get for the night." Verran licked his lips. "The last couple of times I've played, the magic felt 'slippery.' Sorry that I can't explain it better." He paused. "I did get it to work, finally. But in all the years I've used magic, I've never had that happen."

Dawe leaned back in his chair, stretching his long legs. "You know, I was working with some heated copper out in the shed a couple of days ago, and got a nasty burn for my trouble." He held up his right hand with a half-healed burn on the palm.

"I've worked with hot silver since I apprenticed at twelve years old, and I never did that before." He bit at his lip as he thought.

"When it happened, I blamed myself for not being careful. But like Verran, I use a touch of magic in my work—always have. Oh, it's not big magic, not like the warden-mages or even the healers, but it helps me do just a bit more than talent or skill would allow. It's so much a part of me that I rely on it. And I remember thinking, when I burned myself, that it was just like the magic slipped away from me for a moment."

Blaine had been leaning against the wall with his arms folded across his chest. He pushed himself away and began to pace. "From what I've seen down in Bay-town lately, it's like there's been a full moon every night. People are on edge, acting crazy. Ifrem, down at the tavern, told me there's been more fights in the last few weeks than he remembers in all of last year." He shook his head. "I've had a headache for a week that won't go away, and I must have heard a dozen people down at the tavern say the same thing."

A loud cry broke the night stillness.

"That sounded like Kestel," Blaine said, pushing back from the table so quickly his chair nearly fell.

Piran also was on his feet. "Was that a scream?"

"Sounded more like a battle cry to me," Dawe said. They ran for the door, each grabbing something to use as a weapon.

"This way," Blaine said, leading them toward the barns.

They found Kestel standing in the open space in front of the barn. Her clothing was torn and her lip was split. A long knife with a bloody blade was held tightly in her right hand.

"Someone jumped me," she said, her voice breathless. "He got away, but he's hurt."

"We're on it," Piran said, taking off at a run toward the forest, with Dawe close behind.

Blaine realized Kestel's left arm was cradled close to her body and that her sleeve was dark with blood. He turned to Verran, who had followed them out of the kitchen. The minstrel held a frying pan in one hand and a small dirk in the other.

"The pan was handy, and I had the knife on my belt," Verran said with a shrug.

"Take Kestel in and get her cleaned up," Blaine said. "I'm going with the others."

Before long, they filed into the kitchen, cold, snow-covered, and discouraged. "We lost him," Blaine said, hanging up his sodden cloak. "Without torches, we couldn't go far into the trees, and finding someone in a black cloak in the deep brush is damn near impossible."

Kestel sat at the table with her injured forearm on a piece of cloth as Verran carefully stitched closed a gash. A glass of whiskey sat next to Kestel's left hand, and she tossed back what remained of the amber liquid, then cursed fluently, her face taut with pain.

"How bad?" Blaine asked.

"I've had worse," Kestel replied.

"Not too deep, but it will heal faster with a couple of stitches," Verran replied. Kestel winced. "Sorry," Verran said. "I'm a better musician than tailor."

"Do you think it was our 'friend' from the wedding?" Piran asked, exchanging worried glances with Blaine.

Kestel shook her head before Blaine could reply. "No. This was a professional."

Blaine looked at her. "A professional what? Thief?"

Kestel bit back a curse as Verran finished up his stitches. She was silent for a few moments as Verran bound a strip of clean cloth around the wound and then went to pour Kestel another whiskey. "He wasn't a thief. He meant to kidnap me."

"A rapist?" Dawe asked.

Kestel closed her eyes and leaned back in her chair. "Maybe, but that wasn't the intent I got. He said, 'You're coming with me,' and he grabbed me, but there wasn't anything sexual about it."

"What makes you think he was a professional?" Blaine asked.

"He moved like a soldier," Kestel replied. "He knew how to grab someone, and if I didn't have the skills I've got, he would have had me. Fortunately, I had a knife. So did he. But he didn't expect me to know how to use it."

"This makes no sense," Piran said, anger clear in his tone. "Why would anyone want to kidnap you?"

"Did you get a look at him?" Dawe asked.

Kestel shook her head. "He'd made an effort to hide his face. The hothead you and Mick tussled with at the wedding wouldn't have bothered." She managed a wan smile. "Maybe I should feel flattered. No one's tried to kill me since I left court."

"How badly did you injure him?" Blaine asked. "We can put the word out in Bay-town, ask around among the healers."

Kestel closed her eyes. "I stabbed him in the right shoulder. I got him good. It won't heal on its own."

"You look like you could use a rest," Dawe said with a reproving glare at Piran and Blaine. "Why not get some rest? We can go back out with lanterns and see if he left anything behind."

That Kestel would agree to lie down was proof enough that she was shaken by the assault. Verran busied himself cleaning up the blood from the table and putting away his supplies, while Blaine and Piran shouldered into their cloaks once more.

The wind had picked up as they stepped outside. The candles inside their lanterns flickered. "What, exactly, do you think we'll find?" Piran growled, hunching against the cold.

"Don't know. Maybe nothing," Blaine replied, his voice nearly lost to the wind.

They retraced their path to where Kestel had been attacked. Blood stained the snow, which showed obvious signs of a scuffle. They walked back along the route they had taken into the woods when they had followed the attacker's footprints.

Piran searched the snow for anything the attacker might have dropped, careful to check the brambles at the forest's edge for torn clothing. "Look here," Piran called, pointing. "He came out of the woods on the far side of the farm and worked his way around. That's the long way, if he came from town."

Blaine looked down at the snow and frowned. The snow had been churned up where the three of them had run into the woods, obliterating the attacker's prints. But several imprints lay outside the path, and Blaine wondered if Kestel had wounded the man badly enough that he had lost his balance.

Blaine knelt down beside one of the prints and let out a low whistle. Piran came to look over his shoulder. "What?"

"It's a clean footprint, and not one of ours," Blaine replied.

"So?"

"Look at the heel. It's an odd shape."

Piran bent closer. "Doesn't look like Holt's work," he said. Holt, the Bay-town cobbler, was known for the quality of his workmanship and the lack of choices in the styles of shoes he offered. Boot or shoe, for man or woman, Holt made a single, functional style. Since he was the only cobbler in Bay-town, patrons could wear his shoes or make their own, unless they paid a high price for rare imports from home.

"Might be something he bought from a supply ship," Blaine mused. "That's an unusual style. We could ask in town, see if any of the merchants remember boots like that."

Piran straightened. "There's one other group that doesn't buy their shoes from Holt," he said, his voice hard. "Prokief's soldiers."

Blaine stood and dusted the snow from his pants. "I wouldn't have said it looked like a soldier's boot. Toes are too pointy."

Piran shrugged, his expression dark. "Wouldn't have to be regulation issue. Prokief's friends had access to goods that never made it to the Bay-town shops. He was known to have visitors from time to time. I doubt they were required to surrender their clothing, like we were."

Together, they tramped through the snow toward the homestead. "That doesn't make any sense, Piran," Blaine argued. "We've had our Tickets for years. Why would one of Prokief's soldiers come all the way out here to attack Kestel?"

Piran shrugged. "I don't know, but I plan to find out. You've got to admit, between the direction he came from and that boot mark, it's suspicious." He paused. "We're far enough out of town, someone looking for an easy mark—or an easy lay— could find it a lot closer. Ask Verran, but I can't imagine any decent thief imagining that a farmer out in the barn would have coins or jewelry."

"And it's easy enough for a man to find company in town, he'd hardly have to come all the way out here to find a woman," Blaine replied, not liking the direction the conversation was going. Much as he hated to admit it, Piran had a point.

They stomped the snow off their boots outside the door. Piran put a hand on Blaine's arm, stopping him from opening the door. "Tomorrow I think we should take a little trip into Bay-town. Ask some questions."

Blaine nodded. "Agreed. And Kestel's going to hate this, but I think we need to make sure she's got someone to guard her, until we find out what was behind the attack."

Piran smirked. "You get to break that news. Even with her wing clipped, our Sour Rose isn't going to like it."

Blaine's expression was hard. "I don't like it, either. But I'm going to find out what's going on, and if I find whoever did this, I'll make sure he won't come around again."

When Blaine awoke the next morning, he found Verran and Kestel already in the kitchen, arguing about breakfast.

"I tried to reason with her," Verran said, throwing up his hands. "Told her to take it easy, I'd cook."

"I've already been stabbed. I didn't want to be poisoned, too," Kestel returned, though a glint in her eye gave Blaine to know she was enjoying the argument. "Besides, the cut wasn't that deep. It's sore, but not enough to keep me from my chores. I'll be fine." As if to make her point, her knife, cleaned and sheathed, hung at her belt.

"Suit yourself," Verran grumbled, stepping away from the hearth. Kestel's back was to him, so he moved to put bread and jam on the table, along with plates, before she turned. He shot a triumphant glance at Blaine, and poured himself a cup of tea from the kettle by the hearth.

"You're up early," Kestel observed, glancing back at Blaine. She took in the items Verran had put on the table and sighed, rolling her eyes.

"Piran and I have a couple of errands in town," Blaine said, ripping off a hunk of bread and covering it with jam.

Kestel stood, wiping her hands on her apron, and met his eyes. "This is about what happened last night, isn't it?"

"Are you kidding?" Piran answered before Blaine had the chance to speak. He came from his room, still fastening the strings at the top of his shirt. "We know how good you are with a knife. The thief probably bled to death out in the woods. Personally, I'm amazed you didn't gut him. I've seen you dress out a deer."

"Compliments will get you nowhere," Kestel said, breezing

between them. "I've lived with the both of you long enough to know when you're lying. There's probably no stopping you, but be careful."

Blaine and Piran exchanged glances. "You know us," Piran said. "We'll just make a few casual inquiries, nothing to raise suspicions."

Kestel snorted. "You? Not raise suspicions? Since when?"

"I'm wounded," Piran said, clutching at his chest.

Whatever reply Kestel might have made was cut off as a flare of bright light lit the room, blindingly intense. The headache Blaine had fought for days became unbearable, and the pain drove him to his knees. His hands cradled his head. He heard Kestel scream. Two heavy thuds shook the floor. The air around Blaine felt as if he had suddenly been plunged underwater, as if it were too thick and heavy to be drawn into his lungs. His vision blurred, and he collapsed and lost consciousness.

"Mick, wake up." It was Piran's voice, but it sounded far away.

Blaine groaned. He had no idea how long he had been out, but his head still throbbed. He opened his eyes and saw Kestel clinging to the doorpost, wide-eyed with fear and looking quite pale. Dawe and Verran were slumped on the ground, unmoving. Blaine drew a deep breath to steady himself.

"Stay still. I'll see to the others," Piran said. Piran moved over to where Verran lay sprawled on the floor. He was pale, but breathing regularly. Kestel knelt next to Dawe.

"He's breathing," she reported.

Piran climbed to his feet and dipped a rag in the bucket of freezing-cold water that sat next to the door. He wrung out the cloth and walked over to Verran, laying the cold cloth over his eyes. Verran sputtered and moaned, then pushed the cloth aside and opened his eyes.

"What in the name of the gods happened?" Verran groaned.

Piran helped him sit and glanced over to where Kestel was ministering to Dawe, who appeared to be in equal distress.

"You tell us," Piran replied. He moved back to Blaine and helped him stand.

Blaine managed to get to a chair by the table and sat down heavily. "I got a headache that felt like a sword was being rammed through my eye, and the next thing I knew, I woke up on the floor."

"I felt the same thing, and I couldn't breathe," Kestel added. "I was out for a little while, too," she said, touching a bruise on her forehead. She had draped Dawe's arm across her shoulder to get him to his feet and was helping him to a seat at the table.

"You and Dawe were out cold," Blaine said, looking at Verran.

Verran frowned, thinking. "I felt magic stronger than I'd ever felt it before. It burned through me. I thought I'd burst into flames. I swear it felt like my skin was on fire, like my bones were kindling."

"Verran's very poetic. I feel like shit."

Blaine looked up at Dawe, who had climbed to a seat at the table. He looked ill. His eyes had the bleary look of someone with a fever, and his cheeks were flushed. Dawe seemed unsteady in his seat, and his hands clenched the edge of the table. "I thought I was going to burn to death from the inside out. Never felt anything like it before in my life."

Verran managed a grin. "Yeah, but just for a moment, I felt like...a god. It was like my magic suddenly went from a thimbleful to a whole ocean, pouring through me. It was probably just a few heartbeats, but I thought I could touch the sky, like my magic had no limits." His face fell. "And then it was over, and it was like someone cut the strings to a puppet. Next thing I knew, I was lying on the floor."

Dawe sighed. "Leave it to the minstrel to wrap everything in flowery words. I felt the magic swell into more than I'd ever had before. But it was there and gone before I could think to draw on it. For just a moment, though, I felt like I had enough magic to take on all of Prokief's warden-mages and kick their asses." He shrugged. "Then all of a sudden, I was on the floor, waking up." He looked from Kestel to Blaine. "What did you feel?"

Kestel and Blaine exchanged a glance. "I don't think I could have said it quite like you did, but the feeling was the same," Blaine said cautiously.

Kestel nodded. "It was like being filled with fire and then having it snuffed out," she added.

Verran looked askance at Blaine. "I knew our Sour Rose had seduction magic, but you've been holding out on us, mate. What's your talent?"

Blaine shrugged uncomfortably. "Nothing useful up here. I'm better with a sword than I should be, even allowing for what little training I've gotten. Runs in the family."

"I thought someone had clipped me, that's the truth," Piran replied. He reached a hand up to the back of his head. "Felt like my head was smashed open, only there wasn't any blood." He paused, and managed a grin. "Then again, I'm used to that sort of thing. Looks like I recovered a little faster than the rest of you. 'Course, I'm also the only one without a bit of magic."

"So if whatever it was laid us all out, and everyone but Piran has a bit of hedge magic, what do you think it did to real mages? Do you think it took out the warden-mages?" Verran asked.

Piran grimaced. "Probably. But I imagine they're back on their feet by now, and mad as hornets. The bigger question is, what caused it?"

Blaine looked at Piran. "I'd like to find out if anyone else felt what we did. I think that a trip into Bay-town might get us some ale and answers."

CHAPTER SEVEN

THE YOUNG LIEUTENANT WAS ONE OF MANY runners who had reached the castle within the last few candlemarks. His uniform was torn and burned, and his face was bruised. Some of the tears in his uniform were tinged with dried blood. Though it was obvious that the man was making every effort to hold himself together, his pupils were dilated and his face was ashen.

"How many are dead?" King Merrill's voice sounded weary.

"Unknown, m'lord," the lieutenant reported.

"Your best guess, then."

The runner drew a deep breath and shuddered. "Ten thousand."

"Ten thousand dead!" Lord Radenou protested. "Your Majesty, how can that possibly be?"

The lieutenant turned on Radenou with a dead gaze. "You haven't seen what I have, m'lord. My estimate is lower than what I fear to be true."

"What of our mages?"

The lieutenant shook his head. "I know only what I saw, m'lord. But when I reached the high ground some distance behind the battle lines, it appeared that a large portion of Meroven's forces were in disarray. The ground around them was scorched, and I saw what looked to be many bodies. Our catapults could not have reached so far behind their lines, so I would guess our mages inflicted the damage."

"Your commander—what were his orders?"

The young man looked badly shaken. "My commander is dead, m'lord."

"Whoever sent you, what orders did he have to regroup?"

The man swallowed hard, as if forcing down memories worse than nightmares. He licked his lips nervously. "One of the captains was trying to rally the survivors who had fallen back to the hilltop. I don't think he had any orders, m'lord. He told me he hoped to gather enough men to hold the ground."

Merrill's expression was grave. "I see." He paused. "Thank you for your service, and for your valor in bringing me this message." The king looked to the servant who had brought the lieutenant to the War Council. "Find this man a room and get him food. Send a healer to see to his wounds."

"Thank you, Your Majesty," the lieutenant said as he made a shaky bow. When he and the servant had left the room, Merrill turned back to his Council.

From where Connor stood against the wall, the War Council's table sat in a pool of light in an otherwise darkened room. No one had given the order to light the lamps around the edges of the room. To Connor's eye, the shadows seemed to encroach around the king and his Council just as elsewhere, a more dangerous darkness threatened all of Donderath.

"Surely the army can rally," Lord Corrender said hopefully.

"Donderath's generals are good men," Merrill rumbled. "They'll hold the line."

"For how long?" Garnoc leaned forward. "Your Majesty, the

news we're hearing from the runners is quite different from the reports of the generals just last week."

"Much can change in a week during a war."

"Indeed, and yet I wonder if the reports you received might have been...tempered to make them more palatable for royal ears?" Throughout the long session, Garnoc had managed to insinuate the information Penhallow had sent with Connor without ever stating it in a way that would have required naming its source. Faced with the grim reports of runner after runner, Merrill had no choice but to hear what his generals had not dared tell him.

"Can't the mages do more?" Corrender pressed.

"I have given them permission to do whatever they can, to the extent of their ability, gods help us," Merrill replied quietly. It seemed to Connor that the king had aged years in a few days. More gray peppered his brown hair, and fine lines had appeared around his eyes. From all Connor had heard Garnoc tell of the king, it weighed heavily on Merrill's conscience that his health kept him from the front lines. Even with the scryings that the king's seers could do, it was impossible to know just what was happening at the battlefront. Yet on Merrill's decisions, a kingdom would rise or fall.

Later, when Connor tried to put words to the memory, he would say it felt as if the air had suddenly gone out of the room. Blinding pain struck his temples, as if an iron pick had been shoved through his eye, and he fell to his knees, clutching his head. Dimly, he was aware of groans and cries, and of thudding noises that suggested at least some of the men at the Council table had fallen to the floor.

Connor struggled for breath. His heart pounded, its beat deafening. The air had become thick as nectar, making it difficult for his chest to rise and fall. It felt as if everything around him shifted. He curled into a ball, shielding himself with his arms, prepared for tremors that would send glass and statuary crashing from the shelves around the room, but there was only silence. Nothing fell. After a moment, the pain receded, and Connor warily stretched out, climbing to his feet.

"My lords, are you injured?" Connor, much younger than the others at the Council table, ran toward where the men slumped in their chairs. Radenou had been thrown to the floor, as had Merrill. They were surrounded by their stewards, who helped them to their seats.

"What in the realms of the gods was that?" Radenou's voice was angry, but beneath the rage, Connor heard fear.

"The magic," Merrill said, and his voice was not quite steady. "For a moment, it disappeared."

It was the first Connor had heard that Donderath's king possessed any magic, and by the look on the Council's faces, the others were not aware of that fact, either.

"I possess very little magic. Truth-sensing, mainly. Comes in handy, which is why I don't say anything about it, and I'll trust you not to, either." Merrill paused. "But for a moment, it just... winked out. Gone. As if someone had blown out a candle. Then it was back again, and for the life of me, I don't know what to make of it." He looked at the startled faces around the Council table. "What did you feel?"

"I have no magic at all, m'lord," Garnoc said. "I felt a headache like an assassin's knife that nearly put me out of my senses."

Corrender nodded. "So did I—and like Lord Garnoc, I have no magic. Yet I, too, had a headache as if someone had dashed out my brains with a rock. It came on suddenly, and left quickly enough that I could scarcely breathe."

They looked at Radenou, who had regained his seat and was

adjusting his cravat and doublet. He flushed as they stared at him. "I have a bit of magic—useful only for improving my luck at cards. It's as the king said. For a heartbeat, the magic was gone, and then it rushed back like a wave that nearly drowned me. For a moment, it was like magic filled me and threatened to consume me from the inside, and then the wave was gone."

"We won't know how much of the kingdom felt the shift until runners can arrive," Garnoc mused. "Nor whether the effects at the front were harsher—and intended to be so. Perhaps we were merely caught in some kind of backlash."

"Perhaps," Merrill said, but he did not sound convinced. He rubbed his temples with his fingers. "Go back to your rooms and rest. We've already had a long day of it. If more news comes from the front, I'll call for you."

The group filed from the room in somber silence. Garnoc said nothing until he and Connor had reached their suite of rooms, and he saw that Radenou and Corrender had entered their own quarters.

It was the first time since his return from Penhallow's manor that Connor had been alone with Garnoc for more than a few minutes. After waking once more in a ditch by the side of the road, Connor had resolved to tell his master of the blackout and accept the consequences. Before the meeting, there had only been time to share Penhallow's news. Now Connor drew a deep breath, gathering his courage.

"M'lord, there's something—"

"Not now, Connor. I have a job for you," Garnoc said, waving Connor into the room.

"But, m'lord—"

Garnoc shook his head, silencing Connor. "I need you to run an errand for me, to an old friend."

"Penhallow again?"

Garnoc shook his head. "No. Alsibeth will be holding court at the Rooster and Pig. She has far more magic than many believe, and she's been happy to let them underestimate her."

As Garnoc spoke, Connor was already shouldering into his cloak. "Two gold coins should be enough for the information we seek," Garnoc continued, pressing the coins into Connor's hand. He met Connor's gaze. "Without bringing the king's name into it, tell her what happened when the magic disappeared. She's sure to have felt it, too. Ask her what she makes of it, and how widespread she thinks it was. Most of all, ask her if she knows what could cause such a thing."

"Do you think someone like Alsibeth would have more insight than what King Merrill is likely to get from his court mages?"

Garnoc made a dismissive gesture. "Piffle. If Merrill's court mages had been half the sorcerers they think they are, the king would have had them assisting with the war effort. Their 'magic' has more to do with ingratiating themselves to the court ladies than with real power. Alsibeth is a true mage—and she'll tell you the truth, or what she knows of it." He patted Connor on his shoulder. "Now, off with you. Don't dawdle—no telling when the king will get another runner from the front, and I don't want to have to make up a reason to cover your absence."

"Want me to bring back a bucket of ale while I'm there?" Connor asked with a sly smile.

Garnoc chuckled. "Now, that's more like it. I do have a fondness for the bitterbeer that the Rooster brews. Yes, bless you, lad. Bring me back some nice dark ale, and some for yourself as well," he said, dropping a few more coins into Connor's hand. "Now, get going."

* * *

Once again, Connor slipped down the back stair without attracting attention. This time, the guard at the back gate frowned as he headed out of the castle compound.

"Sure you want to do that, laddie? There's an ill wind blowin'."

Connor inclined his head quizzically. "How so?"

"There's trouble in the city. Not sure about what, but the last few men who came from that direction said there'd been a disturbance of some sort. Mind your step and watch your back if that's the way you're going."

Connor thanked the guard and walked on, following the cobblestone streets toward the city of Castle Reach.

Donderath's palace city spilled down the slopes of the hillside on which Quillarth Castle stood. The cobblestone road was broadest closest to the castle, and the largest, wealthiest homes were high on the hillside, just outside the castle walls. Next came the smaller homes of the guild masters and the minor nobles, as well as the villas of wealthy merchants. Homes and businesses became smaller and shabbier the closer one got to the rivers that ran along the hillside's base. Connor squared his shoulders and glanced around. The last blackout on the way back from Penhallow's manor had unsettled him badly. He felt jumpy as a pickpocket, frightened by a simple errand. *If this keeps up, I'll be afraid to leave the castle*, he thought.

Not far beyond the castle gates he felt a warning prickle at the back of his neck. He paused, looking around him, listening intently. The night was silent and the street seemed darker than usual. On a pleasant night such as this, the families who lived in these beautiful homes could often be heard in their courtyards. Women sang, children squealed and laughed, and men gathered by the gates to gossip or do business. Servants should have been abroad in the streets, bringing back water from the common well or trudging up the hill with a cart full of firewood. Yet tonight the street was empty, and the courtyards appeared to be deserted. Even the lights in the windows seemed furtive, and Connor realized that the houses had closed their shutters, odd on an evening that was still quite warm.

He walked on, growing more wary in the eerie silence. His boot steps echoed from the stone of the high walls surrounding the villas, making him feel exposed. The road began to narrow as he passed through another series of walls and gates. The night was still quiet, yet as he continued on his way toward the heart of Castle Reach, he became aware of a different energy in the air. Where the avenues of the wealthy had responded to the flicker of magic with silence, the streets where the merchants and artisans lived were unusually full of people. Clusters of women and groups of men talked in hushed tones, pausing to look over their shoulders. They fell silent as Connor moved among them, watching as he passed by, then going back to their hushed whispers.

"Knocked me off my chair, it did," one man attested.

"Thought I'd gone both blind and deaf for a moment," another reported with a worried tone.

"Didn't know what to make of it. Right as rain one minute and couldn't lift my head off the table the next," a woman's voice carried above the whispers and muted conversations.

Connor kept his head down and went on walking. He knew that the fear and apprehension these people felt would be even greater if they suspected that their king had no more insight into the situation than they did.

The road narrowed once again. It had been a broad boulevard when it left the castle and a wide thoroughfare through the merchants' homes. Now the street was not much wider than the wagons and carts that made their way up and down the hillside bearing goods from the seaport and the produce of farmers from beyond the city, bound for the markets.

The streets of the lower town were crowded. Castle Reach's marketplace, always a busy spot, seemed near to bursting with people. Everywhere Connor looked, people talked in groups of two or three. The throngs were large enough that it might have been a festival night, except that the crowds had a furtive air about them. Connor jumped as someone bumped into him, and he realized that the crowd's tension was affecting him.

"Medals and amulets—better safe than sorry!" A street cart vendor hawked his wares as Connor walked by, holding out a variety of necklaces with a bit of metal stamped with runes to petition Esthrane and the Life Gods for protection. Connor shook his head to discourage the vendor, but the man persisted.

"There's magic afoot. If the enemy can strike at the heart of the palace city, who knows what will come next?"

Connor paused and pretended to consider the amulet, far more interested in the vendor's gossip than his wares. "Will this protect me if... what happened... happens again?"

The pudgy man's head bobbed up and down on his thick neck. "I swear by the gods, you'll be protected."

"You felt it, too?"

Again, the corpulent vendor nodded so briskly that Connor thought he might give himself whiplash. "Aye. Practically knocked me on my ass. I wasn't wearing an amulet. I won't make that mistake again," he boasted, pulling aside the throat of his stained homespun shirt to show five or six crystals and metal disks nestled against the dark hair of his chest.

"Did everyone feel it?" Connor fingered the crystals and turned the amulets over. The metal was thin and greasy, cheaply made. The "crystals" were mere glass, not semiprecious gems. He had spent enough time around Penhallow to gain an eye for both magical items and fine craftsmanship. He doubted these trinkets provided any more protection than one could obtain by whistling in the dark.

"Some more than others," the fat trader replied. "My wife scared the wits out of me, she did. Toppled over as if she'd been struck by the gods. When she came back to herself, told me that—just for a moment—she felt the magic rush out and then swell back, like the tides." He shook his head, eyes wide. "Never saw the like of it. You can believe she's wearing my amulets now, too. Won't take them off for anything."

"Is that what's got everyone talking?" Connor asked.

The trader looked at him as if he were daft. "Aye, it's got them talking all right—and by this time tomorrow, I warrant that anyone who's able will be on the road south, as far away from Quillarth Castle as they can get."

Connor frowned. He looked around at the crowded streets and realized that more than a few handcarts and small wagons were loaded with people's personal possessions, hastily packed and tied down under threadbare blankets. "Why? Why leave the city?"

"It's not just the way the magic flickered. Bad omens lately. Fishing boat sank off the wharves, not a scratch on her. The old crone who reads cards in the square says that every run of cards she lays warns of danger and fire. Old Phearson's cows quit giving milk yesterday. The man who brings eggs to market says the hens have been off their nests." He shook his head, and Connor had the impression that this part of the discussion was not contrived to sell the trader's wares.

The man looked genuinely frightened. "It's bad enough that the big ships aren't sailing. We should have realized something bad was coming. There's talk among the captains about a blockade, but that's not the reason." The man leaned closer, conspiratorially. "King Merrill stopped sending the ships because we don't have enough to feed the soldiers and keep the war going, let alone feeding those criminals at the end of the world. Let 'em starve, I say."

"What of the convicts? Where do they go?"

The trader's smile was mirthless. "The worst of the lot go to the end of a rope, that's where they go. Hangings happen nearly every day since the ships stopped sailing. The rest are conscripted for the war effort. Able-bodied men to the front. Women and those too young to fight go to the cook wagons, or sew uniforms or help the healers with the wounded."

"What about you? Will you stay, or are you packing up, too?"

The trader sighed. "My wife's not well. She won't leave, and I won't leave her. But if I was free to go, I'd already be gone."

Connor gave the man a copper for one of the amulets and went on his way. The tide of people trying to leave the city grew greater the farther down the hill he went. Many were headed for the Forest Road, the main thoroughfare out of the city. Others headed down the hill with their tattered bundles of possessions, and Connor realized why as he reached the wharves.

Throngs of people jostled for position, shouting to be heard. Captains of vessels of all sizes and states of seaworthiness bargained the cost of passage with those who could pay. By the look of it, many of the ships might not make it out of the harbor. Some were trawlers and fishing boats, unsuitable for carrying passengers. Connor's gaze rose to the masts of the larger ships that sat with their sails furled on the big docks. Those made the ocean voyage to the Far Shores, trading for the exotic luxuries for which the nobles were willing to pay dearly. Other ships he recognized as being supply and convict ships. Guards were posted around the decks and gangplanks of all the larger vessels.

He shouldered through the crowd, buffeted by people who were carrying heavy bundles and dragging screaming children. The Rooster and Pig was a brisk walk from the wharves, near the storehouses where the merchants kept their goods, and the Foley Yards, Donderath's largest shipyards.

Half-built ships rose against the night sky like skeletal gods. From the materials and wood shavings littered about, war had not slowed construction on the newest ships. If anything, the yards had an unusual level of disarray, as if the builders had been working more quickly than usual. There were only two likely reasons for that, neither of them good. Either the shipbuilders had been urged to supply new vessels quickly for the war or to breech the impending blockade, or the owners, succumbing to the crowd's fearfulness, had urged their builders to step up their schedules.

The Rooster and Pig's red roof stuck out among the drab warehouses. One of its bright-blue shutters was loose, banging in the wind, like the winking of a whore's painted eye. Yet the tavern served some of the best fresh fish in Castle Reach, along with its signature bitterbeer and cheese bread that brought the most wayward sailor back for more.

Connor was glad for the dagger beneath his cloak and the shiv in his boot. The Rooster and Pig had a better reputation than most of the port-side bars. Fights were few and usually limited to punches thrown over a claim to one of the tavern's trollops. Travelers could spend the night with reasonable certainty that they would not be relieved of their clothing or wallets. Still, with the tension in the air this night, Connor was unsure whether old ways were likely to remain true.

The heavy door opened with a firm push. Every table and

chair was occupied and many patrons stood along the walls nursing their drinks. Men played at dice or cards, and brightly dressed trollops circulated through the crowd, urging high rollers to bet more or conveying luck with a kiss. Connor made his way to the bar, looking for the proprietor.

"Busy day?" Connor greeted the tavern master.

"Busy enough that we never closed from yesterday," the man replied without looking up as he used a pitcher to slosh ale into three tankards in a row.

"I'll have one of your best bitterbeers, and two buckets to take with me when I go," Connor said. That was enough to get the tavern master's attention, and he looked up, then grinned broadly.

"Connor! It's been a while. Doesn't your master let you out?"

Connor chuckled. "Who do you think one of the buckets is for? It's mighty thirsty up the hill these days."

Engraham, the tavern master, was a lanky man, thirty seasons old, with wavy brown hair and light-blue eyes. It was obvious to anyone from court who made their way down to the pub and took one look at the man that Engraham was also the bastard son of Lord Forden. Forden had made no attempt to deny paternity, and it was rumored that Forden had staked Engraham the money to build the Rooster and Pig. Despite the tavern's questionable location, it boasted a well-appointed private back room for gambling that was ofttimes occupied by the wastrel sons of the nobility, and an equally popular set of comfortable rooms upstairs for wenching. If the citizens of Castle Reach sought to drink away their worries, Engraham stood to make a small fortune.

"Is it true?" Engraham brought Connor his bitterbeer and leaned across the bar, lowering his voice.

"Is what true?"

"That Donderath is losing the war. Folks around here are afraid Meroven troops will be marching in any day now."

Connor drank a long draught of his beer and wiped his mouth. "Not to my knowledge. The war isn't going well—I don't think that's much of a secret. Meroven's put up more of a fight than I think anyone—including King Merrill—expected. But if we're on the verge of being overrun, I haven't heard about it…and I do have pretty good sources."

Engraham nodded. "Aye, that you do. That you do indeed." He poured Connor another bitterbeer before the first was empty, the price of information.

"What do you know about the convict ships?"

Connor took another swallow and let the dark ale slide down his throat. "Nothing I didn't learn from a peddler on the roadside."

"Has the king abandoned Velant?" Engraham's blue eyes glinted with uncharacteristic anger. In Connor's experience, Engraham was one of the most easygoing men he knew. Where many tavern keepers would wade into a brawl, fists flying, to restore order, Engraham usually called for a free round on the house, which was equally effective without a loss of anyone's teeth.

"He hasn't said as much, but I see the ships in the harbor," Connor replied.

Engraham swore. "It's not right to send people away and then cut off supplies," he growled. "They're likely to starve without those ships, with winter coming on."

Connor sipped his beer and nodded. Engraham was the result of a dalliance between Lord Forden and a ladies' maid, and while Forden had admitted his paternity of the child, he had wanted nothing more to do with the child's mother. Disgraced and forced by scandal from her position at the castle, the desperate young woman had been reduced to petty theft to get by. She had been caught and sentenced to exile in Velant, and it was only Forden's belated intervention that spared Engraham from going with his mother when he was a half-grown boy. The funds for the tavern were most likely conscience money.

"Have you had any word?" Connor asked, dropping his voice.

The look in Engraham's eyes darkened. "None in several months. Last I heard from my mum was at the beginning of the summer. She has a place as a shopgirl in one of the stores in Bay-town."

"Is there any chance that your father—"

Engraham shook his head. "M'lord was rather clear on that. He may not love his wife, but he's dependent on her wealth. He'd own up to me, but he was just as glad, I think, to have my mum far away." He sighed. "I send her money and warm clothing when I can get Captain Olaf to take it for me. His drinks here are free." He rubbed his thumb and fingers together in the universal gesture for bribery. "No one comes back from Velant. Out of sight, out of mind."

Connor finished the first tankard of bitterbeer and set it down with a thunk. "On that note—is Alsibeth about?"

Engraham jerked his head to the right. "Yonder, in the far corner. It's packed like fish in a barrel in here tonight. Been this way since the magic blinked."

"Worried that most of your patrons will leave the city?"

Engraham shrugged. "Not really. If the worst happens, where can they run that will be better?"

"How about the ones down at the dock haggling with the trawler captains?"

Another shrug. "Assuming they don't capsize and drown,

the best they can hope for is to get to the Lesser Kingdoms, to the south. And what will they do once they get there? I wonder." He shook his head. "And before you ask, I'm not going anywhere, either, least not until fire rains down from the sky or some such sign. After all, where could I get better ale than right here?" He grinned.

"Where indeed?" Connor gripped the handle of the second tankard. "Save me those two buckets of bitterbeer, my friend. I need to talk with Alsibeth."

Crossing the crowded tavern common room was no easy feat. By the time Connor reached the far corner, his toes had been trod upon several times and a third of his beer had been sloshed on the floor as he fended off clumsy patrons. Finally, he made it to the far corner where Alsibeth held court.

Connor and Engraham had often speculated about Alsibeth's age when the seer was out of hearing range. Cascades of dark, wavy hair fell nearly to her trim waist, and a shimmering chain of small gold bells hung from each ear and chimed softly when she moved. She had luminous eyes that were nearly violet, and delicate, long-fingered hands. Connor had never seen Alsibeth dressed in anything except the vibrantly colored silks that draped from her shoulders and swathed her narrow hips. He had as little clue to her birthplace as to her age, but he thought it likely that she could trace her lineage to the Far Shores, beyond Donderath's borders and the Continent itself.

"You're late, Connor. I'd have thought to see you a candlemark ago." Alsibeth did not look up.

"Delayed by a peddler on the road, m'lady," Connor replied. He'd grown used to Alsibeth's uncanny knowledge, and took comments like these as reassurance that other, more important prognostications were also correct.

"Wait a moment." With that, Alsibeth returned her attention

to the items spread before her. She had claimed one of the tavern's tables for her own, and with the number of people who came to ask for her to read their fortune, Connor had no doubt that Engraham made his money back several times over in spite of the loss of a table. Alsibeth had spread the table with a silk covering in blue like the color of the deepest ocean. In a semicircle around her were the tools of her divination: burning candles in a variety of colors and heights, a wide bowl of clear water, a small bundle of sage that smoldered in its pewter holder, and a small wooden "tree" hung with dainty bells.

Alsibeth passed her hand through the sage smoke. Without touching it, the bell tree trembled. Alsibeth listened carefully to the sound of the chimes and raised her face to the anxious woman who stood next to the table, awaiting the prediction.

"The one you trust is not telling the full truth. He does not lie, but he withholds information. You would find this information to be important. Until you are told everything, resist the urge to put your trust in this person."

The patron's eyes widened, and she nodded, clearly taking the meaning of Alsibeth's reading. She gave a shallow bow. "Thank you, m'lady, thank you. I'll do as you say." She placed several coins into a basket that sat on the edge of the table and hurried away.

"I must rest," Alsibeth said to the group of watchers who clustered around her. "Leave me for a while, and come back later."

Her audience drifted away into the tavern crowd, and Alsibeth motioned for Connor to have a seat next to her. Her violet eyes watched him intently for a moment, and then she nodded. "Yes, I felt it." Alsibeth gave him a faint smile. "Your master sent you to find out why the magic flickered."

Connor set out the two gold coins between them. "Yes. He wanted to know how widespread it was, and what caused it."

Alsibeth drew a deep breath and closed her eyes, letting her head fall back. Her dark hair pooled around her, and her earrings chimed softly with the movement. "Everywhere. It was felt everywhere. In Donderath, in Meroven, in Tarrant and Vellanaj, and in the Lesser Kingdoms."

"What caused it?"

Alsibeth opened her eyes and leaned forward. She reached toward the semicircle of burning candles that surrounded her and chose the indigo one. Carefully, she lifted it and held it above the wide, shallow bowl of water, then tipped it until liquid wax puddled around the wick and dripped into the water. The hot wax cooled instantly into fragile, twisted threads that hung suspended in the clear water. Alsibeth inhaled deeply, breathing in the candle smoke and the scent of burning sage and then replaced the indigo candle with a murmured incantation and focused her attention on the bowl.

"The flicker was not natural," Alsibeth said, studying the tracery of the hot wax. "It was caused by the hand of men, but not by their design."

"I don't understand."

"Powerful magic is at work. Men seek to affect the course of the war. They toy with power they cannot fully control. Such unintended consequences will grow more unstable—and more dangerous. They risk far more than they can hope to gain."

"What of the war itself? Can you see the outcome? Will Donderath win?"

Alsibeth stared at the candles. Connor could see the flicker of the flames reflected in her eyes. For a moment, she said nothing, but it seemed to Connor that she listened intently to something he could not hear. "I'm sorry," she said after another pause. "I see nothing but fire." She frowned. "But I hear a name. Valtyr."

Connor startled. Alsibeth smiled. "The name is known to you."

"Yes. But only recently so. It's not a name many would recognize."

"I have heard it before, but not in many years." Alsibeth's voice was soft, pitched only for Connor's ears. Again, he wondered about her age and whether her knowledge was of a name or the man himself.

"Did you know him?"

Alsibeth's laugh was as beautiful as the sound of her bells. "No. Only the stories. Heed the warning you've received. Valtyr's map was created for such times as these. There is no time to waste. You must find what has been hidden." She frowned and tilted her head as if listening to something only she could hear.

"Look to the exiled man."

"M'lady?"

"When the fires come and night falls, look to the exiled man."

"I don't understand."

Alsibeth seemed to come back to herself. Her smile was sad. "I'm sorry. I often don't know the full meaning of the messages I receive."

"Will you read the smoke for me?"

Alsibeth nodded. Her hands gestured gracefully, stirring the smoke from the sage smudge and the scented candle. Connor kept his eye on the bell tree. No part of Alsibeth's body touched the table, and yet the delicate bells that hung from the tree began to quiver although the water in the bowl remained utterly still. He had scarcely taken a breath when the entire bell tree had begun to shake. Suddenly, Connor heard a dull ringing, and realized that the patron's goblets and even the half-filled bottles behind the bar had begun to vibrate. The tavern grew silent. Alsibeth's eyes remained closed. Outside, the city bells began to ring, clanging and clattering as if pulled by a madman. Connor glanced up at the marked candle on the mantle to assure himself it was not yet the hour, not the time for the bells to ring.

As suddenly as the ringing began, it stopped. Everyone in the tavern was staring at them. Alsibeth opened her eyes and met Connor's gaze, paying no attention to the onlookers.

"Don't delay your search. Find the map and keep it with you, no matter what happens." She reached out to take his hand. "I've never feared my own readings, but right now...hurry back to Garnoc, and tell him what you've learned. Time is running out."

CHAPTER EIGHT

BLAINE SHUFFLED TO THE FIREPLACE AND FILLED a bowl with gruel. He poured some hot water into a cup to make the weak tea that was all there was to be had in Edgeland, a brew of native leaves and dried berries that tasted nothing like the tea from home. "Where's Dawe?"

"He went down to the Bay to do a little more shopping," Kestel said, looking up from where she was plucking a chicken. "Don't be shy eating the gruel. I need that pot to stew the chicken and I don't like to waste."

Blaine grinned. "As you wish, m'lady. But you'll be chipping it out of the pot. It's thick as tar."

Kestel shrugged. "Convicts can't be choosy."

Blaine sighed. "Maybe someday colonists can be." He sipped the tea and made a face at its bitter aftertaste. "If we didn't have Prokief's guards at the gates, do you think anyone would choose to stay in Edgeland?"

Kestel set aside the cleaned chicken and wiped off her hands. She picked up her own cup and wandered back toward the table. "Good question. Maybe. There are a lot of folks up here who might not have liked being forced to come, but the truth is, they didn't leave much behind. Fresh start up here. Land, a decent house if you put your back into building it, enough food to get by." She shrugged again. "Dunno. The weather's not to my liking, but it doesn't seem to bother some people."

"Would you go home, if you could?"

Kestel thought for a moment, staring down at her tea. "I understood the role I played back in Donderath. Power, money, and secrets were my trade. There's not a market for those things on the same scale up here." She gave a bitter smile. "I don't know if you'll believe me, but the sex was only ever a small part of it. My patrons wanted me to listen to them, to adore them, to absolve them. They unburdened themselves to me. That was as much of a release."

"And there's nobody as interesting up here?" Blaine replied with a grin.

"Just you, m'lord, and you've only got one secret," Kestel teased. She grew serious. "Would you go back?"

Blaine studied his empty bowl for a while without speaking. "I can't go back to Donderath, not with Merrill on the throne. And even if he pardoned me, I've lost everything. Perhaps if I were willing to go somewhere besides Donderath, but where would that be, and for what end? If I'm to be a beggar, better at least in my own kingdom than in a strange land." He let out a long breath.

"There's no such thing as a fresh start in Donderath. No one would hire a murderer to learn a trade. I can starve here just as well as there. At least here, I've got a way to earn a living and a roof over my head that's partly mine. So long as Prokief keeps his distance, it's tolerable."

Kestel nodded. "I won't say I don't miss the luxuries of court, or the food, or the social life. On the other hand, I haven't had to kill anyone for a long time. That's restful."

"Restful?"

She grinned. "I always found it…distasteful. More so than any of the sex. Messier, too," she said, her grin widening as color stole into Blaine's cheeks. "On the other hand, it's so much less complicated here. Minding the sheep and the rabbits and the chickens. I actually like weaving and spinning—who'd have guessed? It's satisfying to see a skein of yarn I've made myself."

The front door slammed open and Verran stood panting in the entrance. His face was red and his hair clung sweat-soaked to his scalp. "They've taken Dawe to Velant."

"Why?" Blaine motioned for Verran to take the seat he had just vacated, while Kestel went to pour him a cup of tea. Verran paused as he caught his breath, and sipped the tea to steady himself.

"Prokief's got soldiers all over the Bay. Warden-mages, too. The soothsayers in town have been claiming all kinds of omens, from the shape of the clouds to rumblings from Estendall, that volcano out off the fishing waters. Predicting fire and death and blood and darkness."

Blaine grimaced. "Predicting darkness doesn't take much skill. The long dark is about to start. Happens every year."

"Why did they take Dawe?" Kestel pressed.

Verran drained his cup and set it aside. "We were on our way to the cooper to pick up some barrels. Dawe was also going to check to see if the cooper had any more work for him. Two of Prokief's guards stopped us and demanded our papers."

"Dawe hates that," Kestel murmured.

"We would have been all right, except that the guards decided to search us for weapons."

"Prokief's got to be on edge if he doesn't have anything better for his soldiers to do," Blaine muttered.

"We didn't have anything on us larger than hunting knives, but the guard found Dawe's bag of coins. He started making noises about how Dawe must have stolen it, and he and his friend started to push us around, trying to make Dawe confess."

"Because the bastards wanted his money," Kestel said.

"Right." Verran wiped his mouth with the back of his hand, and Blaine saw that one cheekbone was beginning to purple from a fresh bruise. "Now, when I'd seen the guards coming our way, I dropped my share of the coins behind a barrel, so they didn't find anything when they searched me. Dawe wasn't close to anything, so they got his. But you know how that kind of thing sets him off."

Blaine grimaced. Dawe Killick was one of the most even-tempered men Blaine had ever met. He seemed to accept nearly everything—bad weather, lost bets, even his own reversal of fortune that landed him at Velant—with unusual calm, but one thing raised his ire. The bullying of the Velant guards could send him into a rage. He'd had a couple of run-ins with the guards while they were both inside Velant, and a few near-misses since gaining his Ticket of Leave. "Yeah, I know."

"It doesn't surprise me when the guards try to shake me down for some coins," Verran said. "I always have a couple in my pocket for them to find, and use my magic fingers to hide the rest," he said, sliding his thumb along his fingertips, alluding to the pickpocket skills that had helped earn him his conviction. "But when Dawe realized they meant to steal his money outright, he started yelling at the guards. They yelled back, and next thing I knew, there were more guards coming."

He fidgeted nervously. "I'm better at running than fighting, Blaine, you know that. So I gave one of the guards a good shove, and hoped I could drag Dawe free, but the other one had too tight a grip. Before I knew it, four of them were all over him, punching and kicking until Dawe stopped fighting back. I couldn't get him away from them, so I ran before they thought to grab me." He reached beneath his jacket and dropped a pouch on the table.

"Not that it does Dawe much good, but I got his coins back when I shoved the guard. If he would have kept his temper, we could have nipped them back later and none of this would have had to happen," Verran said miserably. "I hung around, out of sight, hoping they'd just leave him on the street and I could get him to a healer. But they took him."

Blaine swore. "Of all the stupid, worthless reasons to get picked up—" He kicked at a chair and sent it skidding across the room.

"We've got to do something," Kestel said.

"Where's Piran?" Blaine asked, looking around.

"He went out to check the traps first thing this morning. He should be back before long," Kestel replied.

Blaine sighed. "He and I can go into town and see what we hear. With luck, Prokief's just trying to intimidate everyone and he'll send Dawe back a little bloody but still in one piece."

"Do you think they'll keep him? Rescind his Ticket?" Kestel asked. She shivered and wrapped her arms around herself, gathering her shawl closer.

Blaine shrugged. "Prokief doesn't have the space or the guards to start locking up every colonist who steps out of line. He can rough us up, push us around, hope that intimidates us into knowing our place, but the truth is there are more of us than there are of his guards. He's got to realize that if he pushes too hard, without reinforcements from Donderath, he can't fight all of us."

"He doesn't have to lock him up," Verran said miserably.

"Throwing back a body once in a while sends a message quite well."

Blaine chewed his lip as he thought. Verran had spoken aloud what had gone through his own mind. "We won't know until we see what's being said in town. As soon as Piran gets back, he and I can head down to the Bay."

"I'm going with you," Verran said.

"You've already had one close scrape with the guards. Don't push your luck."

Verran shook his head, a determined look on his face. "I feel awful about running. I thought they'd just get in a few punches and be gone. If I'd have known they were going to take him to Velant, I'd have fought."

"And ended up in Velant with him," Kestel said. "Mick's right. There's nothing you could have done differently."

"Maybe not," Verran acknowledged grudgingly. "But I'm not going to run away now. I can identify the guards who took him. If we spot them in a tavern, I can use my music and my magic to make sure the ale hits them harder than usual. That should make it easier to get information out of them." He glared at Blaine. "Admit it. Unless you and Piran plan to pound the truth out of the guards, you need me."

"I'd rather have someone stay here with Kestel, especially after the attack."

"Like I need a nursemaid?" Kestel replied. Blaine had not seen her hand move, but a thin steel blade was suddenly in her good hand. "You boys go find out what's going on. I'm quite all right by myself for the evening."

"Just so you know," Verran added, "everyone says there's a storm coming. Not only that, but Estendall's acting strange. Couple of the merchants swore the ground's quaked in the last few days. Heard some fishermen saying that there've been worse than usual waves because the volcano's shaken things up."

"Prokief probably took it as a sign. That man was always as superstitious as he was stupid," Blaine said.

"Just bring Dawe back," Kestel said, looking from Blaine to Verran. "I've gotten used to having him around." Her tone was offhanded, but Blaine saw concern in her eyes. Dawe's dry sense of humor usually won a laugh out of Kestel, and his penchant for building helpful contraptions around the farm had also gone far to endear him to her.

"We'll do our best," Blaine said.

CHAPTER NINE

BLAINE, VERRAN, AND PIRAN JUMPED DOWN from the wagon and gave the driver a coin for his trouble. The wagon's runners crunched across the hard-packed ice of the Skalgerston Bay road as it headed down the street. Blaine's eyes narrowed as he looked from side to side. Soldiers wearing the burgundy livery of the Velant prison regiment were posted at intervals. Two of the soldiers converged on Blaine and the others.

"Papers," the guard demanded, holding out a hand.

Annoyance was clear on Piran's and Verran's faces as they dug for their Tickets of Leave, and Blaine guessed that the soldier could see the same impatience in his own expression. They remained silent as the soldiers took their time examining the Tickets before handing them back with a snap of the wrist.

"What's your business in the city?" one of the guards barked at Blaine.

Blaine met the man's eyes and tapped his Ticket. "Colonist. I can go where I please."

"That can change." The soldiers eyed the three men but did not make a move toward their swords. "Best you stay out of trouble, or there'll be a price to pay."

Blaine and the others said nothing until they had rounded the corner. Piran let loose a string of curses. "What in bloody Raka do they think they're doing? Since when have there been that many guards in the Bay?"

Verran looked both directions to assure that they were out of earshot of the guards. "I'm guessing that Prokief's taking extra precautions." He met Blaine's gaze. "I think you've got part of your answer. Can't imagine Prokief sparing the guards if he hadn't run into the same kind of problem we had with the magic. Now you know what Dawe and I ran into."

"Yeah, but did the warden-mages help cause the disturbance, or were they hit with it like us?" Blaine asked as they turned their backs to the wind and began walking.

Within a four-block stretch along the waterfront, guards stopped them two more times demanding papers. Blaine watched the guards closely as they examined the Tickets of Leave. *Something's scared them*, he thought. *This isn't a normal patrol.*

The third set of guards took so long looking over their Tickets that Blaine began to wonder if the papers were going to be confiscated. "State your business," the guard snapped.

Piran moved to answer, but Blaine laid a cautioning hand on his arm. "Just wanted a tankard of good ale," Blaine said with forced affability. "Not a crime, is it?"

"The Commander's posted new regulations for the city. Best you have a look, or you'll find yourselves in irons."

Blaine felt Piran shift as if to make a response, and he dug his fingers into Piran's arm. "We're here for ale, not trouble. Just point us to the posting."

The guard pointed to a broadsheet nailed to the side of a pipe shop's wall. Blaine could feel his gaze on them as they made their way over.

"Does me precious little good," Piran groused. "Never learned to read much more than my own name."

Blaine scanned through the posting and let out a low whistle. "Something's definitely got Prokief nervous," he murmured. " 'Colonists and sailors will present their Tickets of Leave upon demand. Edgeland-born colonists must show a naming ticket from their town of birth.' He's calling for a curfew at ninth bells, with the threat to confine anyone caught in the street after that time. Taverns have to close before ninth bells or house their patrons for the night."

"And if someone goes out to take a piss in the bushes, do they count that as breaking curfew?" Piran asked indignantly.

"Spare yourself the trouble and just piss out the window," Verran replied.

Blaine returned to the broadsheet. "Uh-oh. 'Soldiers can enter any house at any time to search for illegal mages or unlawful magical items.' And look here: 'Anyone with any magic, however minor, must register with the tax officer in the city. Unregistered magic users will be rounded up and taken to Velant.' "

"He can't do that," Verran muttered.

"Does he think someone in Edgeland caused whatever it was we felt?" Piran asked.

Blaine shrugged. "You know Prokief. Probably." He let out a long breath. "Let's go see what we can find out in the tavern. Maybe someone else will know something."

A walk along the storefronts confirmed Blaine's suspicions. Several of the merchants who carried imported objects from Donderath—fabric, pottery, and the few luxuries to be had in Edgeland, such as trinkets and cheap jewelry—were closed. Merchants who relied on Donderath for their raw materials had sparse goods in the windows of their shops. The grocers in the market stalls displayed none of the foods from Donderath that usually augmented the Edgeland-grown vegetables, freshly slaughtered chickens, roughly milled flour, goat cheese, and jerked game meat from local sources.

Blaine stopped to purchase the salt and cinnamon Kestel had requested that he bring back. He added a small bag of the pipe weed Dawe favored, in the hopes that his friend would return home to enjoy it.

"Sure'n you're joking, aren't you?" the woman behind the stall said. Her breath was heavy with onions and her teeth were stained yellow from the chipped ivory pipe she held in one hand. "Ain't got no spices, and I won't have no more until the ships come again from Donderath. If they come," she added darkly.

She turned out a small bunch of the dried pipe weed into the empty tin Blaine handed her. "That's the last of the smoke weed, too. Either make it last, or figure out how to grow it here." She laughed. "Might as well face facts. Donderath's cut us off. We'll starve this winter, mark my words."

"Is that what everyone thinks?" Blaine asked with a nod to the other merchants down the row of makeshift stalls and pushcarts. The market was less busy than he had ever seen it, and the stalls were nearly empty of wares.

"What'll happen, I wonder, when the long dark comes?" The merchant woman rubbed her hands together. Dirty gloves, roughly knitted, were scarce protection against the cold. "Edgeland was never meant to provide for itself. I reckon the king's found a way to save himself some coin and execute the lot of us, the guards and the guarded together."

"I pray you're wrong," Blaine said quietly, gathering the items he had purchased.

"Pray all you want; the gods can't hear you here," the woman replied, turning to the side to spit into the snow.

Blaine and the others exchanged a glance as they walked away from the market. "She's got a point," Verran said, biting into a hard piece of cheese. "The long night is bad enough when we're not hungry. The fights start getting worse around the second month of dark, and by the time the white nights are back, we're all barely sane."

"Doesn't matter why Donderath's decided not to send more ships," Piran muttered. "What matters to me is what Prokief plans to do about it. That's what's got me worried."

They stopped in front of Crooked House tavern, so named because one side of the building had sunk during a spring thaw. Blaine and the others walked through the slanted doorway, ducking where the building's settling had made part of the lintel lower. Inside, the room had a slight cant to it, like a boat deck in a storm.

"The only people who can walk straight in this place are already drunk," Piran muttered.

Ifrem, the tavern master, hailed them as they entered. He was an older man with a bald head and a close-cropped salt-and-pepper beard. A beating in Velant had given Ifrem a permanent limp, and cost him the sight in one eye, which he covered with a patch. "What'll you have, Mick? Ale or whiskey?"

"Whiskey," Blaine said, dropping a coin on the bar. He looked around. "What's the occasion? You've got quite the crowd in here."

Ifrem poured their drinks and looked around to see who else was close enough to hear. "Strange things going on. Heard the fur trappers telling about odd lights and men disappearing."

Blaine nodded. "We heard that, too."

"Then yesterday, everyone was going about their business and people started falling over. Some of them keeled over right proper. Eyes rolled back in their heads and they went down. Just about everyone else got the headache of their lives." He chuckled. "Can't say I enjoyed the headache, but we sold plenty of medicine afterward," he said, tapping his bottle of whiskey.

Blaine and his friends exchanged silent glances. *So it wasn't just us.*

"How are folks taking it?" Piran asked as he took a sip of his drink. Verran left them to drift over to where the musicians congregated in one corner. He withdrew the pennywhistle that was always in his pocket, and began to play a jaunty tune.

Ifrem shrugged. "Some people think Prokief's mages are up to something. A few thought it was a stroke of the gods. Best theory I've heard is that the warden-mages wanted to identify anyone with a hint of magic—why, I'm not sure, but you've seen the posting?"

Blaine nodded. "Yeah. We were going to ask about that."

Ifrem shrugged. "I've got some guards who are regulars here. Not bad fellows; got into trouble back home like everyone else and got the choice of Velant or the noose."

"Like everyone else," Blaine murmured.

"They were pretty closed-mouthed, even after their ale, but it sounds like there's been trouble up at the prison, and Prokief wants to make sure it doesn't spread into the rest of the colony."

"What kind of trouble?" Blaine asked.

"Couldn't get a straight answer out of them, except that it had something to do with magic."

The door opened, and a sudden hush fell over the crowd. Ifrem's face darkened, and he murmured a curse.

"Looks like we've got our own trouble," Piran growled under his breath. "Prokief just walked in."

Out of the corner of his eye, Blaine could see the crowd part as Velant's commander entered, followed by four burly guards. Prokief was a tall, broad-shouldered man with a cloud of unruly dark hair and a full, dark beard. Rumor had it he had served Merrill too well in a border war some years before, showing a taste for bloodshed and a record for butchery that the king found embarrassing. Merrill had "rewarded" Prokief with the position of Velant commander, in effect exiling him along with his charges.

As soon as the guards had cleared the threshold, patrons began to make their way to the door, jostling one another to leave. Prokief's expression was smug, telling Blaine that the commander relished the fear with which the colonists regarded him.

Prokief nodded toward the large, central table where several men sat playing cards. Without a word, two of the soldiers walked over and upended the table, scattering cards, coins, and chits. "Game's over," one of the guards said. The cardplayers scrambled for the door as the guards righted the table. One of them pulled out a chair for Prokief, who unfastened his cloak and sat down, handing his cloak to the guard.

"A bucket of your best beer, Ifrem, quickly now," Prokief commanded.

Blaine saw Ifrem's jaw clench. "As you wish, Commander," the tavern master said tightly. Ifrem carried over a bucket of beer and set it in front of Prokief, along with a tankard. "On the house," he said stiffly. As he walked back, Blaine caught the look in Ifrem's eyes. Prokief would drink the night away with no intention of paying his tab, so the generosity had been Ifrem's way of gaining the upper hand.

"Damn right it's on the house," Prokief snapped. "Bring me bread and cheese, and another pail of beer for my men. Mind you're quick about it."

Ifrem's shoulders tensed, but his expression was neutral. "As you wish."

Prokief poured himself a tankard and drank it in one draught. He belched loudly, and his guards laughed with gusto, although their humor sounded forced.

"Seems like some of your customers had a little too much to drink," Prokief said loudly. Ifrem stiffened, then went on with his work behind the bar. "Got a few of them back at the prison last night. Drunk and disorderly." He clucked his tongue in mock distress. "What a shame."

"That bastard," Verran muttered. Blaine laid a hand on his arm and gave a warning shake of his head.

"I think one of the men we picked up was a friend of yours, McFadden," Prokief said. "Killick, I think the name was. Passed out drunk in the street. Disgraceful. Some time back in Velant should remind him of his manners."

Ignoring Piran's warning glance, Blaine turned slowly in his seat. "It's illegal to hold citizens who have their Ticket," Blaine said evenly. "King's orders."

Prokief smirked. "The king is a long way from Velant. Here, I decide the rules."

"I'll pay his bond," Blaine replied. "Just let him go."

Satisfaction gleamed in Prokief's eyes. "I don't take orders from you, McFadden. Count yourself lucky I don't haul you back up the hill and throw you in the Hole. I might be tempted to forget you're there this time." He dropped his voice so that only he and Blaine could hear. "Watch your step, McFadden. Merrill won't always be looking."

Blaine was about to say something when a deafening explosion rocked the tavern. The blast shook the ground so hard that glasses slid from tables and bottles fell from the shelf behind Ifrem. The tavern's remaining patrons ran for the door, crowding through the narrow entrance, since the wavy glass in the windows made it impossible to see clearly. For an instant, Blaine saw a flicker of fear in Prokief's face, then the big man pushed away from the table and motioned for his guards to follow, shouldering into his cloak with a flourish. Prokief's guards cleared a path through the crowd outside the door. Blaine and the others followed at a distance.

Far out to sea, a huge plume of smoke and ash rose high into the sky. Flashes of fire rose amid the plume and then fell back toward the water. The ground under their feet rocked once more and then went still. As the crowd watched, billows of smoke continued to rise as high as the clouds. Around Blaine the crowd began to mutter.

"It's Estendall, out there on the edge of the fishing waters. Erupted like a plugged kettle."

"Yadin save us! It's a sign."

"Best hope the winds don't shift, or we'll be tasting ash."

Prokief and the guards strode away toward where their frightened horses were straining at their tethers and rode off in the direction of Velant.

"At least it got rid of Prokief," Piran grumbled.

Ifrem stood next to Blaine, and Blaine heard the tavern master murmur a prayer to the gods of sea and air for protection. Around him, others invoked the names of household deities or the blessing of the High God. Some of them clutched at amulets or rolled a polished stone prayer bead between their fingers, lips moving in desperate supplication.

"You've been here longer than I have," Blaine replied, staring in awe at the island peak enveloped in black, roiling clouds. "When's the last time it erupted?"

Ifrem shook his head. "Not since I've been here." He paused. "Planning to stay the night?"

Blaine shrugged. "With the curfew, don't see as we have a choice."

Ifrem smiled. "Stick around after I close the bar and see to the other guests. I might be able to find an answer to your questions."

That night, a storm came in from the west. From the tavern's doorway, Blaine could see the waves crashing against the storm wall, carrying with them a few of the smaller fishing boats. The crews of the larger boats defied the curfew to take their ships far enough out from the docks to avoid being run aground. Rain lashed the coastline, and high winds snapped the tavern's sign back and forth on its hinges.

Two soaking-wet travelers arrived just as the bells in the tower struck nine times. Shivering and dripping, the two men hung their sodden cloaks on pegs near the door and stomped the water off their boots.

"Bad enough that it's raining so hard a man can't see, but it's got that damned ash in it," one of the newcomers complained as he pushed his way toward the bar. The crowd parted, having no desire to be as wet as he was.

"It's black rain, it is," his companion added. "And the sea's gone wild. Saw a man get swept into the waves when the water crashed up over the seawall and fell back again. Good thing you're down at this end of the street. The shops near the corner will have water up to the ankles, that's for sure."

A palpable sense of fear hung over the crowd that huddled in the Crooked House. Ifrem did a brisk business, with patrons opting for hard liquor over ale to calm their nerves. Blaine and his friends sat in a corner, watching the crowd.

"Mick! What brings you to town on a godsdamned night like this?"

Blaine looked up to see Wills Jothra, the village cooper,

headed their way. "Picked a bad night to go out for some drink, I guess," Blaine replied.

Wills pulled up a stool and nodded a greeting to Piran. "Well, your misfortune is my good luck. Been meaning to talk with you..."

Piran watched the crowd as Wills went into detail on a business deal gone bad. "So that's the long and short of it," Wills said, punctuating the end of his tale of woe by finishing off his tankard of ale. "What do you make of it?"

"Do you think Keffer meant to cheat you?"

Wills shook his head. "Nah. I think he's an idiot, and I think he lost the money he owed me gambling."

"Idiot or not, he buys a lot of barrels for the pickled vegetables he sells, doesn't he?"

Wills nodded. "Aye, when he isn't pickled himself."

"Then give him a choice: Either he pays you cash, with interest, or he pays you in pickles twice the value of the debt."

"What am I going to do with all the ruddy pickles?" Wills exclaimed.

Blaine grinned. "Give one away to everyone who places a new barrel order. Sell them at a discount to the tavern masters. You stay friendly with Keffer, you get value for the debt, and Keffer just might be more careful the next time he owes you money."

Wills grinned and slapped the table. "I knew you'd have a good idea, Mick. Let me buy you and your friends a round."

Blaine and the others toasted Wills, who thanked him again before moving on. Before long, two more men wandered over to ask Mick's advice on business affairs, resulting in two more rounds of liquor.

Blaine shook his head as the last man walked away. "How does a night at the tavern always end up like this?"

Verran had finished playing, and as the musicians packed up their instruments, he walked over to the table, sliding his pennywhistle into a leather pouch on his belt. "Holding court again, Mick?"

"Our friend here wants to know why the confused and beleaguered seek him out," Piran said dryly, his voice slightly slurred from the generosity of Blaine's "clients."

Verran hooked a toe under a stool and brought it close to the table, and poured himself a tankard of ale. "Let's see... because you can read and do figures, unlike the majority of Edgeland folks. Or maybe it's because wherever you came from, much as you won't talk about it with your closest mates," he said, feigning hurt, "you had schooling."

Verran grew serious. "Honestly, Mick, you've done a good turn for more of the settlers than I can count. You've either stood up for them in a fight, kept them out of trouble, or gotten them out of a jam." He shrugged. "That's rare up here. People remember."

"I always figured it was why Prokief had it in for you," Piran added. "Do you think that's why he took Dawe? Because he knows you and Dawe are mates?"

Blaine shrugged. "I wouldn't pretend to know why Prokief does anything," he replied. But that wasn't exactly true. If there had been anyone who hated Ian McFadden more than his own son, it was Vedran Pollard. Time after time, Pollard and the elder McFadden had gone out of their way to quash each other's business dealings, embarrass each other at court, even hire henchmen to poison herds in the fields. It had always amazed Blaine that Pollard hadn't beaten him to murdering old man McFadden. And before his assignment to Velant, Prokief had been Pollard's right-hand man.

There was a crash and the sound of breaking wood, and one

of the front storm shutters tore lose, sending a gust of rain into the tavern. Blaine and Piran jumped up and headed for where their cloaks were hung. "We'll get it," Blaine assured Ifrem, who was busy behind the bar.

Blaine reached for his cloak and paused. "How in Raka did my cloak get wet? I've been here all evening."

Ifrem gave a jerk of his head toward the last peg on the wall. "Your cloak's down there. That's my cloak. I'll grant they look a lot alike. I had to run out to the shed for more whiskey, curfew or no curfew."

Blaine and Piran grabbed tools and a handful of nails and ventured out into the storm. "Not worried about the curfew?" Piran shouted above the storm.

Blaine found the broken shutter snared in the bushes, and together, he and Piran wrestled it into place against the wind. "You expect guards to patrol in this weather?" he shouted back. A glance up and down the deserted, rain-soaked road proved his point. Soaked to the skin, Blaine and Piran headed back into the tavern, where Ifrem was already mopping up the water that had soaked the first row of tables.

"Hang your cloaks by the fire in the kitchen," Ifrem barked. "You'll find some dry clothes in the storage room. I'll pour you a whiskey once I'm done. Your drinks are on me tonight. Much obliged for the help."

By the time Blaine and Piran had dried off and changed clothes, most of the tavern's patrons had drifted to the upstairs rooms or took their places on the benches near the banked fire, ready for the night. When the inn was quiet, Ifrem motioned for Blaine and the others to join him in the kitchen.

"You wanted to know when the last time was that the volcano erupted," Ifrem said. "I don't know, but I've got something that might tell us." He went to a wooden cabinet and reached into the back corner, withdrawing a leather cylinder. Carefully, his rough fingers teased out a yellowed piece of parchment. He motioned for Blaine to clear a spot on the large cook's table, and spread a cloth over the table for a dry surface before he set down the parchment. As he spread it out, Blaine gave a low whistle.

"Where in the Valley of the Gods did you get that?"

Ifrem grinned. "When I first got my Ticket, I apprenticed to the man who owned the Crooked House. That was about five years ago. When he came down with the fever, he called in a witness and gave me this inn." He looked at the others conspiratorially.

"I sat with him in his last hours. And when we were alone, he told me that when he'd first come to Edgeland in the early days of the colony, he'd had a man come to the inn who stayed in one of his upper rooms. The guest was one of the very first to be sent to Velant and then earn his Ticket. Time in the mines broke him, and he wasn't fit to set up his own homestead; that's why he stayed at the inn. Well, long and short of it is, the man took sick and died. Since he owed the old owner for his room and board, the tavern keeper claimed what little was in the man's room in payment. And he found this."

Ifrem tapped the parchment. "From what Evath, the old tavern master could figure, the boarder had been an astrologer and scholar who'd managed to run afoul of someone with the power to banish him. Not sure how he did it, but he managed to smuggle a few of his papers with him. Now, I've always wondered, what would be so important that someone would bother to bring a map all the way to the end of the world?"

"And?" Blaine asked.

"See for yourself." Ifrem spread the parchment carefully with his hands. Piran and Verran helped to hold down the curled edges.

A carefully inked map showed the coast of Edgeland, but neither Velant prison nor Skalgerston Bay were marked. The surveyor had done a thorough job of noting every one of the land's inlets and jagged fjords, as well as the places early explorers had found hot springs or dug for copper or gems. And on the corner of the map, well off the coast of Edgeland, lay a small island marked with a jagged peak and tipped in red. Estendall.

"It's a nice map," Blaine said, straightening, "but what's the big secret? I can understand why Prokief might not want colonists to have a full map of Edgeland, but—"

"Look in the margins," Ifrem replied.

Blaine bent over the map, straining to make out the fine, spidery handwriting by candlelight. "The eruptions of Estendall," he murmured, carefully running his finger down a list of dates. He looked up at Ifrem. "Donderath claimed Edgeland years ago, but didn't really pay any attention until King Merrill created Velant. So who was around to notice the volcano?"

Ifrem shrugged. "Donderath isn't the only land to have ever found Edgeland. Before Merrill's navy drove off everyone else, there were explorers from across the sea who came to Edgeland for the furs. Later, when word spread about the rubies, more came. Ships have fished these waters for a long time. I suspect that the man who made this talked to anyone he met who knew anything at all about Edgeland."

"There's no pattern to the dates," Blaine said.

"Our mapmaker noticed something interesting," Ifrem said. "Every time over the last fifty years that Estendall erupted, there was a major war going on back on the Continent.

Nineteen years ago—look, it's during the Hoagshed War between Tarrant and Meroven. Forty-one years back, it's the War of Decision, between the two rivals for the Donderath throne. I suspect that the dates farther back come from the bard's tales, but our mapmaker found a connection of each one to a major war."

"And you think that Estendall's eruption now has something to do with the war in Donderath?"

Ifrem nodded. "More than that. I think it has something to do with magic."

Blaine pulled up a chair. "I'm not sure that I follow you."

"Look at this." Ifrem pointed to the notation on the map. The map was marked in places with a "u" topped with a ring, a symbol of magic. Some of the locations, Blaine recognized as shrines to the major gods. Others appeared to be natural features, such as caverns or mountain peaks. There was one spot, far to the north of Skalgerston Bay, out in the frozen wilderness.

"That's near where the trappers disappeared," Piran murmured.

Blaine murmured, looking at the other place of magic marked in the far north. One of the "u"-ring symbols for magic sat off the shore of Edgeland, exactly where Estendall spewed its smoke and fire. "What does it mean if a spot is a place of magic?"

Ifrem was silent for a moment, as if debating something with himself. Finally, he sighed and began to roll up the map. "How much do you know about magic?"

Blaine shrugged. "Not much."

"Mages have a hundred different names for magic, but all that really matters are two: *visithara* and *hasithara*. *Visithara* is the name of natural, untamed magic. It's wild, like the sea. *Hasithara* is the name for tame magic, magic that can be harnessed and controlled. Like water in an aqueduct. It's still the same stuff that's in the ocean, but it has been shaped by a person's control."

"So?" Piran asked.

Ifrem rolled his eyes. "The magic that people can control is *hasithara*. The untamed magic is called *visithara*." He replaced the map in the leather container and returned it to its hiding place. "They say places like the ones marked on the map are where the wild power—*visithara*—flows the strongest. People without magic think the gods seem closer there. A shrine or a temple is built, or the people who live nearby bring offerings to the spirits. For someone with the ability to use magic—*hasithara*—their power is stronger in those places. For true mages, supposedly, those places are a *source* of power." He shut the cabinet door behind him and leaned against it. "And according to legend and the bards, when powerful magic is done, it can backlash through those same places of power."

"Are you saying that *magic* made Estendall erupt?" Piran asked skeptically.

"Something happened yesterday that put anyone with a hedge witch's crumb of power flat on their backs," Ifrem replied. "Today, Estendall explodes. We hear hints that the warden-mages' magic isn't working right. I think someone's tapping into the places of power, creating a backlash." He paused.

"Evath told me that the old man he got the map from almost never came out of his room. Seemed to be scared of his shadow. Evath wondered if someone might have been looking for him—or for the maps."

"That's not as crazy as it sounds," Piran said. "I've heard rumors that Prokief has taken bribes from Donderath on more than one occasion to make sure someone in Velant disappeared. It might have taken the old man's enemies a while to catch up with him."

"Do you really think Prokief's mages had something to do with the volcano?" Blaine scoffed. "They're strong enough to bully the convicts, but..."

"Nothing like King Merrill's battle mages," Ifrem finished for him. "Or, we can guess, the battle mages of Meroven and the other kingdoms."

"Gods save us," Blaine murmured. "You think it's the war causing this?"

Ifrem shrugged. "Do you have a better explanation?"

Verran eyed their host. "For an innkeeper, you know a lot about magic."

Ifrem turned away. "We all were something else before we came to Velant," he said quietly.

"I know one doesn't ask about the past up here," Blaine said. "But I have the feeling that whatever is happening stands to cause us all a lot of grief. If there's a way to keep Prokief off our backs—keep him from taking it out on the colonists—I'd like to figure out what it is."

Ifrem was quiet for a moment as if struggling with himself, and then shrugged. "I should have figured you'd ask when I showed you the map. I was assistant to Lord Arrington's senior mage."

Verran raised an eyebrow. "You're a mage?"

Ifrem chuckled. "No. I was assistant to a mage. Chosen because I could read and write and because I couldn't do any magic and therefore couldn't steal any secrets."

"So what did you steal?"

"Nothing of value. My master, the mage, helped to... advance...Lord Arrington's fortunes. After a while, the lord grew worried that my master knew too many secrets. He betrayed my master and had him killed."

"Why didn't they kill you, too?"

Ifrem gave a bitter grin. "I ran away the night my master was taken. I left the city, figuring that Lord Arrington would want rid of me, too. Loose ends, you know. He sent his men after me, and I was pretty sure none of the king's guards would take my side if it came to a fight, so I did the only thing I could."

"You got yourself arrested," Blaine supplied.

Ifrem nodded. "Stole some fruit in plain view of the guards. Once I was in custody, Lord Arrington couldn't easily get to me without a reason. I figured transport to Velant was better than losing my head."

"And do you still think that?" Blaine asked.

"On good days," Ifrem replied.

"So the long and short of it is, you know enough about how magic works to be dangerous, but you can't do any yourself," Verran said.

"Guilty as charged."

Blaine met his eyes. "We understand why you wouldn't want Prokief and his mages to know about you—or the map. Your secret is safe."

Ifrem laid a hand on his shoulder. "I wouldn't have told you if I didn't already know that, Mick," he said. "Trouble is coming. If I can help, I'm happy to do it."

"If trouble comes, we'll need all the help we can get," Blaine replied.

CHAPTER
TEN

WITH ALSIBETH'S WARNING WEIGHING ON HIS mind, Connor declined Engraham's offer of a room for the night. He took the two lidded buckets of bitterbeer and made his way back up the hill toward Quillarth Castle.

Night had fallen and yet the streets were packed with people. He heard snippets of conversation about the strange bells in the city, comments that fell to whispers when he grew closer. He moved as quickly as he could, given the press of the crowd, guessing that Garnoc would be anxious enough for word that he would forgive a bit of spilled ale.

"Got a taste for the bitters, I see," the guard at the gate said with a nod toward his buckets as he waved him through the entrance.

"My master said there was only one thing that would quench his thirst," Connor replied with a joviality he did not feel.

"Might wander that way myself when I'm off duty," the guard said with a wistful look at the buckets. "Been a while since I've had some."

Connor breathed a sigh of relief when he reached the castle without incident. Nothing had interrupted his return, and his memory, thankfully, was intact. *As soon as I give Garnoc my report, I'll tell him about the other times*, Connor swore to himself. *I couldn't live with myself if I've somehow betrayed his trust. No matter the consequences.*

Connor hurried up the back steps and knocked at the door to Garnoc's rooms. He had barely finished knocking when the door opened.

"Did you see her? What happened? Do you know what made the bells ring?"

Connor had expected Garnoc to be sound asleep. The hour was past the late watch, and it was normally Connor's custom to spend the night in town when he was sent on such an errand. That Garnoc was still awake gave Connor to realize that his master had a good idea of the nature of Alsibeth's readings.

"Come in, quickly now." Lord Garnoc looked both ways down the deserted castle corridor before nearly pulling Connor inside the room. "I'm glad you made it back tonight."

Connor held out the lidded buckets. Garnoc took them and set them to the side, motioning Connor to a chair. He listened carefully as Connor recounted his conversation with the amulet seller, the tide of people fleeing the city, the supply and convict ships at anchor, and Alsibeth's dark predictions. When Connor finished, Garnoc stood and poured them both ale from the buckets Connor had retrieved. Connor moved to make his confession, but Garnoc spoke first.

"I know you haven't slept, m'boy, but I don't think there's time to lose." He reached under his shirt and withdrew Penhallow's pendant, pulling it over his head and handing it to Connor.

"Take this. Do you know where the king's library is?"

"Yes, of course."

Garnoc nodded. "Put the pendant on—and keep it on. Go

to the library and look for Valtyr's map." He paused. "Ring for Geddy. We can trust him to be discreet. He also has access to the seneschal's keys. You might need an extra hand. I'll vouch for you if anyone questions, say that you're doing it on behalf of the War Council. Search high and low. I'm convinced more than ever that Penhallow's instinct is correct. King Merrill's called the Council together at dawn. The timing of the gathering suggests bad news."

Connor took a silver bell that sat on the side table and leaned into the corridor, giving it a couple of sound shakes. Within a few minutes, Var Geddy appeared, still rubbing the sleep from his eyes. Geddy was close to Connor's age, a tall, angular young man with dark hair that hung lank and straight around his sharp features, often covering one eye. Geddy had always reminded Connor of a blackbird, clever but twitchy.

"Master Garnoc rang?"

Connor drew Geddy into Garnoc's room and filled him in quickly to the mission as Garnoc nodded in approval. When Connor had finished, Geddy looked from one to the other.

"You want me to let you into the king's library?"

"Yes, that's what we need," Garnoc replied as if it were an utterly normal request.

"In the middle of the night, without *bothering* Master Lynge or the king about it?" Geddy looked skeptical. His master, Lynge the seneschal, was an efficient, intelligent man without a trace of humor. Connor felt a stab of sympathy; if they were caught, Geddy would no doubt be on the receiving end of one of Lynge's notorious tirades.

"No need to wake them," Garnoc answered with a smile. "After all, I plan to take the item Connor retrieves with me to the War Council meeting in a few hours. It's hardly as if we're spiriting something out of the castle. I'd merely like to have some important—and overlooked—information at hand to share with the king."

"Of course," Geddy replied, though he drew out the words, making his skepticism plain.

"Tomorrow night I'll be glad to show my thanks with a few tankards of bitterbeer down at the Rooster and Pig," Connor threw in. "There's a wench down there who caught your eye, if I remember rightly." He dropped his voice conspiratorially and grinned. "I'm friendly with Engraham, the tavern master. I could put in a good word about you to him, and perhaps he can nudge the girl in your direction."

Geddy's cheeks colored, but the offer seemed to overcome his reluctance. "All right. But let's go before the morning servants are about. Just your luck it was that I happened to draw night duty tonight."

Slept through night duty is more like it, Connor thought, but did not say anything.

Connor and Geddy encountered no one on their walk to the king's library. It was still a few candlemarks before dawn, and except for the servants in the kitchen, few in the castle were awake and about. Connor had slipped the pendant under his tunic before calling for Geddy. The obsidian disk was cold against his skin. As they walked, Connor mused how best to explain the pendant to his companion if the search for the map forced him to take the disk from its hiding place.

Think nothing of it. Just a little trinket given to me by an immortal vampire. Probably find a dozen just like it down at the market, Connor thought dryly as he considered his options. *We think it's an ancient magical amulet created by a really powerful mage who's disappeared, but there's nothing to worry about. Right.*

Connor sighed. *As usual, I'll just make something up when—if—the time comes.*

Geddy carried a small lantern to light their way. He kept the lantern's shutters nearly closed and more than once, the thin young man glanced behind them, his pale-green eyes scanning the corridor.

"We're here," Connor whispered as they reached the door.

Geddy handed him the lantern and fumbled in his pocket, then withdrew a ring of keys. "One of these should work," Geddy mumbled. His hands shook as he tried three keys before finding one that turned the tumblers. Geddy tugged the heavy door open and urgently gestured for Connor to enter. With a final cautious look up and down the hallway, he eased the door shut.

Once the massive library door was closed behind them, he let the lantern shine with its full light.

"Do you know what you're looking for?" Geddy set the lantern on a table and moved quickly around the room, lighting a few more candles.

"Yes…and no. Have you ever been in here before?" Connor looked around the room. Quillarth Castle's library was something of a legend on the Continent. King Merrill's great-grandfather valued scholarship, and collected scrolls and manuscripts from across Donderath and the other kingdoms. The library and the tutors brought in for King Merrill's grandfather's siblings became the talk of the land, and sparked a fashion among the nobles. It was whispered that the library contained quite a few occult texts and magical grimoires along with more prosaic histories and tales of great warriors.

"Once or twice, Lord Lynge sent me up with documents for the king to sign," Geddy replied. "From the first time I saw it, I fancied the room. I read well enough to give my master a hand, but I doubt I could read these books. I hear a lot of them have drawings in them, and writing in colored ink with gold. I'd sure like to have a look at those!"

The room was not one of the largest in the castle, but the comfort of its furnishings gave Connor a surprising insight into their usually taciturn king. Its wide, deep fireplace was unlit, but the cushioned chair near the hearth looked well worn, and a lap robe lay draped across one of the chair arms. A side table with glass decanters and goblets offered a selection of brandy and whiskey. Connor had obviously intruded into the king's inner sanctum, and his nervousness at the possibility of being caught increased.

"I doubt what we're looking for is quite that exciting," Connor murmured. "And it's going to be hidden, so we'll need to look sharp." He put his hands on his hips and looked around. "Where could someone hide a map in here that it would stay hidden?"

"Why hide it at all?"

Connor hesitated, unwilling to tell Geddy the whole tale, or to reveal why this particular map was quite so special. "From what Lord Garnoc's been told, several other maps by this map-maker were so desirable that someone stole them."

"Pinched them? From under the king's nose?"

Connor chuckled. "I doubt the king was reading them when the maps were stolen. But yes, from the library, so the story goes. This fourth map must have been hidden better than the others, or maybe the thief didn't realize there was a map he didn't get."

Taking a deep breath, Connor and Geddy set about their work. Connor looked at the high wooden bookshelves packed with scrolls and leather-bound manuscripts and felt panic rise. *Where in Charrot's name do I look?*

Connor began to walk around the room's perimeter. The built-in bookshelves rose higher than his head, and above them, covering the walls of the room up to the ceiling, was a mural of the constellations sacred to each of the major gods of Donderath's pantheon: Mighty Charrot; Torven, the trickster; Esthrane, mother of life; Yadin, the god of sea and ice; Dorcet, goddess of birth. The murals were beautifully painted, and inlaid with gems, decorative tile, and bits of gold and silver.

"You know, with the lines drawn between the stars and all, I can actually see why the fortune-tellers talk about the gods being in the stars," Geddy said, and Connor looked over to see that the young man also was staring at the ornate mural. "Wish you could see the lines like that in the real sky. I never could make it out for myself. Figured the seers were pulling my leg."

Connor had been slowly walking from image to image. He stopped in front of the image of Vessa, goddess of fire. In the artist's imagination, Vessa had wild, red hair that flowed waist-length behind her. In her right hand she held a burning brand, the kind used to light every kitchen fire and cook stove. In her left hand, she held a lightning bolt. At her feet flowed lava from an exploding mountain, setting an entire forest aflame. Volatile, quick to curse and quick to bless, Vessa was a goddess of both life and death.

Connor cast a glance over his shoulder at the fireplace, assuring himself that it was unlit. "Warm in here, isn't it?"

Geddy frowned. "Without the fire lit, I was actually thinking it was a mite cool."

Connor moved away from the mural of Vessa, continuing his trek around the room. A chill ran down his back. He glanced at Geddy. "This is going to sound strange, but has it just gotten a lot colder in here in the last few minutes?"

Geddy looked at him skeptically. "Are you sure you're not ill?

I've been within three paces from you this whole time, and I still think it's a bit cool, but tolerably so."

Connor shifted, and the pendant slid against his undershirt to touch bare skin. The disk was ice cold.

Connor crossed the room to stand once more at Vessa's feet. Within a few breaths, he felt sweat rise on his temples, and noticed that the pendant had grown uncomfortably warm against his skin. He looked up at the mural of the goddess with new interest.

"Hot or cold is it?" he murmured to himself. "Let's see just how warm I am."

"Beggin' your pardon?"

Connor eyed the shelves. "I've got a hunch that it's over here. Give me a hand."

Connor and Geddy started at the bottom shelf, examining every scroll and manuscript, yet the pendant gave no further clue. They found no maps at all, and as their search took them to higher and higher shelves, Connor's nervousness grew that they might be discovered.

He craned his neck to look at the shelves high above his head. "Is there something we can stand on that won't break to reach up there? I'm guessing there's a way to get those books down."

"Aye. There's a ladder over there." Geddy pointed to a small ladder. Unlike the workmen's tools in the barns, this ladder was made of the same rich, polished wood as the shelves themselves.

With the ladder, Connor could reach not only the top shelf but see the mural up close. The artist had captured Vessa's spirit as well as her sensuality. In awe, Connor stretched up a hand to touch the feet of the goddess.

"She's a beauty, isn't she?" Geddy said, but the appreciation in his tone wasn't totally reverential.

Connor flinched as the pendant burned against his skin. The disk was as hot as if it had been in a fire. He snatched it from beneath his tunic, careful to hold it by its leather strap. It glowed with a faint green light. He pulled the strap over his head and held the disk closer to the mural; the green glow grew stronger.

"Hold up there, what's that?" Geddy called up to him. "Where'd you get that?"

"It's supposed to go with the map," Connor replied. "Made by the same person."

"You never told me it was magic. I didn't agree to go looking for a magic map."

Ignoring Geddy, Connor climbed to the very top rung of the ladder to get a better look at the mural. He lifted the disk like a lantern, moving it across the figure of Vessa. When he moved it to the left, the glow dimmed, but as he moved it to the right, the glow intensified until he held it over the burning brand in her right hand. The pendant now glowed brightly. Connor leaned forward to see better. The brand looked to be an inlay of wood.

Holding the pendant aloft with his left hand, Connor began to gently probe the length of the brand with the fingers of his right hand, mindful of his precarious position on the ladder. He felt a small rise, like a knot in the wood, and heard a quiet click. The brand slid out from the wall, revealing a slim wooden box. The pendant's glow was now nearly blinding, and Connor carefully withdrew the box from the mural and climbed carefully down the ladder.

"You found it!" Geddy crowded close to him, eager for a look. "What's so special about it, anyway?"

"Let's have a glance at it and see for ourselves," Connor replied.

"We need to get out of here," Geddy reminded him.

"I've got no desire to take the wrong map back to my master. If it's not the right map, I can put it back and we can keep looking. I don't think we'll have another chance to get back in here."

Connor swiveled the box's top out of the way and gently tapped the box against his hand. Inside was a large piece of parchment, very old, and from what Connor could see, it was indeed a map.

Gingerly, Connor withdrew the map and spread it as flat as he dared on one of the library tables. Geddy stood on tiptoe behind him, straining to see. The parchment was yellowed, and Connor feared it might begin to crack at his touch. To his relief, it did not. The pendant continued to glow, though not as brightly as before. Connor looked more closely at the map, bending over it, and the pendant began to swing over the map. Just as he reached a hand to stop the pendant's motion, it froze in midair of its own accord.

"I saw one of the fortune-tellers down at the pub use a crystal like that," Geddy said. "Is that disk something like her crystal?"

"Apparently so."

Connor studied the map. The pendant hung directly over a series of symbols, runes he had never seen before. He bent closer to take a better look, and realized that the pendant was tugging at him. He lifted it from around his neck. When it lay flat on the map, the tugging stopped for a moment. His fingertips kept a light contact with the pendant, and the disk suddenly began to slide across the surface of the map, drawing his hand with it.

"By Torven's horns! I saw that. Did you move the disk—or did it move you?"

Connor did not answer. He wasn't entirely sure, and he saw

no need in stoking Geddy's interest in what had already been a most unusual errand. The pendant came to rest so that some of the odd cuts in the obsidian surface aligned with the symbols on the map.

"Do you know what those markings mean?" Geddy had edged around Connor, totally forgetting his prior hesitation, and now leaned down from the opposite side of the table so far that his nose nearly touched the parchment.

"I have no idea," Connor replied, mystified.

"Look at the marks on that disk. The way they line up with the squiggles on the map. Do you think that it's some kind of code?"

"I think that's exactly what it is."

Geddy looked up at him, his pale eyes shining. "You think it'll help us win the war?"

"I don't know, Geddy. I hope so. I think that's why Lord Garnoc wants to show this to the king."

A strange, high-pitched whistling noise made both men jump. Geddy rushed to the window. Connor looped the pendant's strap around his neck and hurriedly rolled the map and replaced it in its case. Light flashed outside the window as the whistling noise sounded again, louder and closer this time.

"What's going on?" he called quietly to Geddy.

"Damned if I know, but you'd better see this."

Connor joined Geddy at the window. The rippled glass glimmered with reflected light, but gave him no reliable view. A strange greenish light coruscated across the glass, and outside, Connor could hear shouts. He stuffed the map case into his tunic.

"Come on. Let's get out of here. Maybe we can see better from the bell tower."

Geddy grabbed his lantern, carefully snuffing out the candles he had lit and making sure everything had been returned to its original condition so as to leave no trace of their entry.

When the door closed behind them, Connor and Geddy sprinted down the hall as quietly as possible. They reached the stairwell without being intercepted, and took the stairs two at a time until they reached the bell tower at the top. From here, they could see out over the city and down to the coast.

Geddy glanced upward, and gasped. "Look there!"

A curtain of light splashed across the sky like a glowing ribbon, shimmering with a green cast. It billowed and rippled like a flag caught in the wind.

"Is it just my eyes or is that—whatever it is—getting closer?" Connor asked, catching his breath.

The light had grown greener, and it filled more of the sky. At first, it cut a swath across the night, framed on every side by darkness. But as Connor watched, the coruscating light blotted out the stars and swallowed up the sky's darkness. His heart began to pound, and he felt cold sweat on his back as the hair on his neck stood up.

"I see it too. Let's get out of here." Geddy's face was ashen with fear.

Below the tower, Connor heard voices. He glanced down. A crowd was gathering, though it was not yet dawn. He could hear cries of wonder and alarm amid a babble of conversation. The light in the sky grew brighter and its color became a vivid light green, like the tender leaves of spring. In the distance, Connor saw streaks of gold as shooting stars cut across the strange ribbon of light.

In the distance, bells began to ring. Connor listened, waiting for the bells to stop after a few rings at the hour of the day, but they kept on clanging as if pulled by a demented ringer. The ringing grew nearer, louder. Connor startled at a creaking noise behind him. He turned and saw the large bells swaying slowly. Afraid he would be trapped in the tower with the ringing bells, he moved to shout to the ringer, only to realize that the bells' ropes hung slack.

"Connor, please, let's go. I don't want to be deafened!" Geddy eyed the slowly moving bells with alarm.

Connor frowned. "I don't understand. The bells aren't ringing the hour. But they're not ringing in the alarm pattern. I can't figure out why—"

Connor's voice drifted off as a streak of light crossed the sky. He ran to the edge of the platform and Geddy crowded beside him. The entire sky now glowed with pulsating green light. With a sick feeling, Connor realized that what he had mistaken for falling stars were balls of fire, raining down from the luminous curtain. The fireballs landed explosively, throwing up a hail of dirt and debris where they hit outside the castle walls, instantly igniting everything around them. The sound of the explosions boomed like thunder, echoing from stone walls. Below, in the courtyard, the crowd screamed, fleeing. Behind him, the clapper of the largest bell fell, reverberating with a basso ring that made Connor's bones vibrate.

"It's raining stars," Geddy said, his voice tight. "Gods save us, the stars are falling." Fiery balls of light streamed toward the ground. The air was filled with the screams of those fleeing the onslaught with nowhere to hide. Trapped in the tower, Connor and Geddy watched in horror as behind them, the lesser bells slowly clanged to life independent of a master's hand.

The night sky, clear and star-filled only a short while before, now shone with an unnatural green glow. A haze of smoke drifted above the rooftops, and plumes of fire and smoke lit the night as the bombardment continued. As Connor watched, a new horror emerged.

The green ribbon of light was descending.

Geddy didn't bolt, but a whimper escaped from his clenched jaws. Connor felt his heart race, uncertain of what to do.

The tower bells picked up their tempo, their loose ropes dancing crazily. Beyond the tower, a cacophony of bells played a mad counterpoint to the screams and explosions. Connor covered his ears against the deafening noise.

We could die up here if the tower falls, but we're no safer on the ground, he thought.

"Do you think the mages can keep those fireballs from destroying the castle?" Geddy shouted, leaning over so that his lips nearly brushed Connor's ear.

"Let's hope they're not sound sleepers." Connor paused. "Maybe they're already on the job. Look—nothing's hit inside the courtyard walls yet."

The ribbon of light made a rapid descent, blurring as it moved. Connor was torn between the urge to clap his hands against his ears to block out the deafening clang of the bells, and the instinctive need to brace himself against the ribbon's impact with the ground.

Geddy's lips were moving, and Connor recognized the words as a prayer to Charrot for deliverance.

"How far outside the castle do you figure the ribbon and the fire are hitting?" Connor shouted, focusing on details to banish his fear.

"Don't rightly know. Seems to go all the way to the horizon."

Cries of panic in the courtyard below mingled with curses and desperate prayers. The ground shook and the tower swayed, forcing Connor to steady himself against the windowsill or be knocked to the ground below.

Geddy's next words were lost as the tower bells clanged again. Connor could see his lips moving, but could make out none of the words. His ears buzzed and he was sure that if he survived this night, he might be forever deafened.

Suddenly, there was silence.

For a heartbeat, no sound came. Screams, bells, and the thunder of explosions ceased. The air itself felt unnaturally still, but Connor felt a tingle rush across his skin.

Geddy wrapped his arms around himself as if to hold back the horror that unfolded beyond the window. Connor followed the direction of Geddy's gaze.

From where the ribbon touched ground, a wave of invisible power rippled outward, felling buildings and toppling trees. From his vantage point, Connor could see what those in the courtyard below could not. A swell of power rolled toward the city and the castle, flattening everything before it. Fire surged in its wake, yet this fire glowed as green as the sky ribbon, burning without smoke.

Magic, Connor thought. *Magic fire. Meroven's sorcerers have managed to strike at the heart of Donderath.*

Only seconds had passed, and the silence was still so complete that Connor could not hear his heartbeat, though he could feel it thudding in his chest. Tears streaked down his face, but he could not hear his own sobs.

The curtain of light had plowed through the western end of Castle Reach and bore down on the walls of Quillarth Castle. Connor did not look to see if the crowd below had fled; he could not take his eyes from the beautiful, deadly ribbon of flame.

In the silence, Donderath fell.

The outer walls of the castle crumbled at the touch of the green light, yet still no sound came. The inner walls fell, and then the outbuildings flattened as if stepped upon by an invisible giant. Geddy had fallen to his knees with his arms over his head. Connor readied himself to die.

I should have run when I had the chance. I should have warned Lord Garnoc and the king. Gods forgive me.

For a moment, Connor wondered whether it would be better to cast himself out of the open window than to die in the crush of the tower's collapse, but there was no time to decide. The magic struck the western side of the castle, sending a shockwave through the stone that threw Connor to the floor. He lifted his head and saw the bells careening madly on their yokes, soundless. His own silent screams tore from a raw throat as he grabbed Geddy by the tunic and began to crawl toward the staircase.

The tower shook again, and Connor staggered to his feet, starting down the steps that now bucked and shimmied beneath him. Geddy followed close behind. Connor half fell, half leaped from landing to landing, certain at any moment that the tower would implode around him, and that he would be crushed beneath the huge stones of its walls and the heavy bells above. Behind him, some of the stair treads cracked in two and fell to the tower floor far below. A few small stones shook free of their mortar, and pebbles began to rain down around him.

A final tremor sent Connor tumbling down the steps to the last landing. Geddy landed next to him, bruised and scraped but alive.

In the blink of an eye, the shaking stopped, and Connor realized that the tower stood. Just as quickly, sound rushed back in a mighty roar. His own heartbeat sounded as loudly in his ears as did the clanging of the bells overhead. Yet while his heart thudded as if it meant to tear itself from his chest, Connor realized that the bells' peals had slowed. Through the thick stone of the tower walls, Connor heard screaming and crying. In the distance trumpets sounded a woefully belated alarm for fire.

"Are we dead? Maybe we don't know it yet," Geddy asked, hesitantly looking around.

"Don't know what 'dead' feels like," Connor replied, shakily regaining his feet. "But since we're both bleeding, I think we're still alive."

"Is that a good thing, or a bad thing?"

Connor grimaced. "Not sure yet."

The unbearable tingle that had signaled the onslaught of magic was gone. Connor took a step, afraid he might find that he was no more than a ghost. His shoes crunched the mortar dust against the flagstones of the floor. "Let's see if the others survived."

Connor and Geddy headed toward the nearest door. It opened onto the ground floor of Quillarth Castle. Servants and retainers ran past them as if they were not there, prompting Connor once again to pat his hands against his body to make sure that he was corporeal. Paintings and mirrors littered the hallway. Tapestries lay in a tangle on the floor, and the walkway was littered with furniture that had been overturned or tossed from its original position. Connor caught a glimpse of himself in a shard of mirror, enough to make him accept that he was no revenant.

"What a mess," Geddy murmured. "I've got to find my master."

Connor grabbed him by the arm. "If Lynge survived, there's no telling where he is. Let's stick together—we're sure to find him. I need to reach Garnoc with the things we found. Best if we do that before Lynge asks any questions about where we were."

Geddy nodded. "Assuming both our masters lived through whatever just happened."

A man dressed in servant's clothes jostled Connor, pushing past in a hurry.

"Excuse me—" Connor called, but the man did not stop to answer.

"Can you tell me—" Connor started to ask the next person they came upon, who also ran past as if he could not hear.

"By the gods, get out of my way!" A wild-eyed man shoved Connor and barreled toward the door to the outside, carrying a small chest under his arm. All around Connor and Geddy, servants fled in a panicked wave, forcing him up against the wall. Through the open door, Connor caught the smell of smoke. Outside, the light shifted in a way that first made him fear that the green curtain lingered.

"That's not magic—it's real fire," Geddy said, eyes wide. "The castle's ablaze."

Grimly, Connor began to wade against the tide of people running for the exit. Geddy followed close behind. As Connor worked his way deeper inside the castle, he saw large cracks running diagonally from ceiling to floor, as if the castle had been dropped on its foundation, or the ground beneath it wrung out like a wet towel. Single blocks of stone lay where they had torn loose from their moorings, and grit covered everything.

Connor searched the faces of the servants who streamed past him. Many were covered with dust, bloodied and bruised. All were wide-eyed with fear, and Connor guessed that he looked no better to them.

"Estavan!" Geddy spotted Lord Radenou's valet at the top of the second landing as he made his way up the main staircase toward Lord Garnoc's rooms. Estavan turned slowly, moving as if befuddled by shock.

"Connor? Geddy? What are you doing here? We need to get out!"

Connor shook his head. "Not without Lord Garnoc and Lord Lynge. Where's your master?"

Estavan's pupils were dilated. His face was streaked with dirt, and his dark hair was disheveled. He still wore his night-shirt, and he had a small satchel over his shoulder. "Dead. Missing. I don't know."

Connor gripped Estavan by his shoulders. "Think, man. Where is Radenou? The War Council was to meet at dawn."

"Dawn? We won't be alive by dawn. We need to get out of here." Estavan tore loose from Connor's grip and lurched down the cluttered stairway. Connor began to climb the stairs, cling-ing to the side of the passageway to keep himself from being swept down in the tide of people rushing for the exit.

"Connor? Bevin Connor—is that you?"

From somewhere ahead in the dimly lit stairwell, Connor heard a familiar voice. "Lynge? Where are you?"

"Keep climbing," the voice shouted above the din.

Connor made his way up the stairs. The crowd thinned. In the half-light, Connor could see Lars Lynge, the king's seneschal, looking as if he had thrown on whatever clothing he could find in the dark, a drastic difference from his usual impeccable grooming. Lynge was at least two decades older than Connor, the droll, unflappable manager and the silent mover behind much that transpired within the castle's walls. Lynge looked worried, but there was no trace of panic in his haggard features.

"Geddy! Thank the gods you're safe. I feared the worst," Lynge said.

"Have you seen the king, or Garnoc?" Connor asked as he reached Lynge. Lynge pulled him out of the stairwell into the third-floor corridor. Geddy followed.

Lynge shook his head. "No. I'm headed there myself. Got trapped out in the dependencies when the ruddy fire started falling. You?"

Connor felt the weight of the stolen map against his chest beneath his tunic and gave a warning glance at Geddy. "I'd gone up to the bell tower for a breath of air. Couldn't sleep. Found Geddy up there as well. By Torven's horns! We saw it all, but when we tried to get back down, the world started to shake."

"You saw—how bad is it, beyond the castle?"

Connor took a deep breath. "Bad. Everything looks flattened or burned." He looked around them. As on the first floor, the palace walls were cracked and some of the stones had fallen. Dust covered everything in a gray cloud. Portraits, mirrors, and decorations lay in a broken mess on the floor. "How is it the castle is still standing?"

Lynge met his eyes. "Magic. When the green light appeared in the sky, the king burst into my chambers. He told me to rouse the mages, and to bring them to him immediately, in their nightclothes or naked if necessary. I rounded them up and brought them to the king, then fetched the things they needed for their spells. That's why I ended up in the dependencies—one of them had sent me out to bring back a shovel of fresh horse dung," he said, wrinkling his nose.

They had begun to make their way down the ruined hallway. Debris littered the floor, making it impossible for them to even try to run, though the delay tore at Connor, as he feared for Garnoc and the king.

"So the mages were able to save the castle—"

Lynge nodded. "Barely. As you can see."

"What if there's a second strike? Can we hold out?"

Lynge met his eyes. "There won't be. The magic is gone."

Connor came to a dead halt. "What do you mean?"

Lynge spread his hands. "Can't you feel it?" When Connor shook his head, Lynge sighed. "Of course not. Most can't. I have only a little. But I felt the magic vanish."

"How can magic just vanish?"

Lynge shook his head. "I don't know."

The three men picked their way through the devastated hallway. Wooden doors hung askew from their hinges. Heavy furnishings blocked the corridor. In a few places, Connor saw where overturned lanterns or fallen candles had started small fires. Servants rushed to beat out the flames.

"It could have been worse, at least inside the castle," Lynge said, following Connor's gaze. "If more people had been up and about, there might have been more risk of fire. Bad enough as it is."

Finally, they reached the door to the War Chamber. It was jammed shut, and it took Connor and Lynge together to heave it free. Beyond the windows, Connor could see the first light of dawn, a warm, orange glow.

"King Merrill had summoned the Council to meet at dawn," Connor murmured.

The War Council's chamber had been a well-appointed room. Now it was a shambles. Books, maps, and paintings lay in heaps on the floor where they had fallen from walls or tables. A marble statue lay in pieces, and the room smelled of brandy from a smashed decanter.

It took a moment for Connor to realize that bodies lay amid the wreckage. "Over there," Connor said, pointing. He and Geddy made their way as quickly as they could, stepping over broken glass and shards of pottery and around the remains of splintered chairs and picture frames.

A figure dressed in gray robes lay facedown. Geddy reached

him first, and together he and Connor gently turned the man over. Lynge stepped closer and bent over their shoulders.

"Valshoy," Lynge said quietly. "One of the mages."

Connor leaned closer, feeling for a pulse, but he knew from the man's ashen coloring that the effort was likely to be futile. Though Connor could see no trace of a fatal wound, the mage had neither breath nor heartbeat. He looked up, to see Lynge kneeling over another fallen man, who Connor guessed, by his robes, was another mage.

"Dead," Lynge said in a toneless voice.

Connor moved to the left while Geddy and Lynge made their way to the right. Two more bodies, one on either side of the huge Council table, lay dead on the floor. Like the others, they were unmarked, but dead.

A gasp made Connor look up. With a strangled cry, Lynge ran toward the head of the table. Connor and Geddy joined him a few seconds later. In the dim light, Connor struggled to interpret what he saw. A large velvet-covered chair had overturned, and at first glance, Connor thought a tapestry lay across it. He sank to his knees beside Lynge as he realized what he was seeing.

King Merrill lay unmoving, still seated in his overturned chair. It was clear the king had dressed hurriedly, as he wore none of the trappings of the monarchy, just a tunic and trews and a doublet that he had not bothered to lace.

"Is he—" Connor asked, afraid to breathe.

Lynge bit back a sob. "Dead," he said quietly. "All dead."

"I've got to find Garnoc," Connor said. He rose, hanging on to the bit of sanity that came with purpose. He knew that he should feel grief and shock at the death of the king, but he did not have the luxury to grieve, not until he found his master and knew whether Garnoc lived.

"We'll help you. We should search for the rest of the War Council. With the king…dead," Lynge said, struggling with the word, "they're the closest thing we have to a governing body, until the Council of Nobles can be summoned."

"If there are nobles to summon," Connor added.

Lynge passed a hand over Merrill's unseeing eyes, closing them. The seneschal whispered a prayer of passage, commending the souls of the dead to Torven. A shudder passed through him, and then Lynge collected himself and stood. His face bore the same unreadable expression it held during most days amid the bustle of the court, but in his eyes, Connor saw unspoken grief. "Let's find your master."

Together the three men made their way down the corridor. Ahead, part of the ceiling had collapsed, blocking the way with a tumble of plaster, wood, and stone. Protruding from the rubble were a man's boots.

"Do you think he's still—" Connor began.

Lynge shook his head and pointed to a spreading pool of blood that seeped from beneath the stones. "Doubtful."

They began to dig through the chunks of stone and plaster with their bare hands. Connor took cold comfort in the fact that the boots were unlike any Lord Garnoc owned.

Lynge struggled to shift the last chunk of rock out of the way, revealing its bloodied underside. He sat back on his haunches. "Radenou," he said quietly. "From the size of the rock that hit him, he was probably dead before he hit the ground."

Corrender's rooms were next. Connor knocked at the door, and when no answer came, he tried the knob. Locked. With a glance at Geddy, Connor backed up a step, and then the two of them threw their full weight against the door. It splintered near the bolt and gave way, sending them staggering into the room.

Correnders rooms were a shambles. The bed curtains had fallen to the floor, which was littered with broken glass, bits of shattered porcelain, and everything that had fallen from the room's shelves and desks during the quake.

A body lay in front of the room's large window. Connor was the first to reach Lord Correnders side, and he felt his heart sink as he turned the body over. Correnders was dead, his green eyes wide and staring.

"I don't understand. The king had a bit of magic. But Correnders didn't. There's not a mark on him. How can he be dead?" Geddy looked down at the dead man, puzzled.

Lynge frowned, and knelt next to the body. Lynge glanced down at Correnders right hand, which was clenched around something. Carefully, he reached down and pried the dead man's fingers loose from around a small, ornate blue glass bottle. Lynge lifted the vial to his nose and took a shallow breath.

"Poison."

Connor shook his head. "Why would someone try to poison Correnders?"

Lynge met his gaze. "No one did. No one, except Lord Correnders himself."

"Suicide?"

Lynge shrugged. "Apparently so. The city is on fire. The castle was under siege. Correnders didn't see what you saw from the tower. He had no way of knowing that the Meroven army wasn't at the gates. Correnders was a great general in his day, but that was two decades ago. He once bested Edgar of Meroven's father in battle, and the Merovenians bear a grudge forever. Correnders may have preferred to die by his own hand than to be drawn and quartered by an invading army."

"Do you think that's what awaits us? Edgar's armies marching across Donderath?" Connor was the one to ask the question, but a look at Geddy's ashen face made him guess the other was thinking the same thing.

Lynge drew a deep breath and was silent for a moment. "We have no way of knowing until someone brings word from the front—assuming there's anyone left alive." He turned to meet Connor's gaze. Lynge's eyes had a look of bitter resignation.

"If I were a betting man, I'd guess that whatever the mages sent against us—and whatever our mages countered with—may have exceeded their expectations. Perhaps all our mages could do was hold the castle itself together. Now the mages are dead and the magic is gone. That might mean magic is gone for Meroven as well, and perhaps their mages are also dead. A final strike from each side, calculated to be utterly overwhelming. Edgar's arrogance—and Merrill's desperation—may have doomed both sides."

"You think that our mages sent something like this against Meroven?"

Lynge looked away. "Such a move was discussed, theoretically, as an option if extreme measures were called for." He paused. "And without magic the aftermath of war will be that much more difficult for those who survive."

Connor stood, forcing the fear he felt into determination. "We haven't found Garnoc. If he's still alive, maybe he'll know what to do."

They headed back down the corridor. Connor felt dread like a lead weight in his chest. They reached Garnoc's room and he hesitated, fearing the worst. He used his key to open the door and stepped inside.

Garnoc's rooms were in worse shape than most of the castle they had seen so far. Much of the ceiling had collapsed, shattering the wooden table where Garnoc liked to take his dinner.

"M'lord! Lord Garnoc?" Connor heard the panic that tinged

his own voice as he made his way farther into the room. Geddy and Lynge crowded behind him.

"Connor? Is that you?" Garnoc's voice was weak.

Connor jumped over a pile of rubble in his hurry to reach Garnoc, with Geddy trailing behind him. "Sweet Charrot," Connor murmured as he came around the side of the bed.

Garnoc lay half-buried in debris where a portion of the ceiling near the window had collapsed. It was clear from the dust on the old man's hands and his torn and bloodied fingernails that he had been digging at the debris. A large piece of stone pinned Garnoc's abdomen to the floor. As Connor stepped closer, he could see that Garnoc's legs were twisted at unnatural angles and lay unmoving.

Connor fell to his knees beside his master. "M'lord," he murmured. "You're hurt."

Garnoc was pale, and his thin lips had a bluish cast. Lynge and Geddy kept a respectful distance. Connor took Garnoc's hand. "I'm not hurt," Garnoc said quietly. "I'm dying." He winced and drew a labored breath, then looked up at Connor with a lucid gaze.

"Did you get what you were looking for?" Garnoc's voice was a whisper, too quiet for anyone but Connor to hear.

"Yes, m'lord," Connor replied. "It's safe. But we need to free you."

Garnoc's mouth twisted into a bitter smile. "I'll be free very soon, swept along in the Sea of Souls." He gave Connor's hand a squeeze. "You've done well, m'boy. I couldn't have asked for a better steward."

"I failed you. If I'd have been here, I could have protected you."

Garnoc wheezed a harsh laugh. "You had something more important to do." The laugh became a strained cough. When

Garnoc caught his breath, he gestured toward what remained of the ruined bed with his left hand.

"Bring Millicent to me."

Reluctantly, Connor let go of Garnoc's hand and stood, searching amid the tangle of bedclothes and the fallen plaster for the small gold-edged frame. A glint among the rubble caught his eye, and he bent down, carefully retrieving the small portrait. The frame was scratched and dented, but the portrait itself had survived with little damage. He hurried back to Garnoc and handed him the picture.

"Ah, Millicent. I'll be with you soon." Garnoc turned toward Connor and met his gaze urgently. "Now, m'boy, it's time for you to go."

"I'm not going anywhere without you."

Garnoc squeezed his hand. "I release you from your duties."

"I still won't go. We leave together."

Garnoc shook his head. "I go to the Vale. You must escape." He glanced toward where the pendant hung beneath Connor's tunic. "What you have is too valuable to risk."

"Escape? Donderath is burning. There's nowhere to go."

"Leave the Continent. Take a ship to the Far Shores. Penhallow will find you. Go to the end of the world if you have to. Just make sure you survive—and that you keep what you've found safe."

Garnoc's speech had cost the old man precious energy. He lay back against the rubble, breathing shallowly, Millicent's portrait clutched against his chest. "Go, Connor. That's my last order, as your lord, and as your friend. Go, and leave me to my rest."

A spasm seized Garnoc, sending a tremor through his body. He drew a labored breath, and his eyes opened wide, then his body went slack and his eyes gently closed. Connor bowed his head, weeping.

"Your lord gave you an order." Lynge's voice seemed distant as Connor struggled to pull himself together.

"How can I—"

"You can honor your lord's last wish by doing as he directed."

Connor gathered his resolve as he took a deep breath and choked back his tears. "What of Donderath? What will happen now that Merrill is dead?"

"The king sent his heir into hiding when the war began for just such a situation," Lynge said quietly. "We will gather the surviving nobles, establish a regent, and go on." He paused. "There is no further service you can provide here, Bevin. Do as Garnoc ordered. He had his reasons."

Connor looked at Geddy, who slowly shook his head. "I'll stay with my master. We have work to do here. Your master's given you an order. Your work here is done."

Grudgingly, Connor nodded. "There's nothing for me here, without him. Perhaps the Far Shores will be a refuge."

Lynge nodded. "Go quickly if you mean to find a ship. The city is sure to be in a panic."

Connor stood and made a slight bow. "Thank you, Lynge— and Geddy—for everything."

Just then, they heard someone shouting Lynge's name from the hallway. A moment later, a servant burst into the room. The man was soot-covered and his clothing was torn and stained. "My lord Lynge. A steady stream of messengers are arriving from the manor houses. The power that struck the castle attacked elsewhere first." The messenger looked to be on the verge of panic. "My lord, many of the noble houses are destroyed. The heir to the throne is dead."

Lynge turned to Connor. "Go. Now. Hurry before you lose your chance."

CHAPTER ELEVEN

CONNOR MADE HIS WAY THROUGH THE RUBBLE to the door of Garnoc's room and gave one backward glance, then pushed past the messenger. He paused only long enough to gather a few essentials from his belongings in the room adjacent to Garnoc's. His quarters had sustained serious damage, and it was clear that had he not been on Garnoc's errand, he would be dead.

Connor stuffed some clothing and his bag of coins into a sack, leaving the precious map safe within his tunic and the pendant hidden beneath his shirt. Grabbing his cloak, he made his way through the rubble-strewn corridors.

A river of people filled the streets. Beyond the protection of the castle mages' wardings, the devastation was overwhelming. The air was filled with choking black smoke as flames danced high, consuming entire blocks. Some buildings were leveled, leaving nothing but chunks of stone and snapped timbers. Survivors dug among the wreckage, calling for missing loved ones, while others sat at the edge of the street and wailed in grief.

Smoke stung his eyes and burned his lungs as he shouldered through the crowd. Most of the people were heading up the hill, away from the wharves. Connor was unsure whether that meant that they intended to flee inland, not knowing that those areas had been attacked first, or whether all the ships had sailed.

He breathed a sigh of relief as he reached a bend in the road and saw that the large transport ships were still in the harbor. Struggling against the press of the crowd, Connor made his way toward the waterfront, where he could see workmen loading kegs of beer and liquor onto one of the large ships. Just as he reached the wharf road, a hand came down hard on his shoulder. Expecting a cutpurse, Connor rounded, fist back to swing.

"Easy there!" To Connor's amazement, Engraham, the owner of the Rooster and Pig, was behind him. Like Connor, Engraham wore his cloak although the day was warm, and carried a small sack. "I didn't expect to see you here." He glanced up the hill toward the castle. "Actually, I wasn't sure anyone in the castle was still alive."

"Not many," Connor replied. "Lord Garnoc is dead. There's nothing here for me. I'm taking whatever ship has room for me to wherever they're sailing."

Engraham slapped him on the back. "Then we're heading in the same direction, mate. I have a longtime business relationship with the captain of the *Prowess*," he said with a nod toward one of the convict ships. "Paid my fare and more with those kegs they're loading. Let's see what we can do about getting you on that ship."

Together, they muscled their way through the panicked mob. The wharves were filled with desperate city dwellers pushing toward the ships that were obviously readying for departure. Several burly sailors blocked the mob's path, and it was clear that they were demanding payment from those whom they permitted to pass.

Engraham stepped in front of Connor as they reached the

sailors. "I see they have you greeting passengers, Klark," he said to the broad-chested sailor who stepped out to block his path. The man registered a look of surprise and then grinned, displaying a smile that was missing half a dozen teeth.

"Engraham. What are you doing here?"

"Looking for a ship to take me somewhere else. Know a good one?"

Klark laughed. "No, but there's always the *Prowess*. You can count on Captain Olaf to have room for his favorite tavern master." He paused, looking at Connor. "Say now, who's this?"

Engraham met Klark's gaze. "Connor's a friend, and he's personally drunk enough of my bitterbeer to keep a roof over my head. He's with me." Engraham extended a hand toward Klark, and pinched between thumb and palm, Connor glimpsed a glint of gold.

"Right," Klark said with a glance toward Connor. "There's room for one more. Best get onto the ship. It'll be cheek to jowl."

"Where are we heading?" Engraham asked, clapping Klark on the shoulder in thanks.

"Anywhere," Klark replied. "Anywhere but here."

Under the watchful eye of Captain Olaf's sailors, the passengers lucky enough to gain passage aboard the *Prowess* made an orderly boarding. Once on board, they were herded toward the hold. Connor had only a few moments to look around. The upper decks of the *Prowess* were scrubbed clean, though the ship itself appeared to have weathered a few storms, judging from the worn railings and decking. The crew paid little attention to the stream of passengers, and bent their backs to the tasks of readying the ship to depart.

"Not exactly luxury accommodations," Engraham observed, "but then again, the usual passengers are convicts." He looked toward a tall uniformed man who stood talking with two men in regimental coats. "That's the captain himself, over there."

Connor followed Engraham's gaze. Captain Olaf was taller than average, broad-shouldered, with a muscular build that made Connor wonder if he had worked his way up from dock-hand. His brown hair was gray along the temples, and his face was tanned with permanent creases around his eyes. For an instant, those sea-gray eyes met Connor's, then moved away. He had obviously been of no interest to the captain, but in those few seconds, Connor thought he'd seen both intelligence and cunning in the man's eyes, a good sign if they were to navigate to a safe harbor.

Before he could get a second look, they were being hustled down a narrow set of steps into the crowded hold. Connor gagged at the stench, a mixture of sweat, urine, and old vomit. Though the floor was relatively free of debris, the smell was strong enough that Connor guessed it had worked its way into the wood.

Engraham laughed. "This is one time someone could feel blessed to have no sense of smell. Olaf said that they wash out the hold after each voyage, and sometimes a storm does it for them during the trip. Still, hard to get rid of what hundreds of passengers leave behind, I imagine."

Connor had expected lodgings worthy only of cargo and he was not obliged to upgrade his opinion. A line of small portholes ran along one side of the hull, casting a dim light into the hold. Filthy woven hammocks swung from the support posts, far too few for the number of desperate souls who would crowd into the space. Still, Connor had expected worse. No leg irons were pinned to the walls, no empty manacles littered the floor.

Engraham seemed to guess his thoughts. "Most of Donderath's convicts aren't violent," he said. "Or at least, if they killed anyone, it was more likely to be a friend or relative who had it coming, rather than a random murder. The worst of the lot get hanged. Most of the folks who get sent to Velant aboard these ships are petty thieves, strumpets, and debtors. Hardly a dangerous group." His eyes were shadowed, and Connor wondered if Engraham was thinking about his mother's long-ago exile.

"Where do you figure they'll take us?" Connor asked.

Engraham shrugged. "Don't know. First port that'll let us dock, I figure. If it were up to me, I'd try the Lesser Kingdoms before I headed across the sea for the Far Shores."

They watched out the portholes as the hold grew more crowded behind them. As sailors wheeled the last carts of provisions aboard—including Engraham's kegs—the mood of the crowd on the docks grew surly. The sailors, armed with crossbows, kept the mob at bay as provisions were loaded onto the ship.

Once the mob realized that no more passengers were getting aboard, muttering turned to jeers and shouted obscenities. Bottles and rocks flew through the air, falling far short of the ship.

"Looks like we were lucky to get aboard," Connor observed.

"That we were, although there are still a few other ships left in port."

"Think the mob will do anything to keep us from sailing?"

Engraham shrugged. "This is a large ship. Once Olaf opens up the sails, there's not much the folks on shore can do."

By now, the hold was crowded with people. They milled about the space, murmuring to each other in quiet tones, or praying for deliverance. Connor glanced behind him. Many appeared to have brought nothing with them, while others had a small knapsack or bundle. Most were men, with only a few couples and no children. From what Connor had seen of the refugees leaving the city, families had chosen to make their escape on foot.

Shouts outside drew Connor back to the porthole. The mob on the dock had begun to riot, and men were leaping into the water to swim toward the ship, while others commandeered any raft or battered dinghy that had not already been stolen. As they rowed out from shore, they quickly realized why their boats had been left behind by those who had already fled. Within a few lengths from shore, the decrepit boats began taking on water, rapidly sinking and leaving their would-be masters swimming for shore.

The ship lurched as the sails dropped and filled. Connor saw the lines fall away, freeing the *Prowess* for her journey. His stomach felt a sick tightness that had nothing to do with the sea. As the ship sailed into the bay, Connor had a better view of the coastline. As far as the eye could see, smoke hung heavy over the land. Everywhere he looked he saw buildings that had been destroyed in the firestorm, and in many sections of the city, the fires still burned, fed by the tinder of thatched roofs and dry wood.

Those who stood at the portholes watched in silence. Connor saw the same stricken expression on their faces. Donderath was in ruins, defeated, its people forced into exile. And if Lynge's guess was correct, the other major kingdoms of the Continent might fare no better.

Perhaps now, whatever was causing the holes in my memory will stop, Connor thought. *I can no longer betray Garnoc—or Penhallow. And if I can figure out what to do with the map and the disk, maybe I can redeem myself.* His fear of being found out had tempered to lingering sadness that he might, in the end, have let Garnoc down. *Garnoc never suspected, but I knew, and I didn't have the courage to tell him. What if, somehow, I was compromised by the enemy? Sweet Esthrane, what if they learned something through me that led to all this?*

His thoughts had gone around and around since the firestorm, ending only when he was too exhausted to think at all. *If I unwittingly had a hand in this, then I've borne a price. I'm an exile, I've got no money, no patron, nothing but the clothes on my back. I just wish I knew who was behind the gaps, and what damage I've done.*

Once under sail, the *Prowess* cut through the sea at a brisk pace. Soon the coastline was just a fuzzy image on the horizon. Engraham's eyes narrowed.

"It doesn't appear that the good captain is setting out to sea," he said quietly. "We've put some distance between us and the shore—enough to avoid the shoals—but we're maintaining our course instead of veering away."

It was just after dawn and Connor realized how exhausted he was after the events of the night before. He sank down against the hull, fighting for enough space in the crowded hold to stretch out his legs, though he remained seated. His fellow passengers had grown quiet. All in all, he thought, there had been few hysterics aside from the angry mob on the dock. He looked around at the faces and guessed that he had not been the only one to go without sleep. His fellow passengers, no, *refugees*, looked exhausted.

How in Torven's name did this happen? Donderath wasn't supposed to lose the war. We certainly weren't supposed to end up like this. Connor sighed. *If it never crossed my mind we could lose, I wonder if King Merrill and the War Council seriously thought about it either?*

Engraham slid down beside him. "Do you think it's like this everywhere in Donderath?"

"Lynge—the seneschal—thought so. He was getting reports

when I left that the flames hit the manor houses before they hit the city. The heir to the throne is dead."

Engraham's eyebrows rose. "Truly? Then there's no hope for Donderath. Meroven won."

Connor shook his head. "I don't think so. At least, Lynge believed differently." He glanced around to make sure that no one was listening and quietly recounted what Lynge had told him. Engraham's expression grew grave.

"So if Lynge is right and our mages did to Meroven what their mages did to Donderath, then the four Ascendant Kingdoms may be in ruins?"

Connor nodded. "It'll take months to confirm. Time for riders to reach the other kingdoms, see what remains, and report. But without the king or the heir, what's to become of the people who are left? And if our mages succeeded in killing Edgar and the Vellanaj king, then there's naught but chaos."

Engraham sighed. "Let's hope that the Lesser Kingdoms managed to stay out of the line of fire. They didn't take sides in the war, so there's no reason for them to be targeted."

"Let's hope."

Three days later, Connor felt the ship's motion slow. He poked Engraham to rouse him from his sleep. "Wake up. I think we're getting close."

The hold was dark except for the moonlight that streamed through the small portholes. Engraham and Connor got to their feet and picked their way across the tangle of sleeping bodies to reach the hull. Connor looked out across the moonlit water. He could make out the silhouettes of the buildings, but the town was dark.

"No lights," he muttered.

Engraham shrugged. "Would you expect many? It's not quite dawn. Even most of the taverns are closed by now."

Connor stared at the quiet harbor town. "Maybe. I don't like it."

Resigned to wait until daylight, they went back to sleep. It seemed to Connor that he had barely dozed off before excited voices roused him.

"Can't see anyone on the streets."

"The boats are all gone."

"Look—everything's burned."

Fearing the worst, Connor woke Engraham and made their way to the portholes. His heart sank as he looked out. The harbor town looked deserted. Empty docks jutted out into the bay, littered with bits of wood and debris. Much of the town had burned. Roofless, windowless buildings stared back at them like skulls.

Engraham turned, leaned his back against the hull, and covered his face with his hands. "It's true, then, what your friend Lynge feared."

Connor felt cold dread rising inside him. "We can't know for certain. All we can see is the coast. Surely neither side's mages were strong enough to destroy everything."

"But we don't know that," Engraham argued. "There might be nowhere left to run."

Connor said nothing, unsure of any reply. It was the first time since they had set sail from Castle Reach that he had broken through the shock and exhaustion to wonder about the magic itself, instead of its immediate effects. "I'm sure we can exist without magic," he faltered.

Engraham raised his head to look at him. "Can we? Who'll heal the sick?"

"Even healers use powders and potions. My grandmother could treat a fever with her poultices and she didn't have a wink of magic."

"Ships use mages to navigate," Engraham countered.

"Obviously they have other ways as well, or we wouldn't have left the harbor."

"Mages set wards to keep back floods, to make the crops grow, to bring the rains."

"Crops grow and rains come without magic," Conner replied. "Walls can be built to hold back floods. What we did with magic we can do without, if we have to."

"For how long? How long do you think it will take for people to get restless? Even the poor could scrape together the coins for a hedge witch or a granny conjurer to do magic on their behalf. The merchants and nobles relied on their mages even more."

Connor felt a headache start behind his eyes. "They can get as restless as they like, but if magic is gone, they'll have to learn to deal with it."

"You're a practical man, Connor. I've always liked that about you. But I'm afraid a change like that won't come easily for most people. Seawalls will break. Crops will fail. People will die."

Connor sighed. Much as he hated to admit it, Engraham had a point. For those who had survived the war, the future would be harsh until magic returned. If it ever did.

Connor felt the ship lurch. "We're picking up speed. Captain Olaf must have decided against putting in to port."

"What's the point? If the people who lived there are gone, odds are they've looted everything they could carry. After all, that's what the good captain's men were out doing right before we left."

"Where now?"

Engraham stared out the porthole. "Down the coast a bit farther, I'd guess, just in case things are better in the south. But Olaf won't dare waste much time or go too far out of his way.

We've got too many people on board and no spare provisions, I'd wager. I'd lay my bets that within a day he'll head north-east, toward the Far Shores."

"Then let's hope we find a warm welcome when we get there," Connor muttered. "The Cross-Sea Kingdoms weren't interested enough in the war to take sides."

"You think not?" Engraham chuckled. "I'd bet they were very interested. After all, they trade with every kingdom on the Continent. Wars are bad for business. They don't give a rat's ass about the politics; that much is true. I'm guessing they were hoping that it would boil down to a few skirmishes and insults followed by a return to business as usual. This—" he said with a vague wave to indicate the destruction of the Continent's kingdoms, "will upset the balance. It'll change everything— everything that determines who has power and who doesn't." He met Connor's gaze. "We could get to the Far Shores just in time for another war to break out."

"In that case," Connor said with a yawn, "I'd best get as much sleep as I can."

True to Engraham's prediction, Captain Olaf changed the *Prowess*'s course during the night, and by the stars, Connor could tell that they were heading north once more. The winds were favorable, and it seemed the captain was in a hurry, because the *Prowess* cut through the sea, moving at full speed.

In the hold, the refugees had sorted themselves out into small groups. Some had arrived together, while others had found common cause aboard ship. Men played cards and rolled dice, wagering whatever coins or trinkets they had carried aboard. Most of the women clustered together in one corner. Whether they had arrived alone or with one of the men, during the day the women left the men to their gaming and talked in quiet voices, sang, or prayed. A few had brought needlework or knitting with them, and they worked in the dim light of the hold, listening to the chatter around them.

One woman sat apart in the center of the hold. Crowded as it was, she had a circle of empty space around her, as if her fellow passengers did not wish to get too close. Her clothing looked to have once been of fine materials, velvet and brocade, but now her finery was stained and torn. Connor recognized her as Benna, one of the many fortune-tellers who roved the wharf taverns. Unlike Alsibeth, whose clients numbered among Donderath's wealthy and powerful, Benna and her ilk made their living interpreting the dreams and tea leaves of the fishermen, dockworkers, and day laborers who hung about the wharves or sailed in and out of the harbor.

If the magic is gone, what happens to people like Benna? Connor wondered. *Assuming she isn't a fraud, how does it feel for the magic to disappear? Is it like a song you can't get out of your mind that's suddenly gone?* He watched Benna closely. Everyone around her appeared to be trying to ignore the woman's existence. Benna seemed equally oblivious to those around her. She laid down cards in the manner of fortune-tellers, three rows for Charrot, Torven, and Esthrane, and their lesser gods. One row foretold illusion, darkness, and danger, the province of Torven. Another row spoke to the effects of Charrot's dual nature, of reversals of fortune, change, and unanticipated rewards. The third row gave voice to Esthrane's dominion over love and family, birth and rebirth, and material bounty.

Benna mumbled to herself and reshuffled the cards. Though she patiently set the cards out over and over again, the meaning she sought appeared to elude her.

While Connor had made no effort to meet his fellow

passengers, Engraham worked his way around the hold. Connor suppressed a smile watching his friend in action. Born on the wrong side of the blanket, Engraham had made his way on a combination of charm, ambition, and intelligence. He usually kept the latter two well hidden behind the first, but he and Connor had stayed up past closing on far too many nights for Connor to be fooled. Engraham was a survivor, and now, under pressure and in a strange place, all the skills that had served him well in his past came to the fore once again.

And what about me? Connor wondered. *I can navigate the below-stairs politics at court. Hardly a useful talent without a court. Thank the gods I came from the poorer nobility; at least I've split wood and mucked out the stables. Maybe that'll be good for a coin or two wherever we're going.*

After a while, Engraham made his way back to his spot by Connor.

"Greet everyone in the hold, did you?" Connor joked.

Engraham grinned. "Everyone who was awake."

"And what did you learn?"

"Besides the fact that I overpaid for our fare?"

Connor grimaced. "You know what I mean."

Engraham's smile faded. "For one thing, I learned that Captain Olaf and his fellow ship captains held off taking passengers by a full day beyond when the small ships loaded."

"Oh?"

Engraham nodded sagely. "Smart move—and ballsy. They were taking a big risk staying in port. I'm betting that they figured the small ships would take the refugees who couldn't have afforded to pay much for passage. Might have also figured they'd let the small ships head out of the harbor first and see if they ran into any trouble."

"What else?"

"According to Dorin over there," Engraham said with a nod toward a man with short-cropped gray hair who was dozing against the bulkhead, "we're barely out of sight of the coast. Dorin says he's done a bit of navigating himself and he can tell where we are by the stars. The captain's being very cautious about heading out into open waters."

Connor frowned. "Why?"

"Dorin did a lot of trade with the Far Shores. Owned a number of warehouses down along the wharves. He says that the last ships that came in from the Cross-Sea Kingdoms were in a big hurry to unload and leave. They were afraid Donderath was going to be blockaded."

"Do you think that's likely?"

Engraham shrugged. "If we'd been fighting Meroven alone, I wouldn't give it much thought. Meroven never invested a lot in its navy—it's always put its stock in soldiers. But Meroven allied with Vellanaj, and Vellanaj's navy is formidable."

"Do you think a blockade would still be in effect after all that happened?"

Engraham let out a long breath. "Who knows? It could take weeks for a ship to reach them with new orders."

It occurred to Connor that while much had been made of getting aboard the ship, little had been said in the chaos of the moment about necessities such as food and water.

"Think they took on enough provisions to feed all of us for a long voyage?"

"Actually, that's one reason I wanted to be aboard Olaf's ship," Engraham replied. "He's an honest man. Some of the captains would be the type to take passengers aboard without provisions and let 'em starve. After all, once the ship leaves port, who are they going to complain to?"

Connor shivered.

Engraham grinned wolfishly. "We know they've got ale a-plenty on board. I asked around to see what kinds of provisions the *Prowess* had taken on. Got the right answers, too. Barrels of water and grog, salted fish, hard biscuits, dried beef— enough for a long journey." He paused. "Olaf's used to transporting convicts all the way to Velant. He knows how many people fit in this hold and how much food it takes to make sure they're alive on the other end."

"Well, at least we won't starve, or die of thirst."

Engraham shrugged. "I wouldn't count on a full belly, but staying a little hungry's probably best at sea. Less to retch up when the waves are high. You might lose a few pounds, but I think we can trust Olaf to do right by us."

Just then the ship pitched, sending anyone standing in the hold tumbling and flailing. Connor grabbed at one of the hammocks to slow his slide, and Engraham managed to wrap his arms around a support beam to avoid plowing into the mass of cursing passengers who found themselves tossed hard against the hull.

Connor dragged himself to his feet and braced to be able to see out of the porthole. Two large military ships were close enough to the port side of the *Prowess* that Connor could make out the number of sailors on their decks. Water splashed high into the air as heavy iron balls soared toward the *Prowess*, propelled from catapults on the attacking ships. "We're being fired on!"

The ship leveled out, spilling the passengers across the decking. Above them, Connor could hear shouts and pounding footsteps. Engraham fought his way through the tangle to look out the porthole.

"Those are Vellanaj ships," he said grimly. "We're blockaded."

Connor pushed in next to him. Flaming arrows were arcing

from the attacking warships, falling short of the *Prowess* and disappearing into the water. "If those arrows catch the sails afire—"

Engraham frowned. "If they'd meant to burn us or board us, they'd have done so by now. They know we're a cargo ship. They're not interested in sinking us; they just want to make sure we don't cross the blockade."

The hold buzzed as passengers talked nervously, clustered in groups of two and three. So many people pushed to see out the small portholes that Connor feared he might be crushed against the hull of the ship.

The *Prowess* turned hard once more, but this time, the refugees were faster to brace themselves. People clung to the rope hammocks or wrapped their arms around the support beams to avoid landing in a heap. Connor fought to maintain his view from the porthole.

"They're not pursuing us," he reported.

Engraham nodded. "I'm guessing the Vellanaj ships were ordered to hold their line. They're not looking for a fight; they just want to make sure that no ships get in or out toward the Far Shores."

"We're changing course," Dorin, the trader, shouted.

"Can you tell where we're headed?"

Dorin frowned. "It's daytime—I can't see the stars. But from the sun, I'd reckon we're headed north."

"But there's nothing north of the Continent," one of the passengers protested.

Dorin returned a mirthless grin. "Sure there is. Captain Olaf makes this run all the time. We're headed for Edgeland."

CHAPTER
TWELVE

B LAINE'S SLEEP WAS TROUBLED. DESPITE A FEW
cups of whiskey, sleep had proven elusive and his dreams
were dark.

*Velant's walls loomed high. To the work team headed for the
ruby mines, the stockade might as well have touched the sky.
Guards patrolled along the walkway near the top of the fence.
Torches lit the large open area too well for anyone to hide in the
shadows. Many dreamed of escape, but few if any had ever
succeeded.*

*Blaine shivered. His homespun woolen top and trews would be
plenty warm deep inside the mine, but aboveground, they were
inadequate protection for Edgeland's bitter winds. Shackled between
Piran and another prisoner, Blaine shuffled toward the mine
under the eye of the guards. Their steps made a rhythmic clink-
crunch as they made their way through the crusted snow.*

*A year had passed since Blaine's ship dropped anchor at Velant.
When he had walked off the ship in chains, Donderath and his
former life ceased to exist. Commander Prokief welcomed the new
prisoners with a mock funeral, assuring them that here at the edge
of the world, they were dead to everyone they had left behind. But*

Prokief had plans for his "dead" men. And for the last year, Blaine had toiled in the mines. Dark, wet, bone-chillingly cold, the backbreaking work was not nearly as hard to bear as the torments of their guards, men for whom Blaine knew Velant was also a prison.

"You can move faster than this." The guard lunged toward the shuffling prisoners, laying into one of the convicts with his whip. Manacled at the wrists and shackled to the others at the ankles, the convict could do little to avoid the bite of the flail. Blood spattered the snow and droplets sprayed the other prisoners. The whip fell again and again, slicing through the prisoner's meager clothing, biting into flesh.

The beaten prisoner stumbled, pulling the others with him. Enraged, the guard caught Blaine and Piran with his whip as the tangle of prisoners struggled to regain their footing. The lash caught Blaine across one cheek, opening a cut. Warm blood poured down his face, instantly freezing to his beard in the cold. The second stroke of the whip slashed across his shoulder and chest. The return stroke of the whip cracked down across Piran. Blaine and Piran exchanged glances. Exhausted, hungry, cold, and hopeless, it was the final straw.

Together, they lashed out with their feet, tripping the guard and bringing him down hard to the snow. Using their combined weight, Blaine and Piran heaved themselves on top of the guard, dragging the other men with them. Blaine wrested the flail from the guard's hand and slammed the solid base of it into the guard's skull. Piran pinned the guard's hands and Blaine swung both fists together, striking the guard's face on one side and then the other.

Just yesterday, Blaine had seen four guards beat two of his fellow prisoners to death in the courtyard while the other guards looked on. The battered bodies had been left lying where they fell. They froze rapidly, unprotected from the wind, becoming a ghoulish monument. Today's whipping was one torment too many.

Boots thudded across the snow. Rough hands dragged Blaine and Piran away from the guard. Shouts echoed across the stockade. Two guards helped their comrade struggle to his feet. The guard's face was bloodied and one eye was swelling shut, but he was still alive. As the moment's rage faded, Blaine realized that he was quite likely to end up with the frozen corpses in the parade yard.

"These two—take them to the mages," the captain of the guards snapped, striding across the bloodied snow. Keys clinked in the guard's hands as he unfastened Blaine and Piran from the other prisoners. Before either could take a step, the guard sent a right hook to Blaine's jaw as the captain did the same to Piran, dropping them in their tracks. The beating continued after they fell to the ground, fists and boots flying as the guards returned double what had been inflicted. Finally, as Blaine struggled to remain conscious, the blows stopped.

"Take them away," the captain said. Two guards grabbed him roughly, one under each arm, and began to drag him across the snow-covered yard. Behind him, he heard Piran groan as two more guards hauled him from the ground.

Blaine had stopped fearing death when he had reached Velant. Yet he knew that death was the least of the punishments Prokief and his warden-mages could inflict. He should feel fear, perhaps terror; yet he felt nothing except a numbness that chilled him more than the Edgeland cold. Death would be a mercy, and the torment that might lead to death could not last as long as a life sentence on this godsforsaken slab of ice.

The guards dragged Blaine into the large prison building. He hung like dead weight between the two guards who hauled him along, toes trailing behind him. They stopped in front of two massive doors, which creaked open onto a large open courtyard with a tiled floor and a balcony gallery.

The two guards threw him into the room. Still bound at the wrists, Blaine fell badly and felt his nose break, sending blood streaming down his face. Piran collapsed into a heap beside him. The guards retreated as doors on the other side of the room opened, and for the first time, Blaine felt a stab of fear break through his indifference.

"Sit him up." Commander Prokief's voice was like a rumble of thunder. Black boots stopped just short of where Blaine lay facedown on the tile floor. Guards stepped forward to drag Blaine up and force him to kneel. One grabbed Blaine by the hair, jerking his head up so that he could see the large uniformed man standing over him.

Commander Prokief was a bear of a man, a tall, hulking brawler who had earned his rank through battlefield ruthlessness and then proved too feral to remain in civilized society. Long before his banishment, Blaine remembered hearing whispers that Prokief's connections at court with men like Vedran Pollard made it inconvenient for Merrill to have him killed, and so Prokief was "awarded" the post of commander at Velant.

Blaine glanced at Piran. Piran was supported by the guards, and did not appear conscious. Several deep gashes in his scalp and bruises on his face showed that Piran had not escaped the worst of the beating.

"McFadden and Rowse. Again." Prokief nodded for the guard to tip Piran's face up. Piran's head lolled as the guard jerked his hair.

"Take him to the Hole," Prokief said with a jerk of his head toward Piran. "Three days. If he's alive afterward, put him back in the mines. If not, throw his body outside the stockade for the foxes."

The guards dragged Piran out of the room, leaving Blaine kneeling between his two captors.

"I'm tired of you, McFadden," Prokief said. He stepped closer *and brought the back of his gloved hand hard across Blaine's face, snapping his head to the side. Before Blaine could react, the toe of Prokief's boot caught him hard in the gut. Blaine gasped and retched. The guards held him in his place.*

"Somehow, you're always at the center of it when there's a problem. The others know their place. Why don't you?"

Blaine glowered, but remained silent.

Prokief struck again, snapping Blaine's head in the other direction. "I forgot," he mocked. "You've got noble blood. Lord McFadden." He spat on the ground. "You're the only one with a note next to his entry in the logbook forbidding me from killing you. So, much as I'd like to do Lord Pollard a favor, I can't execute you—more's the pity. On the other hand, if you die of natural causes"—he shrugged—"well, things like that happen all the time."

Prokief glanced at the guards. "Stretch him out."

One of the guards grabbed the chain between Blaine's wrists and dragged him over to the center of the tile floor. Four iron rings were embedded into the tile. The guard unlocked the manacles from Blaine's wrists and another guard put a boot in the center of Blaine's back and sent him sprawling. Rough hemp ropes bit into his wrists and ankles, stretching him spread eagle. One of the guards jerked hard on his shirt, splitting it down the middle and baring his back.

"Twenty lashes," Prokief said dispassionately. Blaine steeled himself. Prokief himself took the whip from the guard, and the knotted leather tendril sang through the air, laying open a welt from shoulder to hip. Blaine grunted and bit into his lip. The lash fell again and again, each time striking in a new spot. He lost count, slipping in and out of consciousness.

Blaine gritted his teeth. His silence enraged Prokief, who brought the lash down harder as the guard counted. "Sixteen...Seventeen...Eighteen...Nineteen...Twenty."

When the last lash fell, Blaine lay still, lost in pain and shock.

"Douse him with salt water," Prokief commanded.

A guard went to grab a bucket from near the wall. The weight of the water hurt as much as the salt that stung in the fresh, raw wounds, and Blaine barely bit back a cry.

"Take him to the Hole. No food or water. Three days." He paused. "Ejnar, come here."

Dimly, Blaine heard the swish of the warden-mage's gray robes as the man's soft boots stepped around the rivulets of blood on the tile floor. "Commander?"

"Use your magic to keep him from dying. I want him alive when he leaves here, even if he's barely breathing."

"Done, Commander."

Blaine could hear the satisfaction in Prokief's tone. "Give him something to remember me by while he's down there. Fever and cramps, eh? It would be pleasant to hear him beg for death."

"As you wish, Commander."

Ejnar had no sooner spoken than Blaine felt a wave of fire building inside his body. A moment earlier, soaked to the skin and spread-eagled on the ice-cold tile, Blaine shivered uncontrollably. Now, he felt sweat breaking out on his temples, only to subside a moment later with shuddering chills. His gut clenched, and the pain would have doubled him over had the ropes not kept him flat against the floor. Blaine's breath came in shallow gasps as the pain hit again. He writhed, twisting against the ropes that held him until the skin at his wrists and ankles were raw. Every movement stretched the savaged skin on his back, yet it was impossible not to move. After only a few moments, the scream Prokief coveted tore from Blaine's lips.

"Make sure he remains conscious." Prokief turned from Ejnar to the guards. "When his time's up, drag him out when the prisoners are in the yard. Let them see the price of insolence."

Blaine sat up with a start, eyes wide and heart pounding. It took him a moment to get his bearings. Despite the room's shutters, the arctic daylight streamed in around the edges, giving him enough to recognize that he was at the Crooked House. He had dozed in a chair near the banked fire, and the tattered blanket Ifrem had given him was dangerously close to the hearth, knocked askew as he had fought against the dream.

"Back in the Hole, huh?" Verran's voice helped anchor him to the present. Blaine closed his eyes and swallowed hard, trying to slow his rapid breathing. His heart thudded so hard against his ribs that he imagined the inn shook with the pounding.

"Drink this." Blaine opened his eyes to find Verran standing in front of him, a tin cup of whiskey in his hand. Gratefully, Blaine accepted it, taking a gulp of the raw liquor. The remembered pain was fading, though Blaine would always carry the scars, both on his back and in the dreams that woke him, sweating and trembling, more nights than he cared to admit.

"Let me tell you," Verran went on, resting a boot on the chair next to Blaine and leaning forward. "Sharing a room with you and Piran is a bit like a front-row seat at the madhouse."

Blaine took another sip of the whiskey and willed himself to relax. "Entertaining, are we?"

Verran shrugged. " 'Entertaining' isn't the word I'd have picked. More like watching a corpse in a gibbet—you don't want to look, but you can't stop." Verran came around to sit on the front of his chair and leaned toward the fire. He poked at the embers, bringing them up to a glow, and threw a small log onto the grate, guessing that Blaine would not go back to sleep tonight. "I was there when they fished the two of you out of the Hole. You looked like the wrath of the gods."

"I don't really remember."

Verran snorted. "I don't think either of you were conscious. I figured Piran would make it. He's a soldier. But I have to say, I wouldn't have bet money on you, even if the mines did put muscle on your bone."

"I couldn't let Prokief win," Blaine said quietly. What little he remembered of his time in the Hole was focused on the rage he had directed at Prokief, rage that was really meant for his father, for the king, for everything about this accursed place. Blaine finished his whiskey, letting it burn down his throat, wishing it would blur the memories and knowing it would not.

"Yeah, and if I knew you'd keep getting dreams about it, I don't know whether I'd have agreed to share the bunk room with you at the homestead," Verran said, attempting a lighter tone. "Gods! Piran's always waking up with his fist ready to strike and you wake up like this more nights than I care to count. At least Dawe's a sound sleeper, or I'd never get any peace."

"Where is Piran?" Blaine looked around the darkened room.

"No idea."

Outside the inn, the sea had grown wild, and the rain was gray with ash from the volcano's explosion. Dark rivulets of water streamed down the walls of the buildings, leaving dirty streaks behind.

"As if we didn't have enough to worry about, I wonder what the blast will do to the fishing," Blaine mused.

"We've got bigger problems, boys," Ifrem said. From where he stood in the doorway, he pointed toward the seawall. "There are all kinds of wardings on the town: wards against fire and spells against mice, and a little witching to keep weevils out of the bread and make the meat keep longer." He nodded toward the raging sea. "If the magic's unsteady, then so are the spells to hold the seawall."

Ifrem turned to the crowd that pressed up against the window. "If you want to stay dry, I'll need some men to latch the storm shutters." A few of the men grumbled and then shouldered into their oilcloth cloaks, some heading out the front door to secure the ground-floor windows, while others tramped up the steps to do the same for the second floor.

"Where's Piran?" Blaine asked once again.

Ifrem shrugged. "Out in it, I guess. He came through here a bit ago, but he was mum when I asked him where he was going."

"Do you think he got caught breaking curfew?" Verran asked, casting a nervous glance toward the rain-soaked streets.

Blaine shook his head. "I don't think Prokief's guards are loyal enough to patrol in this kind of weather. If I know him, he's spending the night with a lady friend."

Blaine had never gotten completely used to nights that never grew dark, nor days where the sun never rose. The candlemarks passed and the bell tower rang out above the sound of the storm. Ifrem's weary guests pitched in, using rags to stop up places where the storm sent rivulets of water beneath the door or around the windows. By third bells, most of those who had jammed into the common room were soundly asleep wherever they could find a seat.

Blaine did not care to attempt sleeping again, though Verran managed to doze. A foreboding that had nothing to do with magic hovered in the back of his mind, and the more time passed without Piran's return, the more worried he became. The storm had ended by fifth bells and Ifrem's guests began to stagger to the door once curfew was over.

Ifrem brought Blaine a cup of *fet*, a strong, licorice-flavored drink brewed from the roots of one of Edgeland's trees, prized for its stimulant properties and cursed for its bitter flavor. "Some night," Ifrem said, grimacing as he sipped his *fet*.

"Yeah, some night."

Ifrem cocked an eyebrow. "Don't waste your time worrying about the likes of Piran Rowse. He's out wenching, or emptying the purses of some poor marks who don't know better than to play him at cards."

Just then, the door burst open. Piran stood in the doorway, rumpled and soaked. "Mick, we've got to get out of here. Where's Verran?"

"Upstairs. What's going on? Where did you go?"

Piran shook his head. "Out with a lady friend. That's not important. We need to get out of the Bay."

Blaine frowned. "What's wrong?"

"Some fighting started over in the marketplace. The guards can't contain it."

"I've got no desire to be here when Prokief sends reinforcements," Blaine said, starting to his feet.

"He won't," Piran said. "Velant's on fire."

CHAPTER
THIRTEEN

———

BLAINE AND VERRAN DONNED THEIR CLOAKS and joined Piran in the street. Debris from the storm littered the roadways. What were once small boats lay in broken heaps, dashed against buildings that had lost shutters, windows, and signage to the storm. The whole town was streaked with ash, and black puddles splashed an inky mixture as crowds moved in the narrow streets.

Despite the looming dark cloud of Estendall's ash, more people milled about in the streets than Blaine could remember seeing at one time. A nervous energy crackled through the crowd.

"Look there!" Piran pointed toward Velant. Elevated on a cliff above the sea, Velant burned like a torch on a hill.

"The whole bloody thing's up in flames," Verran muttered.

"And Dawe's in there somewhere," Piran said grimly.

Blaine shook his head in amazement. "I thought you meant a building, but—"

"Death to Prokief!" The cry came from somewhere in the mob around them and quickly became a chant. The crowd jostled shoulder to shoulder and the chant seemed to come from all directions, building in intensity.

"Disperse! Leave now!" Over the shoulders of the men in front of him, Blaine glimpsed a grim-faced line of soldiers blocking the end of the main street. One row of soldiers were on horseback and two more rows were on foot, perhaps fifty men in all. The soldiers were wearing helmets and light armor and were armed with crossbows that were aimed at the crowd.

"Get out of our way! We've got a score to settle." A large man burst from the front of the mob, waving a broken board. Before he had taken more than a half-dozen steps, a quarrel twanged from the bow of one of the foot soldiers, catching the man full in the chest.

The mob scattered but did not yield. Blaine pulled Verran into an alley. Piran followed a moment later, his arms full of rocks and debris.

"Take some," Piran said, handing some of the rocks to Blaine. "It's about to get ugly."

Blaine grabbed Verran by the arm. "You can't help down here. Get back to the homestead. Warn Kestel. Do what you can to put up some defenses. Piran's right—this is going to get worse before it's sorted out. If there's a way to help Dawe, we'll do it."

"You might need these." Verran dumped out a pouch on his belt, and a variety of keys clanked into his hands.

"Where did you get those?" Blaine asked, taking them from Verran.

Verran smiled. "I've been pinching them from the soldiers at the Crooked House for a while now. Thought it might come in handy someday. They're drunk enough to figure they lost the keys somewhere on their patrol. I don't know what they open, but more than one of them are likely to work at Velant."

Blaine grinned. "You're the best of the worst, Verran."

Verran made an exaggerated bow, with a gesture that swept an invisible hat in a wide arc. "At your service."

"Keep the looting to a minimum on your way home," Blaine cautioned.

"Spoilsport," Verran groused. "On the other hand, Velant has a warehouse down by the docks. With the storm, there could be a door loose—"

"Just get home and make sure Kestel's safe. If this goes badly, we'll need a place to fall back to."

Blaine watched Verran sprint into the distance, and returned his attention to the mob in the street. A chunk of ice whizzed past his head, clattering against the building behind him. Bay colonists had squared off against Prokief's badly outnumbered troops. Armed with storm debris and hunks of ice, the colonists took shelter in the doorways and alleys, hiding behind refuse and overturned barrels. The soldiers had scattered as well, firing off arrows from cover until driven back by a hail of rock-hard chunks of ice and debris.

"They can't have as many arrows as we've got pieces of ice," Blaine said, hefting a chunk in his hand.

"Uh-oh," Piran muttered. "Warden-mages."

Blaine glanced up long enough to see three men in gray robes appear near the soldiers' last position. Their robes matched the color of the uniforms of Velant's soldiers and had their own unusual embroidery to signify rank. One of the men had steel-gray hair and a closely trimmed beard. The man next to him had a gaunt face, and his robes hung on him as if there were no body beneath them. The third mage was short and portly, with brown hair and a shining pate in the middle.

"Watch out!" Blaine warned, bracing for the attack.

A noxious cloud formed out of thin air, gradually dispersing in the direction opposite where the soldiers had taken refuge. The streets were suddenly loud with the sounds of coughing and gagging, and the angry townspeople began to fall to their knees, clutching their throats or grasping at their chests.

Blaine and Piran pulled their scarves around their mouths and noses, but the magicked cloud diffused through the cold air, closing around them until they were gasping and retching, digging at their tearing eyes.

In the distance, they heard the roar of angry voices and the sound of thuds and crashes.

"Mages can't control all of us at once," Blaine gasped, his throat raw and burning.

"Hit them in shifts," Piran choked.

Blaine was already dragging himself to his feet. In the square, colonists surged forward. Armed with fishing spears and broken boards, they took up barrel tops as shields and wielded nets and ropes from the fishing boats with dangerous accuracy.

Soldiers in groups of two or three battled gangs of six or eight colonists. Though the soldiers were armed with swords, the colonists were no strangers to street brawls, and in their hands, knives could be equally deadly.

A hail of rocks and ice flew through the air toward the mages, only to stop as if hitting an invisible wall and dropping to the ground. One of the mages held up his hand, palm out, and a crippling wave of pain felled Blaine, Piran, and the colonists around them. Men cursed as they twisted and writhed with sudden, agonizing muscle cramps. But from behind the mages, a roar of voices shouted curses, growing closer with every second. As quickly as the pain came, it disappeared as the new mob drew the mages' attention elsewhere.

Blaine felt his temper rise. Prokief had never turned his mages loose beyond the Velant walls. In the distance, smoke billowed from the towering flames that rose over Velant. He gripped his hunting knife in one hand and stepped back to send a heavy chunk of ice flying toward a soldier he spotted peering from around a corner. The ice clipped the soldier on the temple and he dropped without a word.

"Come on," Blaine shouted, motioning for Piran to follow him as the crowd rushed forward again.

The mob had reached the icy commons in the middle of the town. The three mages held their position at the northern edge of the commons, but more colonists had taken to the street, and protesters streamed into the narrow alleys. Prokief's mages, realizing that the crowd was growing beyond their ability to control, sent bursts of magic into the mob, dropping men in their tracks with pain or sudden dysentery, only to shift their magic in another direction a moment later. It was enough to slow the crowd, but not stop their advance, and each wave of magic stoked the mob's anger.

Half a dozen protesters ran at the mages with a battle cry, fishing spears raised. The three mages drew together, and thrust out their hands. The attackers screamed and staggered as blood began to stream from their mouths, trickling from their ears and eyes and gushing from their noses.

Blaine was in the center of the mob. He was tall enough to get a glimpse of what was happening, while Piran was unable to see even when he jumped into the air.

"What's going on?" Piran yelled above the cries and curses of the crowd.

"The mages just killed the men who rushed them."

Screams of rage rose from the crowd. Voices carried on the cold night air, cursing Prokief and the mages, damning the king and the guards to Raka.

"I don't think they got the effect they wanted," Piran noted. The entire commons was jammed with people; men stood shoulder to shoulder, pressed so tightly against one another that it was impossible for an individual to leave the center of the mob. Panicked by the deaths of the attackers, the mob began to stampede toward the rear. Shouts and curses filled the air as men were pushed and shoved, and screams echoed from those who stumbled and were trampled beneath the press.

"Here comes another salvo!" Blaine shouted as the mages prepared to drive off the mob with a blast of magic.

For a few seconds, magic hummed in the air, crackling overhead like lightning. Blaine felt a searing blast of pain that made his vision swim, and he fell to his knees. And then…nothing.

In the crowd, men stumbled, shaking their heads with baffled expressions on their faces. "What's going on?" a frightened voice asked.

Blaine struggled to his feet, still trying to clear his head. He sought the flicker of magic within him. Always, it had responded to his call. Now it was gone.

"The magic's gone!" someone in the crowd shouted. The cry was taken up by others and echoed across the commons.

"If the magic's dead, the mages are nothing but men," Piran shouted. "After them! They can't hurt us now!"

The retreating mob made a sudden shift. Footsteps thudded against the icy ground as the crowd converged from every side, running as fast as the press of bodies would permit toward the mages, who stood back to back, hands raised in hapless defense.

"Get back!" the tall mage shouted, and spread his fingers wide, snapping his hands forward as if to cast his magic against the raging mob.

"Go to the gods," shouted one of the men at the front of the mob, a broad-shouldered fisherman who held a well-worn fishing pike in one hand. With a lurch, he thrust the pike forward,

204 • GAIL Z. MARTIN

catching the tall mage just below the ribs, hoisting his writhing body aloft impaled on the pike.

A cheer rose from the mob, and the other mages turned to run, but the crowd hemmed them in, cutting off their escape.

Blaine caught a glint of light off the broad blade of a hunting knife before it sang through the air, severing the head from the body of the short mage. The portly warden-mage was the last of the trio left, and he sank to his knees, ashen, hands upraised in supplication.

"Please, please spare me—"

Colonists who had endured the tortures of the warden-mages when they were convicts turned a deaf ear to the mage's plea. Blaine winced at the sound of the wood against flesh and bone as the rioters massed around the mage, striking over and over with their makeshift weapons until the man's screams were silenced. The crowd hesitated for a moment, as if unsure what to do now that the mages were dead and the soldiers had disappeared.

Blaine scrambled up onto the low stone wall at the edge of the commons. "Now is our chance to take Velant," he shouted. "Without the mages, Prokief can't hold the prison. There are more of us than there are guards. To Velant!"

The crowd took up the chant, and soon the walls of the town rang with the cry. "To Velant! To Velant!"

Blaine climbed down as the crowd shifted and hundreds of colonists began streaming up the road toward the prison, leaving the bloody bodies of the warden-mages where they lay. Velant's flames flared in the perpetual twilight of the white night sky. Black smoke billowed upward, temporarily blotting out the stars that never set.

The wind whipped around them, coming off the ocean with a ferocity that numbed skin and tore at the colonists' coats.

After routing the guards and mages at the commons, the mood of the crowd had turned vengeful. Men brandished their weapons as they headed up the rutted road toward Velant.

"You sure about this, Mick?" Piran asked, glancing at Blaine as they trudged up the hill toward the prison.

Blaine shrugged. "Prokief's vulnerable. The mages can't help him. We outnumber the guards. Something's gone wrong up there, or the place wouldn't be on fire. We won't get better odds."

"Do you think he started it? The fire?"

Blaine considered the possibility for a moment. "No. If the fire were just starting now, I'd say that Prokief might have started it rather than surrender. But it was burning before the magic failed, before the mages died." Blaine shook his head. "Prokief would never have thought he could lose as long as he had the mages."

Piran squinted, trying to make out Velant's buildings through the smoky haze that had settled over the snow-covered landscape. "What about Dawe?"

Blaine ducked his head as a blast of wind swept snow into the air. "I don't know, Piran. I hope we can find him."

Velant sat on a high bluff above the ocean, a commanding enclave with one large stone building and several large wooden structures surrounded by a timber stockade of sharpened pikes and a high stone wall. The stone building and the wall had been quarried by the original convicts under the threat of starvation and the lash. It was a dark, hulking presence, intended to intimidate all who entered beneath Velant's massive iron gates.

"Halt! Go back!"

The voices of the guards at the gate rang out over the ice. As the prison behind them burned, a line of guards stayed at their posts. When the mob drew closer, a hail of arrows flew from behind the crenellations in the wall. Several men in the crowd fell, but many of the attackers had brought makeshift shields, and they raised them overhead, taking the brunt of the attack. The crowd fell back, just out of arrows' reach.

"Surrender, and we won't have to kill you," Blaine shouted. He had reached the front line of the crowd halfway up the hill, and now found himself among the vanguard of the mob. Piran was beside him, his jaw set and his mouth in a hard, determined line.

In response, rocks and ice pelted the crowd, hurled by slingshots and small catapults. The crowd scattered but did not disperse. Instead, they turned over the empty wagons outside the prison, wagons that carried convicts to the mines or out to the fields. The guards were helpless as the crowd began to pull the wagons apart to fashion themselves more cover.

Outside the gates, six gibbets hung from tall posts, each with a rotting corpse inside the iron man-shaped cage. Crows scattered from the carrion as the crowd approached. The sickly sweet smell of death mixed with the smoke.

"Get out of the way! Let us through!" The crowd parted as several large men came from the rear, carrying a large tree that had been hurriedly cut and stripped of its branches. More men ran from the crowd to help carry the large trunk, while others fell into step, holding the wagon boards to provide as much shelter as possible to the crew of what Blaine realized was to become a battering ram.

"Give them room!" Blaine shouted, and Piran echoed the call for the crowd to step back.

The guards at their posts sent arrows and stones down against the invaders, but they bounced uselessly against the improvised shields. Velant had been built to keep its prisoners inside, not with the intent to keep invaders out. The large iron gates relied on mages and guards, not the strength of metal and stone.

"Heave!"

The large tree trunk swayed backward, then crashed into the iron gates, borne on the hands of two dozen men.

"Heave!"

Again and again, the battering ram smashed against the gates. The crowd had taken to making sport of pelting the guards with balls of ice thrown hard enough to draw blood. Shouts rose from the crowd whenever their volleys scored a hit on any soldier unwary enough to show himself between the crenellations.

"Heave!"

Smoke hung heavy in the air, too heavy even for the stiff wind from the ocean to dispel. After the initial resistance, the guards appeared to have abandoned their post, since their arrows and missiles were useless in repelling the attack.

"Heave!"

The iron gate gave a final squeal as it yielded under the weight of the heavy battering ram. Shouts of victory rose from the crowd. Blaine chanced a look down the slope and was amazed to see it filled with colonists, both men and women, stretching halfway back toward town.

"Practically the whole bloody colony turned out for the show," Piran muttered.

"Let's hope Kestel and Verran had the brains to stay home," Blaine replied.

The battering-ram crew gave one final swing and the iron gate tore from its hinges in a mangled heap. Men scrambled forward to clear it from the path, and the ramming crew, still beneath their shields, led the entrance into the prison enclosure.

A crash sounded behind them and Blaine caught a glimpse of teams of men bringing down the hated gibbets, leaving them in a tangle of bent iron, broken wood, and decaying corpse flesh on the trampled snow.

The crowd streamed forward, shoving their way into the courtyard.

For the first time, Blaine got a good look at the source of the fire. Two of the dormitory buildings were charred ruins. Another building, where the women convicts were put to work as bakers and laundresses, was ablaze. Blaine turned toward the hulking stone building, the symbol of Velant's tyranny and Prokief's power. Flames streamed from the windows, scorching the stone. Parts of the roof were on fire and bits of burning wood fell to the ground, sending up showers of sparks.

Blaine ran a few steps to the body of a fallen Velant guard and took a sword from the corpse's hand. He hefted it, satisfied with its grip.

"We'll go after the guards," Piran said, marshaling a few dozen men from the crowd, who fanned out, searching among the buildings for the soldiers who had deserted their posts.

"We'll look for survivors," Blaine replied, gathering a group of his own.

The smell of burning wood and charred flesh hung heavy in the cold air. It appeared that the fire had started in one of the dormitories and that some kind of effort had been made to put it out, judging from the buckets and tracks in the snow. A similar effort had also failed at the second dormitory, but little seemed to have been attempted to save the stone building or the laundry.

Dozens of structures ringed the wall. Some held foodstuffs, while others housed tools, weapons, and gear. The stables appeared untouched by the fire, though even at a distance

Blaine could hear the whinnies of terrified horses and the crash of hooves against wood as the frightened animals tried to escape their stalls.

"Fan out; take the buildings in groups of four," Blaine said. "Stay sharp—you're as likely to find guards as convicts." He held his stolen sword tightly.

They headed into a barn. It was smaller than the dormitories, but still one of the larger buildings, with a large first floor dedicated to wagons and farming equipment and a loft for storing grain. Blaine paired off with another man while the remaining two colonists headed in the opposite direction.

A soft thud drew Blaine's attention and he motioned for his companion to follow him. Carefully, they rounded the corner of a farm wagon, weapons raised.

"Please, don't hurt us." Cowering against the wall were several dozen men and women. They were dressed in the rough, homespun uniforms of new convicts and their faces were soot-covered. Despite the cold, they wore no cloaks and they huddled together against the chill. Blaine searched their faces in vain, but did not see Dawe.

Blaine nodded to the other searchers, who lowered their weapons. As he drew closer, he could see that many of the survivors had seeping burns on their arms and faces. "What happened?"

The man who had initially spoken got to his feet. He was in his middle years, with a face lined from a life lived out of doors. While he was missing several teeth and had a wide scar across one cheek, his blue eyes glinted with intelligence. "Fire started in First Hall just after dawn."

"Was it an accident, or was it set?"

The convict shrugged. "Don't know. It's been bad here in the last few days. Rumors said the magic wasn't stable no more, that Prokief's mages were losing their hold. Maybe it's true, maybe it isn't. Rations have been scarce since the last full moon. Friend of mine in the kitchens said that the last supply ship never showed up and he didn't think there'd be another one, maybe ever. We've been eating thin gruel and spoiled meat for weeks."

Blaine nodded. "The warden-mages can't hurt you. We've broken down the gate. You're free."

The convict looked at him skeptically. "For now, you mean. What happens if the ships start coming again from Donderath?"

Blaine gave a shrug of his own. "Then we're all dead men. You can stay if you want to."

"No, that's quite all right," the convict hastened to answer. "Rather have a few weeks of freedom than die in this cursed place, and they've been dying in scores lately. First, a fever, then the flux. Seemed like the guards or the mages killed someone near every day." He shook his head. "I'm happy to leave. We were already dead men in here, just waiting for the day our lot came up. I'll take my chances out there, anytime."

Blaine nodded again. "We don't know where the guards have gone, or Prokief. Until we find out, you're safest in hiding, for now. As we find more survivors, we'll send them here. Once we've accounted for everyone, we'll use the wagons to get you into Bay-town." He paused.

"Do you know anything about the colonists who were taken in Bay-town yesterday? I'm looking for a friend of mine who was arrested."

The group's self-appointed spokesman shook his head. "Until the fires started, we hadn't been out of our buildings. When everything started to burn, the guards tried to put out the fires, and when they couldn't, they ran away and left us to fend for ourselves. We know nothing about what's gone on in the town."

Blaine sighed, though he was not surprised. "It was worth a try," he muttered, turning away.

Blaine and his fellow searchers turned their attention to the rest of the barn, but found nothing. They stepped back into the twilight. The walls of the laundry building were aflame and its roof had collapsed. Thick smoke blanketed the prison yard.

Bodies littered the parade ground. Many lay just outside the burning buildings, those who had jumped to avoid the flames or who had managed to drag themselves outside before succumbing to the smoke. Quite a few guards were among the dead as well. He wondered whether they had been overcome by smoke or set upon by rebellious inmates.

Across the courtyard, Blaine spotted Piran and his volunteers. They had rounded up more than two dozen guards, who were kneeling, hands clasped atop their heads in surrender. Piran and his men had armed themselves from the pile of weapons they had collected. Others among the colonists busied themselves looting the prison's granary and storehouse, while some were leading wild-eyed horses out of the stable. Given the size of the mob that had accompanied them up the hill, Blaine had no doubt that the rest of the prison's farm animals would also be liberated in short order.

"We've got to find Dawe," Blaine said to the man who had come with him in search of survivors.

"Aye, and I'd like to find my friends as well," the man replied. Blaine got a good look at him for the first time. He had an angular, pox-marked face with unremarkable blue eyes and high cheekbones. His woolen cap was jammed down on a shock of light-brown hair that appeared to have been hacked more than cut to fall shoulder-length. "I'm Taren," he introduced himself.

"I'm Mick, Mick McFadden."

"What do you think's become of Prokief and the rest of the mages?"

Blaine shook his head. "I've been wondering the same thing myself." He lit a lantern for Taren and then one for himself. "Come on," Blaine said to Taren. "Let's keep moving. Prokief had to have at least two thousand prisoners inside Velant, not counting the ones who were out on the farm or in the mines. We haven't found nearly all of them."

"Assuming they're alive."

Blaine drew a deep breath. "Yeah, assuming that."

Blaine held his scarf against his face for scant protection from the smoke and gestured for Taren to follow him. He flung open the doors to a large barn and heard a hurried rustle and hushed whispers.

"If you're convicts, we've come to free you. You've nothing to fear," Blaine shouted into the dim interior. "And if you're guards, give yourselves up. The prison has fallen."

The barn remained quiet. Blaine nodded to Taren, and they entered slowly, their swords raised. The barn smelled of leather and sawdust. After a glance around, Blaine realized it was one of the workshops where convicts made the leather gear needed by the miners, and on the other side of the barn, half-finished nets were strung from beam to beam, the work of those assigned to provision the fishing fleet.

"Come out. Show yourselves," Blaine shouted. "You won't be hurt."

Footsteps shuffled in the gloom. Shadows began to move, and figures rose from where they had hidden, stepping into the faint light. As the convicts gave up their hiding places, Blaine did his best to make a quick head count, and guessed that close to two hundred prisoners had sought shelter in the barn.

"You're free," Blaine said. "Stay here out of the cold. We're trying to account for survivors, and then we'll see about getting you out of the camp."

Blaine and Taren moved down the line of buildings along Velant's outer wall. A slight movement in the shadows between buildings caught Blaine's eye and he motioned for Taren to be still. Swords at the ready, they moved as quietly as the snow-covered ground would permit.

"Show yourselves! The camp has fallen. Surrender, and we won't hurt you."

In response, two dark forms fled to the other end of the narrow alley. Blaine and Taren took off in pursuit. When they rounded the corner, the figures had disappeared. Blaine blinked to adjust to the sudden change from shadow to the glaring snow.

"They can't have gone far," he said. The closest building was a large shed. Taren saw it as well, and nodded. Silently, they moved toward the building. Blaine had hoped to follow the tracks of whoever had run off, but with the fires and the general chaos, the snow was hopelessly flattened by dozens of footprints.

"In here," Blaine murmured as he led the way. The barn was silent, but something seemed out of place. Cautiously, he moved into the half-lit center of the first floor. The light from his lantern cast deep shadows around the barn's walls. A carriage, testimony to Prokief's pretense of finery, sat on one side of the building. Yokes and plows took up most of the rest of the floor space, as well as a large sledge and a huge troika. Tools for the prison's large farm leaned against the wall, and some tools lay abandoned on the ground, as if their users had seen the fires and fled.

Taren pointed, and Blaine nodded. Next to the carriage lay a bit of fresh snow on an otherwise dry floor.

Blaine and Taren split up, moving around the carriage without making a sound. They both set down their lanterns in preparation for a fight. Taren had armed himself with a stolen sword, though Blaine would have been surprised if the man had ever before wielded such a blade. It had been many years since Blaine had labored in his father's salle under the tutelage of an arms master, and since colonists were forbidden from owning swords, he'd had no opportunity for recent practice. Before, he might have counted on magic to enhance his abilities, but now he was on his own.

Together, Blaine and Taren jerked open the doors to the carriage. The two men inside hurled themselves at their discoverers, and Blaine realized they had found Prokief and Ejnar, his favorite warden-mage.

Prokief fell on Blaine with a fury, screaming with incoherent rage. The man wielded a sword, raining blow after blow. One of the blows slashed Blaine hard on the left shoulder, sending searing pain down his arm. Blaine gritted his teeth and parried with his broadsword. Out of the corner of his eye, Blaine spotted Taren skirmishing with Ejnar, who was dressed in singed and dirty mage robes. Taren was holding his own; Blaine returned his attention just in time to parry another deadly blow from Prokief's sword.

Blaine scored a slice on Prokief's arm, and a hail of curses greeted him as his opponent gave a pounding set of blows that pressed Blaine to parry. Blaine felt his temper rise. His fighting magic might be gone, but sheer anger rose to replace it.

Prokief swung hard for Blaine's head and Blaine dodged, though the tip of the blade grazed his temple and a trickle of blood started down his face. He heard Prokief laugh.

"You never had it in you to be the kind of soldier your daddy was," Prokief taunted. "And he was a piss-poor excuse for a man if there ever was one." He grinned. "No matter. You're a dead man, and you don't even know it yet. Pollard made sure of that."

"Pollard? What's he got to do with anything?" Blaine barely moved in time as Prokief hammered home several more blows, relying on sheer brute force. Blaine parried, feeling the shock of the blows in his bones, wondering if he could turn the attack before Prokief shattered his arm.

"I told you the day would come when Merrill wouldn't be around to care what happened to you," Prokief jeered. "The ships have stopped coming. Looks like that day is finally here. I'm going to enjoy this."

Training and anger took over. Blaine struck back with full fury, using the sword with a two-handed grip, driving Prokief back pace after pace.

Prokief scored again, slicing into Blaine's shoulder. Blaine pressed forward, guessing that Prokief was waiting for him to tire. Blaine had fought well so far, but Prokief was a professional soldier. From the gleam in Prokief's eyes, Blaine guessed that the commander was toying with him. In a fair fight, stamina and skill tipped the odds in Prokief's favor.

Blaine smiled. *In a fair fight.* He dove for a scythe that lay abandoned on the barn floor, swinging it with his left hand in a deadly arc that sliced through Prokief's jacket and opened a bloody slice on his chest.

"You insolent cur!" Prokief grated, but the blow had rattled him enough that Blaine saw the opening he needed. With his full strength, Blaine brought his blade down on Prokief's wrist. Both the hand and the sword it clutched fell away in a shower of blood and the man sank to his knees. Blaine glimpsed the flash of steel in the dim light and jerked aside just as a shiv flew from Prokief's left hand.

Blaine lunged forward and sank his blade deep into Prokief's chest, pinning him to the side of the carriage. Blood seeped from the wound, spreading across Prokief's smudged and torn shirt, and a trickle of blood started from the corner of Prokief's mouth.

Prokief regarded Blaine balefully. "Did you start the fires?" Blaine demanded.

Prokief had grown ashen from the loss of blood, but still Blaine kept an eye on Prokief's remaining hand. Blaine stepped back. Hatred and arrogance glinted in Prokief's eyes.

"No, but I should have." A bitter smile touched Prokief's lips. "Don't expect to take back your title, Lord McFadden. Donderath's losing the war. By now, your lands and women either belong to Meroven—or to Lord Pollard." He coughed up blood.

With a growl, Blaine scooped up the fallen dagger and with one broad movement drew its blade across Prokief's throat. Prokief, forever silenced, hung limply from the sword.

As the adrenaline of the fight drained away, Blaine came back to himself, realizing that he was breathing hard and that his hands were shaking. The sound of a nearby scuffle jarred him into the present and he jerked back on the sword, letting Prokief's corpse slump to the ground. Blaine grabbed his sword and ran.

On the other side of the carriage, Taren was still fighting off his opponent. Given that both men held their swords as if it were the first time, it amazed Blaine that they had not already killed each other from sheer blundering.

"A hand here, Mick, if you please!" Taren's sleeves on both arms bore several fresh slashes tinged with blood. The mage had fared no better. A slice down one cheek oozed blood, and

Taren had managed to get in a good cut to the mage's right thigh. From the panicked look on his face, Blaine guessed that Ejnar had never had to fight using anything except his magic. Taren's arms shook with the weight of the sword as he held it in a white-knuckled, two-handed grip.

Blaine raised his sword and gestured for Taren to step back. "I remember you," Blaine said, stepping in to engage Ejnar's wild thrust.

"All convicts look alike to me," Ejnar muttered, doing his best to swing for Blaine's throat, an off-balance stroke Blaine easily parried.

"Oh, it was you, all right," Blaine replied grimly. "Prokief turned me over to you right before he threw me in the Hole."

Ejnar chuckled. "Pity he let you out."

Blaine's sword caught Ejnar's strike, though the force of it sent a jolt down his arm. While their swords were caught against each other, Blaine shoved forward, pushing Ejnar's arm out from his body, and giving him a clean shot to send Prokief's dagger straight into Ejnar's chest.

Blaine heard steel whistle through the air, and abruptly, Ejnar's head toppled from his body as his corpse collapsed in the opposite direction. Behind Ejnar stood Taren, ashen and wide-eyed, his bloody sword gripped with both hands.

"We couldn't let him live," Taren said breathlessly. "What if the magic came back again?"

Blaine nodded. "No, we couldn't."

"Prokief?"

Blaine let out a long breath. "He's dead."

A mixture of relief, bewilderment, and horror crossed Taren's face. "Prokief's dead? Truly?"

"Truly." Blaine shook himself out of the moment. "Leave the bodies. Bring your sword. We still haven't found Dawe."

"Or the other survivors," Taren put in, gingerly stepping around Ejnar's corpse.

"I think I know where to look—in both cases."

Taren followed Blaine to the next and last large barn. This barn held bales of wool sheared from the prison's sheep, and bundles of cloth woven on the looms that the female prisoners worked in half-day shifts. Blaine and Taren yanked open the doors. Blaine nodded toward the many footprints that had tracked through the thick dust on the floor.

Before he could call out, figures began to step out from where they had hidden. Some clutched farm implements and other crude weapons, but many looked ready to flee.

"You're safe," Blaine said, raising his hands and holding them out from his body. "Prokief's dead. The mages can't hurt you."

Men and women began to move out of the shadows and into the light. More and more came, leaving Blaine amazed that they had all found places to hide. From the shuffling he could hear in the loft above, even more of the convicts had taken shelter up there.

"We'll find a way to get you into town as soon as possible," Blaine said. "After that... well, we'll figure something out," he said. As he spoke, Blaine realized that without Velant, Baytown and the other small settlements had lost both persecutor and heavy-handed protector. Without Velant's guards, there was no one to keep order. And without Prokief's military organization, no mechanism existed to assign colonists to homesteads.

Blaine scanned the crowd. "Is Dawe Killick among you?"

No one answered, and Blaine bit back a curse. He looked around, and saw that Taren and two men in convict garb were trading good-natured punches and backslaps. As the newly freed convicts milled around the barn, Blaine stepped back outside.

He was quite surprised when Taren joined him. "I thought you found your friends," Blaine said with a jerk of his head toward the crowd in the building.

"I did. They're a little shaken up, but otherwise fine." Taren paused. "But you haven't found the man you're looking for."

Blaine shook his head. "No, and I'd think if he were in one of the open buildings, he'd have come out by now." Blaine scanned the blacksmith's forge, a stone building open on one side, and several long sheds that also stood open on one side to shelter oft-used items and firewood. "But there's one place we haven't looked yet." He looked around the barn, and spotted a large coil of rope hanging from a peg on one of the posts. He grabbed it, and headed for the door.

Fearing the worst, Blaine strode across the open yard. He spared a glance toward where Piran had gathered at least a hundred soldiers and was in the midst of accepting their surrender. The looters had also grown more organized, forming a human chain to hand bales, boxes, casks, and jugs from hand to hand from the storage barns to wagons. A flash of light caught Blaine's eye and he watched as a flaming arrow soared through the air, ripping through the flag that flew above the prison, Donderath's flag, the banner of the kingdom that had exiled and then abandoned them.

Near the northern edge of the enclosure, close to the latrine trench, was an area with several sunken places in the icy ground. Just the sight of them made Blaine's stomach clench.

"You think your friend is in there?" Taren asked quietly.

"Yes." Blaine kicked the snow away from the first of the sunken areas, revealing a square metal door with a large padlock. Taren cleared the snow from another door a few feet away.

"Here, see if one of these fits." Blaine dug out the handful of keys Verran had stolen from the guards in town, taking half for himself and tossing the others to Taren. Blaine knelt and realized he was holding his breath. He fumbled the lock and blew on his fingers to bring back feeling in the cold. After trying several keys, one turned in the lock, and Blaine dug his fingers under the cold metal and shoved with all his might.

These were the Holes, shafts sunk deep as wells into Edgeland's frozen ground. They served as Prokief's greatest threat and, often, as his personal oubliettes. Blaine had barely survived the Holes, but many others had not lived through the experience, dying alone in the freezing darkness. Blaine set his jaw, expecting the worst. If Dawe was down one of these Holes, he had already been there for at least a day.

The darkness of the shaft was impenetrable compared with the permanent twilight above. "Dawe! Dawe Killick! Are you down there?"

Blaine's heart sank as his voice echoed but no reply came. He stood and walked over to the blacksmith's forge, taking a thin piece of wood from the stack and dipping it in pitch, then using the smith's flint and steel to strike a spark to light the torch. Blaine carried the torch back to the Hole and leaned as far in as he dared, holding the torch to see. The shaft was empty.

He heard Taren shove the lid away from another of the Holes. The smell that rose from the shaft was unmistakable. Someone had died at the bottom of the oubliette. Blaine joined Taren and once again held the torch as low as he dared. He recoiled, swallowing hard to keep from retching. The body at the bottom had been down there far longer than Dawe had been absent.

Together, Blaine and Taren headed for the two remaining Holes. Blaine wrested the next door free. The smell that greeted him was of shit and blood.

"Dawe! Dawe Killick!"

"Mick?" The voice that answered was faint and shaky. "By the gods! I must be dead or dreaming."

"Neither. Can you stand?"

"Doubtful."

Blaine cursed under his breath. "All right. I've got a rope. I'll make a loop in it and toss it down. Can you manage to get the loop under your arms?"

"Yep."

As Blaine tied a solid knot in the rope, he looked over toward Taren. "Anyone in there?"

Taren nodded. "Not much better off than your friend, I wager. Once we bring him up, we'll need to do the same here."

Blaine tossed the rope down to Dawe, and waited. The rope jerked. "I'm ready," Dawe rasped.

Together, Blaine and Taren pulled on the rope. Length by length they drew it up from the bottom of the shaft, until Dawe's head and shoulders appeared. Dawe's face was purple with bruises, and one eye was swollen shut. His lip was split. But to Blaine's great relief, his friend had not been whipped and had been thrown into the Hole fully dressed.

Blaine looked around and grabbed a sooty piece of oilcloth from where it was stretched over the blacksmith's wood to shelter it from the snow. "As soon as we get someone out of the other Hole, we'll steal you a coat," he said.

Dawe was shaking with cold, and his swollen lips had a bluish tint, but he managed a semblance of a smile. "I'm not complaining. I thought for sure I was going to die down there."

Blaine and Taren hauled up the second man from the Hole. Though he had been able to get the rope under his arms, the man looked much worse than Dawe, with several gashes that had the smell of a wound gone bad and a chalky, gray cast to his skin.

"Let's get them both to shelter and find them coats," Blaine said. But when Taren went to get under the other man's shoulder to help him to the barns, it quickly became apparent that it would take both Blaine and Taren together to carry the man to safety.

"Take care of that man first," Dawe said through chattering teeth. "I'll be all right for a few more minutes."

Blaine took the prisoner's shoulders, while Taren got his feet. Together, they hefted him across the open space and into the closest of the barns. The surviving convicts gathered around them as they entered.

"That's Ivar!" one of the convicts said in recognition. "Good thing you could get into the Hole. He's been out there for a couple of days."

"Go find some clothes," Blaine said to the convict. "We'll need two coats—there's another man who's waiting for us to come back." The convict ran for the door and came back a few minutes later with two uniform coats plus shirts and pants.

"We can care for Ivar," one of the women assured Blaine. "Go get your friend."

Blaine and Taren went back to where Dawe waited. He was shaking with cold, but he managed a wan smile. "Thought you got lost," he said.

"Let's get you inside and into some warmer clothing," Blaine said.

Dawe eyed the uniform coat and managed a smile. "Can I be a colonel? I've always wanted to be a colonel."

Blaine chuckled despite the situation. "Can't guarantee the rank, mate. I wager my helper stripped the first corpse he came to."

After they got Dawe to shelter, Blaine looked around at the convicts, who were now refugees from the burned prison.

"I'm going to go see about arranging for transportation back to Bay-town," he said. "And if there are coats and blankets to be found, I'll get them to you."

He looked to Taren, his accidental deputy. "Stay here. Try to get a good count of how many people we've got who can't make the walk back to Bay-town. I'll need that for the wagons." He didn't say it, but the survivors he and Taren had found were just a fraction of the convicts he had expected to find inside Velant. Unless several hundred could be accounted for from the mines and fields, the death toll from the fire had been terribly high.

Blaine headed out of the barn and found Piran walking his way. "Are the guards accounted for?" Blaine asked.

Piran nodded. "All that didn't run off. We found several uniforms behind one of the buildings. My bet is that a dozen or so guards chucked their uniforms and changed into convict garb when it became clear Prokief wasn't going to hold the gate."

Blaine shrugged. "As long as they don't give us any trouble, that suits me. They'll have to learn to live with the other colonists unless they plan to row home." He paused. "And the rest? Did they surrender?"

"Without a fight. Threw down their weapons and knelt down as pretty as you please."

"Before they scatter, let's find out what they know about the war in Donderath. It could be worse than we know. Besides, we need to get some kind of oath from them that they won't turn on us if a ship from home does happen to turn up."

"Do you think that's likely?" Piran's expression was grim, and Blaine was sure his friend guessed the answer.

"No, I don't. I think we're totally on our own now."

"Any sign of Prokief?"

"Dead." Briefly, Blaine recounted the fight he and Taren had in the carriage barn, and the deaths of Prokief and Ejnar.

Piran gave a low whistle. "So you got to be the one to kill Prokief, huh? Can't say I'll mourn him. Saves us the bother of hanging him."

"Did you find any other warden-mages?"

"Yeah." Piran's expression hardened. "We spared the soldiers, but the mages we killed. Can't chance having the magic come back."

Blaine looked out over the ruins of the camp. "We're rid of Prokief, but we're going to have a whole new set of problems with all these new colonists who've got nowhere to go. The guards won't be harassing us, but they won't be policing, either." He met Piran's gaze. "We'd better figure out how to keep a lid on things with the long dark coming, or we might not be around by the time the sun rises again."

CHAPTER
FOURTEEN

IT WAS THE MID-MORNING BEFORE BLAINE, DAWE, and Piran, exhausted from the night's work, caught a ride on the last wagon out of Velant bound for town. Taren had taken a group of men and a few wagons out to the mines and the prison farm to search for convicts or guards who did not know that Velant had fallen.

"Guess it's better this happened while we still have light," Piran muttered, leaning against the side of the wagon with his eyes shut.

Blaine shrugged. "Only a couple of weeks until the long dark falls. We'll have a few thousand people who have nowhere to live and no work to support them. It could get nasty pretty quickly if we're not careful."

Piran opened one eye and looked at him. "You know, for a convict, you think like a damned officer."

Blaine grinned. "Someone has to. Prokief ran the colony as much as he did the prison. We'll have to choose some kind of governing body if we don't want total chaos."

Piran closed his eyes again. "Wake me when you're done. I'm a soldier. I take orders."

"I don't know—you did just fine on your own organizing the guards' surrender."

"Don't tell anyone. Once the officers find out you can think, they either shoot you or promote you, and I don't like either choice."

Dawe was quiet, and his eyes were haunted. Blaine thought his friend still looked ashen and haggard. "Feeling warmer?" Blaine asked with a gentle nudge.

Dawe nodded. "Thanks for getting me out of there. I was pretty sure I was going to die."

"Kestel would have killed Piran and me if we hadn't figured a way to rescue you. I'd have been afraid to sleep in my own bed if we hadn't succeeded."

Dawe gave a weak laugh. "And she'd do it, too," he said quietly.

"Let's stop in town to get you some food and drink before we head all the way back to the homestead."

Dawe nodded and stifled a cough. "I could do with some whiskey." He coughed again and Blaine glanced at him with concern.

"Need to see a healer?"

Dawe met his eyes. "What for? The magic's gone—remember?"

"Let's hope that wasn't the only thing we had going for us, or we've got bigger problems than whether a colony full of convicts can avoid robbing each other blind without guards."

Dawe met his gaze. "I'm really not worried about that last part. Do you have any idea how many of the people here stole bread or clothes to live, or didn't do what they were accused of?"

"You're right, although some of us earned our sentences," Blaine replied. "But I'd wager most of the murderers in Velant killed one person who had it coming, and won't make a habit of it." He grimaced. "On the other hand, we both knew some bad seed who will make trouble for everyone."

"Hire the guards." Piran's voice startled Blaine, who had thought the other was asleep. Piran opened his eyes halfway to meet his gaze. "Seriously. They're military. They'll follow orders. Weed out the few rotters who enjoyed pushing people around."

"He's got a point," Dawe said. The tonelessness in his voice made Blaine wince. "Most of the guards were as much prisoners as we were. They could have made it worse for us than they did. We all know who the bad ones were. My guess is that they'll be found dead within a week. After that, the rest will probably be grateful for a job."

Blaine chuckled. "You may be right."

The rest of the ride back to town was quiet. Blaine kept replaying his final conversation with Prokief in his mind. *Why Pollard?* he wondered. *Vedran Pollard hated Father almost as much as I did. If he'd hated him just a little bit more, maybe Pollard would have been sent to Velant and I'd have been spared the trouble.* He struggled to remember much about Pollard: tall and sinewy, with hawk-like features and a nasty temper. Pollard and Ian McFadden couldn't be in the same room together without harsh words escalating to threats and, on more than one occasion, to blows.

Still, I always had the feeling Merrill liked Father better than he liked Pollard, and that Pollard knew it, Blaine mused. *And as far as I can remember, Pollard never spared me a second glance. What would make Prokief connect me with him?*

A half-forgotten memory triggered. There were always rumors that Prokief had a wealthy supporter back home, someone who sent him luxuries in return for—what? The rest of the old rumors surfaced in memory. Once in a while, a convict would disappear without a burial or even a confirmation of death. Blaine always assumed they were victims of the warden-mages, or the Hole, but there had been whispers that the men who had disappeared had been spirited back to Donderath, with bribes sufficient to make the ship captains turn a blind eye.

Prokief was Pollard's man, Blaine thought. *It would certainly explain why Prokief had it in for me. But if so, without ships from home, even Prokief would be cut off. So what did he mean, that I'm dead and don't know it?*

There would be no answers to his questions just now, but Blaine resolved to see if the remains of Prokief's office harbored any clues. The wagon bumped its way along the rutted icy roads and Blaine found himself looking out toward the wharves, to the empty piers where the supply ships from Donderath usually sat. When they rounded the turn into Bay-town, the streets were alive with people. The town had a festive air about it, and Blaine could hear music playing in the distance.

"Would you look at that?" he said, grinning. Bay-town merchants had taken advantage of the situation and an impromptu street fair ranged down the main waterfront, where just the night before, waves had slammed inland. In the distance, Estendall still billowed smoke, its eruption all but forgotten amid the news of Velant's fall. Blaine looked behind them. High on its cliff, clouds of smoke rose from Velant's ruined buildings like a twin volcano.

Piran sat up and took in the scene. "I could use some ale myself, come to think of it," he said as the wagon rumbled to a stop. Piran and Blaine jumped down and gave Dawe a hand, each of them gripping him by the arms to help him down. They were followed by the other newly freed convicts, who regarded the town wide-eyed, as if expecting guards to appear to drag them back to the prison.

From the sound of it, the Crooked House was already doing a good business despite the early hour, and Blaine guessed that its patrons had been up all night. The tavern was crowded shoulder to shoulder. The room buzzed with excited talk, and musicians strained to play above the din.

Ifrem was behind the bar, filling tankards of ale at a brisk pace. To Blaine's amazement, Kestel was helping dispense drinks to the crowd, sashaying through the tavern like a barmaid carrying a tray of tankards with her uninjured arm. From the grin on her face and the excitement in her eyes, Blaine guessed Kestel was as caught up in the celebration as the rest of the crowd.

"I'll bet you two silvers that if Kestel's here, so's Verran," Piran said with a nudge to Blaine's ribs.

Blaine bumped into a drunk who was wavering on his stool. The man slipped to the ground, and Blaine snagged the stool and nudged it behind Dawe with his foot. "Sit. We'll get you food and drink. You'll be warm enough in here, I wager, with half the town pressed in the room."

"And as much smoke from the pipes as there is from that damned volcano," Piran muttered, stifling a cough.

Blaine nodded. He looked around, aware that something was different and not quite sure what had changed.

Two of the whores who had flounced among the inn's patrons the night before stood near the fireplace. Both of them looked older and harder than Blaine remembered, and he wondered if it had been a bit of magic that had added to their glamour. In a corner, the woman who often told fortunes for Ifrem's guests sat staring at her cards, a baffled expression on her face. Near the bar, two people Blaine recognized as healers were talking, gesturing unhappily.

Blaine led the way, edging through the crowd toward where

Ifrem stood behind the bar. The townspeople who had filled his common room had ordered ale and whiskey, but Blaine noticed that most people stood with a half-full tankard in hand.

"Use a little magic to sweeten the taste of your wares?" Blaine asked quietly. Ifrem glowered in response, providing the answer.

Kestel returned to the bar after delivering a full tray of tankards. "Dawe! Thank Charrot you're safe!" She wiped her hands on her apron and embraced Dawe, giving him a peck on the cheek. Some of the patrons grinned and winked, and a few cheered. Kestel laughed.

"I'm glad you're safe, too," she said to Blaine and Piran, blinking away tears. She hugged each of them hard enough that Blaine realized just how worried she had been.

The musicians finished their tune and a few moments later, Verran elbowed his way through the crowd. "Glad you're back," he said, clapping them on the shoulder.

Ifrem poured Blaine a tankard of ale and waved off payment. Blaine took a sip and his eyes widened at the taste; it had a strong note of burned mash, proof that Ifrem's mages had definitely improved the flavor of the ale, though from the demand for drinks, the tavern's patrons did not seem to care.

Verran sighed. "I can play right well without magic, but a little glamour always helped increase the coins people threw our way."

"And your luck with the ladies?" Piran asked.

Verran grimaced. "Another casualty. 'Twas always my music and my magic that won me the lasses." He gave a gap-toothed grin. "I've got the music, but losing the magic will make it harder to win me a lady for the night."

"Look on the bright side," Blaine said with a nod toward two whores in the corner who had lost their beauty along with their magic. "At least without magic, you'll know for certain what your lady friend really looks like."

"Ah, but she'll have had an equally good look at me," Verran said, his regret only partially feigned. "I might as well resign myself to solitude now."

Ifrem paused after filling several tankards and leaned across the bar, catching Blaine's eye and giving a quick jerk of his head to summon Blaine and Piran closer. "Good to see you boys back in one piece. Thought you'd want to know—while you were burning down the prison, some of the merchants and the fishing-boat owners and such got together to figure out what to do in case things changed in a big way."

Blaine nodded. "Good idea. Prokief is dead. His soldiers surrendered. But without the guards, there's no law to speak of—"

"Which isn't good for the townsfolk," Ifrem finished. He raised an eyebrow. "Funny to hear this coming from a former convict, but civilized people do need some law, so long as it's just."

"No more curfews, no more papers," Piran supplied.

Ifrem's mouth was a hard line. "No more demanding payments from merchants to avoid having our stores looted or our windows broken." He paused to fill a few more tankards. "On the other hand, we can't have highwaymen on the roads and in the alleys. Bad for business."

"And what did this group of your merchant friends decide?" Blaine asked. He leaned against the bar, beginning to feel the activity of the last several hours in every aching bone and muscle.

"They formed a group they're calling the Freedmen's Council to govern the colony, at least until someone comes up with something better. Folks got wind of it and demanded there be representatives from the colonists who aren't merchants—"

Blaine held up a hand, having a good idea of where Ifrem was going with this. "Oh no. You're not roping me into—"

"Your name came up far more than anyone else's," Ifrem said. "You've got a reputation as a fair man."

"Just wait till they find out you were the one who killed Prokief and Ejnar," Piran put in. Blaine rolled his eyes, but Ifrem looked from Piran to Blaine.

"Truly?"

Blaine turned away uncomfortably. "It's not like I set out to do it. I was looking for Dawe—"

"They're both dead? Praise the gods!" Ifrem stood back from the bar. "Prokief and Ejnar are dead. Mick's the one who done it. Next round is on the house!"

With that, Blaine found himself the toast of the evening as townspeople he barely knew made it through the crowd to shake his hand and offer their thanks. He was unused to the attention and uncomfortable with the acclaim. When he had just about made up his mind to see if he could escape out the back door, Kestel sidled up to him and took his arm.

"Give the hero a little room, he's been up all night," she admonished the crowd of well-wishers. "You can thank him tomorrow. Prokief will be just as dead." With that she deftly steered Blaine out of the thick of the mob toward a table in the kitchen.

"Sit down. You look awful. Who clipped you on the side of the head?"

"I don't remember," Blaine said, touching his fingers gently to his throbbing temple. His hand came away sticky with blood.

Kestel got a cloth and dipped it in a bucket, then wrung it out. "Here. It'll take the sting out. Wait here while I go get Dawe and Piran." She returned in a few minutes with the other two men and sat them down at the table with Blaine like errant schoolboys.

"Eat. Drink a whiskey—it's good for digestion."

She turned her attention to Dawe. "Eat as much as you want. Ifrem's buying." She crossed the room and rummaged in a small chest, returning with a variety of tins and a mortar and pestle. As the men ate, she ground dried herbs and mixed them with a few drops of wine to make a paste, then began to bind up the worst of Dawe's injuries.

"You know, I got banged around pretty good, too," Piran muttered half-jokingly.

Kestel regarded him primly. "Ah, but you're the rough and tough professional man-at-arms, aren't you? I wouldn't want to affront your dignity by assuming that you minded injuries that were less than the loss of a limb."

"I like a bit of comfort as much as the next man," Piran groused.

Kestel gave a loud sigh. "Men! You're all babies. All right, Piran dear. I'll get to you after I finish up with Dawe. Mick's got a couple of nasty gashes, too. You'll have to wait your turn."

They were finished with their food by the time Kestel finished tending to Dawe. He looked tired and haggard, but some of the pain in his eyes had lessened. As she finished, Dawe took her hand and turned it over, kissing the back. "Thank you, m'lady."

Kestel shook her head. "Don't get all courtly on me. I just figured you might as well be in one piece if I have to live with the lot of you."

It took much less time for Kestel to apply her poultices to the worst of Blaine's injuries, and he was surprised at how quickly the mixture relieved the pain. Finally, she straightened and looked at Piran.

"All right. Your turn. Now, where are you hurt?"

Piran thrust out his right forearm. It was badly bruised, but the skin was not broken.

"You're not even cut!"

"Probably nicked the bone," Piran muttered. "One of the guards tackled me and slammed me into the hitching rail. Lucky I didn't break my arm."

Kestel gave an exaggerated sigh, but Blaine could see the affection in her eyes. "My poor dumpkins," she clucked. "Does it hurt awfully?"

Blaine and Dawe stifled their laughs. Piran reddened, but did not retreat. "As a matter of fact, yes. And for your information, soldiers feel pain like anyone else. Only more of it."

Blaine could see Kestel biting back her laughter as she took lavish care applying the homemade ointment to Piran's arm and binding it with a strip of cloth. For good measure, she fashioned a sling for him out of one of the serving maid's rags. "There you go," she said, patting him on the shoulder. "Now off with you—and if you're planning to use that injury for sympathy, remember that the ladies will still expect you to bear your weight on your arms, regardless."

Piran smiled broadly as Blaine and Dawe guffawed. "You know me too well, Kestel."

"You four are the children I'll never have," Kestel said with mock irritation. "Now be gone. Ifrem needs Mick upstairs, and I need to go help Verran in the tavern before there's a riot over the ale."

A few moments after Kestel disappeared into the common room, Ifrem entered the kitchen. "I trust you've left some food for my paying customers?" he said, raising an eyebrow. Blaine noticed that Ifrem was limping.

"What happened to you?" Blaine asked. "Lift a keg wrong?"

Ifrem swore and shook his head. "No. Damnedest thing happened last night after you bedded down and the storm eased up. I went out to see to the guests' horses in the barn, and a man jumped me. Why he thought I'd have anything of value on me, I can't imagine."

"Did you get a look at him?"

Ifrem shook his head. "He had a cloth across his face. Came at me with a knife, and might have gutted me if he'd been a little faster. Made a clean slice through my cloak, but since the coat's big on me, I wasn't where he thought I was. I had a bucket in my hand and swung it as hard as I could. Caught him hard between the shoulders. Then he ran away."

"You get hurt?" Blaine nodded toward the way Ifrem held himself, favoring one side.

Ifrem shrugged. "Like I said, he got in a good slice with his knife. Didn't go deep, but it put a crease in me below the ribs that hurts like Raka." He sighed. "Could have been worse." He grimaced. "All these years, and no one's ever tried to rob me. Now I think everyone's lost their minds."

Just then they heard a muffled groan as Dawe tried to stand but sank back down into his chair. Ifrem looked at him with concern. "Come on, Dawe. There's a cot in the back that cook uses sometimes. You can sleep until Mick and the others are ready to head home." He escorted Dawe to the back of the kitchen and got him settled, then returned to where Blaine and Piran waited.

He looked at Blaine. "The Council would like to see you, Mick. I'm pretty sure they want to offer you a seat."

"I don't think I'm Council material," Blaine protested.

Ifrem shook his head. "I don't believe that, or I wouldn't have put your name in for consideration. You've got a good reputation as an honest man—and odd as it sounds coming from a convict, that counts for something. We need someone like you representing the colonists." Ifrem paused. "Besides, you've got more education than most of the folks in Edgeland. I know you can read and write, and figure, too."

Blaine glanced sharply at Kestel, wondering if she had exposed his secret, but she gave the slightest shake of her head. "I guess it won't hurt to hear them out," he said.

Ifrem grinned. "That's great." He looked to Kestel and Piran. "Keep the bar running for me while I take Mick upstairs. Your drinks are on me."

Blaine followed Ifrem up the narrow back stairs. The Crooked House was the largest tavern in Bay-town, with several rooms upstairs where guests could sleep off their whiskey and a large room used for dances, which was now occupied by eight men and women seated around several tables that had been pushed together. They looked up when Ifrem entered, and Blaine could feel the weight of their gazes on him.

"I told you he'd show up tonight," Ifrem said. "He's just come from Velant, so he can give you an eyewitness account."

Blaine recognized the faces around the table. Peters, the fishmonger. Wills Jothra, the barrel maker. Trask, the butcher. The dry goods merchant, whom everyone called Mama Jean. Annalise, the candle maker, who was also the village's broker in potions and household spells. Adger, the whiskey man, who ran the distillery and kept the folks of Skalgerston Bay supplied with more than homemade ale and wine. And Fiella, head of the Whore's Guild, who owned the two largest brothels in town.

There were two empty chairs. Ifrem sat down next to Adger, and motioned for Blaine to take the other seat.

"It's true, then? Prokief's dead?" Peters leaned across the

table. His voice was as rough from the weather as his hands were red from seawater.

Blaine nodded. "Both he and Ejnar." At Peters's prompting, Blaine gave a shortened retelling of what had happened at the prison, making sure to give Piran and Taren their due. When he finished, the Council was silent, its members deep in thought.

"I didn't think I'd live to see Prokief dead," Annalise said, her voice harsh. "I intend to light candles to thank the gods."

"I don't know what we'll do with so many new colonists all at once—and no ships from home," Wills Jothra mused.

"Actually, I was thinking about that," Blaine said. "With no ships expected from Donderath, we won't get any new shipments of the things we used to trade for. We'll need everything from pottery to iron and we'll have to do for ourselves."

He looked around at the Council. "We may not need to mine rubies, but we'll still need the copper. Prokief never bothered mining for iron because Donderath sent the tools and implements, but if we ever want new, we'd best have a source of our own." He spread his hands. "There's no reason we can't make almost everything Donderath used to supply. Fabric, pottery, even dyes and perfumes—we don't have to rely on the kingdom to provide it."

Trask, the eldest of those assembled, nodded. He was a broad, stocky man, as thickly set as the hogs he slaughtered. "What of the guards?"

Blaine shook his head. "Some were killed—but most surrendered without incident. I believe Piran could make a town watch out of them, make them into guards who work for us instead of against us."

The Council members whispered among themselves, but

gradually frowns eased into more neutral expressions. "It is an idea worth considering," Peters said.

"But what if Donderath's ships suddenly appear in a few weeks, or a few months?" Fiella asked. Fiella was an angular, bony woman whose dark eyes glinted with intelligence and old wounds. She was reputed to drive a hard bargain, but was also known to keep her girls clean and well fed and to pay them better than she had to. Kestel had once told Blaine that Fiella had murdered more than one patron who got rough with her girls and had made sure the story spread to assure that her visitors remembered their manners. Now her eyes held fear that was close to panic.

"We've been over that," Wills Jothra replied impatiently. He pushed a stray lock of middling brown hair behind his ear. Through Dawe, Blaine knew that Bay-town's cooper had once been a furniture maker for Donderath's aristocracy, convicted of theft on evidence supplied by his competitor. "I doubt Donderath cares whether the convicts are imprisoned or drowned, so long as they never return. We deal with the ship captains, not the king. If we can make it worth their while and remain the king's dumping ground, Donderath may leave us alone, especially if they've got other problems."

"And you don't think that the king will care that his 'governor' was murdered?" Mama Jean asked, leaning forward. Grocer Bosq's widow was at least twenty years younger than the old man who had left her his name and his store. Her face and figure left no question as to what had attracted the old man, but Mama Jean had a nose for business as keen as any man in Bay-town.

"No, I don't," Ifrem replied. "I'd heard from more than one source that Prokief barely evaded the gallows himself. He was disliked among the king's commanders, and the king sent him here because it solved two problems at once." He paused and poured himself a glass of dark amber whiskey from the flagon on the table. "If it's true that the war's gone badly for Donderath, it's possible the king meant to cut us free. We're just Donderath's oubliette. Maybe it was time to forget us altogether."

Adger harrumphed and shifted in his chair. The wood protested beneath his bulk. The distiller was a coarse-featured man, with a pockmarked face and a broad nose that testified to how much he sampled his own wares. "We have always existed at the pleasure of the king," he said, his voice rumbling through the nearly empty room. "What has changed? King Merrill was free to starve us or slay us whenever he chose. If he meant to kill us, a noose is far cheaper, and he could have hanged the lot of us back home without the expense of a sea journey.

"Ever since Donderath discovered rubies and copper in Edgeland, there's been reason to have a colony here," Adger continued. "If we had less damnable weather, the king wouldn't have had to populate his mines with convicts." He drew a wheezy breath. "Let the mining continue. Make rubies and copper the currency of the realm. And if Donderath sends its ships, show the king he has lost nothing save the expense of upkeep on his miserable prison."

That seemed to satisfy the others. Ifrem cleared his throat. "If discussion is at an end, we have one remaining piece of business." He looked at Blaine. "I recommend Mick McFadden as our ninth and final member, as the representative of the colonists." Ifrem looked around the table. "How votes the Council?"

Adger fixed Blaine with his gaze. His eyes seemed too small for his large head, but it would be a mistake, Blaine knew, to underestimate the distiller's street savvy. "Aye," Adger said. "He's got as much at risk as any of us, bein' the one who put a knife to Prokief." He thumped his broad hands on the table, and it shook. "I'm for it."

One by one, the others gave their assent. Ifrem grinned. "That makes it official, Mick. You're the colonists' voice on the Council."

Blaine felt the events of the last few days beginning to catch up with him. He blinked hard and tried unsuccessfully to stifle a yawn. "Thank you for the vote," he said. "Now, if it's all the same to you, I'd like to get some rest before I fall over."

"Take your rest," Trask replied, "but don't stay away. It'll be the long night soon, and we've got work to do before then to see to changes." He dropped his voice. "We'd best have our plans in place, or Bay-town's likely to go up in flames like Velant."

CHAPTER
FIFTEEN

I WOULDN'T MIND THE MAGGOTS IN THE BREAD so much if the grog was stronger," Dorin said.

Connor nodded. "Talk with the tavern master. It's his grog."

Engraham shook his head. "Don't blame me. I bartered good rum for our passage. I suspect the captain's watered it."

"To keep those of us down below from feeling rebellious, I wager," Dorin said.

"Hard to work up much spirit for rebellion when you're heaving up your guts," Connor added.

"That, too," Engraham allowed. He glanced toward the portholes and turned his attention back to Dorin. "Any idea where we are?"

Dorin consulted the scratches he had made in the wood that tracked their days at sea. "We've been out for thirty-nine days. Stars tell me we're still on a northern heading. I've always heard it said that it took forty days, if the seas were favorable, for a convict ship to reach Velant." He shrugged. "And it's definitely gotten colder. My guess is that we're nearly there."

Connor shivered. It was late summer, and Donderath had still been warm. Now Connor was glad that he'd grabbed his cloak as well as his pack. The Cross-Sea Kingdoms might have been warm this time of year, but Edgeland was another matter entirely.

"What happens when we get there?" Connor asked, looking from Dorin to Engraham. "After all, Velant's a prison. Can they turn us away?"

Engraham frowned. "I don't know. Edgeland itself is very large."

Dorin nodded. "Aye. The sailors would talk when my men and I would go to unload the ships. They spent time in Skalgerston Bay, the port town. From what I heard, you might have opportunity to open yourself a new tavern," he said, clapping Engraham on the shoulder. "I heard that the whiskey up there is potent, but raw. A good distiller like yourself might find his skills in demand."

"So if there's a colony, there's hope that there's somewhere for us to go," Connor said. "I've no desire to live through the voyage just to starve or freeze."

"Well," Dorin replied, "there's no guarantee. Edgeland's not exactly a paradise. I've always reckoned that if the king could have gotten colonists by asking nicely, he wouldn't have had to ship convicts all the way to the end of the world. On the other hand, what I've heard 'round the docks is that people make a go of it. The convicts who live long enough to earn their leave papers get a bit of land and their freedom—so long as they don't try to leave Edgeland."

Engraham nodded. "I'd quibble about it being 'freedom,' because there was no hope to ever leave. But between the crops that will grow and the fish, the colonists don't starve. There are trees enough to have wood to stay warm through the winter, and rubies and copper to trade for coin."

Connor thought for a moment. "The *Prowess* was one of the last four big ships to leave Castle Reach's harbor. I don't know what the war did to the other ports, or whether any of their boats had luck dodging the blockade. But I think it's safe to say there won't be many supply ships behind us."

Engraham shook his head. "Probably not. It was a miracle that more ships didn't burn and sink in the harbor. No telling how it went for the other ports."

"Vellanaj can't hold its blockade forever," Connor replied. "The war is over. Sooner or later, the ships will find out and go home. I'm guessing that they only blockaded our main ports. We haven't seen any sign of them since we veered north."

"What are you getting at?"

Connor shrugged. "If Edgeland has rubies and copper, maybe there'll be a way to trade with the Far Shores once the blockade is over."

Engraham considered it for a moment, and nodded. "Assuming that Meroven doesn't come calling."

Dorin snorted. "Assuming that Meroven is in any better shape than Donderath. For all we know, our mages gave them the same pounding we got. Odds are, no one from the Continent is going to think about Velant or Edgeland for a long, long time."

Connor remembered what Lynge had told him the night of the battle. "A friend of mine in the castle was pretty convinced that we hit them as hard as they hit us. It's possible that the four major kingdoms are in ruins—and the Lesser Kingdoms aren't in good shape, either."

"Which would make Edgeland not just a colony, but an independent land," Engraham said quietly. "The question is— how happy will the prison's commander be to see shiploads of people he doesn't control?"

*　　*　　*

Despite Dorin's assurance that their journey was near its end, Connor slept poorly. Over a month at sea in the crowded, noisy hold had taken its toll. Fever and flux had killed a score of passengers, whose bodies had been consigned to the sea. As rations became sparse, seasickness was less of an issue. All but the fattest of those who had come aboard now looked as if they were scarecrows, with their clothing hanging off gaunt frames.

Once they had broken away from the Vellanaj blockade, the *Prowess* settled into a schedule. The passengers had two opportunities a day to come on deck when the weather permitted. The farther north they sailed, the more turbulent the sea became. It had grown cold enough that even the crowded hold was uncomfortably chilly.

Connor pulled his cloak around him and shivered. Engraham looked up from nursing a cup of watered grog. "Look at the bright side. At least the cold makes the stench bearable."

Connor grimaced. "After this, I'll probably never be able to smell anything again."

"That might be a blessing," Engraham agreed. "Then again, I imagine that the folks on the *Vanguard* would prefer the smell of their ship to being tossed into the ocean."

Connor shivered. Two weeks after leaving port, the four convict ships had been caught in a terrible storm. He'd heard curses and shouted orders from the captain to the sailors on deck, and below, in the hold, men prayed desperately for Yadin to save them. Those aboard the *Vanguard* had not won the favor of the gods. The ship had taken a wave badly and its main mast snapped. Another wave rolled the ship, and it sank before anyone from the other ships dared respond.

"Or the ones aboard the *King's Revenge*," Connor replied. Late one night, the ships had sailed into a stretch of icebergs. The *Prowess* had slowed to a near stop and Connor had watched from the porthole as the sailors had used poles to push the smallest ice out of the way as the ship carefully maneuvered around the huge, sharp-edged chunks. The *King's Revenge* had not been so lucky. It had been out in front, moving at a good speed, before the icebergs were sighted. Unable to stop, it had plowed into an iceberg. Jagged edges hidden by the rough seas had torn through the ship's hull. The remaining two ships had taken on the refugees and crew who could be pulled from the water, as well as any stray barrels of provisions, but the ship sank before a boarding party could retrieve its supplies.

Engraham was quiet for a few moments. "I hate to say it, but we might do better in Edgeland with fewer new arrivals," he said quietly. "After all, they've got no reason to welcome us. Times are hard through the winter. Why should they welcome more mouths to feed?"

"It's also more hands to fish and work the land," Connor replied.

A piercing cry made Connor jump. Everyone in the hold turned to the center of the room, where Benna, the seer, sat bolt upright from where she had been sleeping, with a look of terror on her face.

"The ship will sink. I saw it in my dreams. We're going to die. Cold, the water is so cold," she said, shuddering and wrapping her thin arms around herself, rubbing her skin to warm it.

"Ignore her," one of the men nearby said with a dismissive gesture. "She was never right. She told me my wife would come back to me, and instead she drowned."

His companion elbowed him. "And if you drown, too, perhaps she'll come back to you in the Sea of Souls."

A look of horror crossed the first man's face, and he moved farther away from Benna. "Crazy old woman," he said.

"How can she tell us anything since the magic's gone?" Another man gave Benna a shove. It sent the thin woman sprawling, but she collected herself with quiet dignity.

"Dreams speak, magic or not," Benna replied, though the men had turned away from her. "I saw this ship break into pieces and sink beneath the waves. I saw bodies on the water, many bodies. They floated to the feet of the exiled man, and he gathered them in."

Connor flinched, remembering Alsibeth's prediction. *The exiled man will return.* He forced himself to look away. *Not like there's a shortage of exiled men*, he thought, *with all the ships Merrill sent to Velant. None of the men he exiled returned, I wager, or are likely to do so now.*

Her prediction made, Benna seemed to shut out the throng around her and began to lay out her cards again. Whatever caused her dreams, she appeared in no hurry to try to sleep again.

Connor felt equally restless, though he could claim none of Benna's dubious clairvoyance. The refugees filled the hold, packed tightly enough that it was impossible to avoid being jostled. Nor were the odds favorable that any but the shortest passengers would be able to stretch out full length for long without being tripped over or cursed for taking up more than their share of space. Connor, Dorin, and Engraham had laid claim to enough deck among the three of them that one at a time could sleep fairly comfortably while the other two kept watch. Dorin, for his part, had proven to be pleasant company, ready with a joke. Between him and Engraham, there appeared to be no end of anecdotes and tall tales, and their banter helped to pass the long hours.

Dorin stood and walked over to the nearest porthole. Even from where Connor sat, he could guess that it was a gray day. Dorin squinted, standing on tiptoe to see out. He looked thoughtful when he returned.

"Well?" Connor asked. "Any idea of how soon we'll get to Edgeland?"

Dorin shrugged. "Hard to tell without the stars. I wager we're close—no more than a day, if that. But I don't like the look of the clouds. I'd say we're in for a storm tonight. It's a bad time for it."

Engraham leaned in. "Why? We've had our share of storms since we got on this tub."

Dorin's mouth was a thin line, his lips pressed tightly together. "It's being so close to Edgeland that makes it dangerous. There are shoals off the coast. In a storm, it'll be hard to steer a ship like this through the channels, or see the shoals. They shift about with the tides."

"Captain Olaf's been making the Velant run for years. I'm sure he's seen his share of bad weather before," Engraham said reassuringly. "Why would it be any different now?"

Dorin looked up to meet his gaze. "Because there's no magic."

"What does that have to do with anything?" Connor asked, frowning.

Dorin looked at Connor as if he were a dim child. "Sailors use magic every bit as much as those of us on land. Maybe more so. Olaf and his sailors depend on it. Wouldn't doubt that there were protection spells on the ship itself before the magic died, to keep away the sea worms and the barnacles and keep the seams tight."

"It's possible to navigate without magic," Connor argued.

Dorin nodded. "Aye, that it is. But few men who make the

sea their livelihood do so without magic of their own or mages aboard. They *might* know how to do all those same tasks without magic—or maybe it's been so long since they've needed it, they've forgotten."

"Do you think Olaf can handle it?" Engraham asked.

Dorin shrugged. "Don't rightly know. But I'd wager that the shoals won't be where they were the last time he came to Velant."

"Why not?" Connor couldn't help being drawn into the conversation.

"The commander at the Velant prison would have had his own mages," Dorin replied. "A good mage can set a binding on shoals and dunes and other things that move with the winds and waves, to keep them in their place. Just like I warrant that the mages had a protection spell on their harbor's seawall to keep high tides contained. Without magic—"

"We're left with dead reckoning and sheer luck," Engraham finished.

"Aye, that's the gist of it," Dorin replied. The man's face twitched, and he looked away, reflexively putting an arm across his abdomen.

"What's the matter?" Connor started toward Dorin, but Dorin shook his head.

"Nothing," Dorin replied. His grimace told Connor that Dorin was lying.

"Are you sick?" Engraham moved to help Dorin, but Dorin waved him away.

"Nothing that can be helped," he said, and his features tightened in pain. "I suspect that the food was spoiled enough that it didn't agree with me. I'll be fine."

Everything about Dorin's voice and manner made Connor doubt that, but he held his peace.

"I'll be fine," Dorin repeated. "Just need to rest." Gingerly,

Dorin eased himself down onto the rough planking of the hold's deck, pulling his cloak around him. Connor and Engraham exchanged skeptical looks, but said nothing.

The hold was lit by several lanterns that hung from hooks set into the heavy crossbeams overhead. Days had grown shorter the farther north they traveled, something Engraham called the "long dark." Now that Connor thought about it, the lanterns had stayed lit all day. As if the cold and darkness triggered an urge to hibernate, the passengers in the hold had grown quieter these last few days, huddling in their cloaks and talking in hushed voices. Even the games of chance drew no loud outbursts, though at the beginning of their trip, dice and cards had sparked many a tussle. Perhaps the refugees had already lost everything of value worth fighting over, but Connor thought it more likely that, consciously or not, they felt the darkness and cold closing in around them.

Engraham withdrew a well-worn pack of cards from a pouch at his belt. Without asking, he dealt a hand for himself and Connor. Connor sighed and picked up the cards, sparing a glance in Dorin's direction. To Connor's eye, Dorin looked unusually pale. Now that he watched carefully, he could see that Dorin's breath seemed shallow. Dorin groaned and drew his knees up, then relaxed in his sleep.

"Wind's picking up. Hear it?" Engraham drew a card from his hand and laid it down.

Connor paused, listening. Outside, he could hear the wind howling past the ship. Before long, the sound of rain lashing the hull and waves slapping against the ship drowned out the wind. The *Prowess* was a large, stable ship, but it didn't take long for it to seem as if it were merely a cork on the choppy sea.

Connor tried to focus on the card game. Engraham's expression gave no hint to his mood, but Connor noticed that the other gripped his cards more tightly than necessary. Around them, hushed voices prayed to Yadin for deliverance, or chanted prayers to their household gods to watch over them.

Dorin moaned in his sleep. Connor glanced at him with concern, and saw that Dorin's face now looked flushed with fever.

"Do you think he's all right?" Connor asked.

Engraham shrugged. "Let's hope we make landfall soon. There's got to be a healer in Skalgerston Bay."

By the time Connor and Engraham had played another hand of cards, it was impossible to ignore the sound of the storm outside. Refugees crowded to the portholes, but saw only blackness and drops of rain sliding down the glass.

Dorin had pulled himself into the fetal position and lay moaning in pain. Connor laid aside his cards and knelt beside him. "Gods, his skin is hot."

Engraham took a rag and held it under a stream of water that dripped down from the grate to the deck above until the cloth was soaked. He wrung out the cloth and brought it over, bending down to put it across Dorin's forehead. "It's seawater, cold as ice."

Dorin opened his eyes. "Whiskey," he murmured.

"What hurts? How bad is the pain?" Connor asked. He looked around, but no one looked likely to come forward as a healer. Once or twice, he had helped a healer nurse Lord Garnoc back from stomach ailments, but Dorin's problems appeared to be much more severe than anything Garnoc had suffered.

"It's in my belly," Dorin said, panting with the pain. "Been aching for several days now. Thought I needed to take a good shit. But it's something else. Something's wrong."

Connor reached out tentatively to poke Dorin gently in the

abdomen. It was a gentle press, barely depressing the skin, but Dorin stiffened and cried out. "Can't stand no pressure there. Had to take off my belt because it pressed too hard. Oh gods, I think I'm dying."

From the look on Engraham's face, it was clear that he thought Dorin's prediction might be true. Engraham reached into a pouch inside his shirt and withdrew a small bottle. He took out the stopper. "Open your mouth," he said to Dorin. Dorin complied, and Engraham jostled a few drops of a dark liquid onto Dorin's tongue.

"What is that—poison? Oh gods, you're trying to kill me."

"It's laudanum, you fool," Engraham said quietly. "Bitter as Raka, but it should do something for the pain. I don't have much, but it doesn't take a lot."

Within minutes, Dorin's features had relaxed, and his body was no longer rigid with pain. When it appeared that he had fallen asleep, Engraham motioned for Connor to move a few paces away to talk. With the pitching sea and the crowded hold, that was a challenge. "What do you think is wrong?" Connor asked.

"I'm no healer, but I've seen my share of bar fights," Engraham replied. "He acts like someone who's been punched hard in the gut, hard enough to break something inside. When that happens, it goes bad quickly, and it's an awful way to die. They take fever, and then the sickness goes to the blood. The chirurgeons can't do much unless there's a full healer available."

"He hasn't been in a bar fight," Connor argued.

Engraham shrugged. "I've heard tell that something can break inside without being hit. Different cause, but same outcome."

"So he's going to die?"

"Unless we get to Edgeland soon and their healers still have magic, it's likely." Engraham grimaced. "Then again, with this storm, our odds might not be much better."

He nodded toward the rivulets of water that were pouring down through the grating from the upper deck. "Remember what we talked about, the way ships used magic? I've been keeping an eye out, especially when we're allowed on deck. The *Prowess* is an older ship. It's seen a lot of wear. Transporting convicts made a captain and crew decent money, but not like ships that transported goods from the Far Shores."

"Not as long a voyage, either," Connor noted.

"Agreed—and a cargo of prisoners doesn't draw pirates like a hold full of spices or gold might. But the point is, Captain Olaf didn't have a lot of money to spend on the ship. Wouldn't be surprised if he cut a few corners, now and again, with something mages could patch. But with the magic gone—"

"So are the patches."

Engraham nodded. "We've weathered several storms, and each one put strain on the ship. Be ready, because if the ship runs into trouble, we might have to get out quickly."

And go where? Connor thought. The idea of setting out the ship's dinghy at night with no hope of dawn did not appeal to him. As if he could read Connor's mind, Engraham gave a mirthless smile. "Don't worry, in water this cold we'll barely have time to worry about it. There are worse ways to go. At least we didn't burn."

"What about Dorin?"

Engraham looked back to where Dorin slept restlessly. "Pray to Charrot that we don't have to worry about it."

They took their seats beside Dorin. Connor listened to the wooden timbers creak as the *Prowess* lumbered through the storm. Above them, through the grating, they heard the angry shouts of the sailors on deck and heard running footsteps as men hurried to follow orders. Below them, Connor swore he could hear the ballast shift when the ship moved sharply.

A sound like thunder and a man's scream on the other side of the bulkhead brought Connor and Engraham to their feet. "What in the name of Torven was that?"

From the other compartment, they heard shouts and then a dull rumble that made the deck vibrate beneath their boots. "I'm pretty sure the hold next to us is for cargo," Engraham replied. "We've eaten through the food and drunk the grog, but I don't know what other cargo our good captain was carrying when we set sail. By the sound of it, the cargo shifted and some poor sap got hit by whatever moved."

They sat back down. Connor cast a nervous glance toward Dorin. The laudanum had done its work. Dorin's face was no longer creased with pain, though his breath was shallow and his fever had not broken. *He's probably not even conscious*, Connor thought. *The rest of us are dying a thousand times over, waiting for something to happen. If it does, Dorin won't even know. For him, it might be a mercy.*

Connor had faced what seemed like certain death in the bell tower the night Donderath fell. He and Geddy had gotten out unhurt except for a few bruises and scrapes. He had escaped the firestorm in Castle Reach without singeing a hair. *Perhaps I tempted the gods by getting aboard a ship. Or maybe it's Yadin that doesn't care for me. Did I show poor faith in Esthrane and her land gods by taking to the sea? Sweet Vessa—if I've given offense, I promise to make it right. I don't want to drown.*

At the memory of Vessa's name, Connor remembered the mural in King Merrill's library. Stealing the map seemed like a lifetime ago. Throughout everything, the map remained sealed in its wooden box under his shirt, along with the obsidian pendant. Neither item had stirred since that first night. Restless, Connor tried to remember all the names of his household gods, the deities of garden and hearth, of wells and trees to whom his mother had regularly made offerings and given thanks, but their memory eluded him.

Did the gods perish with the magic? And if they didn't, without magic are they still gods? Connor had a moment of fear that perhaps the gods would hear his musings and strike him down, and an equal fear that perhaps there was no one left to hear his prayers and perhaps never had been. *Is it worse to be abandoned by the gods, or to think that there never were gods to begin with?* He listened to the prayers and chants of his fellow passengers with a stab of jealousy.

A palpable fear had taken root in the hold. Unlike the other storms, even the terrible flight from their ruined kingdom, tonight the fear of death clung to his fellow refugees. Men fingered smooth rune stones and women caressed prayer beads. Crazy Benna, the seer, had made black streaks on her face and arms with the lampblack, a mark of mourning or contrition. She had managed to light a bundle of sage from one of the lanterns, and its sweet, smoky scent fought with the stench of unwashed bodies.

As the ship was suddenly swept skyward, Connor's stomach lurched. The ship came down hard, with a terrible crunch and the crack of breaking beams against something much more solid than water. There was a sickening moment of silence, when the world itself seemed to hold its breath, and then the *Prowess* listed hard to port, crashing against whatever it was that had stopped the ship's forward motion.

Portholes shattered, and icy seawater began to stream in. People screamed and scrambled to keep their footing. Connor hauled Dorin to his feet and shouldered under his arm. Hazy with the drug, Dorin opened his eyes and stared at Connor as if trying to place him.

"What's going on?" Dorin slurred.

"We're sinking."

Already, the seams along the port hull were giving way, and wood splintered under the weight of the ship and the sea waves. "Get to the stairs!" Engraham shouted above the screams and cries. Connor wrapped one arm around Dorin's waist and was attempting to make his way through the crowd when the ship shifted beneath his feet. It felt to Connor as if Yadin himself had lifted the ship in the palm of his hand and thrown it into the air once more.

Awkward and heavy, the beleaguered ship could not hold together. Connor watched in horror as boards peeled away from the ribs of the ship, and the deck above him separated with a loud snap. The portion of the deck connected to the stairs collapsed, trapping those who had nearly made it to the questionable safety above. The ship trembled, and Connor heard a mighty crack that reverberated through every board as the keel of the *Prowess* snapped. The whole forward section ripped away from the aft, and the ship tumbled back to the ocean, spilling its fragile cargo into the black waves.

All around Connor, bodies plummeted through the air. He was pelted with fragments of wood, and with the fractured contents of the hold. He still had a hold of Dorin when the deck dropped out from beneath his feet, but as he fell, Dorin's dead weight tore out of his grip, and Connor tumbled into the sea.

Connor screamed, but he knew enough not to flail his arms and to hit the water's surface as cleanly as he could. He gulped a lungful of frigid air before his body knifed beneath the waves. A few powerful strokes of his arms brought him to the surface, but he ducked beneath the water just as quickly to avoid the bodies and debris that came raining down all around him. Screams echoed in the strange dim glow of a perpetual night that was blacker than twilight but not true dark.

A large barrel floated by, and Connor grabbed at it, hoisting himself mostly over it. He immediately reconsidered as the air began to freeze his clothing to his skin. The sea was a bone-chilling cold, and Connor had no illusions about how long they would stay alive. For an instant, he envied Dorin, who had likely drowned or been killed upon impact.

"Connor!"

Certain he was hallucinating, Connor tried to maintain his grip on the barrel and look around. In the near darkness, he could barely make out the shadows of people and flotsam. Only a few of the body-shaped silhouettes were upright. Most floated on the water, a sea of corpses, amid the wreckage of the *Prowess*.

"Connor! Over here!"

Connor followed the sound, willing his shivering arms to propel him toward Engraham's voice. He found the tavern master clinging to a section of hull that was almost raft-size.

"Where's Dorin?"

Connor shook his head. "I lost him. When we fell, I couldn't hold him—"

"Probably for the best," Engraham said. "I didn't think you'd have approved, but it crossed my mind to just give him the rest of the laudanum and let him drift off in his sleep."

"Might have been a kindness," Connor agreed through chattering teeth.

Engraham had thrown a couple of mid-length boards atop his section of hull. "We're not far from shore," Engraham said, and pointed. Connor could make out a solid line of darkness in the twilight, and farther away, the glow of lights.

"I think we can paddle ashore." Engraham hauled himself atop the makeshift raft, threw a length of salvaged rope to Connor, and pulled him close enough to help him onto the raft. He handed him a broken board. "The storm's dying down, but we've only got a few minutes before we're too cold to think straight. When that happens, we'll die. We might still freeze on shore, but I'd rather die with dry ground under my feet."

Together, they rowed toward the dark shore of Edgeland. The winds had lessened, but the water was still rough. Connor kept his eyes fixed on the horizon, willing himself not to see the corpses that floated on the water, not to think about the ship that had once been assembled out of the bits of broken wood scattered across the ocean. He heard the shouts and cries of the other passengers who bobbed in the water, and he could make out their dark shapes swimming toward the shore or clinging to larger debris. His whole body was trembling violently, and his teeth hit against each other hard enough that Connor was sure he would break a tooth. His hands were clenched around the board, but he was cold enough that he doubted he could have forced his frozen fingers to let go.

As the shoreline loomed, the raft scraped against the rocky shallows. Connor toppled onto his hands and knees. The rocks may have split open his skin, but he was too cold to know or care. Together, he and Engraham staggered the last few feet out of the water and collapsed on the brushy shore.

Connor fought to remain conscious. He thought he heard voices, but dismissed it as the visions of the dying. He heard the sound again: unfamiliar voices, shouting something he couldn't quite make out. There were footsteps, and then someone grasped Connor by the shoulders and rolled him onto his back.

"This one's alive!" the stranger's voice shouted. "What about yours?"

"So's this one, but they won't be for long in this cold."

Connor heard a groan and recognized Engraham's voice. "Take us—" Engraham struggled to say.

"Don't fret yourself," the stranger said. "Whatever it is, you can tell us later."

Connor's rescuer lifted him and carried him a few paces to a wagon. He set Connor down and wrapped him in a rough blanket. Another man wrestled Engraham's lanky frame into the wagon, tucking the blanket around him when it was clear Engraham was shivering too badly to do it for himself.

"Don't know where you thought you were going, but you're in Edgeland, if you wondered," one of their rescuers said. "We saw the ship from the lookout tower, and when we lost sight of you in the storm, we feared the worst."

Several other men walked up to the wagon. "Did you find anyone else?" Connor's rescuer asked.

"Maybe a dozen or so alive," the voice answered. "Otherwise, just corpses."

Connor's rescuer nodded. "All right, then. Let's get the survivors back to town and into dry clothes. We can scavenge the wreck tomorrow."

Engraham grabbed at the man's sleeve. "Take us—" he struggled to say, but the seawater in his throat choked him.

"Where do you think we can take you?" the man asked. "You're at the end of the world." He paused. "Is there someone here you know? Is that it?"

Engraham nodded his head. "I have a friend here," he managed to whisper. "Take us to Lord Blaine McFadden."

CHAPTER
SIXTEEN

M ICK!" PIRAN ROWSE'S VOICE CARRIED THROUGH
the cold autumn night. "Mick McFadden!"

Blaine looked up. He was just getting back to the Crooked
House tavern after several candlemarks spent searching Edgeland's coast for survivors of the shipwreck, and he could barely
feel his hands. The long dark had come a few weeks ago, and
with it, Edgeland's icy cold.

"Over here!" he shouted.

Piran shouldered through the crowd outside of the Crooked
House. Some of those assembled were the tavern's regulars,
excited to have news. Others had come to be on hand should
survivors be found. That included Kestel and Verran, who had
gathered anyone with any healing experience. Dawe and Blaine
had been part of the search teams, heading up and down Edgeland's rocky coast with wagons looking for survivors or usable
items that could be scavenged. Blaine sighed, wishing for nothing more than a glass of brandy and a warm bed.

"Did you find survivors?" Blaine tried to ignore a headache
that was building just behind his temples.

Piran nodded. "Twelve that my group found. Maybe a few

more among the other searchers. Everyone else—" He let his voice drift off, but Blaine understood. Given the freezing-cold water and the chill air, it was a miracle any of the passengers managed to get ashore alive.

"What are the odds that they'll stay alive—at least long enough for us to find out what they were doing out there?"

Piran shrugged. "Most of them were in pretty bad shape. They've been taken to the healers. I wouldn't bet money on some of them." He paused. "A couple were able to speak when we picked them up." He nodded toward the doorway to the Crooked House. "Just took those two inside to let Kestel and the others fix them up. Get some hot soup into them and a nip of brandy, and they'll probably be fine as long as fever doesn't set in."

"Convicts?" Blaine asked.

Piran frowned. "Not so we could tell. Didn't see a brand on them, or irons."

Blaine looked out over the dark sea that stretched from the wharves to the horizon. "Then what in the Sea of Souls were they doing way up here? Were they from Donderath?"

"They answered our questions in Donderan just fine." Piran paused. "Mick, do you know of any other McFadden who's a prisoner here?"

Blaine gave a bitter laugh. "No. It's not a common name. I'm the only black sheep." He paused at the odd look Piran gave him. "Why?"

"Because one of our new guests asked to see 'Lord' Blaine McFadden. That wouldn't be you, Mick, would it?"

For a moment, Blaine felt as if the cold had stolen his breath. "What else did he say?" Blaine asked when he found his voice again.

Piran's eyes narrowed, and Blaine knew his friend recognized the evasion. "Not much. Had lungs full of seawater. Said this Lord McFadden was his friend."

"Sweet Esthrane," Blaine whispered.

Piran laid a hand on Blaine's arm. "You're a lord, Mick? A bleedin' lord? We've been mates for what—six years? And you didn't bother to mention it?"

Blaine let out a long breath. "As far as I'm concerned, 'Lord' McFadden died on the ship from Donderath. I lost my lands and title when Merrill passed sentence. I'm not lord of anything—not anymore."

"King Merrill passed sentence—in person? By Torven, Mick, you've been holding out on your mates. Let me get this straight—the king himself sentenced you?"

"Don't be so impressed. All it did was win me exile rather than the noose—or worse. Merrill had been friends with my father."

"So isn't your father Lord McFadden?"

"Who do you think I killed?"

Piran stared at him, dumbfounded. "Do the others know?"

"Just Kestel."

"You told Kestel?"

"I didn't have to. Kestel recognized me from court."

"From court." Piran gave Blaine an incredulous look. "So all her blather about being a rich man's fancy whore—she was telling the truth?"

"Kestel was the most sought-after courtesan in King Merrill's court. She was also a damn good spy—and an assassin."

Piran let out a low whistle. "Well, that's a few notches up from where I'd figured, even though she's easy on the eyes." He shook his head. "Were you ever going to let the rest of us in on the whole story?"

Blaine shrugged uncomfortably. "What would have been the

point? What I had, I lost. Who I used to be doesn't matter up here. I'm a murderer, a convict, and an exile. And I've gotten rather used to being Mick instead of Blaine. I'd just as soon leave Blaine dead and buried."

Piran gave him a knowing glance. "Don't know if that's going to be possible, Mick m'boy, once our new guests tell their stories."

Blaine sighed. His breath steamed in the cold air. "Then we'd best get in there and see if we can contain the damage."

Blaine and Piran walked into the crowded tavern. It might have been his imagination, but Blaine felt the eyes of the crowd on him as he and Piran made their way to the back room, where two of the survivors had been taken.

They stayed out of the way against the wall as Kestel and one of the Bay-town healers saw to the castaways' needs in the warmth of the inn's kitchen. Verran had tagged along and was lending a hand. Without magic, the healer would be limited to potions and poultices.

Blaine looked at the two men. On the bench closest to him lay a man whom Blaine guessed to be in his late teens or early twenties. He was of average height, with dark-blond hair. It was hard for Blaine to tell much about the man's waterlogged and worn clothing, but from what he could make out, the cut and cloth had once been quite good.

Neither he nor his friend have the look of a laborer, or a farmer, Blaine mused. *Perhaps merchants, or lesser nobility. The blond man might even have worn such an outfit at court if he were a valet or squire. Interesting.* The man would have been barely apprenticed when Blaine had been sent to Velant. Doubtful that he would be the one to have gone looking for a long-disgraced lord at the edge of the world.

The other man was probably a few years older than Blaine,

perhaps in his early thirties, Blaine guessed. He had wavy brown hair, and Blaine felt sure that when the stranger opened his eyes, they would be blue. With a start, Blaine knew where he had seen the man before. *Engraham*, his memory supplied. *Lord Forden's bastard. Now what's he doing so far away from the Rooster and Pig?*

Ifrem came down the back stairs carrying an armful of dry clothing.

"See if any of these fit," Ifrem said. "They're odds and ends from what patrons have left behind, but they're dry and fairly clean." He set the clothing on a worktable and went out front to tend the bar.

Kestel and Verran began stripping the blond man out of his soggy clothing. He was barely conscious, unable to give more assistance than to keep himself from falling off the bench. Blaine saw a look pass between Kestel and Verran, and Kestel's hand brushed against the folds of her skirt with an object Blaine couldn't quite make out. *Never let me forget to add "master thief" among Kestel's many accomplishments*, Blaine thought. *What could she have found worth taking? Petty theft isn't Kestel's style.*

Without comment, Kestel and Verran finished getting the man changed into the mismatched garments Ifrem provided. On the other bench, the second man whom Blaine was increasingly sure was Engraham was only a bit more responsive as the healer got him changed into dry clothing. The healer plied both men with tea, and Blaine could smell the potent herbs in the brew that would ward off both chill and fever. To Blaine's relief, neither man seemed up to talking, and the healer's potion put both of them to sleep. After a murmured discussion between Kestel and the healer, the healer left the room and Kestel headed over to where Blaine and Piran stood, with Verran on her heels.

"The healers were more than happy to let me take the first shift," Kestel reported, answering their unspoken question. "There are several more castaways to care of, and these two seem to be in the best shape."

Verran reached out and poked Blaine in the shoulder.

"What was that for?" Blaine asked, giving Verran a questioning look.

Verran grinned. "Never poked a lord before. By the gods! I've been bunking in the same room with nobility for years now and I never knew it."

Kestel rolled her eyes and gave an elaborate sigh. "Sorry, Mick. I'm guessing Piran's already told you that our new neighbor washed ashore looking for his old 'friend' Blaine."

"Yeah, he told me." Blaine watched Engraham's sleeping form with mixed feelings. Curiosity at what had brought Engraham to Edgeland looking for him. Worry that their darkest fears about the war in Donderath might have come true. And more than a little resentment that Engraham's arrival could blow apart everything Blaine had worked to build since he'd gained his Ticket of Leave.

"Do you know him?" Kestel asked.

Blaine nodded. "He looks like Engraham, who ran the Rooster and Pig tavern down on the wharves. Lord Forden's bastard son." He looked at Kestel. "Have you ever met him?"

Kestel nodded. "I'd have put money on it being Engraham. I had clients who liked to gamble in the back room at the Rooster and Pig. Forden's friends liked to play cards there along with their 'companions.' Place had the best bitterbeer in Castle Reach."

"What do you think he's doing all the way up here?" Piran asked.

Kestel shrugged. "By the time he and his friend got here,

they could barely sit up long enough to get a dose of elixir in them. They're lucky to be alive."

"If it's luck that brings anyone to Edgeland," Verran murmured.

Blaine met Kestel's eyes. "You pocketed something off the first man. What was it?"

Kestel smiled. From a hidden pouch in the folds of her skirt, she produced a slim wooden case and an obsidian disk on a leather strap. "Something I thought looked interesting. Now, if you were thrown into the sea, what would be so important to you that you'd make sure you took it with you?" She weighed the wooden box across her palms.

"Let me take a look," Blaine said. Kestel handed it over. Blaine carefully wiped down the wood with a rag to make sure no seawater would drip into whatever was hidden inside. The cap stuck, but he carefully pried it loose.

"Papers," he said, looking into the dark interior. "Just papers."

Gently, he teased the rolled parchment from its hiding place. He glanced at the two sleeping men on the benches, but neither Engraham nor his companion stirred. Kestel motioned him over to a worktable, and cleaned off the surface so he could stretch out the parchment. Blaine caught his breath when he saw the map.

"It's just a map of Donderath," Piran said. "What's so special about that?"

"Not a treasure map, is it?" Verran asked, his eyes alight.

"It just might be," Blaine murmured. He glanced up at Kestel. "Can you see if Ifrem can come in here?" He glanced around the kitchen, but there was no one else except his friends and the two sleeping castaways. "And let's keep this just among ourselves, huh?"

Kestel gave him a questioning look, but went out to find

Ifrem, and returned a few minutes later with the tavern master in tow. Blaine looked up, giving Ifrem a nod to come over and look at the parchment still stretched between Blaine's hands on the table.

Ifrem let out a low whistle. "Where did you get this?"

"One of our new friends had it hidden under his tunic," Kestel replied.

Blaine met Ifrem's gaze. "A mate to the other map?"

Ifrem bent closer, studying the parchment. "To my eye, it looks like it. Unless it's a very clever forgery."

Blaine shrugged. "Why bother with a forgery?"

Verran eyed the map with curiosity. "So it's a map of all the places where magic's very strong—or places where magic doesn't work?"

"So it would seem," Ifrem replied.

Piran snorted. "If Donderath's had the same problems we've had, magic doesn't work anywhere. Not sure what use that map is now."

Kestel laid the obsidian disk down atop the map. "Do either of you know what this is?"

Ifrem touched the disk gently with his fingertips. He slid it carefully across the map so that the runes that appeared to be scattered at random on the parchment filled the slits in the pendant's surface. "Offhand, I'd say it's a key to the map. I can't read the runes, but I'm betting someone could." He picked up the disk and carefully examined it. "There's also no telling whether it needed magic to work."

"Looks to me like we've got a map of places that don't matter anymore and a disk that doesn't do anything," Piran observed. "Let's hope that we get more useful stuff from what we can scavenge tomorrow. Something that actually works—or that we can eat."

Blaine carefully rerolled the map and replaced it in the wooden box. He offered it to Ifrem, who took it and nodded.

"I'll put it with the other," Ifrem said.

Blaine looked back at their sleeping guests. "What I can't figure out is—what were they doing with the map, and why did they bring it here?" He sighed. "And what in the name of the gods was Engraham thinking when he asked for me?"

Kestel followed his gaze with a worried expression. "I don't know, but we'd better find out before we let them out of our sight."

Blaine and his friends took turns sitting up with the shipwreck survivors throughout the night, napping on pallets near the banked kitchen fire. Ifrem joined them once the crowds thinned and the tavern officially closed, a few candlemarks after midnight.

"A copper for your thoughts," Ifrem said after Blaine had gone for several minutes without talking. Ifrem poured them both another finger of whiskey. Blaine swirled the dark liquid in his glass and took a deep breath.

"To tell you the truth, I'm dreading having them wake up," Blaine replied. "I'd been hoping that Donderath would just forget about us and let us go our own way."

"Every new ship of convicts was another reminder," Ifrem said quietly. "Pasts never stay in the past—not even here."

"Yeah, but Donderath always stayed at a nice, comfortable distance. This," he said with a wave of his hand toward the two men, "brings it all too close."

Ifrem looked at him. "So you were a lord, huh? Do you think Prokief knew?"

Blaine hesitated and then nodded. "He knew."

Ifrem looked at the two castaways. "I wonder what brought them all the way up here. We're not exactly on the main shipping lanes."

"I'm afraid we're going to find out," Blaine replied, knocking back the remainder of the whiskey. "And I don't think we're going to like what we hear."

"Wake up! They're coming around," Kestel hissed in Blaine's ear. Blaine blinked his eyes several times and then scrambled to his feet.

Engraham and the other man were beginning to stir. The blond man thrashed as he awoke, falling from the bench before Verran could steady him. He landed on his hands and knees, eyes wide and wild, looking around himself in panic.

"You're safe," Kestel reassured him. "Safe on Edgeland."

"Velant?"

"Velant burned. You're in Skalgerston Bay—Bay-town. Take it easy. You've been through a lot."

The blond man stared at Kestel with wide eyes, and Blaine wondered whether he was more surprised to discover himself still alive or to find his caretaker to be a beautiful woman. He allowed Kestel to help him back onto the bench. He looked around the room. "Where am I?"

"You're a guest of the Crooked House," Verran said with a flourish. "Best tavern in all of Bay-town."

"What's your name?" Kestel asked, and the man reoriented on Kestel's green eyes.

"Connor. Bevin Connor."

Engraham awoke with a groan, drawing their attention. Verran helped him sit. Engraham squeezed his eyes shut as if fighting off a bad headache. "Did we make it?" he asked in a raspy voice.

"That all depends," Piran replied, "on where you intended to go."

"Edgeland."

"Well, then, congratulations. You're here."

Verran poured a cup of water and pushed it into Engraham's hand. "Drink something. Your voice is nearly gone."

"What happened to your ship?" Kestel asked.

Engraham drank slowly, nursing his raw throat. "Broke apart in the storm. Did the other ship make it?"

Blaine and Kestel exchanged puzzled glances. "What other ship?" Kestel asked.

Engraham and Connor looked at each other. "Four ships left Castle Reach. One went down in a storm. One hit floating ice. We lost sight of the other. We'd hoped they'd made it."

Kestel shook her head. "Not to Edgeland. If they were going to put into port, it would be here. I'm sorry."

Engraham had not taken his eyes off Kestel since she spoke. "I know you," he said quietly.

Kestel gave an enigmatic smile and nodded. "I got invited on more than one occasion to bring good luck to the gamblers in your back room."

Engraham looked around the room, and his gaze fixed on Blaine. "Lord McFadden," he said.

Blaine took a deep breath and let it out. "I go by Mick these days. How are you, Engraham?"

A shadow of a smile crossed Engraham's features. "Alive. That counts for something." He paused. "May I present a friend of mine, Bevin Connor, steward to the late Lord Garnoc."

"Why in the name of the gods did you come here?" Blaine asked.

Just then, Connor sat upright as if stung. His hands patted down his loose shirt, and one hand slipped inside the neckline of his tunic to feel around his throat. "They're gone," he exclaimed. "I must have lost them when the ship went down," he said in despair. "I had brought some things of value with me, and they're gone."

"The map and the pendant are safe," Kestel assured him.

"Which leads us to another question: What are you doing with that map?" Blaine asked.

Engraham cleared his throat. "Perhaps it would be better if we started the story from the beginning."

Blaine nodded. "Probably so. But answer me one thing. Will there be more ships from Donderath—ships with soldiers and convicts and supplies?"

Engraham shook his head slowly. "There are only refugees. Donderath has fallen."

Blaine and the others listened in dumbstruck silence as Connor and Engraham took turns telling their tale of Donderath's last days. Kestel wept as Connor described the fall of the castle and the death of King Merrill. Piran blanched at Connor's account of how badly Donderath's army had been beaten. Verran and Ifrem sat motionless, as if the shock was too great to elicit any reaction at all.

"The Lesser Kingdoms were destroyed as well?" Kestel's voice was a hoarse whisper.

"I'm sorry," Engraham replied. "What we saw from the coast looked no better than what we left behind in Castle Reach."

"What of Meroven and Vellanaj? Did we take them down with us?" Piran's eyes blazed and his voice was as tightly clenched as his fists.

Connor shrugged. "Lynge, the seneschal, believed so."

"And the magic?" Verran asked.

Connor shook his head. "Gone. I thought that it was something local just to Donderath or maybe to the Continent itself.

But even when we were in the middle of the ocean, the magic didn't return."

Blaine looked at Engraham. "Why did you ask for me?"

Engraham gave a sheepish grin. "Because besides my mother, you're the only person I knew up here." He sighed.

"My father, Lord Forden, spoke well of you," Engraham continued. "He was in my tavern the night we heard about the murder. Father was rather well into his brandy—as usual—but his reaction startled me. He went on a rant about how it was time someone took care of Ian McFadden, and what a son of a bitch he was. Seems my father knew your aunt, Dame Judith, well enough to be privy to some family secrets. He never faulted you for what you did."

Blaine looked away.

"Truth be told, I think he wished he'd had the courage to kill your father himself," Engraham continued. "You weren't the only ones Ian McFadden ever hurt. He had a reputation for being a mean-tempered blackguard."

Blaine swallowed hard. "I didn't know that."

Engraham snorted. "People were hardly going to say it to your face, now were they?"

"It's true." Everyone turned to look at Connor. "I heard Lord Garnoc talking about it to Millicent. He went to the king on your behalf, when it happened. Urged Merrill to be lenient."

"Who's Millicent?" Verran asked.

Connor opened his mouth to reply and then closed it, searching for words. "His wife. It's . . . complicated."

"Why?" Blaine asked, feeling light-headed. "Why would Garnoc care? I'm not sure I met him more than a couple of times."

"Lord Garnoc was a good man," Connor said, looking down. "His youngest son would have been about your age, but he died of a fever when he was just a young boy. Garnoc told me once that just a few weeks after his son's death, when he was still sick with grief, he saw you and your father at court. You did something that displeased your father, and he caned you. All Garnoc could see was that here was someone with a living son who was too stupid to appreciate it. He was so mad with grief that he said he shoved your father aside and broke the cane over his knee, offering then and there to adopt you if your father didn't want you."

"I remember that," Blaine said quietly. "I was terrified. I didn't know what to fear more—father's rage or a strange man with wild eyes who wanted to take me home with him." He forced a sad smile. "I can't bear thinking what would have been different if father had said yes."

Connor bit his lip, struggling with his own emotions. "Lord Garnoc was a good man," he repeated. "It was an honor to serve him."

"Did Garnoc know about the map?" Blaine asked, frowning.

Connor nodded. "He sent me to the royal library to find it. Just as I did, the firestorm struck. By the time I got back to Garnoc, it was too late."

"How did he know about it?" Blaine pressed.

Connor paused for a moment. "Lord Garnoc had many sources of information," Connor replied. "He received a tip. Garnoc hoped the information would be useful for the war strategy." Connor's voice became bitter. "Obviously, we were too late."

"Engraham—you mentioned that your mother is here. On Edgeland?" Kestel asked, breaking the tension.

Engraham nodded. His cheeks colored. "Yes. Lord Forden did not acknowledge my mother. He didn't step forward at all until my mother had been convicted for stealing to keep the two of us from starving. Father intervened on my behalf, but my mother was sent to Velant." Engraham's voice was bitter.

"How long ago was she sent here?" Kestel asked gently.

"Fifteen years," Engraham said. He sighed. "I know it's unlikely that she's still alive. But if she's here, I want to find her."

Kestel nodded. "The ones who are hardy enough to survive the ship passage stand a good chance of living through the first year in Velant. Those who survive more than a year or two in Velant usually figure out how to stay alive long enough to get their Ticket. Once you got out of Velant, your chances got a lot better," she said with a wry expression.

She met Engraham's gaze. "Let us put out the word. Among the five of us, we know a lot of the colonists. I'd wager Ifrem knows even more folks—especially the ones who've been here the longest. If she's here, we'll find her for you."

"Thank you," Engraham said. "It means a lot to me."

Ifrem cleared his throat. "We've got a problem."

Everyone turned their attention to the tavern master. "By now, everyone in Edgeland knows that we've fished survivors out of the sea—and they're going to guess that they came from back home. There are going to be all kinds of rumors flying around. People will be in a panic that the ship was full of spies sent from the king, soldiers to put down the uprising, new convicts—you can imagine where people's imaginations will take this."

"That's why the front room is even more filled than usual at this hour?" Piran said.

Ifrem nodded. "Everyone out there wants to be first to hear the news."

"So how do we tell them that it's worse than the king sending soldiers?" Kestel said, thinking aloud. "How do we tell them that everything they knew is gone?"

Blaine looked at Connor. "Do you have any idea how badly places outside the palace city were hit?"

Connor flinched. "We heard that the manor houses had been destroyed first."

"All of them?" Blaine said with a pained expression.

Kestel laid a hand on his arm. "I'm sorry, Mick."

By the time the Council assembled, Ifrem had moved their two new guests to the large room upstairs. Connor and Engraham told their stories, omitting any mention of the map or the amulet, as the Council listened in stunned silence.

For a few moments after the report was finished, no one moved. Trask, the butcher, and Mama Jean, the dry goods merchant, were openly weeping. Wills Jothra, the cooper, looked stunned. Peters, the fishmonger, sat without moving, his face ashen. Fiella, the head of the Whore's Guild, had a distracted look on her face, and Blaine wondered if she was mentally calculating the impact to her profits. Adger, the distiller, was looking at Engraham as if he were trying to decide whether the newcomer posed a threat to his business. Annalise, the potions master and chandler, had closed her eyes and was swaying back and forth, fingering her prayer beads.

"By Charrot, I didn't expect that," Peters said finally. "All these years, I've wished we'd never see another convict ship. And now we won't—ever again."

"We won't see another supply ship either," Fiella said with a practical glint in her eye. "So whatever we can't make ourselves, we won't have."

Trask had collected himself. Red-eyed, he looked at Connor. "So both the king and the heir are dead?"

Connor nodded. "Aye."

"There will be chaos." Fiella's voice was clear. "Without the king and the army, there is no law. We're fortunate to be here, far away."

Mama Jean sniffled and wiped her eyes on her sleeve. "On the other hand," she said, swallowing hard, "there's no one telling us we can't send out ships of our own to trade."

Adger made a dismissive gesture. "Who are we going to trade with? The Continent is in ruins."

"The Far Shores," Mama Jean replied, lifting her chin defiantly. "They might be glad of our copper and rubies."

"Or they might send up their own troops to take them, now that Donderath doesn't have a garrison here," replied Jothra.

"Once the Cross-Sea Kingdoms realize that their trade with the Continent is gone, they're likely to have problems of their own for a while," Engraham said. "An upset like this will do more than wipe out personal fortunes. It could topple kings."

"Meaning the Far Shores will be too busy to bother with us—for good or ill—for quite some time," Ifrem finished. "We're truly on our own."

CHAPTER
SEVENTEEN

A FEW CANDLEMARKS LATER, A RESTLESS CROWD gathered in Bay-town's commons, undeterred by the cold. Blaine rubbed his hands together to warm them, despite his heavy cloak and his fur-lined mittens. "Have I mentioned how much I hate the long night?"

"Only every day, and sometimes twice," Kestel replied. She looked as cold as he felt, even though she wore a fur hat, a wolf-fur coat that went to her shins, and the warmest boots she could buy from the village cobbler.

"As damnably cold as it is, it hasn't kept people from turning out," Blaine observed.

"And Ifrem's probably betting they'll all head back to his place for a nip of whiskey and a chance to hash out what they've heard among their neighbors." Kestel was bouncing in place, her breath clouding on the cold air. It was late afternoon, but the sky was perennially twilight, a cold winter sunset that would last for five more months.

Blaine elbowed Kestel as Ifrem and Peters led Connor and Engraham to the front of the gathering. The crowd grew silent, waiting. Ifrem stepped up atop a bench to be seen and heard.

"You've already heard the talk about a shipwreck off the coast last night," Ifrem said, shouting above the wind. "We've still got search teams out along the shore, but it appears that the survivors we found the first night are the only ones. Two of those men are here to tell their story—and it affects all of us."

With that, Ifrem stepped down and gestured for Connor and Engraham to take his place. Blaine and Kestel waited in the back of the crowd as Connor told his tale, recounting the last candlemarks in Quillarth Castle before the fall of Donderath. As he told about the king's death, some of the men shouted in victory and raised fists. Several women collapsed to their knees, wailing, whether out of veneration for the king or grief over loved ones presumed dead, Blaine did not know. Some of the crowd began to cheer and dance.

"Order! Order!" Peters shouted above the din. "Hold off on your cheering—you haven't heard all they have to tell."

The crowd quieted nervously, and Connor yielded the tale to Engraham. As Engraham recounted the firestorm that left Castle Reach a burning ruin, it seemed as if the entire crowd held its breath. When he spoke of charred bodies, of townspeople fleeing with only the possessions they could carry, of children being thrust into strangers' arms as boats pulled away from the harbor, the crowd's mood, celebratory only moments before, grew somber.

When Engraham finished his tale, the crowd was silent. Peters and Ifrem moved to the front. "What this means for us," Peters said, raising his voice to carry on the cold autumn air, "is that there won't be any more supply ships from Donderath. If the rest of the kingdom saw the same damage as Castle Reach, then 'home' as we knew it is gone. Without a king, we're free men and women. Edgeland has become an independent land. We're no one's convicts—we are citizens."

The crowd buzzed with conversation. From the expressions Blaine could make out in the twilight, most of the colonists were struggling to shift from shock and sorrow to some semblance of jubilation over their newfound freedom. His own feelings were a tangled mess, and he resolutely pushed them aside, unwilling to examine them in public.

Kestel tugged at his sleeve. "Look there." She pointed toward the front. Dozens of people had surged forward with questions for Connor and Engraham, leaving Peters and Ifrem struggling to keep order. But as Blaine followed Kestel's gesture, he could make out one figure that moved through the crowd like a hunting dog intent on its quarry. The figure was dressed in a bulky, nondescript coat, with a woolen shawl over head and shoulders. Whoever it was stood a head shorter than many in the crowd, and the figure often had to zigzag through the press of people to move forward.

Blaine watched the figure as it got closer to where the two refugees stood. The determined spectator did not push to the front, but instead, slipped into the spaces left when the rest of the crowd shifted. Finally, the figure reached Engraham and waited until he finished answering a question before laying a hand on his arm. Engraham turned, and the figure lowered her shawl. Blaine was close enough to tell that the newcomer was a woman with short, dark hair peppered through with gray. Engraham froze for a moment and then clasped her in an embrace as the woman threw her arms around his neck. Blaine chanced a look at Kestel, who wiped the back of her hand across her eyes.

"I guess Engraham's mother found him," Blaine said.

Kestel nodded. Her smile was wistful. "At least something good came out of all this."

The crowd began to disperse, and even the energetic questioners at the front gradually drifted away. Engraham and his mother walked away arm in arm, oblivious to anyone else. Ifrem and Peters were deep in conversation. Connor stood alone for a few minutes, looking around as if unsure what to do. Finally, he began to drift after the last of the crowd.

Kestel broke away from Blaine and ran to catch up with Connor, forcing Blaine to do the same. "Ho there!" she hailed him. Connor looked up and took a moment before he recognized Kestel from the tavern. "Where are you headed?"

Connor looked nonplussed. "Not really sure," he admitted with a self-conscious smile. "Ifrem's asked Engraham to give him a hand with the tavern." He shrugged. "I figured I'd see if there's anyone with a room to trade for work."

Blaine could guess what Kestel was going to say before the words escaped her lips. "Why don't you come with us? We've got room for one more and plenty of work to be done. We could use an extra hand with the farm. You'd at least have a roof over your head while you got your bearings."

Connor glanced nervously at Blaine, seeking confirmation, and looked relieved as Blaine nodded. "There are five of us, but we can fit you in," he said, and guessed that Kestel's offer had been as calculated as it was generous. He had no doubt that Kestel wanted time and privacy to pump Connor for all the gossip she had missed about the now-destroyed Donderath court.

"I daresay the herring fleet will go out again, despite the dark, now that we know there won't be boats from home," Blaine continued. "We could use another pair of hands for the nets. Gods know, we'll need the fish more than ever."

"Sure," Connor said after a moment. "That would be great. Thank you." He had the look of someone struggling to make sense of utter chaos, and Blaine felt a stab of pity. *The poor fellow's seen his world go up in flames, made the passage to Edgeland under conditions that were probably even worse than what the convicts faced, and survived a shipwreck. It's a wonder he's not barking mad.*

"Come on," Kestel said, linking arms with Connor and steering him toward the road. "Let's round up the rest of our crew and hire a wagon to get us home."

They found the others back in the Crooked House. Verran was tending bar to allow Ifrem the chance to attend the meeting in the commons. Dawe and Piran seemed to be taking advantage of the temporary lull in business to grab a good table near the fireplace and line up several glasses of ale.

"Connor's going to be staying with us for a while, until he gets his bearings at least," Blaine announced.

Kestel shot Connor a glance. "Until we know what's what, I figured it was a good idea to keep you—and your map— somewhere safe."

"Much obliged, m'lady," Connor replied, still looking a little dazed.

Piran guffawed. "Need to have a healer take a second look at the man's head. He's callin' our Kestel a lady."

Kestel gave Piran a good-natured backhand. "As if an oaf like you would know a lady from a lark."

Connor glanced at Blaine. "Are they always like this?"

Despite the somber revelations of the evening, Blaine chuckled. "Most of the time, they're worse."

Piran waved Connor to an empty chair in between himself and Dawe. "Have a seat, my good man. If anyone needs a drink this night, it's you." He pushed one of Dawe's tankards of ale toward the empty chair.

"Thief," Dawe accused, grinning. "Share one of your own tankards, thank you!" He took back the ale and then slid it right back into place and met Connor's gaze. "Here you go, Connor. This one's on me."

"By Torven! You're mad." Piran shook his head with exaggerated frustration, and pushed one of his tankards to Connor as well. "Drink up, young man. You look like you could use the whole cask."

Patrons began trickling back into the tavern, and Kestel quickly went to help Verran at the bar. Ifrem and Peters trailed several dozen of their fellow townsmen into the Crooked House, and Ifrem caught Blaine's eye.

"That went fairly well, considering,"

Blaine shrugged. "For now. Tonight, they'll drink. What about tomorrow? I think the Council needs to spend some time thinking about what this means for the colony. Once everything sinks in, we could have some new problems."

Ifrem frowned. "Like?"

Blaine sighed. "I'll wager that the fear of a ship full of new soldiers showing up at any time has kept some of the troublemakers in line. Now that we know that's not going to happen, we probably need to take a second look at our patrols and recruit some new officers." He paused, realizing, now that the evening's adrenaline had ebbed, just how tired he was. "And now that we can be pretty certain there won't be any supply ships, we've got to be doubly sure that we've got enough food to get us through the winter."

Ifrem nodded. "And here's something else to chew on. Our new friends could only speak about Donderath's fate and what happened to the Lesser Kingdoms. What if Meroven didn't get hit as badly? Or Vellanaj? They could send ships our way to lay claim to Edgeland. By Raka, that might even occur to the Cross-Sea Kingdoms, if anyone remembers that we're up here." He met Blaine's gaze. "We'd best rebuild some sea-facing defenses, and fast."

Blaine sighed. "Yeah. But not tonight." He paused and

looked toward where Dawe and Piran plied Connor with ale and he knew that in their own jovial way, they were as adept at pumping the newcomer for information as Kestel. "I heard you've taken Engraham under your wing."

Ifrem snorted. "Damn straight. Wanted to get him before Adger did. I'm likely to offer him a better deal, that's for certain. Besides, I remember the Rooster and Pig quite fondly. Excellent bitterbeer. If he and I could re-create something like that here..."

Blaine shook his head, chuckling. "You'd beat out every other tavern in Edgeland."

Ifrem clapped him on the shoulder. "Now you're thinking like a businessman."

"Connor's going to be living with us. That'll keep him and his map away from prying eyes."

Ifrem nodded. "Good thinking." He looked thoughtful. "After the dust has settled, now that we know Merrill and the heir are dead, do you think anyone will want to go home?"

"I don't know, Ifrem. Your guess is as good as mine."

The next morning, Blaine roused Connor from sound sleep by shaking his shoulder. "Come on, mate. We've hired a wagon to take us back to the farm. Wake up and get moving."

Connor sat up and blinked, as if trying to take in his new surroundings. "I thought you said we'd go in the morning," he said, looking at the darkness outside the windows.

"And morning it is, ninth bells even," Blaine replied. "You're at the top of the world and it's the long night. Sun won't rise much above the horizon until spring."

Connor groaned. "I thought you were kidding about that."

"I wish I were," Blaine said as Connor hurriedly dressed.

Blaine pushed a piece of bread with jam and a cup of *fet* into Connor's hands. "Here. Eat something. Helps ward off the cold."

Blaine waited as Connor downed the bread and swallowed the bitter drink. "Ifrem found you a cloak among the clothing that's gotten left at the tavern. Should do until you can get settled and do some shopping."

Connor wiped his mouth on the back of his hand and set aside his empty cup. "I can't believe how good you and your friends have been to Engraham and me. I don't know how to repay you."

Blaine slapped him on the back. "Well, in the short run, information will do. I don't think Kestel's through with you, and I've got some questions of my own. And in the long run, you'll find where you fit here and make your own way, like the rest of us."

The rest of Blaine's housemates were waiting in the semi-darkness when Blaine and Connor reached the street. Connor looked up and down Bay-town's main road in amazement. The streets were as busy as one might expect mid-morning, except that it was dark as twilight.

"Climb in," Piran said as their wagon arrived. Blaine and the others scrambled into the back of the wagon, grateful for the thick straw strewn in the wagon's bed and for the coarse, scratchy blankets the wagon master had thrown in for them. They huddled together, wrapping the blankets around themselves with their backs to the wind.

"Do you ever get used to the cold?" Connor asked between chattering teeth.

"Not really," Piran replied. "But it all depends what you compare it to. After you've spent time in the mines, or out on the herring boats, where you're frozen to the bone, this feels like a summer breeze."

Kestel slugged Piran in the shoulder. "Don't lie to him. By comparison, summer gets quite tolerable, though it's never as warm as in Donderath."

"Once you learn to dress for it, it's not so bad," Dawe said. His eyes were all that were visible beneath his fur-lined woolen cap and a heavy scarf that muffled his voice.

"Speak for yourself," Verran muttered. "The only time I've been warm since I've been here is when I'm practically sitting in the fireplace."

Blaine was quiet as they rode, taking the measure of their new companion. Connor had held up well, given his ordeal, though he looked haggard. He bantered carefully with Piran and the others, as if he were not yet sure how to take them. Kestel had clearly taken him under her wing, and Connor had reacted gratefully, but had not read any sexual invitation into her actions. *Good so far*, Blaine thought. *Once we thaw him out, let's see what else he knows about doings at court before the Great Fire. Old news to him is still fresh to us. More importantly, let's see if he's heard anything about Aunt Judith or Carensa. By the gods! What I'd give for word from home.*

"Welcome to the farm," Verran said with a grandiose sweep of his arm when the wagon stopped. They climbed down from the wagon's bed and Blaine paid the wagon master. As the wagon pulled away, Connor took in his new lodgings.

"Once the wind dies down and we've got blood in our fingers and toes again, we'll take you out around the back and show you the rest," Dawe said, slinging an arm around Connor's shoulders. "You'll notice the garden here where Kestel keeps the gods happy," he said with a nod toward the shrines to Charrot, Yadin, and the household gods. "If there are any you want to add, I don't imagine she'd mind."

Piran and Kestel were the first inside. Piran went immediately to set a fire in the fireplace, while Kestel lit lanterns. The inside of the house was almost as cold as the outdoors, but the building sheltered them from the wind. They watched, fidgeting with cold, as Piran got the fire going and then hovered near the fireplace as flames licked at the logs.

Kestel sighed and heaved a kettle toward the fireplace. "Water's frozen solid," she said. "Be a while before I can make tea—or dinner."

"I'd best go feed the livestock," Blaine said once he'd warmed enough to have feeling in his hands. "They'll be hungry and I'll need to chip a hole in the ice for them to drink."

Kestel gave him an odd look but said nothing as he slipped out the back, leaving Connor and the others inside. Blaine hurried across the open ground to the barn, where the bleating of goats and sheep greeted him. Chickens clucked at the cold wind that gusted through the small building as he hurriedly entered and shoved the door closed behind him.

The animals' body heat kept the small barn well above freezing. Blaine got to work, glad that the activity would keep him warm, and relieved to have a few moments to himself. He went through the routine of the chores out of habit, free to let his mind wander.

Connor said messengers were arriving at the castle when he left, with word that the manor houses had been hit first. Would Meroven have possibly thought to strike Glenreith? After father's death and the scandal, I can't imagine Glenreith being important enough to attract notice.

Blaine was glad to see that the barn had stayed warm enough to keep the water trough from freezing, though a skin of ice had formed. He used a stick to break up the ice, making it easier for the animals to drink. Kestel had left plenty of feed, knowing that it would be a day before they could return, but

Blaine checked to assure himself that the manger and feeding bins were filled. He put his back into mucking out the worst of the pens for the sheep and goats, promising them outdoor time at the warmest hours of the day. Despite the outside cold, he was sweating, and he brushed a lock of hair out of his face with the back of his sleeve.

The work warmed him, but did little to distract his thoughts. *Carr would be nearly grown by now,* Blaine thought, though he had difficulty picturing his younger brother as more than a child. Mari, the sister for whom he'd given up his freedom and his fortune, would be a woman of twenty-two now and he wondered, with a pang, whether she had managed to rise above his father's actions to make a life for herself. Aunt Judith would be approaching her fifth decade, if fever and heartbreak had not claimed her.

What about Carensa? he wondered. *I begged her to forget me. Did she? Or did my shame ruin her life, too?* None of the questions were new. Usually, Blaine struggled to put them from his mind at the edge of sleep or wakefulness, when he could not completely banish dreams of home. The appearance of the Donderan refugees made the old loss ache, like a badly healed wound that had never closed.

Blaine washed his hands in cold water from a bucket and dried them on a rag, still lost in thought. He knew the odds were slim that Connor had heard any recent news about his family, but he couldn't help hoping that there would be some tidbit. In the years since his exile, there had been a few letters from his aunt, but it was difficult—and expensive—to get such things delivered to Edgeland. All mail and packages for convicts or colonists had to be screened by Commander Prokief, and rumors abounded that he was as capricious as he was greedy when it came to censoring the incoming items.

After the first year, the letters from Aunt Judith stopped coming altogether. By the time Blaine made a handfasting with Selane, Judith's letters had not come for a long time. But as fond as Blaine had been of Selane, he suspected that he would not have mentioned the marriage to Judith, just as he was grateful not to know for certain whether Carensa had found someone else.

The outside door opened and Blaine turned to see Kestel's hooded form in the doorway. "Did you forget your way back to the house?" she asked. She closed the door behind her as the animals squawked their protest at the cold rush of air.

Blaine shook his head. "Just needed a little time to think about everything Connor and Engraham told us. By Charrot! I'd come to accept that we would never return to Donderath, but the idea that there's no Donderath to go home to, now that's going to take some time."

Kestel nodded. "I think everyone's struggling with that. I knew most of the people Connor mentioned, at least to see them at court. It's hard to believe that so many are dead." She cocked her head and looked at him. "You're worried about your family, aren't you?"

Blaine shrugged. "Sure. I mean, Glenreith was never a wealthy holding. My father didn't have the kind of influence many of the peerage have—had. And the manor was far enough from Quillarth Castle that we were hardly in the thick of the social swirl. I can't help hoping—"

"That maybe the Merovenians overlooked it?" Kestel supplied.

Blaine sighed. "Yeah. It was hardly a strategic target."

"Unless you're only looking to inspire terror. Knocking out a country's leadership would have assured a lack of organized and well-armed defenders."

"Except for the part where the magic goes horribly wrong and wipes out both sides."

Kestel grimaced. "I don't imagine either side seriously thought that was ever a possibility."

Blaine leaned against one of the rough barn timbers. "Who would have dreamed that it might actually be lucky to be in Edgeland? If the war mages were strong enough to knock out magic all the way up here, I hate to think about the destruction back home." He sighed. "I never dreamed I'd be a free man again, or that there'd be any price too high to pay for it."

Kestel took his arm. "Come on. The fire's warmed up the kitchen enough for me to put some wassail on the hearth, and once the water boils, I'll get a soup going. There's bread and cheese enough for dinner. And I don't want to miss what Connor has to say."

Blaine allowed Kestel to lead him back to the house. Inside, Connor, Piran, and Dawe were laughing heartily.

"What did we miss?" Kestel asked. Kestel's whole manner was more animated than usual and her eyes were alight. She had pulled back her hair with a comb, a simple thing that drew attention to her high cheekbones and her green eyes. Blaine had the feeling Kestel knew just how to ply Connor for all the information they wanted.

Piran wiped the tears of laughter from his eyes and Dawe slapped his thigh, still chuckling. "You have to understand, Kestel, we've not heard any new jokes in how many years?"

Verran gave an exaggerated sigh. "I've already asked if our guest knows any new songs he could share with us. Unfortunately, he says he's got a tin ear for such things."

Connor looked apologetic. "You might have more luck if you ask Engraham. He was surrounded by musicians at the Rooster and Pig. My existence at court was more administrative than social, I'm afraid. Lord Garnoc, my master, was up in years and a widower. He rose early and retired just after supper on most nights."

Kestel nudged the cook pot closer to the fire and then drew up a stool. She gave Connor her warmest smile and laid a hand gently on his arm. "You have no idea how exciting even the tiniest scrap of news is when you've been gone as long as we have," she said, meeting Connor's gaze. "Please, tell us anything, everything." She poured him a cup of wassail. "Your arrival is the most interesting thing that's happened in ages."

The poor fellow doesn't stand a chance, Blaine thought, smothering a smile. He had little opportunity to see Kestel go to work on a "source" and it was clear that exile had not blunted her skills. Connor smiled self-consciously and took a sip of the wine.

"If you say so, m'lady," he replied. He was silent for a moment, as if searching for a suitable story. "There was an incident with Lady Henereth's chambermaid a few months ago that was quite the talk of the court."

"Arabella Henereth?" Kestel asked, leaning forward. "We attended quite a few balls together. Please, spare no detail!"

Connor warmed to Kestel's request, and as one story led to another, he proved that his memory had not been impaired by the arduous journey north. Blaine, who had paid little attention to gossip at court before his exile, found the stories more interesting than he had expected, especially when Connor mentioned people Blaine had all but forgotten from his old life. As Connor talked, Kestel bustled around the kitchen, readying vegetables for the pot. She sent Dawe out back to slaughter and pluck a chicken for the stew. Between tasks, she kept Connor's cup liberally full of wassail. Before long, a delectable aroma filled the small house.

Connor fell silent for a moment, having answered all of Kestel's many questions. Blaine leaned forward.

"Do you recall any news from Glenreith?" he asked, meeting Connor's eyes. "Anything about Lady Judith Ainsworth, or perhaps Lady Carensa of Rhystorp?"

Connor thought for a moment, then shook his head. "I'm sorry, m'lord...I mean, Mick. Nothing comes to mind."

Blaine sighed, and leaned back, looking away. "That's all right," he said quietly. "I had to ask."

Kestel laid a hand on Blaine's shoulder in passing as she came back to the group, and he knew she would have understood the urgency in his question, and his disappointment with the answer. She took her seat next to Connor, slightly flushed from the exertion of readying dinner. "You're the best company we've had in ages," she said to Connor with a smile.

"He's the only company we've had in ages," Verran grumbled good-naturedly.

"Don't mind him," Kestel said. "Verran doesn't like to share the stage with anyone." She leaned closer. "But what I'm dying to hear more about is your map."

Connor paused to take another sip of wine. "That's an interesting story," he said, letting out a long breath. "It begins with a vampire."

That announcement got even Piran's attention. "Vampire?" Piran nearly choked on his wine.

Kestel looked thoughtful. "There were two vampire factions in Donderath: those belonging to Lanyon Penhallow, and those belonging to Pentreath Reese. Which 'family' was your source a part of?"

The relaxed mood of a moment before had shifted, and Blaine felt a new tension in the air. Connor looked as if he were considering his reply. Despite the offhanded way Kestel had asked the question, there was obviously some unspoken issue of great importance, one that only Kestel and Connor seemed to understand.

"I heard it from Lanyon Penhallow himself," Connor replied. Kestel looked skeptical. "How is it that you are so well acquainted with such a *long-standing* member of the peerage?"

"It can't hurt anyone now to admit that my late master was a longtime conduit of information for Lord Penhallow, who found it personally difficult to attend court."

Kestel nodded knowingly. "So Garnoc was Penhallow's spy?"

Connor shrugged. "One of many, I'm sure. You know how it was."

"Yes, I do," Kestel replied with a hint of a smile. "I made Lord Penhallow's acquaintance on a few occasions. He was... always a gentleman."

"The night before the firestorm, Garnoc sent me to Penhallow to give a report on how the war was going. Penhallow gave me the obsidian disk you saw and told me it was important for me to find the map."

"Why?" Blaine asked, leaning forward.

Connor met his gaze. "Lord Penhallow believed Edgar of Meroven intended to conquer the entire Continent, and planned to use his mages to do it. King Merrill didn't like using mages and he avoided using magic as much as he could. Penhallow didn't think Merrill was hearing the full truth from his generals, didn't realize that Meroven was poised to make their final assault.

"Penhallow couldn't go to the king directly, but he was trying to warn him. He was afraid that in a magic war, the places on the map where magic was strongest would be the hardest hit, and the null places would be safest for... refugees." Connor's voice dropped as he finished.

"So Penhallow expected the attack?" Dawe asked, his voice tinged with outrage.

"Feared it, is more accurate," Connor replied. "Penhallow said he had witnessed such an attack long ago, in another place, and had survived only because he was already dead." He stared at the fire as if replaying the conversation in his mind. "It's rare to see emotion from one of the Elders," he said quietly. "But Penhallow seemed troubled by the memories. He intended to take his entire household away from Rodestead House that night, to someplace safe."

"A null spot on the map?" Kestel asked.

Connor shrugged. "Perhaps. I believe he hoped King Merrill would have time to evacuate the city."

Kestel pursed her lips as she thought. "Why send such a message with you? Or rather, with Garnoc? Why didn't Penhallow take the message to the king himself?"

Connor sighed. "I asked the same question. Penhallow said that Merrill wasn't fond of the undead. He didn't think Merrill would believe him. But he did tell me that if Donderath fell, I was to find a mage named Vigus Quintrel and give him the map and pendant."

"So why didn't you?" Piran asked.

Connor shook his head. "Because Quintrel had already gone missing when Penhallow gave me the message. Even Penhallow didn't know where he had gone. After that, with the firestorm and the fall of the castle, Garnoc ordered me to take the map and pendant out of the kingdom for safekeeping. I'm guessing that Garnoc figured I could come back later, when it was safer, and look for Quintrel." He paused. "I didn't get a chance to ask a lot of questions. Garnoc was dying. His last order was for me to take the map to safety. I obeyed."

Piran eyed Connor skeptically. "How do you know Penhallow wasn't lying to you? After all, he's a vampire. They're not like us."

Connor chuckled. "No, they're not. For one thing, they're dead. For another," he said, beginning to wrap up his sleeve on his left hand, "they have their own magic. And their own way to communicate when it's important." He bared his arm, and the white scars were visible in the firelight.

"Blimey! You let him bite you?" Piran asked, drawing back with a look of revulsion.

"Taking blood from me let him access my memories, see what I saw and hear what I heard," Connor said. "In exchange, it gave me his protection. We had a bond."

"But he couldn't protect you from what happened," Kestel said quietly.

"Even Penhallow couldn't prevent what was about to happen," Connor replied quietly.

Kestel shot a meaningful glance at Blaine. "I'm more curious than ever to put Connor's map next to the one Ifrem has and see if we learn anything. There are places of power here in Edgeland, and null spots too, if Ifrem's map is to be believed. Perhaps Connor's pendant will shed some light on the subject."

"The pendant used magic, at least for what it showed me in the royal library," Connor said. "With the magic gone, it may be useless."

"Ifrem said the person who brought the map to Edgeland had stolen it," Blaine mused. "Could the two maps be related?"

Connor looked up sharply. "Lord Penhallow also spoke of stolen maps. He said that a mage named Valtyr had made the maps, and three of them were stolen by Nadoren."

"One of which managed to find its way to Velant," Kestel mused. "How interesting."

Blaine frowned. "Are you thinking someone brought the map all the way up here for a reason?"

Kestel shrugged. "Who knows? Maybe it's just a coincidence. On the other hand, where better to keep something valuable out of prying hands than at the end of the world?" She smiled in a way Blaine knew meant trouble.

"I think that we need to pay Ifrem a visit and have another look at his map," Kestel said, grinning. "And I definitely think it's worth a visit to one of these 'places of power' Ifrem's map shows in Edgeland—and a null place, too, if there is one."

"You're forgetting about those hunters that disappeared," Piran said, looking uneasy. "What's to say they didn't get too close to one of those spots on the map and it made them vanish?"

"Maybe," Kestel allowed. "We know Estendall's a place of power. Now we've got a pretty good idea that the volcano's eruption might have had something to do with all that magic being lobbed around by the two armies. And we know that what happened in Donderath knocked out magic all the way up here. The question is—did the magic go away forever? And is there anything we can do to bring it back?"

CHAPTER
EIGHTEEN

"THIS IS MADNESS." PIRAN HAD BEEN GRUMBLING under his breath since they left the road and headed onto the sledge trail. Connor had said nothing, but was inclined to agree.

Ahead of him, Dawe's loping stride left wide-spaced marks in the frozen crust of the snow. Blaine and Kestel were in the lead, with Ifrem's map safe inside Blaine's pack. Blaine had retrieved it from the innkeeper the night before. Verran had stayed behind to tend the farm, and Connor found himself feeling rather jealous.

Penhallow's obsidian disk hung from its leather strap around Connor's neck, secure within his tunic. It had warmed from his body heat, but unlike the night it had led him to the library's hiding place, the disk showed no hint of magic, neither glowing nor changing its temperature.

"I never thought they'd decide to set out like this," Connor said apologetically.

Piran snorted. "That just means you don't know Mick and Kestel very well."

True enough—but I'm learning. Connor tried to get his mind off the numbing cold. On one hand, his rescuers had gone far beyond what Connor could have hoped in terms of hospitality, offering him shelter and a ready-made group, no small gift in a strange and forbidding land. They had taken pity on his lack of skills, since little of what he knew from court was any good in Edgeland. He'd found his new friends to be quite companionable, yet his court-honed instincts also suspected that their easy acceptance was hardly casual.

In short, he wondered how things might have been different if he had not arrived with the map and pendant.

The air was mercifully still, which made the cold tolerable, despite Piran's complaints. Connor wore every stitch of clothing he had been able to scrounge together, as well as a heavy coat, scarf, mittens, and a fur-lined hat, plus boots with heavy woolen socks. Even in the harshest of Donderath winters, he would have been roasting in such an outfit. Here in Edgeland, it barely kept him from freezing.

"Does that blasted pendant of yours tell you anything?" Piran asked, his breath fogging on the cold air.

"Not a thing," Connor replied. It was cold enough that it hurt to breathe through his mouth. "How do you tell night from day around here? For all I know, we're out here in the middle of the night."

Piran snorted. "We've got the town bells and the notched candles. Other than that, it's anybody's guess, or you read the stars."

Connor shielded his eyes against the falling snow. Lord McFadden—or Mick, as he preferred up here—had arranged for a trapper to take them as far as the road's end on a horse-drawn sledge. That had been preferable to slogging through snow that was knee-deep where it wasn't drifted and hip-deep or worse in other places. Connor was not yet used to the wide, sinew-woven snowshoes laced onto his feet, contrivances his companions wore as easily as if they had been doing it all their lives. Connor struggled with the odd, wide-legged stance and the rolling gait, afraid he would pitch headfirst into the snow with every step.

"Look on the bright side," Piran said. "We hardly ever get blizzards this early in the season."

"Blizzards?" Connor repeated, trying to stay in the tracks of those who had gone on ahead so that it wasn't quite so difficult to walk. Dawe's stride was enough longer than his that he would have had to leap to go from step to step, but Blaine was closer to his own height, and Kestel was a good bit shorter. The footprints gradually blurred into a trail of sorts.

Chagrined, he realized there was a reason his new friends had taken this particular trekking order, placing him at the rear. Piran, who didn't seem to be having difficulty walking, was probably there to make sure Connor didn't vanish into a drift or collapse of fatigue. Under other circumstances, Connor might have felt embarrassed, but right now, he was too tired and cold to care.

"Yeah, real whiteouts," Piran answered. "It's when the snow and the wind make it impossible to see your hand in front of your face. I've heard of men who froze to death between their house and their barn because they couldn't find their way to shelter. Nasty stuff."

Connor stifled a groan. Piran chuckled. "Don't mind the trek today; Kestel and Mick have a nose for trouble. The rest of us get dragged along into one damned fool thing after another."

While Connor didn't doubt that Kestel and Blaine had a gift for finding trouble, he also imagined that Piran, by the look of his oft-broken nose, had no problem getting into scrapes on his own, without help. And despite the grumbling, neither Piran nor Dawe had made any serious objection to the expedition. Verran had voiced the most qualms and, as a result, was the one who stayed behind. Yet even Verran's vocal concerns had more to do with the weather than with the wisdom of the journey.

Connor returned his attention to what he could see of Blaine McFadden, disgraced lord of Glenreith. He could barely glimpse Blaine's shoulders and the top of his hat in the light snow that swirled around them. Although Engraham had talked a little about his "friend" in Edgeland, Connor had imagined a much different man than the one who had taken him into his home. It was obvious that Blaine's housemates and many of the villagers looked to him as a leader. Yet there was nothing of an aristocratic mien about him. The Blaine McFadden Connor had met would have been right at home among the dockworkers at the Rooster and Pig back in Donderath, perhaps more so than in the salons of Quillarth Castle.

Had it always been so? Or did Blaine camouflage himself with more than a new name up here?

"That trapper thought we were crazy," Connor said after a pause.

Piran laughed. "We are. Don't doubt that a bit. But now that the warden-mages are gone for good, it would be a fine thing to have the magic back again. Gods know, we need it up here."

"Oh?"

Piran had pulled his woolen scarf across his mouth to warm the air as he spoke. His scarf rapidly gained a fine covering of ice as his breath condensed and froze. "There weren't any powerful mages up here 'ceptin' the warden-mages. Guess the king had other ways to deal with rogue magic users than exile. But a lot of the folks here had a little magic; you know, to keep a fire lit all night, or make bread rise right, or nudge crops to grow a wee bit better. Didn't appreciate it until it was gone how much that magic made it a mite more livable up here."

"*Is* it livable without magic?"

Piran met his gaze. "Well, now, that's the question, innit?"

Connor was relieved when Blaine and Kestel signaled for a stop. They had walked at least two candlemarks, perhaps more, after the road's end. He longed for a fire to warm his hands and a hot meal, but he knew what provisions had been packed in his own backpack: dried fish, a hunk of bread, and a wineskin with watered wine. They found shelter in a shallow cave and sat down to eat.

"A flask of brandy would be nice right about now." Connor sighed.

Piran chuckled. "It's a death wish to drink hard spirits when you're in the wild." He paused to tear off a hunk of bread and wrap it around one of the dried fish. "Brings your blood to the surface so you feel warm, but all the while you're losing heat. Then you get sleepy and figure it's the brandy, so you decide to sit down and rest. When you fall asleep, you freeze to death." He shook his head. "Don't worry. There's whiskey enough for all of us once we get back to the house."

Connor was quiet for a while, chastened by Piran's response and the continued revelation of just how little he knew about surviving in his new home. No one said much, although Blaine and Dawe conferred in quiet tones.

Finally, Blaine stood and stretched. "We're almost to the place where the trappers were last seen. We'll be there within half a candlemark. If I read Ifrem's map right, it should be near one of those places of power. If there's anything left of the magic, we're likely to find it there."

Connor looked around at the group. They all looked as cold as he felt, despite their years of exposure to Edgeland's harsh weather. Dawe and Kestel were out here because, like Blaine, they had some minor magical ability. Blaine was the leader; it had been his idea to come. Piran was along as muscle, in case anything went wrong. *And I'm here because of that damned map and pendant,* Connor thought.

They didn't waste much time eating. Connor had the distinct impression that everyone else wanted to get back to the homestead's warm fire just as much as he did. Without the normal rise and set of the sun, Connor found his internal sense of time was completely haywire and he wondered how long it took to grow used to it, or whether anyone truly ever did.

It wasn't long after they left the shelter of the cave that Blaine, who was in the front, slowed down and held up a cautioning hand to warn the others. Connor looked around the barren, snow-swept landscape. They had begun the day's trek on nearly flat ground, heading into the foothills of the mountains that loomed on Edgeland's inner horizon. As they had climbed higher, the flat land had given way to rolling hills, and then to a path between steep cliffs topped with frozen overhangs of snow.

Connor could imagine why the trappers liked these valleys. Snow clung to the needles of scrubby bushes, and icicles hung from the pine boughs of the larger trees. Unlike the open landscape closer to the settlement, this area offered hiding places for the foxes, rabbits, and other game. Except for the carved stone markers that peeked above the snow from time to time, indicating a rough trail, there was no indication that any humans made their dwellings here.

They picked their way around boulders and piles of loose rock that had tumbled down from higher places. Several times, the remains of rock slides forced them to work their way over difficult terrain to get back to the path. The slopes of the mountains were covered with birch, juniper, and aspen trees, but in some places, it looked as if large swaths of the trees had been flattened, with trees snapped or uprooted and the rest a tangled mess of branches.

Connor strained to see what had caught Blaine's attention. Dawe and Piran lit two of the torches they had carried in their packs. Blaine turned his back to the slight wind and motioned for Dawe to bring the torch closer as Blaine unrolled one of the maps.

"We're close," Blaine said. "If the map's right, the place we're looking for should be just on the other side of that pile of rocks." He pointed to where a landslide had collapsed part of the pass's cliff wall into a jumble of boulders.

"How will we know when we get there?" Piran asked through his woolen muffler.

"Leave that to Dawe and me." Kestel turned around to search for Connor. "Can you dig out that pendant of yours, Connor? Let's see if it reacts to the map or the place."

Reluctantly, Connor nodded and took advantage of the pause in the wind to reach under his coat and dig out his pendant. Despite the warmth it held from being against his skin, it lay dead against his palm, dark and shining.

"Keep your wits about you," Blaine cautioned. "We saw a lot of rock slides on the way here. I'd rather not get caught in one. Let's go." Blaine rolled up the map and stowed it in his pack, then signaled for them to move forward.

As they neared the edge of the valley, Dawe caught up with Blaine and pointed to several places along the cliffs. Connor's gaze followed Dawe's gesture. The rough rock walls were pockmarked with openings large and small, and Connor repressed a shiver, wondering what might be watching them. Humans were probably not the only ones who went hungry during Edgeland's winter.

Piran had grown more watchful as they made their way through the valley. "I don't see any tracks," Piran muttered. "This is fresh snow. There should be foxes about, and stoats. Mountain goats and reindeer, too. I haven't seen any tracks except ours since we entered this damned valley."

"Maybe the trappers got them all," Connor replied.

"Keep your voice down!" Piran cautioned in a harsh whisper. He pointed up at the precarious snow ledges that cantilevered from the edge of the valley's crags. "I've got no desire to have that snow down on us." He turned, and his torch's light cast long shadows across the snow and rocks. "Edgeland's harsh, but there are animals all over if you know where to look. I've got to wonder why there aren't any here."

Connor shivered, and for once, it had nothing to do with the cold. "Does anything bigger than a fox live up here?" he asked in a low voice. "I mean, anything that might hunt us?"

Piran gave a mirthless chuckle. "For a long time, Commander Prokief was the only predator we had to worry about. Him and his warden-mages. Out here—I've heard tell that trappers see some of those big white bears once in a while. They come and go, but they're bad news. Trappers say one of those bears'll hunt a man for days if it catches the scent."

They came to a stop. "We're here," Kestel said quietly. A natural alcove in the cliff face greeted them. While the rock itself was majestic, it had been hallowed by the gifts of many pilgrims. Weather-worn beads hung draped over rocks and the branches of a lone pine tree. Small, faded flags fluttered in the wind, held aloft by tattered lengths of twine. Here and there, the cliff face had niches carved into it, deep enough to hold a candle. The charred nubs of several candles remained frozen where they had gone out.

"Look, over there," Dawe said, pointing. A large clearing between two slopes made an open space around the shrine. Not far across the clearing, the land ended, but whether to a ledge or into a sheer drop, Connor couldn't see from where they stood. The snow was pockmarked with odd circles, some that appeared to go down several feet. The trees on the mountain's slopes were broken, scattered like kindling.

"Maybe it was the quake, when Estendall exploded," Kestel replied.

"Maybe," Blaine repeated, but he sounded unconvinced. Connor and Piran moved closer, suddenly unwilling to be far from the rest of the group.

"Let's do what we came here to do," Blaine said, keeping his voice low and glancing up at the snow that clung to the high outcroppings. "Dawe, Kestel, move into the shrine area. See if you can feel any magic. Connor, let's get that disk of yours into position and see if anything happens."

Kestel reached out and took Dawe's hand. Dawe gave his torch to Piran and squared his shoulders. Together, Dawe and Kestel walked carefully toward the shrine, moving slowly, as if they were testing the magic with every step. Connor followed them, holding the obsidian disk at the end of its leather strap flat on his palm in front of him. He glanced back to where Blaine and Piran stood, braced as if ready for an attack.

"Something feels wrong," Kestel murmured. Dawe nodded. "Is it magic?" she asked in a half whisper.

"Damned if I know, but it feels... twisted," Dawe replied.

The obsidian disk on Connor's hand began to move of its own accord. "Something's happening!" Connor hissed. It was all he could do to stifle a shout.

The disk began trembling, then started to slide from side to side although Connor's palm was level. It did not glow, but Connor felt a tingle where his skin touched the disk's glassy surface.

A high-pitched screech filled the air and a circle of light opened around where Dawe, Kestel, and Connor stood. Kestel and Dawe clapped their hands against their ears and fell to their knees, their faces twisted in pain. Connor watched the disk on his palm thrash from side to side, taking on an eerie blue glow. Outside the circle, Connor could see Blaine and Piran. They looked as if they were calling out to him, but he could hear nothing. He saw Blaine stagger, as if some of the effects reached him even outside the circle of light.

The circle of light formed a coruscating curtain, and Connor felt his heart pound. The light was far too similar to the deadly magical fire that had taken its toll on Castle Reach. But where the fire that destroyed Donderath had burned, Connor thought, this power was cold, even colder than the ice around them, leeching the warmth from his blood and bone.

Dawe and Kestel were on the ground, writhing. Dawe moaned, teeth gritted, and Kestel whimpered between labored breaths. Terrified, Connor did the first thing that came to mind. He grabbed the disk in both hands and held it up, a meager shield against the light.

The faint blue glow grew brighter, surrounding the disk like a nimbus. The screech that accompanied the circle of light that imprisoned them grew louder, sending a searing pain through Connor's head that made him stagger. Outside the light, Connor saw a sudden wind buffet Piran and Blaine, guttering their torches and driving them back from the shrine.

Light struck the medallion in a bolt of cold fire. The blast threw Connor on his back, tearing the obsidian from his grip and snapping the leather strap that held it around his neck.

Dazed, he expected to see the amulet go flying, even as he awaited the onslaught of the pain that racked Dawe and Kestel. Instead, the disk hovered, trailing the bits of broken leather, as more and more bolts struck it.

The bolts sheared off from the curtain of light, and with each one that struck the disk, the curtain wavered and grew thinner, dimmer. In the distance, Connor could now hear the howl of the wind and make out the warning shouts from Blaine and Piran, and the anguished cries of Kestel and Dawe.

A crack like the loudest thunder reverberated from the mountains around them, followed by a gust of wind that raised a blanket of snow in the air and then dropped it, threatening to bury them. The ground rumbled, and Connor looked toward the twilight sky. The curtain of light winked out, and in its place came a glistening wave.

"Avalanche!" Blaine shouted.

Snow crashed down from the peaks, swirling toward them like an incoming ocean wave, and just as unstoppable. Caught in the rush of snow, Connor tumbled head over heels. When the snow momentarily freed him from its grip as they surged down the slope, Connor gasped for air, only to be buried again an instant later. He had lost sight of his companions, enveloped in cold, shifting darkness. Connor did not know whether he would suffocate before the press of the snow crushed him, or whether he might be dashed against the rocks or plummet from the drop at the end of the clearing. But he was very sure that he was about to die.

Something thin and hard smacked against the side of his head. Connor felt it slide down his body, until the smooth surface stroked against his hand. Reflexively, he grasped it, and realized that the disk had found its way back to him just in time to witness his death.

For a moment, he was airborne, falling through space as the avalanche carried him across the clearing and off the ledge. He gulped air as the snow loosened around him, bracing himself for a killing impact as he fell back against the rocky ground. He landed hard enough to jar the breath from him, but the landing was onto deep snow that cushioned his fall. Just as quickly, a smothering blanket covered him again, tumbling him like a twig in the surf.

Finally, slowed by its own momentum, the avalanche drifted to a stop. Trapped in a pocket of air, Connor forced down panic. It was completely dark, and he feared that any movement might collapse the precious pocket around him. Completely disoriented by the fall, he had no idea whether he should dig down or up to reach the surface. His whole body ached, battered and bruised.

The awful cold he had felt earlier in the day was replaced by a seductive, sleepy daze. The air around him was stale, and it was becoming difficult to breathe. For a fleeting instant, the idea of digging occurred to him, but it would require far more energy than he possessed. Resigned to death, Connor closed his eyes and let sleep take him.

CHAPTER NINETEEN

CONNOR STIRRED. HE WAS LYING ON SOMETHING hard and he hurt all over. He had a blurred memory of the avalanche, of sleep, and then nothing.

Gradually, Connor realized that he was breathing, and that if he concentrated, he could feel his heart beating. He wiggled first his fingers and then his toes. Aching muscles protested, but his body responded. Connor abruptly noticed that he was wearing neither gloves nor boots.

Surely I'm dead. I wonder what the Sea of Souls looks like? For a moment, he struggled between fear and curiosity, before the need for certainty won out and he opened his eyes.

He lay on a plank floor in a dimly lit cabin. The air smelled of burning wood and an odd scent Connor couldn't place. The ceiling above him was made of hewn timbers holding up a roof of flat boards. Turning his head to one side, he saw Blaine lying nearby, covered with a thin woolen blanket. If the others were here, he could not see them without sitting up, which he wasn't quite ready to do just yet. Beyond Blaine, in the corner, the carcass of a deer hung by its hind legs, fresh enough that blood was dripping into a bowl beneath it.

Connor's head throbbed. As he came to himself, he realized just how many parts of his body hurt. Gingerly, he flexed his arms and legs to reassure himself that nothing was broken, a minor miracle. He guessed that he would be covered in head-to-toe bruises for a while, a trivial price to pay for surviving.

"You and your companions are safe."

The voice startled Connor and his heart reassured him of his status among the living by beginning to pound. Moving carefully, in case he had not discovered the true extent of his injuries, Connor sat up.

The cabin was a small rectangle, smaller than the kitchen at the homestead. A small stone fireplace at one end sent the warmth of a roaring fire into the room. The smell of roasting meat and baking bread filled the air, along with a hint of juniper from the cabin's wood and the logs in the fire. On shelves around the cabin's walls, Connor spied an astrolabe, navigator's instruments, and a few figures carved from wood. A table and bench and a bookcase sufficed for furniture. Skinned and tanned hides hung from the walls, and several hides covered the floor. Connor recognized most as deerskin, along with what appeared to be that of a huge bear. With a start, Connor realized that the cabin had no windows.

Piran and Dawe lay to his left, while Kestel lay beyond Blaine. None of them stirred, but all were breathing. Their coats and outer garments had been removed, and each was covered with a homespun blanket. He turned toward the voice that had awakened him.

A man sat in a wooden chair near the fireplace, his face a play of light and shadow as the fire flickered from the wind outside. His dark hair was drawn back to frame his pale skin. The man's looks suggested intelligence, perhaps aristocracy. Their benefactor—or captor—sat with both hands clearly in view on the arms of the chair. From what Connor could see in half-light, the man was tall and he wore a tunic and trews and high boots.

"Who are you? How did we come here?"

The man gave a half smile. "My name is Arin Grimur. You and your companions are here because I pulled you from the snow."

"Thank you." Connor found himself unwilling to look the man directly in the eye. Despite their rescue, Connor felt uncomfortable, although he could not figure out why. "How did you find us?"

"Your blood called to me."

Connor's heart skipped a beat. He glanced toward the deer in the corner, and to the bowl of fresh blood beneath it. It had been the scent of blood that Connor had not been able to place when he awoke. "How so?" he managed, knowing that his voice was pinched with fear.

Arin Grimur chuckled, revealing the tips of overly long eye-teeth. "Don't be afraid. The marks of your master protect you. Even here, Lanyon Penhallow's reputation is known and respected."

Connor reflexively laid one hand over the marks on the inside of his arm. "Why did you save us?"

Grimur regarded him for a moment before answering. "Lanyon Penhallow is my maker. Although he and I parted ways decades ago, I bear him no ill will. If he chose to give you his protection, then you have mine as well."

Connor realized he had been holding his breath. "Thank you," he repeated. He glanced worriedly at his friends, who still had not stirred. "Are they—"

Grimur gave another disquieting half smile. "They are alive

and well. Bruised, perhaps, but no serious injuries. I thought it best to let them sleep until you and I had been introduced."

Connor frowned. "I thought that magic didn't work anymore."

Grimur shrugged. "The effect that a vampire has over mortals—'glamour' some call it—is a part of what we are. If it *is* magic, it's a very personal, very old magic." Grimur did not move, yet in the next breath, Blaine and the others began to stir.

Piran sat bolt upright, tensed to fight. "Where are we?"

"Safe," Connor said as Blaine and Dawe also sat up and looked around. Kestel was the last to stir. She gave a catlike stretch, winced, and then sinuously rose to a sitting position.

"Who's he?" Piran asked, his voice wary.

"A friend," Connor replied. "And our rescuer."

Piran looked around the cabin. "Why in Raka aren't there any windows?"

Kestel's gaze had fixed on Grimur. "Because our host is a vampire," she said quietly.

Grimur gave a nod. "Very good. How did m'lady know?"

Kestel gave an enigmatic smile. "One of my patrons at court was a sometime guest of Lanyon Penhallow—and Pentreath Reese."

Grimur's eyes narrowed at the second name. "Penhallow's friends are welcome here. Reese's are not. Which are you?"

If Kestel felt concerned to be questioned by a vampire, her expression revealed nothing. "I'm Connor's friend," she replied. "You asked how I recognized you; I've seen others of your kind. They were my patrons, nothing more."

Blaine had been watching their host warily during the exchange. "Where, exactly, are we?"

Grimur turned his attention to Blaine as if he were taking

Blaine's measure. "In my home, in Edgeland. Not far from the location of your…accident."

"You mean when we got hit with a ton of snow?" Piran asked, rubbing his neck. "After the spooky lights knocked us flat on our asses?"

Grimur chuckled, a disquieting sound. "Precisely."

Blaine's expression hardened. "What do you know about the accident? What happened up there?"

Grimur stood in a languorous movement that reminded Connor of a snake unwinding its coil. He walked over to the corner, lifted the bowl of blood from beneath the unlucky deer, and carried it to the table. Connor eyed the carcass, which was obviously slain just a few candlemarks ago, after Grimur would have brought them to his house. *A substitution for dinner?* he wondered.

"You found one of the places of power, a 'node' where, under normal circumstances, magic is more powerful than usual." He paused to pour the fresh blood into an empty wine bottle and to stopper the opening. "These are not normal circumstances."

"Magic died," Blaine countered doggedly. "So what was that?"

"It was magic," Kestel answered quietly. "But not normal magic."

"Wild magic," Dawe replied, rubbing his temples as if the attack lingered in a headache.

Grimur nodded. "More precisely, 'feral' magic. Mages call it '*visithara*.' Something has wrenched magic loose by the roots, so to speak, and this is the consequence."

Grimur hesitated as if debating something, then unstoppered the bottle and poured himself a goblet. Connor watched, both fascinated and revolted. "Don't worry," he said with a chuckle, noting the direction of Connor's gaze. "When I realized I would have guests, I hunted well. Would you feel better knowing that the carcass of another deer—one cleanly drained of its blood—is buried in the snow behind the cabin?"

"Do I have to answer that?' Piran's bravado belied his uncertainty.

"I would be a poor host not to offer you refreshment after your ordeal," Grimur said, ignoring Piran. "Usually, I have no need of the meat, but I thought that a venison soup might do, given the circumstances. As for the bread," he said with a shrug and a wave of his hand in the general direction of the hearth, "I still enjoy the taste of a fresh loaf from time to time, although I no longer require its nourishment."

Connor saw the warning glance that flashed between Kestel and Blaine. "We are indebted to you," Kestel replied. "Your hospitality is most appreciated."

Grimur's lips twitched as if he found the notion of indebtedness amusing. Connor did not want to dwell on the idea, unsure of just what, if anything, it might require of them. "Most courteous—and courtly," Grimur said with a slight bow to Kestel as he walked back to his seat. He held the goblet of blood indifferently.

"As for the magic," Grimur said, crossing his long legs, "it is a force of nature. It can be damaged, temporarily altered, but ultimately cannot be destroyed by mortals." He paused to take a sip. "So far as we know."

"Meaning what? That it will come back?" Blaine asked.

Grimur gave an eloquent shrug. "Perhaps. What form it takes and whether or not it can be controlled by mortals as it once was I have no way of knowing."

"You're saying that magic was domesticated?" Dawe's tone was sharp with disbelief.

"In a manner of speaking," Grimur replied. He seemed

mildly amused at their uneasiness. "That's what my friend Valtyr believed."

"The mapmaker?" Connor looked up abruptly at the name.

"Ah, so this must belong to you." Grimur withdrew the wooden box with Connor's map from the shadows behind his chair. "And this?" he asked, holding up the obsidian disk.

"That's also mine," Connor replied.

Grimur swirled the blood in his glass, watching it coat the goblet's bowl. "Valtyr was a master mage. He was also, quite literally, afraid of his shadow. His shadow side, so to speak. And of the shadow side of others. Magic, like all types of power, lures the weak into hubris. They begin to believe that they're invincible, immortal."

"Like you?" Blaine asked, an edge to his voice.

Grimur's laugh was deep and rolling this time, edged with bitterness. "I am immortal, but, like all of my kind, not invincible. We may not be mortals, but we are not gods. Time has taught me that lesson quite memorably." He stared toward the fire as if looking into the past. "I was also a mage, but that power has vanished.

"Valtyr understood that power corrupts," Grimur continued after a pause. "And he was aware, more so than most mages, that the power he wielded did not come from anything inside himself. Mages are channels through which power flows easily. Those without magic are somehow blocked to the flow of power."

"I thought magic sprang from the gods," Dawe replied warily.

Grimur chuckled. "Oh, the temple guardians would like you to think so, but what we know as magic is quite different from the powers of the gods. Magic has no source in Charrot and his sorry band of revelers, unless you believe that the world and every power in it sprang from his loins like the lesser gods."

"You don't believe in the gods?" Piran asked, less a challenge than a question. Connor had the impression that Piran's devotion was haphazard at best.

Grimur sobered. "Oh, I believe, not because I want to, but because I know them to exist. I have known Torven's touch. The gods are real. Best you not attract their notice."

They fell silent for a moment. Finally, Blaine looked up. "A group of trappers went missing right before the magic died. They had come this way hunting fox. Might they have stumbled into the kind of wild magic we encountered?"

Grimur finished off the blood in his goblet and nodded. "Another reason why I have rarely ventured outside of late. Over the last several months, the magic has grown erratic. I had chosen this location for a cabin because, among other reasons, the place of power that you found was a boost to my own power—before the magic disappeared."

Grimur toyed with his empty goblet before setting it aside. "You happened to be in the wrong place at the wrong time, with artifacts that had magical properties. Magic calls to magic. I also assume that some of you have some magic, and that it triggered the incident at the shrine. Is that correct?"

Kestel and Dawe nodded hesitantly, as if unsure how much to disclose to this new benefactor. Connor shared their hesitation. Though Penhallow had always kept the letter of his agreements, Connor had heard rumors that others among the immortals did not consider their word as a bond when given to mortals. Grimur had not retrieved them to feed upon; that much seemed clear. Still, Connor doubted Grimur had saved them out of sheer altruism. Exactly why their host had rescued them remained to be seen.

Grimur nodded. "What you experienced was a storm, of sorts. Magic has come untethered from the places of power and from those who used to wield it. It's like an untamed horse, full of potential and dangerous to everything around it unless properly harnessed. Something snapped the bonds that kept the magic harnessed. Such a thing has happened before—and Valtyr knew it." He rose and lifted the lid on a cauldron on the hearth, poking at its contents with a wooden spoon.

Grimur straightened and turned to them. "Come, you must be hungry after your ordeal. Eat. As long as it's been since I was mortal, I still recall that conversation was best over a shared meal."

Grimur set the table with an assortment of wooden bowls and pewter goblets. However the vampire had come to live at the edge of the world, he made the small cabin a comfortable home. *Did he choose to come here, or was he exiled? And if so, by whom?* Connor wondered as the group sat down. By their expressions, Connor guessed that his companions shared his uneasiness over dining with a vampire. His stomach growled, unconcerned.

Kestel tasted her stew and looked up, smiling. "This is very good."

Grimur smiled and gave an exaggerated, courtly bow. "M'lady is generous with her praise," he said. "I thought I might be out of practice. I rarely crave mortal food, and have very few guests."

Connor and Blaine exchanged glances, and Connor guessed that the same question occurred to Blaine as flashed through his own mind. *Who else might be among Grimur's guests?*

Grimur watched them eat, an attentive host. Connor thought that he saw a flicker of longing in Grimur's gaze, as if the vampire might be momentarily wistful for mortal hunger.

"After you've slept, I will guide you back to the sledge road."

"Thank you," Blaine replied. "Does that pose a risk for you?"

Grimur shrugged. "Every exposure poses risk. I choose to live alone, but I can go about during the long night without harm. And the way here is difficult to remember, if you were so inclined to return."

"How did you come to be in Edgeland?" Kestel asked, setting her empty soup bowl aside. "I doubt the king exiled you."

Grimur looked away, remaining silent long enough that Blaine was unsure the vampire meant to answer. "I was not exiled by a king," he said finally. "I had been a mage in the employ of a master mage. Then I was brought across. The mage hated the *talishte*—vampires. He cast me out. I remained with my maker, Lanyon, for many years, and then tired of civilization. And so I came here, and here I have lived in peace."

"Do you think that magic can be…harnessed…again?" Dawe asked.

Grimur shrugged. "Over the centuries, I've seen the damage man can do to the world around him. Forests leveled. Streams and rivers fouled. Farmland rendered useless. Sometimes magic was involved, but more often it was caused by the malice of men. And yet, over time, the world healed itself. Trees grew back. Waters cleansed themselves. Cropland became usable once more."

"So there's a chance that the magic might heal, too?" Blaine pressed.

Grimur nodded. "Perhaps. But such things don't heal quickly. And while it is wounded, we bear its pain."

"Immortals, too?"

Again, Grimur nodded. "And perhaps even the gods."

CHAPTER TWENTY

THANK THE GODS YOU'RE NOT DEAD!" VERRAN met them at the door to the homestead. He looked beside himself with worry, and he fussed over each of them as they trundled in the doorway, shook off the snow, and unfastened their heavy coats and boots. "Where in Torven's name have you been? I didn't sleep all night."

Blaine pounded the snow from his boots and shrugged out of his cloak. "We were attacked by rogue magic, caught in an avalanche, pushed over a cliff, and rescued by a vampire, who put us up for the night."

Verran laughed. "How long did it take you to think that up?"

Dawe hung his hat and coat on pegs near the door, gave his boots a final stamp, and heel-toed them off. "He's not making it up."

"Actually, I thought it was a rather productive outing," Blaine replied.

"And we learned that there's a vampire prowling around the wilds," Piran muttered. "I thought that was important."

"Which he'd rather not have us make too public," Connor put in. "I think he likes his privacy."

"Point taken," Blaine said, pouring himself more brandy. He was just beginning to feel the chill recede from his fingers and toes. They filled Verran in, while the musician listened, wide-eyed.

Verran rose to get himself another bowl of stew. He returned to his seat and licked traces of broth from his fingers. "Oh, almost forgot. Ifrem sent word, looking for you. Seems there's an emergency Council meeting tonight, down at Crooked House."

Blaine swore. "Great. Can I mention that a trip into town—let alone an evening with the Council—is not on my list of favorite things to do?"

"Look at the bright side," Dawe said, elbowing him. "Maybe Connor's buddy has taught Ifrem how to brew a proper bitterbeer."

Blaine pulled his cloak around him, heading into the night, toward the road to Bay-town. Verran's stew had filled his stomach and warmed his blood, though the bitter wind was making a quick end of any lingering warmth.

The road ahead of him was deserted. Moonlight cast the snow in shades of blue, and Blaine repressed a shiver. His boots crunched through the frozen top skin of the snow, and his breath misted despite the heavy scarf he had pulled over his face. He sincerely hoped that Old Man Jordenson would be on time. Jordenson had a homestead just a ways up the road from where Blaine and the others lived, and he made a nightly run into Bay-town and back to deliver produce and pick up ale or whiskey. He passed Blaine's homestead every night at sixth bells, and returned from town a few candlemarks later, usually around tenth bells. For a few coppers, Jordenson was happy to give his fellow homesteaders a ride in and back. Blaine's teeth chattered, and he devoutly hoped that this was one night Jordenson would not be late.

Behind him in the darkness, he heard the snow crunch. Blaine stopped, motionless, listening. One hand fell to the knife sheathed on his belt. Wolves were common in Edgeland, and Blaine had no desire to face one out here alone on the road. After a moment, when there was no sound except for the wind, Blaine continued walking toward the meeting point, his senses on high alert. Twice, he froze, listening, sure he had heard something in the shadows. By now he was certain that he was being watched, although he saw nothing to provide a clue to his pursuer.

The meeting point, a small wooden shed at the end of the lane, was just ahead. By Blaine's reckoning, Jordenson should be along any moment. *After all that happened, I'm probably just tired, and nervous. My imagination is playing tricks. Who would be crazy enough to be out on a night like this, besides Jordenson and me? A wolf would have attacked by now, if it meant to. Probably just some wild dogs.*

Blaine approached the wooden shed and heard the twang of a bowstring. Pure instinct drove him to the ground, landing him facedown in the snow. He lay still for a moment, listening. He heard boot steps, coming closer, and then another sound, the creaking of wagon wheels straining against the rutted snow. There was a muffled curse, then footsteps retreating as the sound of the wagon grew closer.

Cautiously, Blaine stood, knocking the snow from his cloak. A hunting arrow had embedded itself into the wall of the shed, at just the height that might have taken him through the back had he not thrown himself down.

Blaine turned, scanning the shadowy horizon, looking across

the snow toward the forest. He saw no one. He hesitated, sure that he would find footprints in the snow, but unwilling to miss his ride into town.

"That you, Mick?" Jordenson called as his wagon rolled up to the shed. "You wantin' a ride into Bay-town?"

Rattled from the near miss, Blaine nodded. He stepped up to the shed wall and snapped the arrow free. There were no unusual markings, no pattern to the fletchings, no remarkable workmanship. Only one thing set this arrow apart from hundreds of arrows in the quills of hunters across Edgeland. It bore a military tip, barbed and strong, capable of piercing even plate armor. Only one place in Edgeland was permitted such arrows: the armory at Velant.

"I said, do you want a ride to Bay-town?" The irritation in Jordenson's voice broke Blaine out of his thoughts.

"Sorry," he said, hiding the arrow in the folds of his cloak. "Yes, I'd appreciate it. Damn cold night."

"By Torven's stars! You've said that right." Old Man Jordenson accepted the coins Blaine paid for a spot in the back of the wagon, and reined in his skittish horse.

"Keep a sharp eye out, will ya?" Jordenson said as Blaine settled into the horse blankets and straw in the wagon. "Old Betta's been skittish the last few miles, and I'm wondering if there be wolves about."

Blaine's gaze scanned the tree line. *Not wolves*, he thought. *A hunter. And the question is, why was that hunter hunting me?* "I'll keep watch," Blaine replied, glad for the shelter of the wagon as Betta jerked the wagon into motion.

The wagon creaked as it labored through the snowy ruts. Blaine was glad to see the lights of Bay-town come into view, glittering against the snow and the water, a welcome beacon. Down the coastline, Blaine could just glimpse the shadow of the fortifications that were being rebuilt to guard against unwanted visitors from abroad. He turned, looking for the familiar shadow that was Velant, but the ruins of the prison camp blended completely into the twilight sky.

The crowd at the Crooked House was fairly subdued. A few men played at dice or cards, protesting loudly when their luck went bad. A cluster of men gathered around the fire, swapping tales. Engraham was tending bar, and if he minded the shift from tavern master to bartender, he didn't show it. "Hey there, Bl—I mean, Mick," he said with a ready smile. "Ifrem was hoping you'd show up. Everything all right?"

Blaine shrugged and put down enough coins to pay for a glass of whiskey. The wagon ride into town had once again chilled him to the bone and soured his mood. "Right as it can be, I guess," he replied. "How are you catching on to the new job?"

Engraham grinned. "What's to catch? This bar's not that different from the Rooster and Pig, 'ceptin' the fact that the whiskey's rougher and we're more likely to ferment potatoes than wheat." He nodded toward the room full of patrons, who seemed oblivious to his comments. "Don't think they rightly care what we ferment, so long as it helps them forget their troubles."

"You and your mum doing all right?"

Engraham nodded. "Aye. Funny thing, how someone close to you as your mum can become sort of a stranger when you lose enough years together, but we're working on it. After all, I was just a lad when she was sent away, and I show up a grown man—there's some adjusting to do, for both of us. But odd as it sounds, I'm glad I made it here. If I can't be in Donderath, I don't know where else I'd feel more at home."

Blaine thanked him for the drink, tossed an extra coin to

him for his trouble, and headed up the back stairs. The Council was already assembled in the upper room. By the sound of it, they'd been gathered long enough for tempers to flare.

A thump that sounded like a man's fist hitting the table rumbled through the door. "Dammit, Adger, be reasonable. What you're reporting is nothing but hearsay."

Blaine opened the door. Peters the fishmonger was half-standing, his fist still against the table. Adger, the distiller, sat across from him, his face flushed with anger.

"This 'hearsay,' as you call it, comes from three different, independent sources," Adger argued. "And all three say they've seen wild magic out on the far ice, dangerous magic. We're in danger."

Peters sat down, scowling. "Who says so? A bunch of drunken trappers?"

"Perhaps, but I've seen the wild magic and have the bruises to show for it," Blaine said. The Council fell silent, and they all turned to look at him.

"And how did that happen?" Peters snapped.

Blaine sat down in the remaining empty chair at the table and sipped his whiskey. He did his best to recount their adventure without betraying Grimur's secret or the existence of the map and pendant. When he finished, the others were silent for a few moments.

"Those trappers that disappeared, do you think that's what happened to them?" Trask asked.

Blaine shrugged, unwilling to repeat Grimur's tale. "That would be my bet. We were pretty lucky to get out of there alive."

Peters leaned back and crossed his arms over his chest. "We thought the magic was gone, but maybe it's just broken. Could it fix itself?"

Blaine shrugged. "Who knows? It didn't break itself. We know from what Connor told us that the mages on both sides of the war broke the magic. We also aren't sure the magic is 'broken' everywhere in the world," he added.

"That does us little good," Adger grumbled. "Our ships can't reach the Cross-Sea Kingdoms, and as it is, we'd be asking them to conquer us."

"I agree," said Jothra. "But it raises an interesting question. If it required mages to break the magic, does it require mages to fix it? And if the mages of power are dead on the Continent, and we have none here, where could we find mages we trust to set things right?"

The group was silent for a few moments, then Ifrem cleared his throat. "As interesting as the speculation is," Ifrem said, "we have a more pressing problem, which is why we convened. Trask and Mama Jean have completed their inventory of our food stock. I'll let them share what they've found."

Trask looked uncomfortable, and not just because his broad, muscular body was wedged into one of the tavern chairs. He drummed his fingers nervously on the table, like a schoolboy caught playing truant. Mama Jean's expression was unusually pinched with worry, making her look older and worn.

"Might as well cut to the worst of it," Trask said in a voice still thick with the accent of the Donderath hill country. "We've counted colonists and we've inventoried what's in the warehouses. We've also figured out about how much food each homestead can raise for itself, and what amount of surplus they can generally bring to market. We also managed to find most of Prokief's receipts for supplies from the homeland and tallied what the Bay-town merchants bought from Donderath suppliers." He shifted uncomfortably in his chair.

"I'll say it if he won't," Mama Jean interrupted. "From what we can figure, we don't have enough food for everyone in Edgeland to make it through the winter."

Outcry erupted around the table, until Ifrem pounded his fist to settle them. "There'll be time enough for riots when word gets to the street," he said sternly. "We're supposed to be the governing body."

Blaine had been quiet as the others had expressed shock and outrage. Mama Jean's news had not really surprised him. He remembered growing up at Glenreith, watching his mother fret and argue with the manor's seneschal over what to plant for the next harvest, always with an eye toward having enough to last the winter. Though the ships from home had been slower to arrive in recent months, no one had really expected them to stop altogether. Without ample preparation, hunger was certain.

"By our count we've got enough for several hundred fewer people than we have," Trask added. "There weren't many newcomers on the ship, but they're still mouths to feed. Normally, the colony only loses a few dozen over the winter to fever and accident. So we all need to do with a little less, and come up with a way to find a little more, if we're to get through 'til spring."

"What are our options?" Annalise might be a seer, but she was also a good merchant, and she understood a ledger. "It's too late to plant more crops until spring. We don't dare eat through the seed stock or kill too many of the animals. We have no choice except to ration what we have and hunt for what we don't."

"I don't fancy telling the folks out there that we'll need to ration," Adger said. "And with trappers disappearing out on the ice, there won't be a lot of enthusiasm for going hunting too far afield."

"We could take the herring boats out." Everyone turned to

look at Blaine. "I know we don't usually fish beyond the bay after the long dark sets in, but if we have to, we have to."

"The waters are more dangerous in the winter," Peters said.

Blaine shrugged. "And the fish are in different places than they are when we're in the white nights. We're at Yadin's mercy, even more than usual. But a full catch on just a few boats can bring in enough fish to feed most of Bay-town, at least for a while." He paused. "One ship can bring in six tons of fish, if we take all we can carry. A few outings of the fleet, if we're successful, should keep us in herring. If we get lucky, we might get a whale."

"Herring for breakfast, lunch, and supper," Adger growled.

Mama Jean turned on him. "Washed down with your rotgut." She looked back to the group. "We have enough flour, if we portion it out to make it last, to go until spring. So you can have coated herring, herring and biscuits, herring and pancakes..."

Despite the tension, the group laughed. "All right, then," Ifrem said. "We need to leave here with a plan."

"I'll rally the fishermen," Blaine said, dreading Piran's reaction to learning he was about to be drafted for more herring duty.

"I'll gather the merchants and work out a fair rationing system," Annalise replied.

"I'll help you," Mama Jean volunteered.

"Adger and I can roust up some hunting parties," Peters said with a glance toward Adger, who scowlingly acknowledged. "If we could bring down a few walrus, instead of small game, we can salt and dry the meat for later, when the storms are bad."

"I'll work with Engraham to make sure we can adjust the mash to brew whatever we've got in the storehouses," Ifrem said.

"What do we tell the colonists?" Annalise's voice brought silence.

"Tell them the truth," Blaine replied. "The only way we're going to make it through this is to work together. They deserve to know."

"We'll need their cooperation if we're going to take the fleet out," Ifrem agreed. "And it wouldn't hurt to send gleaners out to the Velant farm fields. We brought in the cabbages, but I can't say that we dug for all of the potatoes and root crops in those fields. I'll gather a harvesting team."

Ifrem looked from face to face. "Edgeland is going to need its leaders more now than ever before. Right now, that's us. We've got to help keep the peace and get people working together."

Blaine thought about the long dark in years past, and how, inevitably, toward the end of the sunless period, even at the best of times, Edgeland saw its peace disturbed by brawls, suicides, and murder. "Then Charrot help us, because we'll have our hands full," he murmured.

Blaine waited until the Council adjourned and its members had filed downstairs before he removed the arrow from its hiding place within his cloak. He had signaled Ifrem to stay behind, and now he laid the arrow on the table between them.

"What do you make of this?" Blaine asked.

Ifrem studied the arrow, then lifted it for a better look. "Looks like military issue to me. Where did you find it?"

"Someone shot it at me earlier this evening," Blaine replied dryly. Ifrem listened as Blaine recounted his story, and sat down, frowning at the arrow in his hands.

"Light's bad this time of year. And a lot of the weapons went missing when Velant fell. Maybe someone mistook you for an elk."

"Maybe," Blaine replied, unconvinced. "Or maybe there's more to it." He leaned forward. "First, someone tried to kidnap Kestel from the homestead."

Ifrem chuckled. "Someone who didn't know Mistress Kestel's reputation at court, I warrant. Where did you hide the body?"

Blaine shook his head. "Kestel said whoever it was, was a professional. He got away, although she slashed him good." He gave Ifrem a meaningful look. "Then you were attacked, not long afterward."

Ifrem held up his hands in protest. "What could that have to do with anything? Probably a drunk who thought I had a few coins on me." He paused. "And I doubt anyone mistook Kestel for you."

"No, but everyone knows she's part of my 'family,'" Blaine replied. "Someone might assume that she'd be easy to grab, figuring that I'd come after her. And as for your attack, you said it yourself—our cloaks are nearly identical. What if you weren't meant to be the target?"

Ifrem frowned and leaned back, studying the arrow anew. "I'll grant you that our cloaks are similar, and we're nearly the same height. But this is all guessing. The three attacks could have nothing to do with one another. Kestel's a pretty woman. Perhaps one of Prokief's soldiers thought she'd make an easy target, and learned his lesson the hard way. What happened to me might have just been a botched robbery. And you could have run afoul of a hunter with bad eyesight."

Blaine shrugged. "Maybe."

"Besides, why would anyone be out to kill you, Mick?" Ifrem set the arrow back on the table. "Most of the colonists like you. And Prokief's dead."

Blaine met Ifrem's gaze. "Prokief said something odd just before he died. He said I was a dead man and didn't know it yet."

Ifrem's gaze widened. "That puts a different slant on things. What did he mean?"

Blaine gave another shrug. "Don't know. I meant to have a look at Prokief's papers, whatever survived the fire. But I don't know what became of them."

Ifrem brightened. "That I can help you with." He rose and rummaged in a trunk at the back of the room. When he returned, he had a wooden box that was soot-scarred and smelled of smoke. He set it on the table. The box was carved with Prokief's initials. It was plain that the lock had been smashed. Ifrem opened the lid.

"Mama Jean insisted we send someone back to Velant that first night, to see if we could find bills of lading or other documents to help determine whether Prokief was hiding any food or equipment. Any of those kinds of papers I gave to her for the inventories. These I kept, just in case they turned out to be important." He pushed the chest toward Blaine. "Go ahead. Have a look. They didn't mean anything to me."

Blaine removed the papers from the box and spread them out on the table. He paged through a sheaf of papers filled with cramped handwriting in faded ink. After a few moments, he looked up. "These appear to be reports from Prokief's spies. I'd say he had spies everywhere, but he kept a close eye on the warden-mages. Maybe that's how he kept control."

Ifrem nodded. "Makes sense. Anything else?"

At the bottom of the stack of papers was another parchment, this one with a broken wax seal. Blaine frowned and picked it up. The parchment was fine stock, and the wax seal bore an ornate symbol with a "P." *"P" for Prokief?* Blaine wondered. Another possibility crossed his mind. *Or "P" for Pollard?*

He opened the parchment. "This is dated from four months ago. It must have come on one of the last ships from home." He scanned down through the writing, noting that whoever had written it had a strong, flowing hand, completely unlike Prokief's clumsy script. The farther he read, the greater his suspicions became.

"Something's got your attention, Mick," Ifrem said. "What's so interesting?"

Blaine sat back in his chair. "I'd bet a day's wage this letter is from Prokief's patron back in Donderath."

"Prokief had a patron? That's news to me. How'd he get sent here?"

"Maybe his patron wanted someone positioned in Edgeland," Blaine suggested. "There were always rumors that some prisoners who disappeared actually got sent home on the sly."

Ifrem grunted. "I always thought those rumors were wishful thinking. More likely, they were buried out in the fields."

Blaine set the letter on the table. "According to the letter, Prokief was to receive payment as agreed, plus various hard-to-find items like good wine and caviar, and a 'special workman.'"

"A workman?" Ifrem echoed. "What in Raka does that mean?"

"This workman," Blaine read, picking the letter back up, "was supposed to be turned loose against the target if there was a 'significant change' at home."

"A change? Like the war going badly for Donderath?" Ifrem replied, leaning close for a look at the letter. "Gods, Mick. Someone sent Prokief an assassin?"

"What if Prokief had a patron with the money of a lord and

the morals of a cutpurse?" Blaine replied. "Someone who might have need of henchmen who were sent away to Velant, and could give them a job if they happened to find their way back home? Someone who could pay Prokief well to do his bidding?"

"You have someone in mind?"

Blaine nodded and held out the wax seal for Ifrem's inspection. "Vedran Pollard."

Ifrem nodded. "Pollard did have a reputation as a blackguard."

"Second only to my father," Blaine added, not bothering to hide the bitterness in his voice. "They hated each other."

Ifrem fixed Blaine with a look. "Enough to send an assassin to kill you?"

Blaine shrugged. "Would Pollard flinch at having a man killed? Probably not. Why he'd care about killing me when I'm already at the end of the world, I can't imagine."

"If Pollard wanted you dead, why did Prokief wait so long? He could have killed you when you were in Velant."

Blaine sighed. "No, he couldn't," he admitted, looking away. "Prokief told me that himself, one of the times he sent me to the Hole. Apparently, Merrill's order of exile specifically forbade Prokief from killing me." He grimaced. "Although Prokief certainly tried to make sure I had plenty of opportunity to die of 'natural causes.'"

Ifrem let out a low whistle. "Never knew you were quite so special, Mick. But you said it yourself—why now?"

Blaine's gaze returned to the arrow. "I don't know, Ifrem. But if I want to stay alive, I think we'd better find out."

CHAPTER
TWENTY-ONE

———

"BRING IN THOSE NETS, YOU SLACKING BASTARDS!"
Captain Darden's voice rang out over the windswept deck.

Connor bent his head to focus on the fish he was gibbing, but he stole another glance toward the rail, where teams of men put their backs into hauling bulging nets of fish onto the ship's sea-soaked deck.

It was Connor's second week aboard a herring buss and already he had the calluses to prove it. He glanced with grudging admiration toward where Blaine and Piran moved in rhythm with the dozens of other men who were on their shift at the net. Eight-hour shifts, by turn gibbing, sleeping, and hauling, all under a twilight sky where the sun would not rise for four more miserable months.

Connor had done little hard work and he knew it showed. As the third son of a minor noble, he'd had education but no inheritance prospects, and he had been appointed as Garnoc's assistant as soon as he was old enough for fostering. Lord Garnoc, a longtime friend of his family, had taken him on. It was a job that required discretion, but could hardly be considered physically taxing.

Salt water sloshed around Connor's feet and sea spray stung his eyes. Despite the oilcloth garments and heavy boots, he was wet to the skin and nearly frozen. His fingers were numb with cold and the repetitive motions of his job. *Grab a freezing cold, flopping fish. Chop the head, slit the gut, cut the tail, toss, repeat.* His hands were nicked in a dozen places where the sharp scales or the tip of his own blade had cut into the flesh, and the seawater burned with every touch.

He watched Blaine and Piran put their backs into the haul, jumping aside in the last minute as nearly a ton of fish slid and slithered across the deck. Blaine, or rather, "Mick," had adapted quite well to his convict/colonist life. *How long did it take him to toughen up? When he first got here, was he soft and useless... like me?* Blaine had said little about his life before Velant, though Connor was acquainted with the scandal from the gossip at court, and Engraham had talked some on the voyage to Edgeland. Connor felt guilty at his curiosity, especially as McFadden obviously wanted to leave his past buried.

While Piran, Verran, Kestel, and Dawe had become Connor's housemates, he couldn't help considering Blaine as his patron, just as Lord Garnoc had been. Patronage brought protection, and obligation. *Mick's given me his protection. He's gone out of his way to keep me—and my map—close by. But why?*

"Pick up the pace, or you'll get us all in trouble." The man next to Connor hissed a warning, and Connor dug his knife into the next fish, making quick work of it as his thoughts continued to churn.

So far, Mick's asked nothing of me except to go along on that godsforsaken trip onto the far ice, Connor thought. He shook his head, lost in thought as the fish flopped through his hands— chop, gut, cut, drop—and the gibbers' knives kept a steady rhythm on the barrelheads.

Blaine hadn't wanted Connor to go with the herring fleet. His own time on the water had come after a few years in Velant's mines had hardened him. But Connor had refused to stay behind. As one of the last new mouths to feed, Connor had felt guilty. In the end, Blaine had relented, though Connor had overheard Piran and Dawe betting on how long it would take Connor to retch once the boats left the bay. Ruefully, Connor admitted that Piran's bet of two candlemarks had won.

"Hope you like to eat fish better than you gib them," the man on Connor's right remarked. "If what the Council says is true, we'll be eating naught but fish 'til the sun rises."

Connor shrugged. "I'll eat what I have to. I've been hungry before." He didn't add that hunger hadn't been a part of his privileged upbringing. No, he'd learned those harsh lessons aboard the doomed ship that brought him to Edgeland. He'd discovered that when he was hungry enough, he could force himself to swallow maggoty bread and wash it down with brackish water. By comparison, salted herring was a lordly repast.

Uncomfortable as it was aboard the herring buss, Edgeland had one unquestioned benefit in Connor's mind. Since the night of the Great Fire, there had been no more mysterious blackouts, no gaps in his memory. Still, his guilt lingered, and when he lay awake in the middle of the night, fears of what might have happened in those missing candlemarks haunted him.

"Wonder what they're not telling us," the man to Connor's left said, never looking up from his work. Connor jumped, feeling a flash of guilt until he realized that the comment was not directed to him personally. The gibber's hands flew, processing twice as many fish as Connor could, even though Connor's speed had doubled since they'd left port. "Most of them that sit on the Council are merchants, ain't they? Mebbe with no ships comin' from back home, they want to charge us more for what they've got."

"Then why send us out to get more fish, if'n they want to charge us more for what we got already?" the first gibber argued. "You've got the brains of one of these herrings, Tad. They'd be tryin' to keep us from fishing more, so as to drive up the cost."

Tad shrugged ill-humoredly. "You mark my words; those Council folks got an angle. Everyone's got an angle."

Connor said nothing, wondering silently if Tad and the other gibbers realized that one of the Council members whom they suspected of profiteering was just a few feet away, cursing at a heavy net full of herring. A shrill whistle interrupted whatever Connor might have said.

"Unknown ship, off the port side!" the bowman shouted.

Gibbers stood, craning their necks, and haulers shifted for a better view. In the perpetual twilight, it was difficult to make out anything in detail. At first, there was just a darker shadow against an indigo sky, blocking the stars. As they drew closer, Connor could see the outline of a vessel that stood eerily silent in the water. It was a sailing vessel like the one that had brought him to Edgeland. Its sails hung in tatters, ragged streamers lashing the wind.

"Why innit moving?" Tad asked.

"What's it doing out here?" another man wondered aloud.

"Maybe it's got supplies from home!" A hopeful voice sounded from behind Connor.

"Or maybe it's full of more refugees, mouths to feed," a different, bitter voice replied.

"Hard to port!" Captain Darden's voice cut across the wind. "The rest of you, back to work!"

Unwilling to risk a bite from the overseer's lash, Connor hurried back to his seat. Though the fishermen were now all free men, Captain Darden's discipline at sea had not changed. A large man who went by the moniker of Plow paced up and down the deck, with an intimidating flail in one hand and a bullwhip in the other. Connor eyed Plow warily, and went back to his gibbing.

"Know why he's called Plow?" Tad asked.

Connor cast a watchful glance over his shoulder to make sure the overseer was out of hearing range. "No, why?"

Tad guffawed. "Because he's as big as the ox that pulls one, and dumb as two."

The man on Tad's other side elbowed him. "Enough. You'll scare the new guy." The speaker was an older man named Ev with gray-flecked hair and beard, whose short, muscular body made Connor guess he might have been a sailor before ill luck sent him to Velant.

"Truth is, since the prison closed, ain't no one got a taste of that bullwhip, though it makes a mighty fine crack in the air. Most of us pick up the pace when we hear it, havin' had a lick of it in the past," Ev added. "No one who's carrying his share gets the flail, either, not on Darden's ship. Can't say on the others."

Plow edged closer. Connor and the others bent to gibbing until Plow had shifted his attention elsewhere. The ship had changed course, and when Connor dared a glance seaward, he saw that the new ship was closer than it had been before.

Their own buss had picked up speed, and after the last haul, the nets had remained on board. In the half-light, Connor could see several of the other fishing boats converging around the larger ship, which made no move to elude them. The strange ship had a ghostly look to it, silhouetted against the horizon's faint light. The distance had closed enough for Connor to get a good look, yet he glimpsed no one aboard its decks, and no movement in the rigging save for the ragged canvas of its sails. He repressed a shiver that had nothing to do with the miserable weather or the seawater that sloshed around his ankles on the deck.

"Unknown ship, show your colors." Captain Darden's voice boomed through a speaking trumpet. By now, the herring buss's fishermen had idled at their tasks and stood for a better look. Even Plow strained to see what was going on. Darden's challenge echoed across the water. Aboard the ghost ship, nothing stirred. As their fishing boat drew closer, Connor glimpsed the name on the larger ship's prow, *Nomad*.

"*Nomad*, fly your colors and show your crew, or you will be boarded."

Aboard the herring boat, no one spoke. It was ridiculous, Connor thought, for a fishing boat to threaten a much larger ship. The *Nomad* appeared to be a merchant ship, made for hauling cargo, nearly the same size as the *Prowess*, on which Connor had sailed. No flag flew from its mast. It appeared to be adrift.

"*Nomad*, this is your final warning. Fly colors or be boarded."

Another few moments passed with no reply. Captain Darden turned his speaking trumpet toward the crew. "I need twenty volunteers to go aboard and see what we've got."

Blaine and Piran raised their hands. Connor did too, driven now by curiosity. So did half of the men on deck. Plow made his way through the men. "You, you, and you," he said, pointing to Blaine, Piran, and Connor. "Not you," Plow snarled at Tad. "And not you, old man," he sneered at Ev.

Captain Darden directed their boat closer to the ghost ship. Now Connor could really see the difference in size between the two craft. The silent ship had three masts, and at least three decks above its storage and ballast hold. Up close, it towered over the herring busses, which ringed it like insects.

"Send a few shafts into the hull," the captain called. "Give the men something to climb." He gestured toward the harpoons that the fishing boat carried, just in case they got lucky enough to spot a small whale.

Half a dozen fishermen took up harpoons and sent them flying into the hull of the derelict ship, linking their buss with the ship. The harpoon ropes formed two parallel lines from near the railing of the buss to the deck of the taller ship.

"Ready now, climb!"

Connor's eyes grew wide. He had expected a rope ladder, or some other, normal means of boarding. One of the volunteers stepped up onto the fishing boat's railing and leaped, catching the first line. With a bit of a swing, he caught the second, making his way up the side of the ship like one of the trained monkeys from the Cross-Sea Kingdoms Connor had once seen at court.

The next man was not so agile, and he fell from the third line into the sea, only to be hauled back into the fishing boat, soaked and shivering, to the catcalls and jeers of his fellow sailors.

Blaine was next, and then Piran, who came to the railing cursing loudly enough for all to hear. At last, it was Connor's turn, and he murmured a prayer to Yadin as he took his place on the railing. Swearing under his breath, Connor jumped. He closed his hands around the rough hemp of the harpoon line and swung, grasping the next line. Refusing to look down, or to afford the audience aboard the fishing boat a backward glance, Connor fixed his gaze on the next line, and then the next, until he'd swung and jumped for the railing of the anchored ship.

His arms were shaking and his grip faltered, but two pairs of strong hands grabbed him by the shoulders and hoisted him on board, tumbling him onto the deck like a net of fish. "I just want you to know, I helped you on board even though I had a bet you wouldn't make it," Piran grumbled as he gave Connor a hand up.

Aboard the *Nomad*, no other signs of life stirred. The slack lines of the ruined sails slapped against the masts; there were no other sounds beyond their own shuffling on deck.

"Let's split up and search." As usual, it was Blaine who stepped into the breach. "The men from our boat will search the crew and officer quarters." He looked to the dozen men who had also scrambled aboard on the starboard side of the *Nomad*. "You there, take the hold. See if there are supplies we can use." He looked to the two groups of fishermen who had climbed in from the port side. "Your group—take the second deck. See what you find. Last group, search on deck. We're looking for survivors, logbooks, supplies, and anything that gives us a clue about how the ship came to be here in this condition. Move sharp—we've still got fish to catch."

Connor suppressed a smile and shook his head. Blaine's fellow convicts might know little of his noble background, but they deferred to him nonetheless. On Blaine's part, taking charge seemed to be something that came naturally, and Connor wondered if Blaine was aware of it. From what he had seen of Blaine's determined efforts to blend into the background as "Mick," Connor guessed not.

As they headed down the narrow steps to the first deck that housed the crew and officer quarters, Connor steeled himself to stumble over corpses. Yet no bodies littered the crowded passageways, which gave no hint of violence or disease.

"Where in Raka did they all go?" Piran asked, putting into words what Connor bet they were all thinking.

"And why did they go anywhere?" one of the other men asked from behind Connor.

"That's what we're here to find out," Blaine muttered. "Piran and Connor, come with me. The rest of you, go in teams of two or three and make sure you open every cabin. No looting, mind you. Darden'll see we get a share of the spoils when we get back to port."

Blaine led them into the largest cabin at the bow of the ship. It was obviously the captain's quarters, though as a merchant vessel it was modest compared to what Connor had heard about on warships. Its furnishings, though sparse, befit a captain. A large desk, perfect for ledgers and bills of lading, sat in the center of the room. A smaller dining table and two campaign chairs sat near the mullioned glass panes at the stern. Between two support posts swung an empty rope hammock with a pillow and woolen blanket. Near the foot of the hammock was a brass-bound trunk.

Blaine began to rummage through the drawers of the main desk, while Piran began to work at the trunk's lock with the knife. At a loss for what else to do, Connor made a slow circle of the rest of the room. He opened a door, and found the captain's formal uniform hanging neatly inside, as well as a pair of polished high black boots and a heavy cloak.

Connor's boots crunched on glass and he looked down. A small oval frame lay on the floor, as if it had been knocked from one of the railed ledges in the wall. He bent to retrieve it, and found a small oil painting of a comely young woman and a small child. He smiled, remembering Garnoc and Millicent, imagining that the mysteriously departed captain of the *Nomad* had wanted to keep his loved ones near him during his long voyages.

"Looks like the ship's seen some rough seas since the crew vanished," Connor observed. Though the order in the captain's closets and drawers attested to a normally tidy nature, now that Connor looked around the room, the floor was littered with objects that looked to have fallen from the desk or table, or been tossed from the niches in the bulkhead. Glassware and dishes were tumbled against a corner of the room. As Connor completed his careful inspection, he found little else of note, save for a large tin of hard biscuits, obviously the captain's own stash, which was almost full.

Blaine had lowered himself into the captain's chair, and sat at the desk with a leather-bound journal in front of him. "According to this, the *Nomad* set sail from Aquesta in the Lesser Kingdoms just after the defeat in Donderath. The captain refers to the 'Great Fire' and talks about the night the magic died. His family was killed in the fire, which apparently leveled quite a bit of the countryside."

Blaine paused, and his finger slipped down along the lines of cramped, neat writing. "Apparently he intended to dock at Castle Reach, but found the city no better off. He says here that they set sail for the Cross-Sea Kingdoms on the Far Shores, but that doesn't make any sense." He looked from Piran and Connor. "How in Esthrane's name would the ship have ended up here if he meant to reach the Far Shores?"

Piran shrugged. "I've heard there's a powerful current that goes from the open ocean off of Donderath north toward Edgeland. We don't know how long the ship's been adrift. If the current took it, and there was no one at the wheel, the ship might have just been swept here like driftwood."

Blaine flipped through several pages of the captain's log,

then frowned and skipped ahead, only to flip back. "There are only two weeks' worth of entries. Whatever went wrong must have happened not long after they set out." He flipped to the end of the journal.

"*Second of Tormun, sixth hour by the stars. I fear the stress of knowing that our homeland is in ruins hangs heavy on my crew and passengers. Despite the efforts of the guards, fights have become a constant and tempers are short. It cannot help matters that our supplies are inferior. Several of the barrels of grain looted from a warehouse near the docks after the Great Fire were badly spoiled, but we had no choice except to mill the damaged grain and make the best of it. Afterward, whether because of the bad grain or the rough seas, quite a few of the passengers took sick.*"

Blaine turned the page. "Listen to this. *Fourth of Tormun, tenth hour. I fear we are cursed. The winds fight us, and the sea has been violent, so that we have made hardly any progress these last few days. Belowdecks, many are sick, some so much so that they imagine visions and terrors that are not real, and must be confined or bound. Our food supplies are indeed poor quality. Some of the men report a strange burning in their hands and feet, and a few have taken fits, writhing and foaming at the mouth. Yadin save us, but I fear for this ship.*"

Blaine let out a long breath as he flipped to the last entry. "*Surely we have angered the gods. The passengers and my crew flee from terrors only they can see. Many have jumped or thrown men overboard, while others have killed themselves or those around them in their panic. Only the first mate, the navigator, and I appear to be spared from the madness, but what can three do against three hundred? I was accosted by one of the crew, a man quite out of his wits, who came at me so violently with a belaying pin that I expected to die, and might have except that a fit took him and sent him scrabbling on the deck like a beast with a broken back. I have made every offering in my knowledge to appease Yadin, but it is not enough. Charrot save us; we are bound for the Sea of Souls.*"

Blaine closed the journal. "That's the last entry."

Pounding on the door made them all jump. "McFadden, you've got to see this," a man said, poking his head into the room. Blaine and the others followed the man down into the hold.

"We've found no bodies," the man explained. "Rager told me that a ship like this should have a dinghy or two, and they're gone, so some of them might have thought they'd row for land, but I can't imagine why. Especially when we found all this," he said, and opened the door to the ship's galley.

"They had dried meat and cheese enough to last for weeks, along with plenty of salted fish and grog. Barrels of wheat, too, which should have kept them, even though some of it went a bit funny."

"Something about the wheat looked funny?" Piran echoed with a strange look on his face.

"Aye," their guide explained. "It smells off, and some of the grains are dark."

"Show me," Piran said with sudden fierceness.

Baffled, Blaine and Connor exchanged questioning glances. They followed the fisherman into a storage room filled with sacks of grain. Piran fell to his knees beside one of the sacks and stabbed it with his knife, letting the grain pour out into his cupped hands. Connor was close enough to see that about half of the kernels were a dark brown, instead of their normal light gold.

Piran let out a string of curses that were potent even for him. He looked up at Blaine and Connor with a pained expression. "Bad grain," he said. "Ergot. I saw this once on campaign.

Something turns the humours of the grain poisonous. All the things in the captain's journal—the fits, madness, visions—the poison in the grain does that." He shook his head. "Poor blokes never knew what hit them. If they didn't die from the fits, they likely pitched over the side."

"But the captain said he and the officers weren't affected," Blaine countered.

Connor remembered something he had seen in the captain's quarters. "The biscuits!"

"What?" Blaine and Piran both turned toward him.

"There was a partially eaten tin of hard biscuits in the captain's quarters. What if he and the officers didn't eat the spoiled grain? If they had their own supplies, they wouldn't have caught the madness."

Blaine drew a deep breath. "If you're right, then it's likely the *Nomad*'s crew died or deserted her not long after that last entry in the journal." He shook his head. "With the crew gone mad, the captain and his officers were dead men."

Their fisherman guide looked on in horror. "What do we do, then? There's food and drink aboard, and we need both back home."

"We can't take the grain," Piran said, standing and dusting off his hands. "That's for certain, or we'll end up like they did."

"Piran's right," Blaine said. "But the other supplies should be salvageable. I'll talk to Darden, explain why we need to throw the grain overboard. He'll make sure there's no trouble about it."

"What about the ship?" Connor hadn't realized he had spoken aloud until they turned toward him. "What we've seen of it, the ship itself isn't damaged. I hate to leave it out here."

"We found fresh sails down below," the fisherman who had led them to the galley replied. "So if anyone's of a mind to rig new sails, it can be done."

Blaine nodded. "Let's make a report to Darden. I daresay that among the four fishing boats, we've got enough sailors to get the *Nomad* back to Bay-town." He looked to the fisherman. "Go tell the others not to eat any breads or biscuits that they find, before we bring trouble onto our own boats."

"Right," the man said, and left them alone in the galley.

Piran looked at Blaine. "You know, a ship like this could make it back to Donderath," he said quietly.

Blaine's expression was unreadable. "I thought of that, too."

CHAPTER
TWENTY-TWO

▄▄▄

"EVER THOUGHT YOU'D BE SEEING EDGELAND from the deck of a ship like this?" Piran shouted above the wind in the *Nomad*'s sails as they neared the port of Skalgerston Bay.

Blaine shook his head. "Never thought I'd be on board any ship bigger than a fishing buss again." He glanced around, looking for Connor, who was nowhere to be seen. *He didn't come to Edgeland as a convict*, Blaine thought. *He doesn't understand how sweet it is to be on deck like a free man.*

A crowd mulled near the docks, trying to figure out what to make of the ghost ship. Blaine and Piran hurried down the gangplank and shouldered through the mob, with Connor scrambling behind them. Ifrem hailed them from the doorway to the Crooked House.

"Brought back quite a fish there," he said with a nod toward the *Nomad*.

"Question is—do we keep it or throw it back?" Blaine replied.

Ifrem nodded, and Blaine knew that the tavern master recognized the real question: *Now that some of us can leave, do we? Who goes and who stays? And if we leave, where do we go?*

"A ship like that can hold four or five hundred people," Ifrem mused quietly. "That could take quite a strain off the colony, if people were of a mind to leave."

"And go where?" Blaine asked, watching the wind billow in the *Nomad*'s sails.

"If things are as bad as Engraham and Connor told us, Donderath may be in need of some sturdy colonists."

Blaine met his gaze. "Go back?"

"Go home."

"Home didn't want us, remember?"

It was Ifrem's turn to shrug. "King Merrill didn't want us. Merrill is dead."

Blaine looked away, uncomfortable with the feelings that stirred at Ifrem's words. "The only home I'm anxious to see is the homestead, and my bed. That's where I'll be if the Council has a mind to discuss anything. Just make sure they leave me time to get some sleep. Otherwise, I'll be crankier than usual."

"How could we tell?" Ifrem cracked a smile. But by that time, Blaine had rejoined Piran and Connor in flagging down a cart.

Blaine, Piran, and Connor climbed into the back of a farmer's wagon and covered themselves with the feed sacks and horse blankets they found there. No one was in the mood for conversation, and Blaine wedged himself into a space between hay bales where he was sheltered from the wind and relatively safe from falling overboard. Exhausted, he leaned against the bales and dozed.

"Hey, Mick, wake up. We're home." Piran's voice cut through the fog of sleep as a strong hand shook Blaine's shoulder. Blaine blinked, trying to clear his head. They were back at the homestead. The small house was lit up, offering the promise of warmth and shelter. Blaine jumped down from the wagon.

"Did you catch anything?" Kestel greeted them merrily, standing in the doorway, her cloak clutched around her.

"Bigger than you can imagine," Piran said with a grin. "We caught ourselves a whole ship!"

Dawe ambled forward and helped to take their heavy cloaks and fishing gear. "A ship?"

"An abandoned merchant ship," Connor supplied, stripping off his coat and stumbling as he tried to remove his boots. "No one on board."

"What did you do with it?" Verran wanted to know from where he stood in the doorway to the small sitting room.

Piran shrugged. "Sailed it back to port. I guess what happens now is up to the Council," he said with a look toward Blaine.

"Don't look at me," Blaine said, his mood still off from the dream. "I'm just one lone voice, not the whole damn Council."

"Well, we've been busy while you were out trawling," Kestel said, hustling them into the sitting room. A cheery fire warmed the room, and on the hearth, in the embers, a cauldron held what smelled like venison stew. Verran helped her fetch bowls, which she filled, and Dawe brought two freshly baked loaves of bread from the kitchen.

"Sit. Eat." Kestel was trying and failing to suppress an ear-to-ear grin, with a look Blaine had come to associate with a successful scheme. "And we've got company."

"Company?" Blaine asked between gulps of stew.

"That would be me." Blaine and the others turned. Arin Grimur, their vampire rescuer, stood in the doorway.

Blaine looked questioningly at Kestel, then from Grimur down to the bowl in front of him. "Is that where the venison came from?"

Grimur gave a slight smile that revealed just the tips of his elongated eyeteeth. "I felt it was only right to bring a gift when I came to visit. Some of the trappers are willing to give me blood in exchange for my protection. Between them and the deer, I fed well enough to keep me satisfied until I return to my home."

"We certainly wouldn't want you feeling peckish," Piran muttered, unconsciously raising a hand to rub his neck.

To Blaine's amazement, Grimur chuckled. "I assure you, I pose no threat. You're quite well protected." At that, Grimur's gaze slid for a moment to rest on Connor, who looked away.

I wonder if Connor understands his ties to that vampire back in Donderath any better than we do, Blaine mused.

"Arin came down to study the maps with us," Kestel said, taking a seat between Blaine and Grimur as if Blaine's lack of a hearty welcome had not escaped her notice.

"Maps?" Blaine asked with a warning glance.

"I persuaded Ifrem to let us borrow his map. We put it alongside Connor's and took a good look at that obsidian disk of his. I think we've figured out something—something important," Kestel said, ignoring Blaine's wary look.

"Which is?" Piran's voice sounded as unconvinced as Blaine's.

"We think we know how we might be able to restore the magic," Verran replied.

When they had finished eating, Kestel and Dawe cleared away the dishes. Verran brought the chairs in the room closer to circle the table, while Grimur spread the maps open and laid Connor's obsidian pendant in the center of Ifrem's map.

"Here's the map of Edgeland Ifrem had," Kestel said, a hint of glee in her voice. "And here's Connor's map of Donderath. Do you see anything alike?"

Blaine frowned and studied the two maps. "The same 'u'-shaped symbols that Ifrem said stood for magic places and null places. Some odd gibberish that no one seems to understand." He looked up at Kestel. "Am I missing something?"

Kestel's smile was triumphant. "Verran's the one who spotted it. Look at what happens if you put the two maps on top of each other."

"If you do that, you won't be able to see the one on the bottom. Big deal," Piran said irritably.

Kestel rolled her eyes and gave an exaggerated sigh. Grimur did not move, but it seemed to Blaine that the vampire actually repressed a smile.

"Don't be so literal, Piran," Kestel said. She reached for a gossamer jumble that had been set to one side. Blaine had assumed she had cast aside a shawl, and he frowned when Kestel picked up a fine silk scarf that was nearly see-through. She stretched the delicate fabric tight between her hands and held it over the Edgeland map. "Now do you notice something?" Kestel looked pointedly at Blaine.

Marked on the fine silk in dark strokes were the symbols of magic and null. And it was clear at a glance that those symbols on the silk matched the symbols on the Edgeland map.

"What's on the scarf lines up with the map. Of course they do, if you copied them. Hard to see why you'd sacrifice a silk scarf for that," Blaine replied.

Kestel moved the scarf, still held taut between her hands, until it was over the Donderath map. "Connor, you're a clever man," she said with a glance to tell Blaine that the comment was a gentle dig at him for missing...something. "Tell me what you see."

Connor leaned forward. "The pattern is the same from map to map," he said, looking to Kestel for corroboration. She let one end of the scarf fly into the air in celebration.

"Yes!" She waved Blaine and Connor closer to the maps. "The pattern of power and null is identical on these maps of Donderath and Edgeland. Which means…"

"That you think those nodes are a key to the missing magic," Blaine finished for her.

"Exactly." She brought out another drawing, this one on yellowed parchment. Blaine moved closer for a better look at the new drawing. "Grimur was kind enough to bring us something else," Kestel said. "Look at this."

"What is it?' Blaine strained for a good look, but saw only a network of regular lines, almost like a spider's web.

"They're called 'meridians.'" Everyone turned to look at Grimur. "That drawing was made by Elos Torinth, a mage who was a contemporary of Valtyr."

"The one who made the maps," Blaine replied.

Grimur inclined his head in acknowledgment. "Exactly. Torinth believed that the meridians were the places where wild magic, *visithara*, was strongest. The meridians and their power are a natural force, according to Torinth, and in addition to the lines, there are also 'wells' and 'deserts,' where power is much stronger or weaker."

"The nodes," Kestel murmured. "Places of power and no-power."

"Yes." Grimur gestured toward the yellowed parchment. "But there is also something very interesting about the parchment that you haven't noticed. On it are marked the locations of the twelve old noble houses, the manors—actually, fortresses—of the original Council of Nobles who supported Donderath's first king."

The others crowded closer for a better look. "Quillarth, Rhystorp, Doranset, Glenreith," Kestel read, with a glance to Blaine as she read the name of his family's manor. She read the other names, a familiar litany from court. Kestel paused. "There are thirteen names. But only twelve old houses."

Grimur nodded. "Quillarth was not originally the castle of the king. King Merrill's line won the crown in the Lowland Insurrection three hundred years ago. Mirdalur, the thirteenth location, was the fortress—castle—of King Hougen, Donderath's first real king."

Blaine frowned. "I've never heard of Mirdalur."

"That's because it was destroyed a long time ago," Grimur said, a wistfulness touching his voice that made Blaine think perhaps Grimur remembered the manor from his long existence. "During the war between Donderath and Vellanaj. Quillarth Castle replaced it."

Grimur gave a knowing smile. "This map has another secret. Do you see a pattern in the locations of the old houses?"

Dawe bent closer, intrigued by the puzzle. "Well, the old houses are clearly built along the meridians," he mused. "Not too close to the 'wells' or to the 'deserts' of power. But they don't match the pattern of the nodes on the other maps." He straightened. "I give up." The others nodded in agreement.

Grimur leaned down and traced several lines with his fingers. "Imagine lines connecting these houses in this way," he said. His touch made a crude stick figure.

Verran frowned. "That's pretty close to the way Charrot's constellation looks in the sky—according to the astrologers, anyhow," he said.

Grimur smiled as if pleased with a prize student. "Exactly. Now look at this," he said, turning the map a half twist and connecting more dots with a finger-stroke.

"Esthrane's stars," Kestel said.

"And this," Grimur added, tracing invisible lines for the third time.

"Torven," Piran said. "Any fisherman worth his salt can sketch those star figures."

"The connection to the constellations could just be luck," Blaine said, struggling to dampen his growing irritation. He had the feeling Grimur was leading them somewhere, and Blaine didn't like being led in the dark. "I understand building the old houses on the meridians. They probably had mages telling them where it would be 'auspicious.' But those star figures are hard enough to see in the sky—they take more beer than imagination, if you ask me. It's all in what you want to see."

Grimur regarded him for a few seconds in silence. Blaine had the uncomfortable feeling that the vampire took more meaning from his outburst than Blaine had intended. "Perhaps," Grimur replied mildly. "And yet, I can attest that in the days of the old houses, astrologers were consulted as frequently as mages, and the omens they read from the stars guided the hand of the king."

"So you don't think it's coincidence," Kestel supplied.

"No," Grimur said. "I don't."

"What does all this have to do with making magic usable again?" Blaine snapped. "And why tell us? We're not mages."

"Because the configuration of fortresses created back when King Hougen took the throne changed magic on the Continent— and I'd bet, here in Edgeland and elsewhere. Before Hougen's time, there were few if any mages of great power. Magic was mostly of the seer and hedge witch variety. After Hougen, we saw powerful mages arise, and magic became an art of war."

"You think something about the fortresses and the meridians 'created' magic as we know it?" Blaine challenged.

Grimur shrugged. " 'Created' is perhaps too strong a word. Perhaps 'harnessed' or 'channeled' might be more accurate. But something changed after Hougen with the role magic played on the Continent—until this last battle between Donderath and Meroven."

"Word came to Quillarth Castle right before I left that Meroven had attacked the noble houses before attacking the king," Connor said. "If at least some of the noble houses were linked, somehow, to the magic itself—"

"It would have been like snuffing out a candle," Verran finished. "Those Meroven sots probably never had any idea that by attacking the old manors they were destroying the very magic they themselves were using."

"This is all very interesting," Blaine said, "but how does it change anything? If what Connor says is true, the manors were destroyed. What does all this information matter if it can't fix the problem?"

"Maybe it can." Grimur met Blaine's gaze.

"How?"

Grimur pointed to a spot on the map. "This is where Mirdalur's ruins still stand. King Hougen's castle. All of the meridians from the other original noble houses pass through Mirdalur, and Mirdalur is the head of the figure that looks like Charrot's constellation. I believe Mirdalur could be the key to putting things right."

"You don't seem to get what I've been saying," Blaine retorted. "None of us have the power to do what you're expecting. And we're in Edgeland, not in Donderath. We're a world away."

"We have a ship," Piran said quietly. "We could get there, if it would make a difference."

Grimur went to a leather bag that sat against the wall. "There is another, older magic that plays a part in this," he said. "I have had this book for more than a hundred years, but until I saw Connor's pendant and the writing on the map that the pendant decoded, I did not know what I held." He walked around the table with the map, toward Blaine. "I have spent the last four nights using the pendant to translate what was written. It's a journal by a mage of great renown, Archus Quintrel. He wrote down what had been an oral tradition among mages until then, the secret to how the magic was channeled."

"Quintrel," Connor murmured, and everyone turned to look at him. "A relation to Vigus Quintrel?"

Grimur nodded. "Vigus Quintrel would be a direct descendant—in name as well as in power."

"Lanyon Penhallow told me to find Vigus Quintrel." Connor paused. "But by that time, Quintrel had vanished."

"Penhallow would have known about the link between Vigus and his great-great-grandfather," Grimur replied. "What Archus Quintrel recorded in his journal tells me that the magic of the meridians was harnessed by an older, more powerful magic—blood."

Kestel caught her breath. "Sacrifices?"

Grimur gave a disquieting smile. "No, m'lady. Not blood shed but blood bound and blood stirred by magic to become a greater magic. Archus Quintrel's journal says that the rise of magic was part of a compact between Hougen and his most trusted nobles. They met at Mirdalur and made a blood oath, binding themselves and their descendants to defend the kingdom. Their blood was the crucible and the seal for whatever the mages did that night. And from that moment on, magic as we knew it stirred on the Continent."

"If the magic was somehow bound to the blood of the old nobles and the king…" Verran began.

"And Meroven struck first at the noble houses, not knowing about the origin of magic," Connor supplied, "then if they wiped out the old families, the magic died with them."

Blaine felt as if he had been punched in the gut. Though he

had heard Connor's story about the fall of Donderath more than once, he had not allowed himself to think about what a strike by Meroven against the noble houses would have really meant. Now, his mind supplied the images that his heart did not want to see. His own home, Glenreith, in ruins, and his loved ones, Mari, Judith, and Carr, dead. Carensa's home, Rhystorp, leveled, and Carensa among the dead.

Kestel laid a hand on his arm. "Mick? You've gone pale. Do you need to sit down?"

Blaine tried to catch his breath, and found his chest tight. "It's just that... my family..."

Grimur's expression softened. "The death of magic doesn't mean that everyone was 'wiped out,' as Connor put it. King Hougen was clever. From what I'm able to piece together, the magic had two sources: the blood oath of the nobles, and anchors to the power that were set within the manor houses themselves, on the meridians."

He paused. "The blood inheritance could have been growing weaker for generations. It wouldn't be surprising if several of the old houses failed to produce male heirs or saw their heirs die in battle without a suitable successor. That might be enough to break the bond. The combined bond between the manor houses and the blood oath might have been enough to sustain the magic, but when Meroven struck at the manors, it could have been the tipping point."

Grimur looked at Blaine. "The blood oath would have passed down through the oldest surviving son, the inheritor of the title. We must be willing to consider the idea that all of the blood heirs may be dead, except for one."

Everyone was staring at Blaine. "Except for you, Mick," Piran said quietly.

Blaine still felt the shock of Grimur's announcement. He

struggled to clear his thoughts. "But...I lost the title when I was condemned. Merrill himself stripped me of it. It would have passed to my brother, Carr, when he came of age."

"I doubt the magic would have been concerned with technicalities," Grimur said. "Legalities don't change blood. To the magic, you would have remained the heir, since you are still alive."

"Meroven might have struck at the noble houses without even knowing about the magic." Dawe snorted. "They probably didn't have any idea about where the magic came from."

"But it would explain the backlash, wouldn't it?" Kestel murmured. "If they struck at a target that was bound up in the source of their magic itself."

"It means there's a chance that you could set it right," Grimur said. "The fact that the magic 'died' tells us that something has broken the old bonds. To do that, from what this book suggests, it would take a combination of destroying the manor houses and having the original pure bloodlines die out to the point where the power of the oath was weakened."

Grimur stared down at the book in his hands. "Unfortunately, bloodlines are more fragile than you might imagine. Infidelity, a barren wife, or an impotent husband can mean that the 'heir' is not the real heir of the blood. A round of plague or pox can wipe out entire families." He shook his head. "You may well be the last surviving Lord of the Blood from the original thirteen houses."

"This is crazy!" Blaine protested. "My magic was no good except in a brawl. I don't know about blood and oaths and meridians."

"It may require nothing more than your presence to reactivate the magic," Grimur replied. "Or perhaps, a token of your blood. The *kruvgaldur*, or blood bond, has not been weakened by the 'death' of magic. It was the *kruvgaldur* that spoke to me of Connor's bond with Penhallow," he said with a nod toward Connor. "And I suspect that through the *kruvgaldur*, Penhallow may yet speak with Connor, even at this distance."

They all turned to look at Connor, who reddened.

"Is that true? Can you communicate with Penhallow, even from here?" Piran demanded.

"It's not what I'd call 'communication,'" Connor said awkwardly. "I get dreams that... aren't my own. On the edge of waking and sleeping, sometimes I think I can hear his voice. I had convinced myself I was imagining it," he said with a sour look toward Grimur.

"And what does your master tell you?" Piran said with an edge in his voice.

Connor reddened further. "Penhallow was not my 'master.' I served Lord Garnoc, who was a fine master. Garnoc had long been Penhallow's eyes and ears at court."

"You mean, his spy," Piran said.

Connor hesitated, and then nodded. "Yes, his spy. When Garnoc got too old to move easily back and forth to Rodestead House, I went in his place."

Kestel smiled at him encouragingly. "Court wouldn't exist without spies," she said, and turned a withering glance on Piran, who shrugged.

"What do you see in these 'dreams'?" Grimur asked.

"I see castle ruins," Connor said slowly, struggling to recall. "Very old." He gave a nervous smile. "I assumed Penhallow was giving me a way to find him if I ever came back."

"Tell me about the ruins," Grimur replied.

"It had broken walls, and walls inside of walls. The ruins stand on a rocky hill. There's a forest, and a deep valley with a river. The base of the tower has an odd shape—like a five-pointed star."

Grimur nodded. "You've seen what's left of Mirdalur. It was rebuilt after the first time it fell, and then was destroyed again. Over the years, mages held their rituals there, sensing the power. For a while, they preserved the site as best they could. Over time, they abandoned the place. No one's used it for decades. I would say that Penhallow knows the site is important. Perhaps he's come to the same suspicions that we have, and if so, he knows exactly where to find a living Lord of the Blood." He met Blaine's gaze.

"I've been tracking the magic storms," Grimur continued. "They're getting stronger, and coming closer together. I believe they're moving along the meridians here in Edgeland. Baytown lies at the nexus of several meridians. How many storms like the one that hit you out on the ice would it take to wipe out the Edgeland colony?"

Not many, Blaine thought. *Maybe just one if it were big enough. And the bastard knows it. He's forcing my hand, damn him.* "I'd rather not find out," Blaine replied.

"You may be the only one who can fix it, Lord McFadden," Grimur said, and Blaine did not pick up any hint of irony in his use of Blaine's long-discarded title. "You could return to Donderath on the salvaged 'ghost' ship. Go to Mirdalur. If we're right, you might be able to set the magic right, stop the storms."

"Donderath? Who said anything about going to Donderath?" Blaine protested.

Grimur shrugged. "We don't know much about how the blood-oath magic worked. But we do know it was done at Mirdalur. That seems like the logical place to attempt to bring the magic back." Grimur met his eyes. "But be careful. If our guess is right and you are the last Lord of the Blood, if you die, the magic may die with you—permanently."

CHAPTER
TWENTY-THREE

BLAINE THRASHED AWAKE AS THE POUNDING ON his door grew louder. It took a moment to shake himself clear of the nightmares from Velant. In the near-darkness, another moment passed before he could orient himself. He took a deep breath as he recognized his surroundings as one of the guest rooms at the Crooked House.

"Mick, we need you out here. By the gods, wake up!" Ifrem's voice was insistent, and from his tone, Blaine gathered that the innkeeper had been shouting for him for a while without result.

Groggily, Blaine swung his legs out of bed. It was cold enough that he had slept in his clothes; good thing, since he had thrown the thin blankets to the floor during his dream-induced thrashing. He made his way to the door and slid back the bolt.

"If it hadn't been my own door, I'd have been of a mind to break it down," Ifrem greeted him ill-humoredly. "For all the noise you make, you're damnably hard to rouse."

Blaine grunted, still blinking to wake up. "What can possibly be important enough for this?" he grumbled. "If the inn were on fire, I'd smell smoke."

"Get your cloak," Ifrem said, pushing Blaine back into his room and toward the peg on the wall that held his coat. "There are riots in Bay-town, and we need every man we've got to settle them."

Blaine splashed cold water on his face from a basin near the door and wiped off the water with a rough towel. In the distance, he could hear muffled shouts. "It's damn cold and the middle of the night. What in Torven's name is important enough to fight about that it can't wait until morning?"

Ifrem shrugged. He looked tired, and his short-trimmed beard seemed grayer than before. The Council had been meeting daily since the herring crews sailed the ghost ship *Nomad* back into port, and the decision was made for a colonist crew to steer the ship back to Donderath. "Piran didn't say. He just stopped long enough to make a request for able-bodied men to help keep the peace." He snorted. "Since that sure didn't mean me, I figured he was looking for you."

The meetings had kept Blaine in Bay-town much of the last few weeks, and while he was grateful for Ifrem's hospitality, he missed his own bed at the homestead. He took his sword belt down from where it hung next to his cloak and belted it on, then swung his cloak across his shoulders. "All right. I'm awake. Where am I supposed to go?"

"Piran was rallying men out back near the stable. Said the trouble was down near the Green."

Muttering curses under his breath, Blaine headed down the back stairs. The winter wind was like a slap in the face as he opened the door, driving clear any lingering sleepiness. Men were streaming toward the open area by the stable, coming between the buildings and through the alleyways. From the rolling gait of more than a few of the men, Blaine guessed that many of Ifrem's patrons had also heeded Piran's call to arms.

Blaine joined the crowd, standing near the back. By now a group of about fifty men were assembled, and Piran stood on top of a wooden cask to address them.

"We've got trouble down on the Green, and we need to put an end to it," shouted Piran, his breath clouding in the freezing air. "Not sure what started it, but we've got to keep it from getting worse. You on the right," he said to a group of men standing a bit apart from the crowd. "Form a line along the storefronts. We'll have scarce supplies enough without any looting going on." He looked to the others. "The rest of you, break up fights, and try not to get pulled into them. The Town Guards are already on their way, but they may need backup. Let's go!"

Blaine could tell Piran had spotted him, and sure enough, when Piran jumped down from the cask, he made a straight line over to Blaine. "Since when are you the constable?" Blaine asked as they began to run toward the village green.

"I guess you could say the constable deputized me. He was heading toward the Green with the Guards, and told me to round up dependable men to even the odds."

"And so you went to the Crooked House? That's your idea of dependable men?"

Piran grinned. "I know the regulars, and I depend on them to have my back in a fight. Hence, 'dependable.'"

They rounded a corner, and found that the fight had moved from the Green and was sprawling down the main street in Bay-town and spilling into its alleys. Blaine and Piran had kept the peace in the Crooked House enough nights to have experience breaking up fights, and with a glance and a shrug, they parted ways, wading into the nearest altercations to separate the brawlers.

"Hey, now! Break it up!" Blaine shouted, shouldering between two men who were trading punches. Before he'd even gotten close, he could smell the whiskey on their breath. A punch grazed Blaine's jaw, and he ducked, landing a blow of his own that sent the man down on his ass in the snow. Rounding on the other man just in time to block a punch meant for his nose, Blaine socked the second man in the gut, doubling him over.

"What in Raka is this about?" Blaine asked, striding over to yank the first man out of the snow. He could hear the second fighter retching in the gutter.

"It ain't right for the ones who are taking that bleedin' ship back home to clean us out of food when things are scarce," the man snapped, unrepentant even though the fight had left him with a bloody gash above one eyebrow and a rapidly blackening eye.

"Who told you that?" Blaine demanded.

The man shrugged. "Heard it around town," he said with a baleful glare.

Blaine shook him free, and stepped back from both of them. "That's what this whole thing is about?"

Another shrug. "There's been talk. The way I figure it, sending people away on the ship might mean fewer mouths to feed here, but what about all the food they'll take with them? What happens if there's naught for the ones left behind? We won't be getting no more ships from Donderath, that's for sure." He wiped his split lip with the sleeve of his sweater.

Blaine sighed. This was an issue the Council itself had already debated and thought was concluded. The *Nomad* had been abandoned early enough in its journey that it was nearly completely stocked, even when the damaged grain was destroyed. Since the wheat rot had only affected a few barrels, replacing them would cause no shortage in Edgeland. Barrels of fresh water and casks of salted herring, something the colonists could easily replace, would be all that was needed to supply the *Nomad* for its journey home. Simple enough, he thought, but probably not something the brawler and his sparring partner wanted to hear.

"All they'll be taking from here is water and herring, and Bay-town isn't running short of either," Blaine replied. "Now, get out of here before the Town Guards get here and start knocking heads together."

The two men limped off in separate directions, and with a sigh, Blaine headed into another nearby fray. He spotted Piran across the way. Piran was scuffling with a broad-shouldered man, trying to pull him off a lanky fellow Blaine recognized as one of the colonists who had successfully applied for passage on the *Nomad*. The ship had room to carry four hundred passengers and crew, and Blaine had wondered how many colonists would jump for a chance to return to Donderath. To his surprise, they barely had enough applicants to fill the ship. Apparently, he thought, he wasn't the only colonist who had finally come to terms with Edgeland being home.

From what Blaine could see, a few hundred men and women were surging their way. Shouting and catcalling, they were in an ugly mood, and although the Town Guards were breaking up fights, the crowd showed no interest in breaking up.

Blaine grabbed a tin bucket and a ladle and scrambled atop the roof of a small shed. He began to bang the bucket with the ladle and shout until the mob quieted and everyone had turned to stare at the madman on the roof.

"You'll not be losing anything except herring and water when the *Nomad* sails for Donderath," Blaine shouted. His throat constricted at the freezing-cold air, and he fought the urge to cough. "If that's what you're fighting about, go home."

"Fine for you to say," shouted a young man from the front of the crowd. "You're one of them goin' on the boat. Takin' all the food—what about them that's stayin' behind?"

Piran had walked up behind the speaker and smacked the man in the back of the head. "Didn't you hear the man? Naught but herring and water—you think you'll miss any of that?" The young man spun to strike back, then thought better of it as he got a look at Piran's size and ready fist.

"Herring and water, folks," Blaine repeated. "And a long, cold voyage back to gods only knows what. You didn't want to be on the boat, and the passengers aren't taking anything you can't replace. Go home."

There were a few shouts from the rear of the crowd, and widespread muttering, but with the combination of Blaine's interruption and the heavy-handed tactics of the Town Guards cracking down on brawlers, the riot's momentum had dwindled to nothing. Under the watchful eyes of the Guards, the colonists began to disperse. Piran fell in with the Guards, rooting out stragglers and encouraging the dawdlers to be on their way, herding them down the street and breaking up the crowd. Gradually, they disappeared around a corner.

Blaine tossed the bucket and ladle down to the ground and started to climb down. He had just turned to let himself down from the shed's roof when he heard a rush of air and felt something hard and heavy slam into his right temple. He fell backward into the drifted snow, and before he could clear his head, a black-robed man came at him, brandishing a wicked-looking knife.

Blaine could feel blood streaming down the side of his face. Whatever had hit him had been hard enough to nearly knock him out, and the best he could do was to raise an arm to fend off his attacker. The knife bit down, cutting deep into his left forearm, as the black-robed man came at him. Before Blaine could reach his sword, the robed man struck again, swinging the blade toward Blaine's chest.

Blaine kicked his attacker in the thigh and rolled. His head swam as he struggled to his feet, and his vision blurred, threatening to black him out. He managed to draw his sword, and the attacker's knife clanged against it as Blaine blocked his swing.

The robed man moved with the sure-footed confidence of a trained fighter, and his single-minded focus left no doubt that he intended to finish Blaine. From the folds of the man's robe, a second knife appeared, and the man came at him again, striking with both blades.

Blaine staggered backward, still struggling to keep his footing as his head pounded. He blinked rapidly, trying to clear his vision, and blocked one blade with his sword. The other blade scored a gash on his left shoulder.

Forcing himself to stay on his feet, Blaine landed several pounding strikes with his sword, but he knew the blow to his head had badly compromised his ability to fight. His attacker danced out of range of his blade, waiting for him to tire, counting on the head wound to force Blaine into a fatal error.

It was hard to think with the pounding in his head, and his vision now showed him a double figure, making it damnably difficult to anticipate the man's next move. Piran and the Guards were long out of sight, leaving Blaine on his own. He was bleeding freely, his blood marking the snow with crimson drops, and his attacker waited with a hunter's instinct for his quarry to make the wrong move.

The robed man sprang forward, coupling speed with momentum sufficient to knock Blaine off his feet. Blaine struck at him with his sword, but the man had gotten close enough for the tip of his blade to graze Blaine's chest.

The attacker drew back his arm, preparing to slash the blade across Blaine's throat, when there was a blur of motion, and the robed man was yanked free with such violence that Blaine heard bones snap and a strangled yelp that was suddenly silenced. Blaine blinked, trying to clear his vision to make out the bulky shape in the shadows.

Grimur stood a few paces away, holding the limp form of a man by the throat. The angle of the man's head made it plain that his spine had been broken. Blaine got to his feet, not quite sure whether he had been rescued or had just changed foes.

Before Blaine could speak, Grimur dropped the body to the ground, sank to his haunches, and grabbed one of the corpse's arms, ripping back the clothing as if it were paper. Grimur sank his fangs into the man's wrist, tearing into the dead flesh, and drinking deeply of the fresh blood. Blaine swayed on his feet, his sword clutched two-handed in front of him, knowing that if Grimur chose to attack him, he stood no chance at all of defending himself.

Finally, Grimur dropped the dead man's arm. His lips were bright crimson, a stark contrast to skin as pale as the snow. Grimur seemed to be deep in thought, and Blaine wondered if he had totally forgotten his presence. After a moment, Grimur stood and regarded Blaine with a trace of amusement.

"Put the sword down, lad," Grimur said. "I've no want for your blood, and if I did, that pig-sticker wouldn't stop me." Shaking with the effort to remain on his feet, Blaine lowered his sword, but did not sheathe it.

"Thanks," Blaine said, his teeth chattering with cold. "But now we have no idea why he was after me."

Grimur chuckled. "Not entirely true. It's possible to read much from the blood, especially from a fresh kill." He licked his lips, and the crimson stain vanished.

"Where in the gods' name have you been?" Piran said as he came running around the corner, only to skid to a stop. His gaze flickered between Blaine, still standing with his sword drawn, Grimur, and the corpse of the black-robed man.

"You have nothing to fear... now," Grimur said. "But we'd best get Mick inside before he falls down. He's lost a lot of blood," he said. His tone was solicitous, but there was just a hint of a pause, enough for Blaine to imagine a lingering hunger.

Blaine sheathed his sword, and swayed enough that he stumbled, nearly falling. Piran got under his good arm. Together, they made their way to the back door of the Crooked House, but by that time, Blaine was weaving in and out of consciousness and Piran was nearly dragging him as dead weight.

Blaine heard Ifrem's voice, though it seemed to come from a distance. Piran was talking loud and fast. Blaine slumped to the floor. An instant later, strong hands lifted him like a child, and Blaine stopped fighting the merciful tide of darkness.

"He's comin' 'round," Piran said. Blaine groaned. The pounding in his head had lessened but not vanished altogether, and it seemed every beat of his heart echoed in his throbbing skull. His body ached and his left arm was immobilized. Just trying to move his arm caused pain, both in the shoulder and in the arm itself.

"Easy there," Piran said. "We only just got you to stop bleeding. The healer was rather cross; I don't fancy having to tell her you started it back up again."

Blaine managed to open his eyes. He was in a room at the Crooked House. Ifrem stood against one wall, and Grimur sat in a chair in the corner. Piran brought Blaine a tin cup and helped him sit enough to take a sip of whiskey.

"Do you remember what happened?" Piran asked.

Blaine sank back against the mattress and closed his eyes.

His voice, when he spoke, was raw, not entirely from the whiskey. "I got clipped in the head by something, a rock, maybe. When I fell, a man in a black robe attacked me. Never said a word, but he meant to kill me. Would have, too, if Grimur hadn't gotten him first."

There was a moment of silence, then Grimur spoke. "I stopped by the homestead to work with Kestel on the maps. She was worried about you, and I said I'd come find you in town. Just as I located you, I found you at, shall we say, a disadvantage. I was happy to even the odds."

Blaine was unable to repress a shudder at the memory of the sound of snapping bone and the wheezing last breath of the robed attacker. "Thank you," he managed.

"As it happened, I was able to get a bit of information from the man before his blood cooled," Grimur went on. "He was a paid assassin, sent from Donderath. Prokief made some use of him, but he'd been put in place here for one purpose: to kill you."

At that, Blaine made the effort to open his eyes again. "Why?" he rasped. Piran held the cup for him, and Blaine took another sip of the whiskey, wishing it would hurry and ease the throbbing in his head.

Grimur shrugged. "The man didn't know and didn't care. He wasn't a stranger to this kind of work. But he did wonder why anyone would pay gold to kill a convict, and why it was important enough to send him to the end of the world to do it."

Blaine drew a sharp breath. "Who sent him?"

"Vedran Pollard."

"Blimey." Piran's voice showed his surprise. "Is that what it's like, bein' a lord? You all spend your time trying to kill each other?"

"That's my experience, anyhow," Blaine muttered.

Grimur chuckled. Blaine struggled to sit up, and Piran

propped him up with pillows. His left arm and shoulder were tightly bound with bandages, and his arm was in a sling. Ifrem offered him a linen sack with ice in it, which did little to help his aching head.

"Pollard again," Ifrem said. "What's Pollard got against you to be worth sending someone all the way up here?"

Blaine knew Ifrem was thinking about the papers they had found in Prokief's chest. He tried to shrug, and thought better of it as pain lanced through his shoulder. Piran was ready with the whiskey, and this time, Blaine tossed it back.

"I wish I knew. There's no way Pollard could have known about the *Nomad*, and without it, no way for me to ever come home."

"Might he be after your lands?" Grimur asked. "No matter what excuse nobles give, in my experience, when there's a fight, it's usually over land."

Blaine grimaced. "The exile took my title, so technically, I'm no longer lord of Glenreith." Another possibility sent a chill down his spine. *In time, the title would have passed to Carr. Unless something's already happened to him—*

"Kings and decrees can't change blood," Grimur said quietly. "You remain a descendant of the original thirteen. You're still a Lord of the Blood."

"And Pollard isn't, on account of how he's a bastard," Piran mused. "So why would he care?"

Grimur stirred from his seat. "Pollard himself might not. But others may. My fellow mages would have been quite interested in you, had they realized that magic was about to be snuffed out."

"Yeah, but Pollard isn't a mage," Piran countered. "Is he?"

"Not that I've ever heard," Blaine replied.

"Mages themselves rarely have the gold to send assassins to the edge of the world," Grimur answered. "*Talishte* do."

CHAPTER
TWENTY-FOUR

———

BEING AT SEA ISN'T SO BAD—WITHOUT THE CHAINS or the herring," Piran observed. He stood next to Blaine on the deck of the *Nomad*. Blaine let the wind blow back through his dark-chestnut hair, and brushed a stray strand out of his eyes, which were almost the color of the sea. He smiled.

"Not so bad," Blaine repeated. "Gods! When you can walk on deck a free man and you're not dripping with herring blood, the sea is actually...beautiful." He tore his gaze away from the ocean and slid a glance toward Piran. "I still can't believe the lot of you volunteered to come with me."

"And miss our chance to be back at court for the winter ball?" Kestel quipped. Kestel's voice carried above the wind. Blaine turned to see her behind him. The wind whipped her red hair into a cloud around her face, and her green eyes sparkled with excitement.

"You masterminded the whole thing, didn't you?"

Kestel smiled. "It didn't hurt that Engraham jumped at the chance to get the homestead now that he's got his mother to take care of. They'll take good care of it, keep the animals healthy, mind the gardens."

"And if we don't come back in three years, it's theirs to keep," Blaine finished for her. "Honestly, Kestel, you drive a better deal than Mama Jean."

Kestel made a show of preening at the compliment. "Just another among my many talents," she said, her eyes twinkling.

Blaine was quiet for a moment, his gaze drawn back to the sea. Over four hundred men and women had volunteered to return to Donderath, enough to ease the burden on the colony's food supply. Few of the longtime colonists had chosen to go back. Most of the volunteers came from the newest convicts. Perhaps they still had hope that the people they left behind had not forgotten them, or maybe memories of Donderath were fresher in their minds. Those who had finally carved out a place for themselves on Edgeland's ice had chosen to stay behind. Blaine would have been content to stay with them.

Even the salt spray in the wind seemed different away from Edgeland. For one thing, it was no longer freezing cold. *Could the air of freedom really be so different?* he wondered. They would be back in Castle Reach very soon. In the pit of his stomach, Blaine felt a knot that mere seasickness could not explain away. Dread. Anticipation. Grief. Curiosity. The knot of emotions sat like lead in his gut.

Kestel laid a hand on his arm. "You've grown quieter the longer we're gone from Edgeland, Mick," she said.

"Still trying to figure out how I feel about coming back," he said, his voice roughened by the wind and perhaps by something else. "I truly don't know whether I would have done it if Grimur hadn't forced my hand."

"I'd have liked it better if he had come with us," Piran grumbled. "Convenient of him to stay behind."

"It would have been difficult for him to travel safely," Blaine replied, shaking his head. "And perhaps, since he was as much an exile as we were, he didn't relish running into old mages or other vampires. But I agree; it would be nice to have a true mage among us."

"It's worth the whole voyage just to have day and night again," Kestel said, pulling her shawl closer against the wind. "By Yadin's chalice! I had almost forgotten that the normal world has sunrise and sunset every day. I think I'll make it a point to watch both, every day, until I'm an old lady. I don't think I'll ever take them for granted again."

Blaine chuckled. "Where are Dawe and Verran? Don't tell me Verran's playing for coins again?"

Kestel shrugged. "Probably. He and Dawe were scheming on how to provision our expedition and just where in Castle Reach to loot first."

Blaine looked at her, slightly aghast. "Loot?"

Again, a shrug. "If Connor's account of the Great Fire is true, the castle and the city are a ruin. By this time, I imagine anything of value's already been stolen," Kestel replied.

"Maybe Dawe didn't tell you," Piran said, "but he's been scribbling again. Tinkering with things, making plans for some of his new machines. He started as soon as we began talking about coming back. Whenever the ship's been steady enough to let him draw, he's been working out dimensions for a new-fangled crossbow contraption. Thinks we'll need it if Donderath's gone back to brigands and warlords."

"Brigands and warlords," Blaine repeated, feeling sick. "That bad?"

"Connor seems to think it was a possibility," Kestel said. "Even so, he thinks we should check out what's left of Quillarth Castle, in case any of his contacts can help us out."

"How about any of your contacts?" Blaine asked, meeting Kestel's eyes.

She gave an enigmatic smile. "Perhaps." Kestel squinted, looking toward the horizon. "How is it that it only took us forty days to go from Donderath to Velant, but now that we're going back, it's been fifty days and we aren't in port yet?"

Piran did not take his gaze off the horizon. "The winds. The current. And we lost several days going around what might have been a magic storm."

Blaine shrugged. "Let's hope our captain and the navigator remember the way home."

"Land, ho!" A voice from the rigging above them rang out. Sailors and passengers alike ran to the railings for a look. Blaine strained to make out the thin fringe of land barely visible on the hazy horizon.

The deck behind them grew more crowded as the ship sailed onward. Gradually, the mirage-like distant blue at the edge of sight grew more identifiable as they neared. Kestel clung to Blaine's arm in excitement, unconcerned as the stiff wind tangled her red curls.

"Can you really see Donderath?" Dawe had edged up behind them. He peered over Blaine's head toward where the sky met the water, searching for the glimpse of land.

"You'll have to tell me about it," Verran grumbled. "I can't see over everyone else."

"Not much to look at yet," Dawe replied. "How long do you reckon it'll take us to put into port?"

"Several candlemarks, I'd imagine," Blaine said. "I'm guessing the closer we get, the slower the captain'll have to go, in case there are wrecks just below the surface. I'd hate to come this far and founder."

Blaine looked around at the excited passengers who crowded to the rails, hoping for their first sight of the home that had once exiled them. *We've had the benefit of hearing Connor's stories in detail*, he thought. *How much do the rest of these people understand that Donderath isn't the kingdom they left behind?* Blaine looked at the faces flushed with the anticipation of a homecoming most had never believed possible. It wasn't hard to guess their thoughts. Reunions with loved ones. Pleasures long denied in Edgeland's relative deprivation. A homecoming to places and people sorely missed. For some, perhaps, even vengeance.

What happens when they realize the extent of the damage? That there is no home for them to go back to? Blaine winced at his own thoughts. Throughout his exile, Blaine had kept a mental image of Glenreith as home. As much as he had hated his father, he had loved the manor and his siblings, his aunt Judith, and the retainers who were, in their own way, a part of the family. He'd nurtured an idea of what Glenreith would be like without his father's dark moods and cruel humors.

Grimur believes that I'm the last Lord of the Blood. What if I'm also the last of my family?

Connor sprawled in his hammock down in the hold. He did not join the rush to the stairs or to the porthole to see out. He knew what the shores of home would look like. The image of Donderath's burning coastline was seared forever in his memory. Bad as it had been when the castle and the port city were engulfed by flames, Connor guessed that what remained would be even worse. Gutted, blackened shells of buildings, looted by desperate survivors. A shadow of a once-thriving kingdom, now feral and lawless. He had seen Dawe's drawings of a small, compact crossbow, even handled the prototype Dawe had secreted on board. He feared that they would need Dawe's contraptions, and perhaps even more fearsome weapons, before they could reclaim Donderath as home.

Though he had done his best to prepare his new friends for the harsh reality, Connor doubted they could imagine the scope of the destruction he had witnessed. The thriving, sophisticated kingdom that had banished his fellow passengers was gone. In its place would be a different, desperate place. Connor had stopped praying to the gods the night of the Great Fire. Certainly on that night, the gods had stopped listening to prayers. He could only hope that courage and stubbornness would suffice.

"Ain't you anxious to see home again, son?" A voice broke into Connor's dreary thoughts. Connor looked up to see a wiry man who he guessed might be his father's age. The man looked as if he were no stranger to hard work, with gnarled hands and sinewy arms.

"I saw it burn," Connor replied. "I know what it looks like."

The man squinted at him. "You're one of the men they fished out of the sea, ain't ya?"

"Yes."

The man cocked his head. "If it's so bad, why'd you leave Edgeland? Why come back?"

"Because it's home," Connor lied. *How do I explain the truth? Because one of my new friends might be able to save the world? Because a vampire master is haunting my dreams?* Unthinkingly, he ran one hand up his other forearm, over the small, white scars that were the traces of the messages he had borne to Penhallow. *Because a man who's been dead for centuries whispers in my mind?* Madness, all of it, Connor knew. But the lie seemed to satisfy the man, who nodded, then continued.

"Aye. I've been in Edgeland for nearly fifteen years, had it better than some, I wager. Lived through Velant. Earned my Ticket. Made a life for myself. But it wasn't ever home. I'm not so young anymore. Mostly worn out. I didn't want to be buried in the ice, if you know what I mean. Here at least, when I go, it'll be home soil around me. That matters," he said with a knowing expression and a nod. "You're young now, but in time, you'll understand what I mean." And with that, the older man wandered back to his place by the porthole.

Connor swayed in his hammock with the ship's motion. In his mind's eye, the hold filled with the desperate refugees who had crowded together in fear and shock on the night Donderath fell. The smell of smoke followed them out to sea, clinging to their hair and clothing long after they had left the coast behind them. He could see individual faces, etched in his memory though they were total strangers. All of them dead now.

Another memory came back to him, of the addled seer on the voyage. *The exiled man must return*, she had said, echoing what Alsibeth, the woman who read omens and bells at the Rooster and Pig, had told him.

What did Alsibeth and the other woman see? Gods, I wish I knew, Connor thought, running his hands back through his hair. *With the rogue magic, nowhere is safe, not even Edgeland. Donderath is definitely not safe. And here I am, a companion of thieves, assassins, and murderers, and a conscript to the whims of vampires. How did I get myself into this? Maybe it would have been better if I had gone down with the* Prowess.

Connor threw himself back in his hammock and closed his eyes. In the recesses of his thoughts, he could hear Penhallow's voice. *Bring them to me*, the voice whispered. *You have done well. But there is more, much more to be done. Bring your friends to me. I have need of them.*

Garnoc had trusted Penhallow, or what passed for trust in the cynical and jaded climate of Donderath's court. Penhallow had warned him the night of Donderath's fall, entrusted him with the pendant. *Penhallow made me the guardian of the pen-*

dant, even though to someone like him, I'm just another sort of servant. Grimur might know what we should do next, but Grimur didn't come back with us. How are we supposed to find Penhallow, let alone Vigus Quintrel? Connor wondered. *What are Penhallow's real reasons?* Connor could not help the suspicions that lingered in his mind. *What if he has his own agenda for Blaine McFadden, the last Lord of the Blood? And what if I'm the tool to betray Blaine like I may have betrayed Garnoc?*

Since they had set sail from Edgeland, Connor's dreams had been dark. *What if whoever made the holes in my memories is waiting for me? How can I stop myself from betraying my friends if I don't even know what happened to me?*

Connor had no answers, and the questions made his head ache. He heard the pounding of footsteps on the stairs, marking the return of the passengers who had gone on deck, and perhaps of Blaine and the others. Rather than betray their confidence or confide his fears, Connor closed his eyes and feigned sleep.

CHAPTER TWENTY-FIVE

"I GUESS YOU REALLY DIDN'T MAKE THE WHOLE thing up," Blaine said to Connor as they stood on the rubble-strewn street that had once been a main thoroughfare in Castle Reach. They had lagged behind, neither the first nor the last to disembark, hoping to provide some cover for themselves among the milling passengers.

"You were hoping?"

Blaine nodded. "Part of me definitely hoped that you were lying through your teeth."

"Sorry to disappoint."

Blaine stood looking around at the once-familiar landscape that now bore no resemblance to the place he had left behind. A hush had fallen over the *Nomad*'s passengers when the ship pulled into port and the enormity of the damage became apparent. Blaine realized now that his imagination, bleak as it had been, had resisted the truth of Connor's account.

Much of Castle Reach's once-thriving wharfside had burned to the ground. Few of the buildings had walls intact that were even as high as a man's waist. Where higher remnants still stood, they bore the scars of flames, roofless and hollow. It was clear that many of the ships in harbor when the fires came had never sailed. Half-sunken hulls and masts jutted above the waters of the bay, forming a treacherous reef.

The faces of the *Nomad*'s passengers twisted in pain and confusion as reality set in. Some collapsed to their knees, sobbing, holding their heads in their hands. A few of the men began to curse, kicking at chunks of rock and bits of scorched wood with all their might, as if the savagery of their wishes might undo the past. The rest wandered like ghosts in the eerie silence, pale and shaken, eyes wide with sorrow and disbelief.

Blaine led his small group through the maze of stupefied passengers and their meager bundles of possessions, until they could talk safely without being overheard. "Let's head for the Rooster and Pig first," Blaine said.

"Here's the key Engraham sent for you," Connor said, pressing the rough metal into Blaine's hand.

Blaine weighed the heavy piece of iron. "Does he really think his tavern would be secure from looters?"

Connor shrugged. "It's a basement with one entrance and a locked iron trapdoor. Even if the tavern burned to the ground, the room shouldn't have been touched. As for looters, I imagine they came for his ale and whiskey, but Engraham traded all of that for our passage to Edgeland."

"We'll see soon enough," Blaine said.

Connor gave him a quizzical look. "Do you need me to lead the way?"

Blaine shook his head. "No. I remember it," he replied, not needing to add that the road he recalled was far different from the charred and littered streets they now walked.

Blaine's hand fell to the pommel of the sword that hung at his hip. Before leaving Edgeland, they had gathered enough of the weapons looted from Prokief's soldiers and the ghost ship to outfit themselves against highwaymen. Blaine carried an officer's sword, and had a sharp dirk in his boot. Piran had claimed a two-handed sword, which hung in a back scabbard, as well as a collection of knives with wicked blades secured on a baldric across his chest. Dawe had unwrapped the small crossbow and held it casually in his right hand, pointed toward the ground. Verran had no visible weapons, but Blaine knew that the thief's real skill lay in his ability to outrun any opponent and scale nearly any wall. Kestel, too, wore no apparent weapons, but her knowing smile gave Blaine to understand that she was armed to the teeth in her own way. Connor wore another "borrowed" sword, a well-balanced soldier's broadsword that he said was a good fit in grip and heft. *It's probably best there aren't any soldiers about*, Blaine thought. *We might be taken for brigands ourselves.*

Once they had gone just a block in from the wharves, the noise of their fellow passengers faded. If anything, the shadowed alleys and ginnels looked bleaker than the ravaged wharf front. While the docks had been empty of visible inhabitants, the narrow streets held a vestige of the traffic that had once made it one of the busiest ports in Donderath. But where Castle Reach's dockside area on an average day would have teemed with people of all descriptions from ports of many kingdoms, the hard-worn inhabitants they now passed looked uniformly bedraggled and wary.

Gone were the merchants with their carts, hawking their wares. For the first time, Blaine realized he could actually smell the sea air in Castle Reach. In the city's glory days, food vendors had crowded cheek and jowl against each other, warring for the coins of the sailors and traders. Now the city smelled of decay, and occasionally, when the wind shifted, Blaine caught a whiff of charred wood.

"Stay together," Piran growled. Piran had moved up to the front of the group, and his expression had taken on an edgy watchfulness Blaine had rarely seen in Edgeland. Out of all of them, Piran was the only one with military experience, and now that he had seen the ruination of Donderath for himself, Blaine found himself very happy to have Piran with him.

"We're here," Blaine announced as they reached the spot where the Rooster and Pig used to stand.

"Too bad the pub isn't," Kestel observed.

The building that once housed the Rooster and Pig had collapsed in a heap of half-burned timbers and fire-scarred shingles. Its falling roof had blown out the glass of its small windows, leaving them vacant and staring, like the empty sockets of a skull.

"What now?" Dawe asked. He had raised his crossbow and stood with his back to his friends, watching the street.

"We dig," Verran replied.

"Maybe not," Connor said. "Follow me."

Connor dodged around fallen roof timbers and the debris that littered the narrow streets and into a darkened ginnel behind the wreckage of the pub. He pushed a broken fence gate out of the way to slip between the charred outer wall of the pub and the building that stood next to it, edging sideways until he came to a spot midway between the alley behind the pub and the street in front of it. "Here," he said, pointing down.

Blaine looked down at the stained bricks that lined the narrow walkway. Connor kicked aside a piece of shingle and shards of broken pottery, refuse that might have predated the pub's destruction. He bent down and began to remove bricks from their place. Connor looked up at Blaine. "Give me a hand."

The space was too narrow for anyone but the two men closest to the spot to remove the bricks. When Connor and Blaine had finished, they had cleared a small rectangle that was roughly the width of a man's shoulders. Beneath the bricks was a dented metal door. Blaine fished Engraham's key from his pocket and jiggled it in the stiff lock. The click seemed to echo from the ginnel's walls, and both Dawe and Piran looked up, watchful for intruders. Together, Blaine and Connor wrested the heavy door open.

"Shit," Piran muttered. He fumbled in a pouch at his belt and pulled out flint and steel. "Anybody got something we can use as a torch?"

"Way ahead of you," Kestel said. She handed him a thick piece of wood wrapped with rags. "Can't guarantee what it'll smell like when you light it, but I'm betting it'll burn just fine."

"Nice," Piran said, taking it from her and nurturing sparks until the rags caught on fire with the distinct smell of stale beer and old urine. "I'll go in first." He glanced at Connor. "Where did you say this goes?"

"Engraham told me it was an escape route for his gaming rooms, in case any of his players' enemies came looking for them. Right under us is a holding room, where people could hide until someone came out here to let them out. There should be a passage back under the pub, and a door that opens into the cellars. What we're looking for should be in the passageway," Connor said.

"Why was a barkeep with a noble father stockpiling food and weapons?" Blaine asked as Piran started down into the opening.

Connor shrugged. "The way Engraham tells it, his 'sources' started to doubt that Donderath would win the war. I guess people were plenty scared that Meroven might invade. If the city came under attack—a normal attack—Engraham intended to stand his ground."

"And he left everything here when he fled?" Kestel asked.

"He sent all his liquor, ale, and wine to the *Prowess*, and took only what he could carry, once he realized the only way out was by ship," Connor replied.

"It's empty. Come on down." Piran's voice echoed from the cellar.

"Someone should stand guard up here," Dawe said. "The rest of you go. I'll stay."

Blaine led the way, followed by Connor. Verran climbed nimbly down the narrow ladder, and paused to give Kestel a hand. Blaine smiled. He doubted Kestel needed any assistance from Verran, but she accepted his proffered hand graciously.

"Even with the torch, I can hardly see anything," Piran grumbled. "But from the cobwebs, it doesn't seem like anyone else has been here recently."

The corridor widened a bit, and Blaine's shoulders no longer brushed against both walls. Piran stopped beside an alcove that had been carved into the rock. "Hold up. There's something here." He passed the torch to Blaine and hunkered down to have a look at three solid-looking wooden boxes.

"They're painted black, so I almost missed them," Piran said. "Locked, too." He swore as he looked around. "You don't happen to have a key for them, too, do you?" he said with a glance toward Blaine.

"I don't think we'll need a key." Verran's voice carried from the back of the corridor, and he began to edge his way forward, squeezing past the rest of them. He took one look at the locks and smiled. "No wonder your friend went to the trouble of hiding them down here. Those locks wouldn't keep any self-respecting thief out for very long."

Verran flexed his hands and drummed his fingers in the air, limbering them up. He reached for a small pouch on his belt and withdrew a few curiously shaped bits of metal. Verran bent to his work, sliding the thin, oddly angled tools into the lock and closing his eyes, gently jiggling the tools until he heard sounds that only he recognized. He twisted the tools once more, and the lock on the first box dropped free.

"Haven't lost my touch," Verran said with satisfaction. He began to work on the second lock, which yielded with less effort than the first. The third lock secured the largest box. Verran's lip twisted as he prodded at it.

"Hurry up," Piran urged. "I don't like it down here."

"If I break off part of a tool in the lock, we'll have to break the box," Verran replied without looking up. "From what I can see, it's solid and heavy. I don't fancy trying to drag it out of here."

Minutes dragged by as they waited in silence. Blaine fidgeted, disliking the feel of the cobwebs that traced ghostly fingers across his face. In the distance, he could hear the shuffling of vermin. Verran swore under his breath, manipulating the balky lock with a jewel smith's patience.

Piran cast a nervous glance over his shoulder. "We don't know where these cellars go. I can hear things back there. We need to get out of here."

"Scared of the dark, Pir?" Verran jibed without taking his eyes off the lock. "I thought Velant would have cured you of that."

Piran answered with a long and creative curse that impugned both Verran's mother's honor and his family tree.

Verran clucked his tongue. "You used that one last week, Rowse. Gotta come up with some new curses if you want them to still sting a bit."

"I'll sting your hide if you don't get moving," Piran muttered.

Verran had just opened his mouth to respond when Piran

was suddenly yanked backward into the darkness of the corridor. A feral growl rumbled from the narrow tunnel walls, and they could hear the sound of clawed feet scrabbling against the stone floor. Piran's scream echoed, rapidly growing more distant.

"Grab the torch," Blaine yelled. "After him!"

"What's going on?" Dawe called from the street.

"Something's got Piran. Get down here!" Blaine shouted, drawing his sword. Without waiting, he and Connor plunged into the darkness.

"What do you think it was?" Connor's voice seemed loud, even though he had nearly whispered.

"Could be anything," Blaine replied. The torch illuminated the cellar passageway in front of them, but Blaine had no idea how many branching tunnels might connect. Castle Reach was an old city, long populated. He'd heard tell that a warren of old cellars, caverns, and aqueducts ran beneath the city, many of them long forgotten by any but thieves, vagrants, and vermin. "Piran!" Blaine shouted. "Where are you?"

"Down here!" Piran's voice was ahead of them, but in the echoes of the brick and stone corridors, it was difficult to judge how far away he might be. Piran gave a cry, and they could hear the distant clang of steel against stone.

Blaine and Connor quickened their pace. Behind them, they heard more footsteps. "It's us," Dawe called softly. "We're right behind you."

A battle in these narrow tunnels would not go well, Blaine thought. He'd drawn his sword in the large cellar, but the tunnel was barely wider than his shoulders, and its roof was low enough in places that his head brushed the ceiling. Fighting with swords in this space would be suicidal.

The tunnel widened. Blaine and Connor skidded to a stop in a vaulted cellar chamber. Blaine slowly turned from left to right, letting the torchlight illuminate the dusty room. A groan sounded in front of them, in the deep shadows toward the far end of the cellar. Connor started forward, but Blaine put a hand on his arm and gave a warning shake of his head.

Dawe came up behind him, with Kestel a step farther back. Dawe's crossbow was at the ready, and Kestel gripped daggers in both hands. That meant Verran had stuck with his task. Just as well; combat wasn't Verran's strong point.

Dawe and Kestel fanned out, one to the left and the other to the right, moving silently as spirits. Blaine and Connor chanced a few steps forward. A warning growl rumbled from the shadows, louder than before.

"Go!" Blaine shouted, beginning to run toward the sound. As he ran, the torch illuminated the back corner of the cellar. Something had obviously made its lair here for quite a while, judging from the bones and rags that littered the filthy floor. Then Blaine caught sight of Piran's prone body, and a glimpse of two red eyes that shone with more than the light of his torch.

The thing behind Piran leaped forward. Blaine heard the twang of Dawe's crossbow, felt the still air stir as the quarrel whizzed past him and thunked into the chest of the beast. It did not slow the attack. Blaine swung with his full might, while Connor braced himself, holding his sword two-handed like a pike for the thing to spit itself when it landed. Connor ducked, shielding his head even as he used his body to brace the sword in place.

With a wild growl, the beast twisted in midair, so that Connor's sword caught it in the front shoulder and not full in the belly. Blaine hacked at the thing with enough force to kill a man, but the beast's thick, rough fur fought against his blade. The torch cast a wavering light, but it showed enough to make Blaine's blood run cold.

The thing that had attacked Piran was wolflike, but larger than any wolf Blaine had ever seen. It was closer to the size of a small horse, thickly muscled, with powerful haunches and a filthy, matted coat of coarse hair. Most of it was black as the shadows, with streaks of gray. The fur would make it difficult to reach vulnerable flesh below, though two of Dawe's quarrels now stuck out from the creature's hide.

The creature had a wide, blocky head with strong jaws. Powerful front feet ended in curled claws. Foam flecked its jaws, and the front of its chest was stained red with new blood. Piran's. Enraged, Blaine gave a cry and lunged at it, with his sword held two-handed, shoulder height, aiming for the heart.

Two silver streaks twinkled in the firelight, then dug hilt-deep into the beast's neck. Kestel's daggers. As Blaine surged forward, Connor shifted his position and thrust his two-handed sword up and forward, anticipating the beast's attempt to move out of Blaine's way. Two more quarrels flew through the air, one catching the beast in the throat and the other lodging in its muzzle.

The beast gave a cry that was more chilling than a wolf's howl, and its blood-red eyes glowed with rage. With surprising dexterity, it evaded Connor's sword, twisting as Blaine sank his blade so that the tip slid along the rib cage instead of penetrating. With a cuff of its massive paw, it swept Connor out of the way and into a wall, his sword skittering in the opposite direction. Blaine tried to yank his blade free, but it was snarled in the beast's matted fur. He was a breath too slow, stumbling wildly as the beast turned sharply, snapping its fangs just shy of Blaine's shoulder.

"Over here!" Dawe shouted to distract the thing. A large rock cracked against the beast's forehead, and it howled again, turning away from Blaine. Kestel had drawn another blade, but she had also fallen back a few paces. A rock the size of a large apple smacked between the beast's eyes, and the creature turned on her with fury.

"Get Piran!" Dawe shouted as he sent another quarrel toward the beast's heart. Connor had regained his sword and scrambled to his feet.

Blaine sized up what he could see of the room in the flickering torchlight. Two more corridors branched from the chamber, leading into darkness. The beast could easily follow them. To Blaine's dismay, Piran had not yet moved, and he was unarmed, no doubt having lost his blade somewhere down the corridor in the grip of the creature. Blaine would not be able to drag Piran to the exit without sacrificing his friends in the effort.

Dawe had drawn the creature's attention, but it was advancing more quickly than he could reload. Kestel's barrage of stones angered the beast but did not look likely to strike a killing blow. Blaine caught Connor's eye and nodded. Together, they roared a battle cry and ran at the thing's haunches, striking to disable it. Blaine went high, sinking his sword deep into the creature's hip, while Connor dove low, slicing his blade across where the beast's hamstrings should be.

The beast gave a maddened howl and reared back, cuffing Blaine and sending him sprawling. As he fell, he glimpsed movement in the shadows, and the dark shape of a man briefly silhouetted by the torchlight. Blaine hit the ground hard, and it knocked the breath out of him. Connor cried out in alarm as the beast went after him. Dawe and Kestel were quickly running out of ammunition, and Blaine doubted that Kestel had the speed to get close enough with her blade. Blaine shot a glance toward Piran. Piran had not moved, and Blaine spotted a dark stain that looked like blood on his shoulder. *We crossed an ocean to die here*, Blaine thought, rallying the energy to reach his feet again.

Connor was doing his best to hold off the beast with his sword. Though dark blood ran from cuts on the thing's forelegs, the blade did not strike deep enough to slow the creature. Kestel's rocks pounded the beast's head and shoulders. A direct hit slowed the beast, a glancing blow enraged it, but the creature showed no sign of tiring. Dawe sent another quarrel into the beast's shoulder, and it screamed in rage.

Out of the corner of his eye, Blaine saw a dark blur. For a heartbeat, he thought it was a trick of the light; then the shadow moved nearly faster than sight could track. The beast reared up, howling in pain, and a dark-clad figure drove a wide blade deep between the thing's ribs. The creature snapped at the attacker, who hung on to the sword's grip with unnatural strength, even when the beast raked it with its long claws. Blaine expected the attacker to fall, but to his amazement, their new defender clung to the sword even as dark blood streamed from bone-deep gashes on its back.

With a wild bellow, the beast reared again. Its new assailant jerked the sword free, dodging the creature's claws, and swung. The sword whistled through the air, coming down hard on the beast's neck. Bone crunched under the two-handed swing, and then the blade was free, and the head rolled to one side while the beast tottered and collapsed.

In the faltering torchlight, Blaine caught a glimpse of their defender. A man clad in black, with equally dark hair that fell shoulder-length. Blaine expected him to collapse at any moment, given the damage he had taken from the creature, but instead, the man looked up, straight at Blaine. "Your friend is dying. I can help, but we need to get out of here now."

Blaine scrambled to his feet, feeling the ache of new bruises and strained muscles. "Who are you?" he asked, making his way as quickly as possible to where Piran lay. "And what was that thing?"

"That 'thing' was a barghest," the man replied. "And I'm Geir, your guide."

"Guide?" Dawe was standing again, and his crossbow was leveled at Geir's chest. "Who says we need a guide?" Kestel had recovered both of her knives and stood next to Dawe.

One side of Geir's mouth twitched in a sardonic half smile. "Why don't you ask Connor?"

"Do you know him, Connor?" Kestel asked, a dangerous edge of suspicion in her voice.

A muscle twitched in Connor's jaw, as if he were angrily clenching his teeth. "Yes. He's one of Penhallow's."

Geir smiled. "Your blood called me. Our master knew you had returned to Donderath as soon as you set foot on shore. He's anxious to see you—and your companions."

Blaine knelt next to Piran. Piran was breathing, but his breath was coming fast and shallow, and blood soaked his shoulder. Gently, Blaine pushed back the torn remnant of Piran's shirt to see the damage. He grimaced. The barghest's fangs had left deep puncture wounds and an open gash. Piran groaned but did not open his eyes.

"Can you save him?" Blaine looked back to meet Geir's gaze.

"If we hurry."

Blaine glanced to Dawe. "Get Verran."

"I'm here." Verran's voice sounded behind them. He was carrying a sack that bulged and rattled.

"And go where?" Kestel challenged.

"Somewhere much safer than here, unless you like the wildlife," Geir replied.

Blaine used bits of Piran's torn shirt and jacket to bandage his wound. It slowed the flow of blood, but would to nothing to stave off infection. Blaine glanced at Dawe. "Come on. Piran's a heavy bastard. It'll take both of us to move him."

Geir sheathed his sword and crossed the room before Dawe could move. In one fluid motion he bent to pick up Piran, lifting him into his arms as if Piran were a child. "We'd best get moving, if you want to save your friend."

Dawe retrieved the torch and came up beside Blaine as they followed Geir. "This could be a trap," he murmured.

Blaine glared at Connor. "Maybe it already was."

"And you're just going along with it?"

Blaine shrugged. "What choice do we have? Piran needs a healer. What are the chances we can find one in time to help?"

"How do we know this guy isn't just hungry? Maybe Geir set the barghest on us."

"No one controls a barghest," Geir said from the front of the small party. "Not even the *talishte*." He paused. "And as for your other question, I've fed well already."

"How were you able to kill the barghest?" Dawe asked. "We weren't having any luck."

"Iron blade," Geir replied in a tone that suggested it was common knowledge. "The iron itself is poison to some beings."

"Where exactly are we going?" Blaine asked.

"Somewhere safe," Geir replied. "Unless you'd rather blunder around in the tunnels. There are all kinds of scavengers— human and otherwise—since the Great Fire. Can't guarantee your welcome."

"And what kind of guarantee can you make us where we're going?" Blaine asked.

"The protection of my master, Lanyon Penhallow. Our quarters are not as comfortable as they once were, but your party will not be harmed. You have Lord Penhallow's word."

Blaine did not voice his thoughts about the value of a lord's word. Instead, he tried to keep up with the brisk pace Geir set. The total darkness did not seem to bother Geir, but even with the torch, the others struggled to make their way through the rubble and debris that littered the tunnel floors.

"We're going deeper into the tunnels than I've ever been before," Verran murmured.

"You've been down here before?" Blaine asked.

"A time or two, to stay out of reach of the guards," Verran replied offhandedly. "In the old days, the upper cellars were a second city, full of illegal whiskey, games of chance, shady ladies, and peddlers selling just about everything."

"A thieves' paradise," Blaine murmured.

"That it was." Verran sighed. "We kept the guards paid off in coin, women, and whiskey, and they left us alone."

"How about the rest of these tunnels? Where do they go?" Dawe asked.

"Don't rightly know. There's an old aqueduct system under the city, been here since the Illoran Conquest. A lot of the buildings have cellars that connect, too. Deeper down, they say there are caves. Wouldn't surprise me. Lots of caves under Donderath," Verran said. "No one I knew ever needed to go beyond the upper cellars, but I heard tell about the low places."

"What did you hear?" Dawe asked, his sword still gripped in his hand.

"People said desperate men made the low places their own, to keep their necks out of the noose," Verran replied. "I heard there were monsters down here, like that barghest and worse." His gaze flickered nervously toward Geir. "And vampires."

Geir spat out a harsh laugh. "And do you always believe children's fables?"

"That barghest was no fable," Dawe countered.

Geir did not slow his stride as he answered. "Yes, beasts like the barghest dwell down here. As for the *talishte*, we had no need for refuge in these tunnels until the Great Fire."

They wound through a maze of cellars, tunnels, and cave passageways. Blaine had given up on trying to mark their way. They had walked for miles, and Blaine hoped Piran would be able to fight off both blood loss and any poison from the barghest's fangs long enough to reach the healer Geir promised.

Blaine glanced toward Connor, who had said nothing, taking up the rear of the group. *Did Connor betray us? Or was he as surprised by Geir's appearance as the rest of us?*

"We're here," Geir announced. Geir led the way up an old set of stone steps to a door. It opened before they reached it, giving Blaine to guess that their approach had been observed. They followed Geir into a large cellar room appointed like the salon of a down-at-the-heels noble. Tapestries and curtains covered the room's stone walls. Torches in wall sconces and oil lamps lit the room as if it were merely night outside. The room was comfortably furnished in the manner of a drawing room, with a desk, a couch, and several upholstered chairs. Each wall had a closed door. Antique Lethurian carpets covered the floors. Blaine wondered when Lord Penhallow would make his appearance.

A blond man stood beside the door. Geir bent to speak in low tones to the guard, who nodded and gave a quick glance toward Connor. In a moment, the man slipped through another door and left them alone in the chamber.

Geir laid Piran on the sofa. Kestel sank to her knees beside him. She looked up in alarm. "He's barely breathing."

Geir touched Piran's forehead, and Piran awoke with a start. "Merely a courtesy, m'lady," Geir said. "My kind have certain abilities that are native to our blood. Among other things, we can slow down a heartbeat and depress respiration. It made the journey easier on your friend."

And it would certainly come in handy subduing prey, Blaine thought.

"Where's the healer you promised?" Blaine asked.

"On her way. But there is something I can do for him in the meantime." Geir motioned for Kestel to move out of the way. He knelt beside Piran and tore his shirt open as if it were gauze, revealing a nasty wound that was already beginning to fester. Geir spat onto the palm of his hand and then pressed his palm against Piran's wound.

"What in Raka did you do that for?" Dawe protested. "Can't you see it's already going sour?"

Geir said nothing, but moved his hand slowly over the raw gash. Verran grabbed Geir's shoulder as if to throw him aside, but Geir was immovable, and the twitch of his arm sent Verran sprawling.

"Look," Kestel said quietly to Blaine, pointing. Where Geir had touched the wound with his spittle, the blood had stopped flowing, and the skin, torn and ragged just moments before, was visibly knitting closed.

Geir stood and went to wash his hands in a nearby basin. He turned back to where the others stood. "Our saliva staunches blood flow and encourages the skin to heal rapidly. It's necessary, given that we don't need to kill the creatures from which we feed."

"And the infection?"

"I will see to that." They turned as a woman with long dark hair entered the room. She was dressed in tunic and trews, like a man. The heavy brocade cloth was of superior quality, though it was stained and worn in places.

"This is Anya," Geir said. "She's a healer."

"How is it that the *talishte* have need of a healer?" Kestel asked Geir as Anya knelt beside Piran. "What can ail the dead?"

Geir regarded her with a half smile as if he enjoyed Kestel's sparring. "While we are indeed undead, there are certain... vulnerabilities... that are more tolerable when eased by a healer. And we take our responsibilities to our human envoys quite seriously."

"You mean 'servants,'" Dawe challenged.

Geir raised his head, looking at Dawe with an unreadable expression. "Not servants in the manner in which you mean the term, as chattel. Longtime retainers, envoys who manage our daytime affairs with our complete trust, members of our household." He turned his gaze back to Blaine. "I believe you would understand the term in that manner from your own experience, would you not, Lord McFadden?"

"A retainer's status depends upon the character of his lord," Blaine replied, hoping he did not look as uncomfortable with Geir's use of the title as he felt.

"Indeed," Geir replied with a hint of cold mirth.

Blaine returned his attention to Anya. She had withdrawn a shallow cup and vials of powder from the pouches at her belt, and a small flagon of what appeared to be wine. Anya poured a portion of the powders and wine into the cup and stirred them with her finger, then poured out the mixture slowly over Piran's rapidly healing wound. Piran gave a cry and lurched, but Anya pressed him back into the couch one-handed, despite Piran's bulk. The mixture fizzed and thickened, gradually disappearing into Piran's skin.

Anya straightened and dusted off her trews, returning the vials and cup to the pouch on her belt. "Your friend will live," she said, her voice thick with an accent Blaine could not place.

"He must rest. A barghest's bite is not poisoned, but they are foul creatures, and their wounds, you see, sour quickly. I'll see to his care while you're a guest here." With that, Anya swept out of the room.

Geir turned back to Blaine and the others. "I need to make arrangements for your food and to assure your quarters are acceptable. Make yourselves comfortable. Lord Penhallow will join you shortly." Geir left by the same doorway that Anya had used. For a moment, Blaine's group was silent, and then Dawe moved to the door Geir had just opened. It did not budge.

"Locked," Dawe reported.

Kestel sat down in the chair nearest to Piran. "What now?"

Blaine turned toward Connor. "That's a good question. How about it, Connor? Did you betray us?"

Connor reddened. "No, or at least, not intentionally. The *kruvgaldur* bond isn't something I initiate or control. Communicating through the bond never happened when I was just Garnoc's messenger."

Connor sighed. "I told you about the dreams while we were at sea. I don't know what Penhallow can read from my mind when we're not in actual contact, or how far away his link can reach. His touch was lighter in Edgeland, only at the brink of wakefulness. The closer we came to Donderath, the more I felt his presence on the fringes of my thoughts."

"Did Penhallow order you to get us into the cellars?" Dawe demanded.

Connor shook his head. "No. Engraham told me about the cache and gave me the key. I had no idea where Penhallow was. He disappeared on the eve of the last battle."

Kestel stood up and placed herself between Dawe and Connor. "Whether or not Connor could have guessed Penhallow knew where we were, it's damn lucky he did. We were losing the fight before Geir showed up."

Dawe turned away grudgingly to find a seat on the other side of the room. Blaine returned his attention to Connor. It was possible, he guessed, for Connor not to know the full extent of the vampire's hold over him. And it was also true that Connor had not hidden the link between himself and the vampire, a connection that had now rescued them twice. Connor had endured the same hardship as the rest of them on the journey back to Donderath, a journey he had not been forced to make. And in the battle with the barghest, Connor had fought as hard and as bravely as any of them, though he was clearly not a sea-soned warrior. Hardly the actions of a man who knew help was on the way.

"Give him a break, Dawe," Blaine said. "For now, I'm will-ing to take him at his word."

Connor visibly relaxed. "I don't believe Lord Penhallow means you harm," Connor said with a glance toward the door. "He may be able to help us. Even if he offers us no other boon, his protection is quite valuable."

"Or at least it was," Blaine replied, beginning to pace. "If he's so powerful, why hide down here? Why flee on the eve of battle? We don't know the landscape anymore. Obviously, Donderath has changed."

They fell silent for a few moments, and then Dawe turned to Verran. "The tools worked, huh?" Dawe asked.

"You made him a set of thieves' tools?" Kestel asked incredulously.

Dawe shrugged. "Figured we'd have to forage once we got here. When Verran showed me what he had, I saw how to make him a better set. Just planning ahead, that's all."

"Don't let him kid you," Verran said. "Dawe built me the best set of tools I've ever seen. He's got real potential as a thief, I'm telling you."

Connor sat on the edge of the group. After a while, Kestel walked over and sat down beside him. "You don't have to keep your distance," she said.

Connor shrugged. "They don't trust me."

Kestel looked at Blaine and the others and turned back to Connor. "Don't take it too hard. Blaine doesn't like surprises. That barghest was a damnable surprise. And I think we're all pretty shaken up over what happened to Piran."

"I didn't intend to betray anyone," Connor said, an edge of controlled anger beneath his voice.

Kestel regarded him for a moment. "No, I don't believe you did intend to, and I'm not convinced that leading us to Penhallow is a betrayal. If he's as powerful as you say, we may need his help, or at least his patronage. What's in it for him?"

Connor was thoughtful for a moment. "While I respect Lord Penhallow's power, I've never had cause to fear him. I can't say the same of many mortals at court, men who were completely without scruples. Penhallow's existed a long time, and he says he's seen magic collapse before. He warned me, and got his people to safety. He didn't seem to anticipate any gain from the upset. If anything, knowing what was likely to happen seemed to make him melancholy."

"Very human of him," Kestel remarked.

Connor shrugged. "He and Grimur and the other vampires I've met seem more like us than not, despite their age. Perhaps even death can't change some things."

"You might be surprised." The voice came from the doorway. Blaine and the others rose to their feet defensively as the door swung open to admit the speaker. Lanyon Penhallow was a tall man. Long brown hair fell loose to his shoulders. His face was angular, neither handsome nor unpleasant, yet striking for its confidence. He moved into the room gracefully, with an air of bridled power, reminding Blaine of a racehorse, or perhaps, more correctly, one of the large mountain cats in the forest. Everything about the man spoke of wealth, from the fine brocade of his trews to the cut of his waistcoat. Blaine met his gaze and repressed a shiver. The power that was only hinted at in Penhallow's manner was utterly clear in his eyes.

"Connor," Penhallow said with a hint of a smile. "I am truly relieved to see you looking well."

Connor gave a slight bow. "Thank you, m'lord. It's been an interesting journey."

"Indeed." Penhallow turned his attention to Blaine. "Lord McFadden," he said, though to the best of Blaine's memory, he and Penhallow had never met.

"I go by Mick these days," Blaine replied.

Penhallow's thin lips twitched in amusement. "Reinventing yourself for Velant? I know something of adapting to suit the circumstances. Why have you come home?"

Blaine did not look away. "Can't you read my mind?"

Penhallow's laugh was deep and rich. "You are not afraid of much, are you, Blaine McFadden?"

"Exile tends to reduce what you fear."

Penhallow's expression sobered. "It does indeed." He turned away, and his glance fell in turn on each of Blaine's companions. "Geir said Connor had brought friends." He smiled when he saw Kestel, who nodded her head in recognition.

"Mistress Kestel I have met before," Penhallow said. "Perhaps introductions for the rest of you are in order." Penhallow moved slowly around the room, listening intently as each of the group made an introduction. Finally, Penhallow stopped beside Piran's couch, and looked down at his sleeping form.

"That's Piran," Connor said. "The barghest caught him by surprise. Your healer and Geir seemed to think he would be all right."

Penhallow frowned as if deep in thought, and then spoke. "Yes, I believe he will be. His life force is growing stronger. Fortunate that Geir caught up with you."

"I had a feeling that bit of luck was arranged," Blaine said neutrally.

Penhallow gave an offhanded shrug. "If you're implying that I set the barghest on you to force your audience with me, the answer is, no. Did I have the sense from the *kruvgaldur* that Connor was in danger? Yes. I had hoped that Geir would intercept you without incident."

"What do you want from us?" Blaine lifted his head challengingly.

"I would like to see you succeed," Penhallow replied, with a gesture that bade them sit.

Blaine shot a glance toward Connor. "What do you know about our plans?"

Penhallow's expression was unreadable. "As I have not had a chance for Connor to brief me, I know very little. But I have gleaned insights through my bond with him, whispers at the edge of wakefulness. You would like to see magic return as it had been. No doubt, Valtyr's maps play a role in your plan. I sent Connor to save the last map the night Donderath fell." He paused. "I suspect that you have learned something important to your quest. Otherwise, I don't think you would have returned, am I correct?" Penhallow asked.

Grudgingly, Blaine nodded. "You're correct."

"Perhaps I can be of greater help if I am fully apprised." Penhallow looked to Connor. "I need your memories."

Connor began to roll up the sleeve to his shirt. His face was blank as he offered his forearm to Penhallow, positioning it so that the vulnerable inside elbow with its throbbing vein was easily accessible.

Kestel gasped as Penhallow took Connor's arm and pressed it against his mouth. Connor stiffened but did not cry out, his eyes focused on the distance as if he were not truly present. After a moment, Penhallow raised his head. Blaine had expected to see blood on the vampire's mouth, but Penhallow's lips were clean, as was Connor's arm. All that remained were two small punctures, and even from where he sat, Blaine could see that the bite was already healing.

"Interesting," Penhallow said, releasing Connor's arm. Connor shook himself, as if coming out of his thoughts, and stepped away.

"Now that I know more about your purpose, I am even more interested in supporting your cause," Penhallow said, leaning forward a bit to meet Blaine's gaze. "I would like to be your patron, and will offer you my protection."

"At what price?" Kestel's voice was sharp. Penhallow looked at her and chuckled.

"You've lost none of your fire, Kestel," Penhallow replied.

"I know your reputation," Kestel replied. "It held that you were a loyal friend and an implacable enemy."

Penhallow gave an eloquent shrug. "That is true."

"So what's in it for you?" she challenged.

"A very businesslike attitude for a courtesan...and an assassin," Penhallow replied.

"Business always comes first," Kestel answered.

Penhallow stretched. Had he needed to breathe, Blaine

guessed the other would have taken a long breath. As it was, his stretch seemed designed to delay comment, or perhaps it was just a vestige of a mortal mannerism. "I don't like what Donderath—and the Continent—have become since the Great Fire."

"I thought predators preferred the wild," Kestel replied.

Penhallow chuckled. "Predators prefer order. The natural order of things has been upset. The wildness that results—in the magic, in the people—is good for no one. I have seen the collapse of many kingdoms in my time. There is profit for no one but the scavengers."

A groan from Piran drew their attention. Piran's eyes opened, and a look of panic crossed his face as he awoke in unfamiliar surroundings.

"You're safe, Piran," Kestel said, crossing to him.

Piran managed to sit up. His shoulder was now completely healed. "Where are we?" He glanced around the room and stopped when he saw Lanyon Penhallow. "Who's he?"

"Lord Penhallow gave us shelter and provided a healer for your wound," Kestel said in an even voice that did not betray her thoughts about the matter.

"Penhallow, the vampire?"

"An inelegant term, but sufficient," Penhallow said with a slight incline of his head in acknowledgment.

"I thought you said we were safe?"

"To the extent that anywhere is safe, you are safe here," Penhallow replied, ignoring the tone of Piran's question.

"If your magic, this *kruvgaldur*, still works, why should you care about the rest of the magic?" Dawe asked.

Penhallow made a gesture to take in the scope of the comfortable room. It resembled the parlor of a well-appointed manor much more than it did an underground bunker of a noble in exile. "With magic, it is possible to rebuild within a generation. Without magic..." Another shrug. "What has been lost may never be reclaimed."

Blaine leaned forward. "You say that you've seen kingdoms collapse before this. Do you know how they regained their magic?"

"Yes—and no. I'm not a mage myself. But I have been told by mages that magic rises from different sources. Perhaps it is the gods' way to assure that magic everywhere is not destroyed." Penhallow paused. "What you have learned from the maps and the book that Grimur gave you is your best hope. Whether or not you have all the pieces that are required remains to be seen."

"That's not very reassuring," Blaine replied.

Penhallow frowned, and sat up straight, suddenly alert, all conviviality gone from his manner. "Something is not right," he murmured. He moved to the door in a blur, all pretense of mortality gone. Blaine caught a glimpse of Geir's face at the door, but could not hear their muffled conversation.

Abruptly, Penhallow turned back to them. "You must go."

"I thought you said we were safe here?" Piran challenged.

"From mortals, yes. It isn't mortals who attack us." He nodded toward the sack full of weapons Verran had taken from the chest in the tunnel. "Take your weapons. Geir will get you out. He'll stay with you, help you navigate. This is not the land you left behind. You'll need him."

"Don't we get a say in that?" Blaine remarked as Kestel and Dawe helped Piran to his feet. Piran waved off their assistance, standing on his own though he was more pale than usual. Verran handed him a sword to replace the one Piran lost to the barghest.

"No," Penhallow replied. "Not if you want to survive. Leave now."

With that, Penhallow disappeared into the corridor. Geir slipped past him into the room. "Come on," he said, striding past them toward one of the other closed doors.

Blaine caught him by the arm. Geir permitted his hold, but turned with an impatient expression. "Who's out there?" Blaine demanded.

"Vampires. Pentreath Reese's get. Reese doesn't hold much with helping mortals. I suggest we leave before introductions are required." Geir shook off Blaine's hand casually, but with enough restrained force that Blaine got the message.

In the distance, Blaine could hear crashing and banging, and a jumble of shouts. He'd seen what one vampire could do. He had no desire to be caught between two warring vampire camps. Blaine looked back at the others, who were watching for his response. The crashes were getting closer. "We've got no choice. Follow him."

Just as they reached the opposite wall, the door to the salon splintered down the center. It smashed to the floor, torn from its hinges. A blur of motion followed, as if storm winds had found their way into the underground. Blaine caught glimpses of men fighting, moving faster than his gaze could follow.

Blaine gripped his sword, ready to defend himself. Connor took a place next to him, his sword drawn. Piran stood ready for the attack, but Blaine doubted Piran could hold his own for long. Verran was on his knees in front of a door on the far side of the room, and Blaine guessed that he was picking the lock. Dawe fired a steady stream of quarrels at the onslaught of attackers, while Kestel lobbed whatever she could find toward the newcomers to slow their advance. After a moment, Verran rose with a triumphant grin and joined Kestel, keeping up a constant barrage of hurled projectiles.

Geir and Penhallow were at the front of the fray. Geir fought with a broadsword in one hand and a short sword in the other, against an attacker that was equally well armed. The two parried and feinted, sizing each other up. Geir struck first, swinging hard with the broadsword. His opponent blocked the swing, slashing with the scythe-shaped dagger in his left hand and nearly scoring on Geir's arm.

Geir twisted away, using his momentum to strike another bone-jarring blow, and while his opponent was able to parry, it drove him back a step, enough for Geir to get inside his guard with the short sword and slice open a long gash on the other's left arm. With a curse, Geir's opponent sprang at Geir, driving forward with his sword. Geir evaded the strike, but the point of the blade tore into his side, and dark blood colored his tunic. Geir countered with a series of pounding blows, each one driving his attacker back, staying just out of range of the scythe blade in the man's left hand.

Not far from Geir, Penhallow kept two attackers at bay. He moved with a fighter's grace, parrying a killing thrust by one opponent as he fended off a two-handed slash by the other that would have cut a mortal in two. While Geir's face showed intent concentration, Penhallow had the look of a predator in his element: focused, remorseless, yet alive with the thrill of battle. Geir moved with cold precision and elegant reflexes. Penhallow seemed to dance, punctuating his attack with kicks and turns, a lethal combination of warrior training and reckless abandon.

More of the *talishte* had joined the fight, pressing Blaine and the others closer to the far wall of the chamber. "Do we run for it?" Dawe asked. Thus far, Geir and Penhallow had been able to keep the attackers away from Blaine and his friends, but as more of the undead swarmed into the room, that seemed unlikely to remain the case.

"I'd rather fight here, where we can see and move, than be overtaken in some damned tunnel," Blaine replied.

Most of the *talishte* battled in pairs or triads, and from the look of it, Penhallow's forces were holding their own, though in this room, the numerical advantage went to the attackers. Just as Blaine spoke, two of the *talishte* split off from the two-man attacks they had been mounting against single vampires and came at Blaine and Connor in a blurred rush of motion.

Dawe's crossbow thudded as he loaded as quickly as the device would allow. Kestel hurled a silver candlestick at one of the vampires, striking him on the temple with enough force to fell a normal man. Verran had begun to raid the bag of weapons they had taken from the ruins of the inn, and sent a dagger wheeling through the air at the second vampire, pegging the man in the left shoulder so that the blade sank halfway into the joint.

Their attackers slowed but did not stop. Blaine heard scuffing next to him and looked up to see Piran beside him. Piran looked drawn and pale, but he held his sword with both hands and his lips were curled in a snarl.

"You should have stayed in Velant," one of the attacking *talishte* sneered as he slashed toward Blaine. Blaine managed to parry—just barely—but the force of the undead fighter's blow made his arm ache to the shoulder. The attacker grinned, sure of an easy kill, and brought his blade sideways for the next blow. Again, Blaine narrowly evaded the deadly tip, but it ripped into his jacket and sliced through his shirt, drawing blood from a shallow gash.

The other attacker had gone for Connor. The first swing was low, nearly catching Connor in the thigh. Connor parried and lurched out of the way as the next blow was a thrust meant to fix him between the ribs. The blade slashed through his shirt, and blood flowed from a cut on his side. The vampire laughed, and Connor's expression hardened. He ran toward the vampire instead of attempting to flee as his opponent expected, gratified when his sword scored a deep gash on the vampire's forearm before the other knocked it loose with a force that sent Connor reeling. One of Dawe's quarrels thudded against the wall, missing its target by a hair's breadth.

Blaine was tiring fast, but his attacker clearly was not. From the gleam in his opponent's eyes, Blaine guessed that wearing him out was part of the strategy. Each of the vampire's blows took Blaine's full strength to deflect, yet the attacker's speed made it difficult for Blaine to wound the vampire, and he had no idea what would be required to kill it.

Piran ran at Blaine's attacker, making up for waning strength with bluster and a bellowed war cry that could be heard even above the din of battle. The vampire wheeled, catching the brunt of Piran's thrust on his blade, but he was a few seconds too late to deflect the blow completely, and the point of Piran's sword dug deep into the vampire's belly, a move that should have dropped a normal attacker in a steaming mess of blood and entrails.

Annoyance glinted in the man's eyes as he focused his attack on Piran, and Blaine struck from the side, holding his sword shoulder height, its grip in both hands, running at the vampire like a horseless jouster. Piran feinted as if striking for the man's chest, then at the last instant took his sword down, slashing hard across the vampire's thighs as Blaine's attack forced the vampire to raise his weapon in response.

Piran's sword bit deep across the vampire's flesh. The pain of it forced the vampire to flinch, just enough for Blaine's wild thrust to slide along the vampire's parry, slip free of the defending blade, and stab, point first, into the vampire's neck. Carried by his own momentum, Blaine's sword skewered deeper, severing the throat and slicing through the neck muscles until the head lolled back, held only by the spine, which gleamed white against the blood. The vampire staggered, falling to its knees, blood washing down its thighs from the gashes that cut to the bone. Piran sprang forward and grasped the dangling head, then gave a vicious twist that snapped the spine and broke the head away from the body.

Only then, as the vampire fell forward and lay still, did Blaine have the chance to glimpse Connor's battle. Blood flowed from multiple gashes on Connor's shoulder, chest, and forearms. By sheer luck, Connor had managed to land a few nicks on his opponent, but it was clear that Connor was rapidly tiring. Before Blaine or Piran could move, they heard a wild shriek and saw the glint of silver in the torchlight. Kestel gripped the base of a heavy silver candelabra in both hands and came at Connor's attacker swinging with her full might. Bone crunched as the blow landed on the vampire's ribs and spine. Before the vampire could turn to face this new threat, Connor rallied. Lurching forward, he rammed his sword through the vampire's chest, catching him full in the heart. Kestel brought down the candelabra again as the vampire fell forward, smashing the bloodied silver down on the vampire's skull with a sickening crunch.

The room smelled of blood and decay. Kestel screamed as the vampire whose skull she had just crushed began to rot more quickly than a corpse left in the sun. Within seconds, its once-ashen skin had purpled and blackened, then began to peel back, exposing decomposing tissue beneath it. A few seconds later, the skin was gone, and the rotted muscles and organs became gelatinous, then sloughed off, leaving only bone. A heartbeat more, and the bone crumbled into dust.

Blaine heaved for breath and looked out over the battle. More of Penhallow's loyalists had joined the fight, enough that the attackers were joined one-on-one, eliminating their advantage. The floor was littered with decomposing corpses, but Blaine had no idea whom the body count favored. Penhallow was in the center of it, holding his own, though his once-fine doublet was torn and bloodied, and he moved as if at least some of the blood was his. As Blaine watched, Penhallow cut down his attacker, only to have another take his place.

Geir was closer to them, but still fighting off an opponent who seemed well matched in both skill and strength. Like Penhallow, Geir was bloodied, with a gash on his left cheek and multiple slashes to his shirt that left the sleeves in tatters. Geir's face was set in a grimace of deadly resolve, eyes hard, lips pressed tightly together, though out of resolve or pain, Blaine could not tell.

Connor cried out as someone yanked his arm, pulling him off his feet and tossing him into the fray in the center of the room as casually as one might throw a rag doll. The motion caught Geir's attention, costing him his focus as his opponent made a vicious slash with the scythe blade in his left hand. The blade cut along Geir's belly, and Geir doubled over, his face twisted in pain. The attacker stepped back for the kill, and Geir jerked upright, spitting his attacker with his sword, driving it into the man's abdomen and up through the rib cage. Blood flowed down, covering Geir's arm, staining his tattered sleeve, and it dribbled from the lips of the dying vampire, whose expression was one of complete astonishment.

Blaine ducked as a fiery blur whizzed past his head. Verran was grabbing anything in his reach, lighting it on fire from the torch he held and lobbing it into the fray. The vampires drew back. Blaine strained for a glimpse of Connor and saw him lying on the floor with Penhallow standing over him, fighting off an attacker while shielding Connor with his body. The fighting was vicious, but there were fewer fighters still on their feet and the air had become as fetid as a charnel house in summer.

"Get them out of here!" Penhallow shouted above the din.

Geir staggered toward where Blaine and the others stood ready for another wave of attack. "Come on," he said, his voice tight with pain. One arm was clutched across his belly, but he stayed on his feet, sword still in hand.

"We can't leave Connor," Blaine protested.

"Penhallow has him. He'll protect him. But we can't protect all of you and still fight Reese's men." Geir gave Blaine a shove toward the door and tore a torch free from its sconce, pushing it into Blaine's hands.

"Run!" Geir shouted, flinging open the door to their escape route.

The corridor was dank and smelled of mold and decaying sludge. Rough rock walls were moist, and partially frozen slime made footing treacherous. They moved as quickly as they dared, and at every breath Blaine expected to hear the pounding of footsteps in pursuit.

No sooner had they cleared the first turn than they heard a thunderous roar behind them. In the near-darkness, Blaine had no idea what was going on, but every instinct told him to keep running, and he did, with the sound of his companions' footsteps pounding behind him. A cloud of dust billowed through the tunnel, choking him and stinging his eyes.

"What in Torven's name was that?" Dawe swore when they finally stopped, heaving for breath and digging at the grit in their eyes.

"Sounded like the whole damn roof collapsed," Verran replied.

"It did." Geir's voice sounded at the edge of the darkness, his face barely visible in the torchlight. "The corridor was snared. Lanyon had it set so that we could seal it off, either to keep invaders out or to put a barrier between us and pursuers." He paused. "If Lanyon was successful, no one will be coming after us. If he wasn't...it should hold them off for a while."

"We've got to go slower. Piran's hurt," Kestel spoke up from the rear.

"Don't listen to her. I'm fine," Piran growled, but his voice was tight, pinched with pain.

"We don't dare stop yet." Geir's voice cut through the gloom. "Keep moving." Geir was the last in line, giving Blaine to know that Geir felt they had more to fear from someone following them than they did from unknown perils in the darkness ahead of them.

Piran had been injured even before the fight, and Blaine had seen Geir take a nasty wound that would have killed him had he been mortal. By comparison, Blaine was in pretty good shape, though his body ached and he was bruised and sore to the bone. His shirt and trews stuck to the blood on his skin where he had been cut in the fight. Although his long-ago salle training had kept him alive, it was obviously inadequate to the perils Donderath presented. If they survived the night, Blaine resolved to sharpen his sword skills.

Dawe had managed to get behind Blaine in the chaos of the escape. Kestel and Verran were in the middle, followed by Piran and Geir. "Do you think Penhallow won?" Dawe asked in a half whisper.

"Don't know. Whoever sent the attack sure sent enough fighters. Question is—were they after Penhallow himself, or did they get a tip that we'd be there?" Blaine replied.

"I don't feel right leaving Connor behind."

Dawe's words echoed the recrimination Blaine had struggled with in his own thoughts. "I didn't like it either. If Penhallow wins, I imagine he'll see to Connor. And if he loses..." Blaine didn't finish his sentence.

Thirst and hunger gnawed at Blaine as much as the sting of his wounds. They made their way through the twists and turns of the rock tunnel for more than a candlemark. Gradually, the tunnel led them uphill, ending in a heavy oaken door that was barred from the tunnel side.

"Now what?" Blaine asked, fatigue and tension making his voice terse.

"Unless you want to spend the night in here, we open the door and see if there's a surprise on the other side," Geir replied.

Blaine and Dawe traded places so that Dawe would have an open shot into the doorway. Blaine threw back the bolt and thrust the torch forward, illuminating the path. Dawe's crossbow was at his shoulder, notched and ready. Torchlight glinted on Blaine's sword. Tired and wounded, Blaine fervently hoped that nothing unfriendly awaited them.

Silence greeted their entrance. "Move forward," Geir urged. "If there were anything waiting, I'd hear or smell it."

Carefully, Blaine and Dawe edged forward. The torch illuminated a wine cellar, filled with dust-covered casks and racks of filthy bottles. Overhead, the ceiling soared in bricked barrel vaults.

Geir brushed past Blaine and headed for a set of shelves that held winemakers' tools. He rummaged around and returned in a few minutes with a yellowed pile of folded muslin. "They use this to strain the wine," Geir muttered. "It'll do to bind up your wounds. Sit."

Behind him, Kestel and Verran wrestled with one of the kegs

and a tap. Kestel brought Geir a bowl of wine that was dark as blood. "To clean the wounds," she said.

Verran brought a full pitcher and offered it first to Piran. "Should help with the pain," he said with a shrug.

Geir handed off the muslin to Kestel. "Ever make bandages?" he asked tersely.

"On occasion," Kestel replied. She grasped the muslin and began to rip it into wide strips. Dawe remained standing, his crossbow ready.

Geir knelt next to Piran. "Let's have a look at you," he said, helping Piran shed his torn and bloody shirt. The wounds caused by the barghest had healed, but Piran had taken several new gashes in the fight with Reese's *talishte*.

Piran eyed the dark stain across Geir's belly where the scythe had cut. "Shouldn't you be tending yourself?"

"Have a look," Geir replied, pulling apart the damaged shirt to reveal a thin, pink scar. "Although I'll admit it hurt something fierce to begin with."

"Yeah, I bet it did," Piran replied with a hint of incredulity.

Geir cleaned the wounds, adding the healing power of his saliva to those that were the deepest and most ragged. Kestel came behind him to bind up the wounds, and Verran kept the pitcher of wine full. After everyone had taken what they wanted of the wine, Verran busied himself digging through the barrels and boxes in the corners of the cellar, emerging with a victorious grin a little while later. He held a large waxed wheel of cheese and a handful of dried fish.

"Dinner is served," he said. He brushed the dust from a worktable and set down the cheese, then carved a wedge out of it with his knife.

"Don't tell me those fish are—" Piran began.

"Yep. Herring," Verran replied.

Piran let out a curse. "I had really hoped never to eat another one of those damned fish in my life now that we're out of Edgeland."

Verran shrugged. "Suit yourself—but I'm hungry and I don't think I'll mind the taste at all with enough of this wine."

Piran groaned. "All right, all right. Pass me a hunk of cheese and some of that damn herring."

Verran refilled the pitcher of wine and moved around the room, dispensing cheese and herring. Geir moved to where Blaine sat.

"You and your people fought well in there—for mortals," Geir said, not looking at Blaine as he tended the gashes Blaine had taken in the fight.

"You did pretty well yourself—for a dead man," Blaine replied.

A faint smile touched the edges of Geir's lips. "I've had a few centuries of practice, and war was my art, even when I still lived."

"Were the attackers after Penhallow—or us?"

Geir worked in silence for a few moments, daubing at the worst of Blaine's wounds. "Pentreath Reese and Lanyon Penhallow have been at odds for a long time. Penhallow prefers to work through mortal intermediaries. He has no desire to wield power directly—at least, not anymore. Reese would set himself up as the dominant warlord. It was only the magic that kept him at bay before—magic and the organized human armies that far outnumbered his own get."

"Does that mean Penhallow is on our side?"

Geir did not look up. "Penhallow has no desire to see Reese rule the Continent. Assuming that such a thing would even be possible, given that there are relatively few of the *talishte*.

Penhallow believes that mortals would inevitably rebel and strike back.

"And besides that, Penhallow loathes Reese on general principles. Reese is an arrogant, domineering ass. Penhallow is more... civilized. For years, Penhallow has made it his business to support anything that keeps Reese from getting what he wants." Geir shrugged. "To a point, it's a rich man's pissing contest. But it goes deeper than that. Penhallow is correct in his belief that Reese would be a merciless tyrant. Even the undead don't care for such a ruler."

Blaine frowned. "Could Reese have had something to do with the war? Or with the Meroven strike that destroyed the magic?"

Another shrug. "Who can say? Reese is a devious bastard. All of the powerful *talishte* have their networks of spies and informers, and their mortal supporters."

"Garnoc, through Connor, made sure Penhallow knew what was going on at court, who had gained King Merrill's attention, what intrigue was playing out," Geir added.

"So that Penhallow could interfere?" Blaine challenged, as the combination of pain and fatigue made him increasingly ill-tempered.

Geir gave a sharp laugh. "Is that what you imagine? A vampire puppet-master pulling the strings and making the king dance? I almost wish that had been true. If that were the case, I promise you Penhallow would never have allowed the war with Meroven to go as it did." He sat back as Kestel bound up the last of Blaine's wounds. "No. If anything, what happened occurred because Penhallow could not openly be at court."

"Why not?" It was Kestel who asked, giving Blaine a pat on the shoulder as she helped Geir tie off the final bandage and sat back on her haunches.

Geir grimaced. "Merrill feared us. There are rumors that his father was set upon by a feral vampire, and forever after, he hated us. Under King Merrill's father, we were hunted almost to extermination."

"But not under Merrill?" Kestel questioned.

"Merrill stopped the persecution, but we think it was because of silver, not scruples. Since we *talishte* have been forced to live in the shadows, both figuratively and quite literally, we have mastered, shall we say, a thriving underground economy?" Geir's laugh was bitter. "There has been a *talishte* hand behind many of the large fortunes on the Continent, as advisers, assassins, and negotiators." He stressed the last word just enough to give Blaine the sense that such negotiations incorporated the politics of speed and unnatural strength they had witnessed in the battle a few candlemarks earlier.

"Some of the nobility had good reason to fear for their continued wealth if the *talishte* were exterminated. They prevailed on Merrill, and he stopped the hunts."

"There is a rumor," Kestel said, looking intently at Geir, "that Merrill might have had an even more personal stake in the matter."

Geir chuckled. "As always, m'lady Kestel has her sources. You are correct. Merrill's oldest daughter was stricken with a breathing sickness. She grew pale, and her blood was not strong enough to keep her alive. The king sought the help of every healer in the kingdom, and from beyond its borders, but no one could help her. She was dying.

"In desperation, King Merrill sent for Penhallow, who was known to him as a *talishte* with integrity. He begged Penhallow to bring his daughter across so that she would not be lost to him. Penhallow complied."

"At what cost?" Kestel asked.

"When the princess had been brought across and Merrill was assured of her survival, Penhallow made it clear that aggression against the *talishte* would put Merrill's daughter in certain danger."

"He took her hostage?" Blaine said sharply.

Geir shrugged. "He didn't need to. Merrill had been so grief-stricken over his daughter's illness that he had not truly thought through the consequences of saving her. When he realized that he had unwittingly given the *talishte* their most powerful bargaining chip, Merrill kept his word about the hunt, but he banished the *talishte* from court."

"Did that include his daughter?" Kestel asked.

Geir nodded. "Merrill was not as fanatic in his prejudices as his father, but his dislike of our kind was deeply ingrained in him. He could make exceptions for economic and political reasons. But he found that he could not stand the thought of what his daughter had become. He gave her a small fortune—the money that would have been her dowry—and sent her away."

"What happened to her?" Kestel asked quietly.

Geir looked away. "Penhallow kept his word to King Merrill. The princess was welcome among us, treated with respect, and protected. But on the morning after the magic died, when we learned for a certainty that Quillarth Castle had fallen and that the king was dead, the princess ran out into the sun." He shuddered. "She immolated herself."

They were quiet for a few minutes. Finally, Geir stood. "We'll rest here for the day. It'll be dawn soon. We'll leave after night falls."

"And go where?" Dawe asked.

Geir moved to answer, but Blaine spoke first. "Glenreith," he said. "My home—if anything's left of it."

"I thought you wanted to get to Mirdalur?" Geir said in a tone that gave Blaine to guess the *talishte* did not like surprises.

"We're tired and wounded and we don't have a plan," Blaine replied. "We heal slower than you do," he said, meeting Geir's gaze. "And we have absolutely no idea what we're walking into at Mirdalur. If Glenreith is standing, we'll have shelter and maybe food, too. A base from which we can plan our next move. Perhaps Penhallow and Connor will meet us there. Even if they don't, we have Ifrem's map, along with that book of Grimur's to go on." He grimaced. "We might only get one chance to set things right—I don't want to foul it up because we didn't bother to get the details straight."

"After the last few surprises we've had, I'd just as soon have the chance to scout the area before we go charging into Mirdalur," Dawe said. "What if Reese's people are already there? I've got no desire to walk into a trap."

"I'm just curious to see where Mick calls home," Verran said with a grin, raising the pitcher of wine in a mock toast and then taking a long draught. "Now that we know he's not a common cutthroat, I'm interested to see where criminals of a better sort hail from."

Blaine shot Verran an exasperated look. "Don't get your hopes up. Titles may have been in the family for a long time, but not money. The manor was down-at-the-heels before I left; if it was attacked in the final assault on Donderath, it may not even be standing." He kept his tone light, but the thought that Glenreith and his family could be gone sent a chill through him that no fire would warm. Blaine realized that Kestel was watching him and he knew that she was observant enough to guess his thoughts.

"We still need to rest here, whether you head for Mirdalur or Glenreith," Geir said. "It's too close to dawn for me to take you elsewhere. Reese's people will also have to go to ground. This place appears to be unused by mortals, but we'll post a guard, just in case."

"And tomorrow?" Blaine asked.

Geir's expression revealed no hint of his thought. "Tomorrow night, we'll head for Glenreith."

"Wouldn't we be safer going by day?" Dawe countered. "Reese's men won't be able to get to us in daylight."

Geir turned to him. "Before the Great Fire, I would have agreed with your logic. But Donderath is a different place than the kingdom you left behind. Bursts of wild magic that come and go without warning. Brigands and highwaymen who aren't afraid to attack armed men. Neither day nor night is safe. But by night, I go with you."

"We'll wait for night," Blaine said. "It won't hurt to get some rest, and let Piran heal. Glenreith is a three-day ride out of the city. Mirdalur is beyond that. Who knows what kind of shelter we'll find tomorrow? Best to take some rest while we can."

Geir volunteered to take the first watch. Blaine and the others made the best of the stone floor in the wine cellar, spreading their cloaks against the chill. Weary from the fight and numbed with wine, Blaine fell into a fitful sleep.

CHAPTER
TWENTY-SIX

R OCK AND FIRE FELL TOGETHER IN A DEADLY rain. The air filled with smoke, making it difficult to breathe. Connor hurled himself out of the way of the largest portion of the roof as it collapsed, but bits of falling brick and stone slammed into his shoulder and thigh hard enough to make him stumble. The roar of falling stone deafened him, and the choking smoke blinded him. *Crushed or burned?* he wondered, sure that he was about to die.

He struggled to his feet, clawing at his eyes. Swords clanged and he heard fighting close at hand. His right hand gripped his sword, though his eyes were tearing so badly he could not see to defend himself. A dark shape appeared in front of him out of the haze. Connor saw a glint of firelight on steel and managed to throw himself out of the sword's way by sheer luck. The blade sliced down, catching his left sleeve and opening a thin, bloody slice down his forearm.

Connor blinked, trying desperately to see. He heard his attacker chuckle, knew the *talishte* was playing with him. Killing one of Penhallow's mortal spies would be quite a coup for Reese's men. This one no doubt meant to make sport of it.

"I'm ready, you bastard. Fight like a man," Connor snapped with bravery he did not feel. His sword skills were barely adequate at best, since he had never been expected to serve as a bodyguard. Even if he could see, he lacked the speed and skill of any of Reese's men. Before his attacker could take him up on the challenge, he heard a sound like a crack of thunder close at hand, deafeningly loud.

"The whole damn thing is collapsing!" Connor heard a voice shout. His attacker made a sudden thrust forward, sinking his blade deep into Connor's side. He withdrew his sword and vanished. Connor sank to his knees, clutching his gut. He heard a roar like a waterfall, glimpsed a shadow falling over him, and was struck by something large with a force that knocked him to the floor. His head slammed against the flagstones, and everything went black.

In his dream, fire and rock fell together outside the grand tower in Quillarth Castle. Connor heard the peal of the bells, watched as the green fiery ribbon of light from the sky descended, saw everything it touched burst into flame. Stones pelted him as he scrambled down the stairs from the belfry. He could hear screams echoing around him; some were his own. The wooden staircase gave way beneath him and a black shadow overtook him. The shadow engulfed him, swallowed him whole, laid him flat on his back. And then, nothing.

Connor's eyes opened, but all he saw was darkness. He was lying facedown on a cold, hard slab. He tried to sit up, but his head slammed against wood. He attempted to reach out with his arms, only to find himself trapped in a small space barely wider than his shoulders. *Gods help me! They've buried me alive!*

Panic choked him and his breath came in short, sharp gulps, his heart thudding so hard in his chest that his ribs ached. *Think, dammit!* He had just enough room to flex his arms, but he could not budge what lay above him. He forced himself to lie still, breathe slowly, and gather his wits. Once the first swell of panic had passed, he realized pain throbbed the length of his left leg. The rest of his body felt bruised and battered, as if he'd been dragged behind a wagon.

I remember… Quillarth Castle… a ribbon of light. No, that's not right. Not right, but if not the castle, then where? Cellars, tunnels, fire. Stone, falling. There was a battle—

Connor's thoughts were interrupted by a distant scratching sound. His heart seized again. *Rats? Please, Charrot, no rats. Crush me, suffocate me, but don't let rats eat me before I'm dead.*

Despite his prayers, the scratching noise grew louder, closer. Connor struggled, but it caused excruciating pain in his leg and served only to remind him just how narrow the tomb was in which he lay. His leg was not the only source of pain. His left side throbbed, and it felt sticky. Despite his dreams of fire, Connor felt a growing coldness.

Maybe there are worse things than rats. Ghouls. I've heard stories of "things" that dig up the freshly dead and eat their flesh. His head throbbed, and from how tender the skin was on one side of his skull, he guessed that a sizable chunk of falling rock had clipped him, hard. Images in his memory blurred, making them unfamiliar and unreliable.

Connor had no idea how long he had been unconscious. *Long enough for them to think me dead and bury me,* he thought. A more chilling idea occurred to him. *Maybe I'm already dead and I've risen as* talishte.

The scraping noise was closer, just on the other side of the wood. Connor braced himself, certain that whatever was digging him out of his grave would rip away the lid of his tomb any minute now. In desperation, his right hand felt around in the darkness for his sword. His fingers closed around the hilt, only to discover that the blade was immobilized.

The wood above him splintered, sending bits of it falling down onto Connor's head and shoulders. The weight lifted off of him, and Connor drank in the fresh air, then groaned at the pain in his ribs.

"Connor." The voice was familiar, but Connor barely heard anything in his panic. Whatever had pinned his leg was suddenly removed, and hands grasped his shoulders, gently turning him over. Bloody fingers reached down toward him, and even though Connor flattened himself, he had nowhere to go.

The hands shook him gently. "Connor."

Connor struggled with all his waning strength, grabbing at the arms that seized him, but it was like wrestling with stone. The flesh was cold, and the grip was strong enough that Connor's blows did not make the grip weaken for a second.

"Look at me." The voice was a command, and Connor felt a honeyed compulsion in the words that subdued his will.

Connor's eyes opened. He saw a dark-haired man bending over him. The man's hair was streaked with dust; blood stained his torn shirt and pale skin. His blue eyes held Connor's attention. Connor let himself drown in their depths, abandoning his fear. And in that trance, memory returned. The barghest. Sanctuary among the undead. The attack. Flames and the chamber collapsing around him. He blinked, and knew the face that watched him with uncharacteristic anxiousness.

"Penhallow," Connor groaned in acknowledgment.

Lanyon Penhallow's narrow features relaxed and he favored Connor with a rare smile. "Glad to have you among the living," he said in an offhanded tone that did not match the concern in his eyes.

"What happened?" Connor's voice was scratchy and his throat was raw. Though the air was cooler than before his "tomb" had been opened, it smelled of blood and smoke. He could taste grit, though his mouth was too dry to spit.

"Let's get you out of there, and we'll have time for tales later. Lie still." Penhallow's voice was colored with the same compulsion that had roused him, and Connor felt himself relax, though inside, he fought a new surge of panic.

Penhallow gripped him by the shoulder, and Connor felt other hands on his legs. Caught in Penhallow's gaze, Connor felt the pain lessen, even when his rescuers lifted him.

"Let me have a look at your side," Penhallow said, as dispassionate as a surgeon. He ripped open what remained of Connor's torn and bloodied shirt. Connor struggled to see, but two pairs of hands pressed him down by the shoulders, keeping him immobile. The glint of worry he saw in Penhallow's eyes gave Connor to know that the wounds were bad.

"Hold him still," Penhallow said to helpers Connor could not see. Penhallow's eyes narrowed as he studied the wounds, and then he spat onto his own palm and pressed his hand against the wounds, and then moved to the deep gash on Connor's leg. Penhallow bit into his own wrist, then mingled blood with spittal in his palm, and covered the gash with his hand.

Connor writhed as liquid fire poured through the raw gash, into the torn tissue and organs, burning through his blood. The fire felt as if it would consume him, driving back the numbing chill. Hands like steel bands anchored his shoulders and his good leg. Penhallow repeated the process twice, and each time, Connor felt as if he had swallowed hot coals.

Exhausted, Connor lay back, utterly spent. A few terse words by Penhallow sent someone scouring the wreckage for wood to use for a crutch. Penhallow leaned back, satisfied. "You'll be sore for a while, and you might have quite a limp for a few days, but you should heal just fine. The *kruvgaldur* has many advantages. So long as you're close to me, you gain strength from my power. It will help you heal."

"What happened?" Connor asked. One of Penhallow's men, a blond vampire with a farmer's build, helped Connor sit and pressed a cup of wine to his lips.

Penhallow shrugged. "Reese came after us. Geir was able to get McFadden and the rest of his party to safety, but using that exit triggered a trap that, unfortunately, worked a little too well. It was only supposed to collapse the tunnel entrance. But these are old chambers. It weakened the roof. After the collapse, Reese's men set the main entrance on fire to trap us." Neither his face nor his voice revealed any emotion. "Reese did not count on the skills of my fighters."

"And I got caught in the cave-in," Connor supplied.

"You got separated from Geir and the others in the fight. I said I would protect you. I failed badly. For that, you have my apology."

Connor looked at him, frowning as more memories returned. "Just before the roof fell, I was fighting one of Reese's men. He ran me through." He shook his head. "I don't remember much of anything after that."

"A support beam and some paneling kept you from being crushed. The sword wound you took was deep, and you were injured further by the collapse. You lost blood while we searched for you."

"You saved my life."

Penhallow shrugged. "You've served me well."

"I think I need training with a sword if I'm to survive what Donderath's become," Connor said tiredly. One of the *talishte* pressed a wineskin into his hand, and Connor savored the wine, realizing that he was actually hungry as well as thirsty. He looked around at the ruined room. What had been a comfortable salon was now a charred wreck. On the other side of the room, two more *talishte* worked to clear wreckage from one of the room's doorways. Three other vampires awaited Penhallow's orders. None of the men were familiar to Connor.

"What now?" Connor asked.

If Penhallow felt any loss over his ruined salon, he did not show it. Connor wondered how many such hiding places Penhallow had throughout Donderath, and perhaps beyond its borders. "Your friends will head to Mirdalur eventually. We'll meet them there, but before we do, I have a few suspicions to follow up on."

While Penhallow's men had cleared an exit, Connor fashioned a crutch for himself. He had no desire to be carried all the way to Mirdalur, even if the weight of a full-grown man was little burden to one of the *talishte*. He tested the crutch and tried to stand. Connor's balance faltered, and he put down his left foot to steady himself, sending pain arcing up his leg. With a grimace, he experimented with the crutch until he could move with a reasonable approximation of his normal walking speed. That would still be much slower than the *talishte* could move, but it was a start. Exhausted, he sat down on a pile of rubble to wait. The cave-in had collapsed parts of several other escape tunnels. They were stranded until the guards could dig through enough rubble to find a tunnel in good enough shape to chance using it for their exit.

"How did you avoid being crushed yourselves?" Connor asked Penhallow.

"Quick reflexes help, although not all my men were so lucky," Penhallow replied. He had stripped to the waist, abandoning the shreds of his silk shirt. His fine brocade pants were bloodstained and covered with dust. Dried blood and rock dust caked his pale chest, the blood a reminder of wounds that had already healed. Connor eyed the amount of blood and frowned. *Just how badly were the "survivors" injured? Badly enough to kill a mortal, I'd bet. The ones that died must have been crushed beyond repair.*

Connor had always figured Penhallow for being a typical noble: aloof, unwilling to do anything that smacked of physical labor unless it involved hunting or riding. Yet Penhallow bent to the task at hand alongside his bodyguards. Stripped of his finery, he had the build of an athlete or a laborer—lean-muscled and whipcord strong. *What's his story? I wonder. Was he born noble? Or could a clever man acquire both title and fortune if he had several lifetimes to work on it?* Musing about Penhallow's origins took Connor's mind off his aching leg. After the example set by Penhallow, Connor felt chagrined not to be taking part in the excavation, but he could find no way of doing so without further injuring himself.

Instead, he picked his way around the rubble, scavenging weapons. His own sword lay in pieces. He found a serviceable replacement among the weapons of the dead and made a pile of the daggers, swords, and crossbows that were not too damaged to use. Penhallow's *talishte* might be confident in their personal strength, but Reese's men had obviously seen an advantage in matching strength with weaponry. And as the puny mortal in the room, Connor found that the pile of weapons rekindled something akin to hope.

CHAPTER
TWENTY-SEVEN

———

THE MOON WAS BRIGHT OVERHEAD WHEN Penhallow's guards finally opened a passage to the outside. "Can you walk?" Penhallow said with a glance toward Connor.

"If you don't expect me to run," Connor replied. His leg throbbed, his body ached all over, and he wanted nothing so much as a few belts of whiskey to numb the pain.

"We'll find a horse for you," Penhallow said in a voice that did not accept argument. "It will slow us down less than having you pass out or hobble across Donderath."

Connor chafed at feeling like a damsel in distress as he waited for one of the bodyguards to return with a horse. His pride demanded that he make a show of swinging up to the saddle without assistance. In addition to his looted sword, Connor had chosen a crossbow with a quiver of quarrels and two lethal-looking daggers. He would not go down easily if it came to another fight.

They rode in military formation, with crossbows at the ready. Connor thought the *talishte* actually looked nervous, something he had not thought possible. *How has Donderath changed to make the undead afraid to travel by night?* he wondered.

Connor looked around. He had never thought about what the conflagration and the death of magic had done beyond the city walls. Now, even by moonlight, the damage took his breath away.

The trees that still stood looked scraggly and diseased, as if locusts had feasted on them. The rock fences that crosshatched the countryside lay in disarray, resembling more a tumble of stones than any actual barrier. Dams had broken, washing away everything downstream. The mighty aqueducts that carried water to the city were broken in multiple places, leaving behind only dry, useless stone arches. Many of the thatched-roof homes had burned. Sod houses had fared better, but even buildings made of stone stood roofless and charred.

They rode in silence for most of a candlemark. Connor possessed none of the *talishte*'s acute senses, but he sensed that the quiet night held more danger than he could see. In the distance, he saw the lantern light of a small village. As they grew closer, Connor realized that a high stockade surrounded the village and that the wall of close-set, pointed logs looked recently built. Ahead, there was a shadow across the road, and a few dark figures were milling about.

The group of riders slowed. At Penhallow's signal, they lowered their weapons, but kept their swords and crossbows in hand just in case the sentries were not as peaceable.

"Ho there! What business be you about in the middle of the night?" A warning tone colored the greeting. A large tree trunk blocked most of the road. Marshland on either side kept riders from going around. The men who had created the roadblock looked equally well armed as their own party, and stood with weapons at the ready, eyeing them suspiciously.

"Our business is our own," Penhallow answered smoothly. "We have no quarrel with you. Let us pass, and we'll be on our way. We want nothing from you or your village."

The man who hailed them barked a laugh. "That's right nice of you, but we be wanting something from you. Your gold and your horses, if you please, since you've got no wenches with you."

"No." Penhallow's voice was toneless.

Connor saw the armed men raise their crossbows. In the split second before he could react, something swept him from his mount. Connor slid to the ground, grateful to have fallen on his good leg. Overhead, he heard the thud of crossbows. His mind registered the importance of the sound a second later. The brigands had drawn first, but Penhallow's men had fired first, in the heartbeat between the brigands' motion and when they could twitch their fingers to loose their arrows.

"You can get up now," Penhallow said laconically.

Connor staggered to his feet and dusted himself off, then stared. Every one of the dark-clad men lay dead on the ground, quarrels protruding from their chests. Two of Penhallow's guards bent to the task of rolling the huge tree trunk out of the roadway, something Connor bet had taken a dozen mortals to place. His heart was pounding although the battle had lasted mere seconds.

"What in Raka was that about?" Fear and unspent anger found vent in Connor's voice.

The two men finished clearing away the tree and swung up to their mounts. Penhallow afforded Connor a glance. "Look around you. This is what the world is like without magic."

"I don't understand."

Penhallow's arm swung in a shallow arc to indicate the countryside around them. "At court, you saw only the great magics, though small magics were always around."

"And now it's gone." Connor supplied, still at a loss to understand the ambush. He swung back up onto his horse.

"A year ago, these were fields, not marshlands. Magic drained the water away, and magic bound the dams and levees together that kept the land from flooding. When the magic died, the wardings and charms went with it. People and livestock died in such numbers, one might have thought a plague struck. In a way, it did. Nature came back with a vengeance, and there was no one to turn to for help."

"Except the *talishte*?" Connor asked.

Penhallow's expression was pained. "There are not enough of my kind to prevail against those odds, even if mortals would trust us enough to seek us out. And few of the vampire lords would bother to intervene in mortal affairs. They are content to sit back, watch the situation sort itself out, and adjust accordingly."

"And you?" Connor's tone was more of a challenge than he intended. Penhallow did not reply immediately, and Connor wondered if he had given offense.

"The last time the magic died, in another place long ago, I withdrew and waited to see what would come of it. The result was not to my liking. I will not make the same mistake again," Penhallow said. There was steel in his voice, and Connor wondered just how badly wrong the last situation had gone. Bad enough, obviously, to stir Penhallow to hedge his bets this time around.

They rode on, leaving the corpses of the dead brigands where they lay. "I still don't understand the highwaymen," Connor said, anxious for a change of subject. "Were they from that village?"

Penhallow shrugged. "Probably. Without law, the survivors form armed camps. First, they loot the dead, and then they horde what they can steal from the living. Over time, the strongest and most ruthless men become warlords, and feud among themselves. After a few decades, or longer, a victor emerges and is crowned king." Penhallow wasn't looking at Connor as he spoke. His eyes were fixed straight ahead, but something in his gaze gave Connor to know that Penhallow looked out over centuries, and not at the road in front of them.

"I don't understand how the magic played a role in that," Connor said.

Penhallow seemed to return from wherever his thoughts had strayed. "Magic, large and small, kept the peace in a hundred little ways." He chuckled at Connor's look of amazement. "You weren't supposed to be aware of it, but we could feel it in our blood. Magic assured decent crop yields, to keep the people from getting too hungry. Hungry people revolt. Mages also made sure there was enough wine and ale for all. Hedge witches and sorcerers alike could use a flicker of magic here and there to diffuse hot tempers, avert riots, make it impossible to raise an angry mob."

He shrugged. "It wasn't a perfect system. But the Long Peace that spanned the reigns of King Merrill and his father was no accident, nor was it all due to wise and beneficent kings," he said with a hint of bitterness.

"And no one noticed?" Connor asked, outraged. "The bloody mages were mucking around with our minds and no one objected?"

Penhallow's smile was mirthless. "It was hardly a conspiracy, or at least it was an open conspiracy. Tell me truly; were you totally unaware of the small magics around you on a daily basis?"

Connor stopped to think. Anger shifted into confusion. "Not completely, although I don't have a wink of magic myself.

I knew the cooks used it to help cakes rise, nursemaids used it to soothe squalling babies, and farriers used a twitch of magic to steady the horses while they worked. I'd heard about the way farmers, shopkeepers, and tradesmen used a flicker of magic here and there, and I appreciated when the distillers, vintners, or brewers used it to keep us from running out of drinks."

Penhallow nodded without looking at him. "Did you mind the magic, so long as it kept you from being inconvenienced?"

Chagrined, Connor let out a sigh. "No." He paused. "And I had an inkling that there were more powerful mages who helped put down riots or scouted to help the war. Now I know more than I wanted to know about what a mage could do in battle."

They rode in silence after that. Connor mulled over the conversation with Penhallow, disturbed by a perspective that, while unexpected, felt like the truth. *I've been blind.*

At Penhallow's signal, they quickened their pace. Just as the horizon was growing lighter, Penhallow veered from the road, heading through a forest down a well-worn lane toward a large, walled house grand enough to be a lord's manor and secure enough to be a fortress. "We've arrived," Penhallow murmured.

Before Connor could ask any questions, a dozen men emerged from the forest. Even in the waning light, Connor could see that these men were well armed, and unlike their previous attackers, stayed far enough back to avoid being the target of arrows.

"Halt. State your business."

"I'm here to see Traher Voss," Penhallow said. "Tell him Lanyon is here, with a few friends."

The leader of the guards conferred with one of the men, who went sprinting back toward the house. No one else moved. After a while, the runner returned and shared a message with the leader.

"You may proceed." At that, the guards drew back, but remained in sight, forming a wide corridor through which Penhallow's group passed. Connor fought the urge to glance over his shoulder, wondering whether Penhallow knew their host well enough to rule out the possibility of being shot in the back. When they reached the doors of the house without incident, Connor breathed a sigh of relief.

Connor noted that the manor house had been fortified, though not recently. The door was oak overlaid with iron straps. Bars covered the windows on the lower floors, and above them, the windows had been narrowed into archers' slits by bricking up more than half of each opening.

Penhallow's men kept their swords sheathed and their crossbows lowered. Connor did likewise, though he felt damnably vulnerable. The room into which they were ushered looked more appropriate to a high-ranking military commander than to a member of the nobility. Swords of every description hung from the walls in ornamental groupings that Connor guessed would not hinder their use if needed. Battle axes, long swords, pikes, and halberds were grouped on both walls and ceilings. A variety of maces and morning stars hung from sconces. Colorful battle pennants fluttered at intervals along the stairwell.

"My, my, my. What have we here?" A voice boomed from the large, curved staircase that graced the manor's main entranceway. Traher Voss came down the steps, rubbing his hands together. He narrowed his gaze as he came closer, assessing them with a shrewd glance.

"Lanyon Penhallow and his pup, just before dawn?" Voss wondered aloud. "Best we get you and your people belowground, and answer questions when we're out of the reach of the sun." He led the way down another long, winding flight of stairs carved into the rock beneath the manor house. Connor did not miss the fact that three burly men from Voss's household guard followed them, and to Connor's eye, at least one of the guards also appeared to be *talishte*. While Penhallow undoubtedly knew about the guards, nothing in his manner suggested that he found the company objectionable.

The staircase descended to a large common room fitted with tables and chairs as if for a group. Rows of doors on either side opened off the room, reminding Connor of a barracks. Voss grinned broadly at Penhallow. "I've invited you to visit me for quite some time, Lanyon," he said. "Now you come in the middle of the night, looking worse for the wear."

Penhallow shrugged. "Reese's men attacked us. Our party split in two. We'll rejoin the others later, but before that, I need to find out what you've been hearing, my friend."

Voss motioned them toward the tables and benches. One of the guards opened the door to what appeared to be a wine cellar and emerged with a flagon of brandy and pitcher of blood. A second guard found goblets enough for all of them. "Just brought a stag in earlier tonight." He paused and poured brandy for himself and Connor, validating Connor's guess that he and Voss were the only mortals in the room.

"Here. Drink this. You look like you could use a couple of fingers of brandy," Voss said, setting Connor's goblet in front of him with a thud.

Connor glanced to Penhallow, who gave a nearly imperceptible nod and took a sip from his own goblet, indicating it was safe for Connor to drink. Voss chuckled, catching the silent exchange. "He's appropriately cautious. Gods above! You all look as if you've been ridden down by a small garrison."

"Feels like it," Penhallow replied. He finished his goblet of blood and poured another, passing the pitcher to the rest of the *talishte* who had traveled with them. Their evident hunger sent a shiver down Connor's spine.

"What's got Reese stirred up?" Voss asked, tenting his fingers in front of him.

"I was hoping you had some intelligence on that," Penhallow replied, leaning back in his chair.

Voss stretched. He was portly, and he had the thick neck and broad shoulders to suggest a past military background. Even past his prime, Voss looked like he could hold his own in a fight, against mortals at least. He was dressed in a dark shirt and tunic, and though it bore no rank or insignia, something about it struck Connor as being the off-duty clothing of a military man.

"Pentreath Reese has been active since the Great Fire," Voss mused. "Rumor has it he's allied with Vedran Pollard."

Penhallow frowned. "I thought all the nobility died in the war or the Great Fire."

Voss drained his brandy. "Pollard's like a cockroach. Nothing kills him. He's his mother's son, all right. Treacherous bastard. He'd been looking for a way to gain more power before the Fire, but I don't think Merrill trusted him. Smart of Merrill. There's a rumor that Pollard sent assassins against any nobles who didn't die in the Cataclysm. No doubt on Reese's orders."

"There can be only one winner, and Reese is immortal. So why hasn't Reese eliminated Pollard?" Penhallow asked.

Voss leaned forward. "You know the answer as well as I do. Reese needs mortals. He can't go about by daylight, and not everything keeps until night. Pollard's ruthless. He's happy to be Reese's enforcer, hoping for a bigger share of the pie in return for whatever passes with him for loyalty."

"So why is Reese after me—this time? Why now? We'd left each other alone, more or less, of late."

It was Voss's turn to shrug. "If I knew anything about that, I'd have warned you." Penhallow's glance was skeptical, and Voss gave a crooked grin. "Yeah, I would have. You're too good a client to lose, and too bad of an enemy to make. I may be mortal, but I'm not stupid." He paused, and poured himself another brandy, refilling Connor's goblet unasked.

"We've long suspected that Reese would like to be the real power on the Continent," Voss speculated. "Oh, he'd have mortals fronting for him, but in Reese's fantasy, he'd pull all the strings. He's probably the one man on the entire Continent who rejoiced when magic died—and the one with the biggest stake in making sure it stays dead."

Penhallow's eyes glinted with interest. "How so?"

Voss's gaze sharpened. "Magic also kept a balance of power between the living and the undead, didn't it?" He interpreted Penhallow's silence as agreement. "You have your own magic, in your blood. Don't bother to try to deny it; I know these things. Yes? So when the common magic dies, what happens to that power balance? It tips, don't it? And it tips to the side Reese favors." He grinned smugly.

Penhallow shifted in his chair. "Uncomfortably insightful, as always," he said, sipping from his goblet. "But there's something Reese either doesn't understand or refuses to see. The death of magic affects us as well, but differently."

Voss frowned. "I thought you were immortal?"

Penhallow shrugged. "That's a relative term. A much-elongated existence, yes, but truly immortal?" He shook his head. "That's for the gods alone." He took another sip of blood. "When the external magic dies, it doesn't just 'tip the balance,' as you put it. It starts to affect those of us who have the old magic in our blood, the *talishte* and the other not-quite-humans. We seem stronger at first, because there isn't external magic to counter us. But over time, if the magic doesn't come back, the lack wears on us. We weaken, lose our focus. Some go mad. It gets very bad after that, for everyone." Penhallow paused to finish the contents of his goblet. "Have you been hit by any of the magic storms?"

Voss thumped his fist on the table. "Damn right we've been hit. One struck out in the fields, where my cattle graze. Came out of nowhere. Lost ten head of cattle and two of my best herders to those storms."

Voss's voice dropped. "The magic changed things. After one of those storms came through, I saw one of my men step into a puddle—just a mud puddle—but he screamed and disappeared like something was dragging him down. When the rest of my men poked in a long branch to pull him out, they hit bottom just a hand's breadth deep. But he was gone. Now, tell me how a grown man can disappear into a puddle?"

Traher Voss shook his head. "Heard of a man whose house was in the middle of one of those magic storms. He got out of a chair and went to walk from his sitting room into a bedroom. Only when he walked through the doorway, it didn't go to his bedroom. It put him outside, on a hill a candlemark's walk from where he lived. Swore up and down he wasn't drunk when it happened, but that damned storm changed where the doorway took him."

"What happened when he got back to his house?" Connor asked.

Voss gave him a predatory grin. "When he got up the nerve to try to walk into his bedroom again, everything was right as rain. Just a normal door. The storm had passed."

Penhallow had been listening to the conversation with an

expression Connor could not decipher. Now he leaned forward intently. "How often are the storms coming?"

Voss frowned. "Believe me, we've tried to find a pattern. No one wants to get caught out in one; might come back with two heads or six arms or some other freak thing. But there's no rhyme nor reason to when they strike."

"Have you mapped where they've struck? Perhaps it's a 'where,' not a 'when' pattern," Penhallow said quietly.

"You know something, Lanyon. Stop fishing around and tell me."

Penhallow sat back in his chair. "I don't *know* anything— but I do have some suspicions. Connor was successful in obtaining Valtyr's map."

Voss's eyes lit up, but his face remained neutral. "Got the map on you?"

Penhallow chuckled. "Yes. As we thought, it marks the places where magic was strongest—and null—throughout Donderath."

"Anything else?" Voss looked intrigued.

Penhallow's eyes glinted, like a fisherman with a big bass on his hook. "Really. I'm wondering whether or not your 'random' magic storms would show a pattern if we put them on a map."

Voss chewed his lip as he thought. "Maybe. 'Course, we only can mark the ones we've heard about. Could be others and we don't know it."

Penhallow shrugged. "Probably so. But even a handful of storms plotted on a map might prove interesting."

Voss nodded. "I'll put someone on it." He paused and watched Penhallow closely. "I don't think you came here in the middle of the night just to talk about maps."

Penhallow shook his head. "Reese stormed my crypt. He and

I had a truce—and he broke it. I'm interested in finding out why."

Voss's eyes narrowed. "I told you that I don't know—and I don't. But knowing Reese, he thought you either had something or knew something that he wanted. Like maybe the map—or, has he learned of the pendant?"

"Maybe," Penhallow allowed. "But for something like that, even Reese is usually civilized enough to ask first." He frowned. "No, Reese intended to kill me; I'm certain. And the odd thing is, I haven't done anything to actively annoy him in months."

Voss laughed. "The important word there is 'actively,' isn't it? I've always thought that just your continued existence annoyed Reese."

"I'm sure of it. But he's put up with me until now. Why change?"

Voss's rough guffaw made Connor jump. Traher Voss rocked his chair onto its back legs and shook his head. "Really, Lanyon. It's Reese we're talking about. If he's trying to kill you, it's because he thinks that you've got the edge on him, that you're a threat."

Connor saw a flicker of something in Penhallow's eyes. "Reese benefits from the magic being gone. So he'd be pretty unhappy if it came back, right?"

Voss's chair settled down onto all four legs with a thump. "Unhappy? That's one word for it. Angry as a branded bull with his balls in the fire is more like it." He gave Penhallow a sideways look. "Is there a reason he might blame you for trying to bring the magic back?"

"Perhaps."

Voss let loose with a creative barrage of curses. "Dammit, Lanyon," he ended his tirade. "Why didn't you say so in the first place?"

Penhallow shrugged. "I wanted to see what you knew."

Voss glared at him. "As if you couldn't get what you needed just by walking in the door."

Connor looked up, taking Voss's meaning immediately. He stared at Voss's long-sleeved shirt, sleeves that covered the vein on the inside of his elbow, the place where Connor had his own scars from yielding blood and information to Penhallow.

"How's your business since the magic died?" Penhallow asked, shifting the conversation.

Voss cursed again. "Wretched—what did you expect?" He sighed. "Oh, the weapons trade has been brisk. But contraband?" He shook his head.

"The market for smuggled goods fell apart completely when the war went sour. After all, without a king to ban things, where's the value in smuggling? The major noble houses were destroyed. Who's going to pay for illicit goodies? And when anyone can run across the border and loot what's left of Vellanaj and Meroven, how can I charge top price for smuggled dainties?" He sighed again, loudly.

"Bloody magic. I made a good living with my stable of rogue mages," Voss complained. "Willing to break all the rules that the 'king's approved' mages wouldn't." Voss sank down in his chair, a dispirited mound. "Just about ruined me, Lanyon. You have no idea."

Penhallow chuckled, and Connor heard a trace of real affection in the vampire's voice. "You amuse me, Traher, and I mean that in the best possible way. You've got the oddest way of being seamy and endearing all at once, with a hint of annoying. It works well for you." He grinned, baring his eyeteeth. It was a gesture that Connor knew could mean many things, depending on the situation. Here, he took it as a genuine smile.

"Did Reese have spies in Edgeland?" Connor asked.

The question seemed to truly surprise Voss. "Edgeland? Who in Raka would need spies there?" He frowned as he reconsidered. "Then again, it's very possible that more than a few of the convicts had been Reese's men at one time or another. Why?"

"We came back on a ship packed full of people," Connor said. "Anyone who wanted to come got passage, no questions asked. There could have been any number of Reese's men on that ship."

Penhallow nodded. "Pentreath Reese is an opportunist. It's what's kept him in existence this long. Could someone have picked up a clue about the maps, or your companions, while you were on the ship?"

Connor thought for a moment. "Possibly. We certainly weren't shouting our business, but it's a tight fit on a ship like that. Can't say for sure that no one overheard." He paused. "Pollard sent an assassin to Edgeland," Connor continued. "We think he was after Blaine McFadden."

Voss looked up. "Blaine McFadden?"

"You know him?" Penhallow asked.

"Knew his father. Real son of a bitch. Always thought it was a miscarriage of justice for that boy to go to Velant for killing the old man. It was just a matter of time before someone did," Voss said. He paused, and then looked up. "Now that I think of it, there is a connection, although it's a distant one. Lord Pollard and old Lord McFadden hated each other."

Penhallow shrugged. "You've just said that everyone hated old Lord McFadden."

Voss uncrossed his arms and leaned forward. "Yeah, but not everyone hates like Vedran Pollard. I always figured Pollard would be the one to kill the old man, and he probably would have if the son hadn't beat Pollard to it." He met Penhallow's gaze. "And Pollard is Reese's man."

Connor looked at Penhallow. "If all of the old nobility was killed by Meroven's magic attack, how did Pollard survive?"

Voss chuckled. "Remember how I said Vedran Pollard was his mother's son? That's on account of how he wasn't his daddy's son. Genuine wrong-side-of-the-blanket bastard, not a blood relation. Got the title because the legitimate heirs died under suspicious circumstances, in ways his mother might have helped along," he said with a knowing wink.

Connor sat back, unwilling to say more in front of Voss and his crew. He glanced toward Penhallow, wondering what the *talishte* knew about their host, not sure just how far Penhallow trusted Voss.

Voss looked at Penhallow. "You're keeping something back, Lanyon. I don't know how Blaine McFadden figures into anything that Pentreath Reese would care about, or into anything to do with magic, but I can tell you that it would frost Pollard's nuts to think that Ian McFadden's heir was back on the Continent."

"Why would Pollard care?"

Voss sat back and crossed his arms. "Ian McFadden may have been a son of a bitch, but we can thank the gods that he spent most of his venom on Pollard. Feuding with each other kept the two of them too busy to do much damage to the rest of us. Old man McFadden might have been a tyrant—or worse—to his family, but his sniping kept Pollard whittled down to size. With both old man McFadden and his heir out of the picture, Pollard's been free to do as he pleased, and he pleases to fashion himself as a warlord."

Voss stretched and yawned. "All this talk has been quite interesting, but I imagine you need to rest. You'll be safe down here. None of my people will bother you, and I'll have my men at the upper door on watch just to make sure of it. There's food and drink for mortal and dead folks in the wine cellar. Make yourselves comfortable; I'm going to do just that as soon as I reach my bed."

At that, Voss lumbered out of his chair and, with a nod to Penhallow, headed up the stairs with his bodyguards behind him. Connor waited until they were gone and the door at the top of the steps had latched before he spoke.

"Do you trust him? Are we guests—or prisoners?"

Penhallow stretched out his lanky frame. "Both, if I know Traher. But Traher Voss has worked with me for a long time. I'm in his blood, as I am in yours. He's not an honest man, but he does understand money and power. We're as safe with him as we'd be anywhere."

Connor's lip quirked as he held himself in check from replying that Penhallow's answer was no answer at all. "What about Blaine? Reese stands to lose a lot if the magic returns. Could he possibly suspect that Blaine might be the key to bringing it back?"

Penhallow grimaced. "I don't put anything past Reese. But if he does know, it might mean that I wasn't his target last night. If he had spies on the ship, and if they passed along information quickly enough, you might have been followed to the tavern when you went to look for supplies. Reese's men would have recognized Geir as one of mine. They wouldn't have had to risk the barghest or go through the tunnels. Once they had you pegged as belonging to me, they just had to wait for you to show up with me and then drop down and try to take the prize."

"If that's true," Connor said, trying to make himself comfortable enough to sleep on one of the wooden benches, "then Blaine's still in danger."

"If it's true," Penhallow echoed, "we've got to get to him before Reese does."

CHAPTER
TWENTY-EIGHT

CONNOR AWOKE FROM DREAMS OF FALLING rock and flames to the sound of shouted curses and a pounding that shook Traher Voss's fortified manor to its foundations. He sprang to his feet, fighting down panic, and winced at the sudden pressure on his wounded leg. After their arrival just before dawn, he had gone to bed exhausted, resigning himself to waking and sleeping on the vampires' schedule. He glanced toward the notched candle and saw that it had burned halfway down, indicating that he had slept through the day and that night had fallen.

Connor grabbed his sword and limped toward the stairs. Penhallow and the other *talishte* were also awake and armed. He joined them, and they headed up the steps, with Penhallow in the lead.

When they reached the top of the stairs, Penhallow slammed the door open. An armed guard stood at the top, his sword in hand.

"What's going on?" Penhallow demanded.

"We're under attack," the guard replied.

A muscle twitched in Penhallow's jaw. "Obviously. Why and from whom?"

"It's Reese." Voss's voice sounded behind them. Connor turned to see their host. He was stunned at the transformation. Gone completely was the genial smuggling lord. Voss wore a long chainmail tunic that fell to mid-thigh, covered with a cuirass of hardened leather and scale mail. He carried a helmet and wore a lethal variety of knives and swords. His dark eyes glinted with anger.

"Are you sure?" Penhallow's voice had a hard undercurrent.

"Positive. My perimeter guards identified him. They moved right after sunset."

"It sounded as if we were being bombarded."

Voss nodded. "We are. Reese has a catapult, and maybe a battering ram. Damn good thing I fortified this place for a siege, because that's what we've got."

"What do they want?" Penhallow pressed.

Voss jerked his head. "We're about to find out, although I can hazard a few guesses. They're sending a messenger under a flag of truce."

"Let's hear it," Penhallow said, following Voss to the manor's large front entranceway.

Connor and the others stood well back from the door as three of Voss's soldiers opened it just far enough to see a messenger standing outside the massive front doors.

"Speak your message," the guard barked at the messenger.

"M'lord Pentreath Reese has sent me to demand that you turn over Lanyon Penhallow and his people or face the consequences." The messenger was a young soldier, and he wore an expression of resignation, knowing that one party or the other would likely be unhappy with his message and that he stood little chance of emerging from his mission alive.

"Not for all the damned souls in Raka," Voss said, striding closer but still careful to avoid being framed in the doorway, where one of Reese's archers might be able to get off a lucky shot.

The young soldier did not flinch, though his eyes had the look of a man condemned. "Lord Reese insists. Otherwise, we will lay siege to your manor, destroy your soldiers, and take the fugitives you are sheltering by force."

Voss's face had grown red. "Where in the depths of the Sea of Souls did Reese get the idea he could demand anything from me? Go back to your master and tell him—" At that, Voss veered into an obscenely creative and anatomically impossible suggestion detailed and vulgar enough to send a blush to the doomed messenger's cheeks.

"Is that your last answer?" the messenger asked, still standing at attention. Connor felt a stab of pity at the fear and hopelessness in the messenger's eyes. He guessed Reese had given the messenger an ultimatum to succeed or die.

"It's my only answer," Voss roared.

"As you wish." The messenger turned slowly, leadenly, his face impassive. He took only a few steps away from the doorway before an arrow fired by Reese's men took him through the heart and he fell down dead on the flagstones.

Voss's men swung the heavy door shut and dropped a massive crosspiece into place. Voss was still cursing fluently in several languages, swinging his sword in a wide arc for good measure, so that everyone stepped far back to give him room.

Running footsteps on the stairs from the upper levels drew everyone's attention. "Commander Voss," called a young man clad in the same quasi-military uniform that Voss wore. "I've got a report from the parapets."

"What do you see?"

The soldier ran a hand back through his close-cropped dark hair. "From their speed, we're sure that most of the men out there right now are *talishte*. But with a spyglass, we can make out wagons and men headed this way. We think Reese plans to keep you pinned down by day with mortals and by night with the *talishte*."

"Any better look at what they've got to use against us?" Voss questioned.

"Yes, sir. We counted a full battle catapult, a small trebuchet, and a battering ram." Just then, a loud boom sounded above them, and a fine rain of dust rained down from the ceiling. "It appears they have resumed bombardment."

Voss cursed, then looked at the soldier and nodded. "Very well. Get someone up to the murder hole and get a fire lit under the water cauldrons. Reese's men'll burn real nice when we pour hot water on them. Tell the mortals among our archers to keep themselves out of sight. Reese's men can get off two shots before a mortal can fire one."

"Aye, sir," the man said. He made a stiff partial bow and headed back up the stairs. Just as the first man disappeared, another man in the same uniform emerged from the steps to the lower floors where Connor and the others had spent the night.

"Commander Voss," the man hailed their host. "We've got a problem."

Voss gave him an incredulous look. "You just figured that out?"

The man shook his head. "Not the problem out front, sir. They've found the escape tunnels. I sent men ahead to check the route, and both tunnels are compromised. One tunnel had been blocked, caved in. There was an ambush at the mouth of the other tunnel. I lost two men, and a third is injured."

Voss sobered and nodded. "Drop the portcullises on both

tunnels and station guards. I'm not convinced a cave-in would stop Reese, and it could be a trick to get us to leave the 'blocked' tunnel unguarded."

"Yes, sir," the man said, sprinting off with his instructions.

"That's all you've got?" Penhallow questioned. "Two tunnels?"

Voss shrugged eloquently. "It's a fortress. The easier it is to get out, the easier for someone else to get in."

"How long can you withstand a siege?" Penhallow asked.

Voss chewed his lip as he thought. "We've got food, spring water, and wine to last quite some time." He gave Penhallow a sideways glance. "I suspect we'll have blood aplenty for you once Reese steps up his attack. Starving is the least of our worries."

Just then another man came hurrying down the corridor. Despite the late hour, he was fully dressed in a dark waistcoat and trews beneath an open, flowing scholar's robe. The man had a closely trimmed gray beard and a squinted look, with severe, hard-angled features. He glowered as he swept down the hallway, his robes swirling around him. "What's all the ruckus? What's going on?"

Despite the circumstances, Voss smiled. "So sorry to have roused you, Treven. We're under siege."

Treven pulled out a pair of wire spectacles on a chain around his neck and fitted them onto his nose. He looked owlishly from Voss to Penhallow and Connor. "Collecting strays or taking captives?" he asked.

"Which are you?" Penhallow inquired before Voss could answer.

The gray-haired man peered over the lenses balanced on his nose to get a better look at the *talishte*, and his gaze flickered briefly to Connor. "Damned if I can tell. Voss tells me I'm here for my own safety. Since I didn't know I was in danger before his people swooped in and gathered me up, I'm not sure about the danger part, but the food is good, the wine is excellent and plentiful, and he has a damn-fine library, so I figure I got the good end of the deal."

"Lanyon Penhallow, I'm sure you remember Treven Lowrey," Voss said hurriedly as one of his lieutenants began to signal for his attention from down the corridor. "And this is Penhallow's pet mortal, Conroy."

"Connor," Connor corrected. "Bevin Connor."

Penhallow glowered at Voss, who seemed oblivious. "And he's hardly a 'pet' mortal."

Voss dismissed the disagreement with a gesture. "As you wish. Feel free to find a safe room on the lower floors, eat my food, and stay out of the line of fire. I've got a siege to manage." With that, Voss hustled off down the corridor to catch up to his lieutenant, leaving the others standing in silence.

Lowrey cleared his throat. "Since I've been here for a month and I take it you're newly arrived, allow me to play host with Traher's resources," he said with a voice that revealed more curiosity than welcome. "I've learned my way around, and if I'm a prisoner, it's a most agreeable prison. Aside from not being permitted to leave, I've had the run of the place and all the food and wine I care to consume." He patted his stomach. "And I can consume a lot."

He paused and looked hard at Penhallow. "If I recall correctly, you're dead, aren't you? Fascinating. *Talishte*, is it? I've been studying your kind for decades. Once we get you settled in, I've got a few questions for you." He headed off down the corridor in the opposite direction of where Voss went. After a few steps, he paused and turned, motioning for them to follow him.

"Well? Are you coming?" He stood with his hands on his hips.

Penhallow chuckled. "After you, Conroy," he said.

Connor glared at him. "That's not funny."

Treven Lowrey led them deeper into Voss's fortress. The interior rooms were to Penhallow's liking, as they were windowless and kept out the sun. They made a detour at the kitchen, where Lowrey was a dour host, gathering fruit, bread, cheese, and a trencher of bread for Connor and a flagon of fresh deer's blood for Penhallow, while pocketing a few small cakes for himself, all the time grumbling about the lateness of the hour.

"Carry these," he said, handing Connor enough goblets and napkins for them all.

"How did you come to be Voss's 'guest'?" Penhallow asked as Lowrey continued his raid on the kitchen.

"Not quite sure," Lowrey replied. "I'd had the feeling I was being followed and watched. One night, as I was going down to the pub, two ruffians grabbed me and tried to throw me into a carriage. To my amazement, two larger ruffians attacked—at the time, I wasn't sure exactly who was attacking whom, or why—and thrashed the first two brigands, then dumped the carriage driver out of the box, forced me into the carriage, and stole it themselves."

Lowrey led them out of the pantry and down the corridor, which was lit with lanterns that hung at intervals from hooks on the walls. "In here," he said, nudging the door open with his foot.

Connor moved around the room, lighting the lamps. It was a very comfortable library, one that reminded Connor of the king's library in Quillarth Castle. Shelves of books covered the walls, stretching from floor to ceiling. The fireplace was dark, but near it were two comfortable chairs and a leather-covered bench. Lowrey appropriated one of the chairs, motioning for Penhallow to take the other. Connor found a seat on the bench, and Lowrey pulled a small table between them for their repast. He spread out their bounty, along with the goblets he had foisted on Connor to carry from the pantry. Lowrey did not settle back into his chair until he had poured a goblet of blood for Penhallow and filled his own goblet and Connor's with wine. Then he withdrew the cakes from his pockets and took a bite.

"Why would anyone want to kidnap you?" Penhallow asked.

Lowrey dabbed a few crumbs from his lips and shook out his napkin. "I couldn't figure it out at the time, but now I'm sure it was because of the magic."

Penhallow and Connor exchanged glances. "Magic?" Penhallow asked.

Lowrey gave them a sour look. "Oh, I see the look in your eyes. Makes me glad you've eaten, you look so hungry. I'm a scholar and a mage, or perhaps, more to the point, an ex-mage. Lost my powers when the magic died." He shook his head. "Apparently in some circles, even without magic I'm dangerous."

"You seem to think it's all a joke," Connor said accusingly.

Lowrey leaned back and crossed his arms. "No, no. It's no joke. It felt quite real when those villains were fighting over me outside the pub. I was afraid someone was going to slit my throat, hoping to pick my pocket of coins, and I had only enough to buy a pint or two at the pub. As I said, I'm a scholar. Not the man to rob. But," he said with a tight-lipped smile, "once I got over the fear, I realized that whatever was going on was a damned sight more interesting than what I'd normally be doing, and I settled in and went along for the ride."

"Who tried to kidnap you?" Penhallow asked. He had poured a goblet of blood and sat back, looking as comfortable as if he were in his own quarters. Connor watched Lowrey closely, trying to come to his own decision about the wiry little man. There was shrewd intelligence in Lowrey's eyes. Yet he knew from court that even scholars in monastic houses often worked as spies and informants for other powerful interests, and that the research they did served purposes more worldly than academic.

"I had no idea," Lowrey replied. "Voss tells me the men belonged to Vedran Pollard, working for another man, a *talishte* named Pentreath Reese. Do you know them?"

Penhallow looked as if he'd tasted spoiled meat. "Unfortunately, yes. Why did they want to kidnap you?"

Lowrey's grin was crafty. "On account of the magic. I've made a life's work of studying cartography and astronomy, which influence magics small and large. To tell you the truth, my magic is very much influenced by the movement of the stars, which is what got me started on the subject. Bit of an obsession, I must confess. I traveled among all the noble houses, searching through their libraries, to compare old maps with new ones and to look for references to the stars in their courses in olden days. Wanted to trace both the maps and the star positions back to the beginning of magic on the Continent, see how it influenced mages over the years."

Lowrey paused and looked from Penhallow to Connor like a schoolmaster quizzing errant boys on their lessons. "You do know that magic wasn't always here, don't you?"

"Yes, we were aware," Penhallow said, staving off what Connor guessed would have been a long lecture.

Lowrey looked disappointed, but rallied quickly. "Traced it

back to a place called Mirdalur, where the first great Lords of the Blood pulled the energies together to bring magic to the Continent. Since the war and all, when the magic died, I'd been trying to figure out whether someone could do what the great lords did at Mirdalur, and bring it back."

"And what did you discover?"

"Well, that was what I was really afraid of when those ruffians grabbed me. I was afraid that someone might harm my research. I'd gone through all those tomes in the noble houses, you know, before the Great Fire."

"So your notes are all that remains of those books," Connor said.

A furtive look glimmered in Lowrey's eyes. "Not exactly," he said. "I, uh, liberated, volumes that were particularly helpful. Those high-born dandies weren't using them. Most of the books were thick with dust and falling apart—shameful treatment for a book, you know. I took them with me, for safekeeping."

"You looted the noble libraries, stole what you wanted, and hid it," Penhallow summarized, his voice more amused than scolding.

Lowrey grimaced. "It sounds bad when you say it like that, but I guess you could see it that way."

"Where are your books now?"

Lowrey gestured to a corner of the library where frayed and aged tomes lay stacked on a table. "Over there. Once Voss explained to me who was after me and why, and that Reese's men wanted to make sure the magic never came back, I told him where I'd hidden the books and he brought everything here. Now I'm the scholar-in-residence, and Voss keeps me quite comfortable."

Penhallow exchanged glances with Connor, who could sense

the other's excitement even though to Lowrey, Penhallow's expression might not reveal anything. "And what did you discover?" Penhallow asked, then held up a hand, forestalling Lowrey, who appeared to be ready to launch into a lecture. "In a nutshell?"

Lowrey frowned at being cut off, and for a moment, Connor did not think the scholar would comply. "It's all very interesting," he said finally, looking wounded at the need to cut his dissertation short. "It took a special combination of place, people, power, and timing to make it happen the first time. Unfortunately, the records from those years are largely nonexistent, but I have some firsthand accounts written by the men who were there, who kept journals.

"Mirdalur was important because the energies ran through it. That made it a place of power long before the great lords convened. It's the kind of place where people built shrines or felt they ought to leave an offering to the gods." Lowrey leaned back.

"Getting all the great lords to work together—that might be the real trick. My theory is that they each had latent magical ability, even if they didn't know it. In other words, they were good 'conductors' for the magic." Lowrey rubbed his hands together, getting excited over the story despite his previous pique. "They were all exceptional men in their own right, which is why they had fought their way to the top as warlords in a brutal age."

He leaned forward. "And I have another theory: that the magic flowing through them that night changed them. I think it not only made them more likely to pass on magical ability to their children, but I think it marked them in their very blood."

"Can you prove any of this?" Penhallow asked skeptically.

Lowrey looked wounded at Penhallow's doubt. "A scholar,

even a scholar-mage, can't 'prove' anything. But he can assemble enough evidence to make the case to a reasonable man. And I think I've been able to put the pieces together to make a pretty solid case."

"So what would it take to bring the magic back?" Connor asked, leaning forward, feeling as if he would burst if no one asked the question.

Lowrey tented his fingers. "I've told you about people, place, and power. Timing is the other element. Whether the first lords knew it or just got lucky, I believe that there are times of the year when the power is stronger. The equinoxes would be ideal, when the natural powers are balanced."

Connor frowned. "We haven't had the solstice yet. The spring equinox is still months away."

Lowrey nodded. "That's correct. You can't rush the natural order of things."

"What else did you discover?" Penhallow pressed. "Is timing the only other piece?"

Lowrey looked mildly annoyed at being forced to tell his story on someone else's terms. "I'm not certain how many Lords of the Blood it requires to raise the power. I would assume that at least one of the heirs of those original Lords of the Blood would be necessary to awaken the magic again. Mirdalur would be my first choice of location, because that's where the ritual worked the first time."

"First choice," Penhallow said intently. "Are there other possibilities?"

Lowrey nodded. "Possibly, although the old lords no doubt had their own reason for choosing Mirdalur, and it is a very strong place of power. In theory, other places of power might work, although you'd want one that was as strong as Mirdalur." He paused. "It's difficult to say with certainty. I've only been able to find bits and pieces of information, you see, and it's quite possible there are still unknowns." He looked at them over the rim of his spectacles. "Unknowns can make for nasty magic."

"What about the ritual itself?" Connor asked, too drawn into the conversation to think about whether Penhallow preferred to lead the questioning. "What did they actually do?"

Lowrey managed a smile. "That's where my research let me put together pieces no one else found," he said with an air of satisfaction. "The first Lords of the Blood worked the ritual using items known to attract and concentrate power: amulets, that sort of thing. There were also thirteen carved pillars at the site to focus the energies. Both the location and the objects themselves aligned with the position of the stars and the natural energy of the land. I've heard legends about Mirdalur all my life, but never anything about the objects, or anything linking its power to the stars or to the site itself."

"How did you discover them?" Penhallow asked. Connor knew that as intrigued as the *talishte* was, Penhallow's long existence had also made him suspicious, a trait that had saved both of their lives on more than one occasion.

Lowrey looked extremely pleased with himself. "The family of one of the Lords of the Blood had fractured enough times that everyone thought there were no relics or heirlooms left. But the family matriarch was a stern old woman, Lady Alarian, and she had a secret. She'd been the one entrusted with the guardianship of her family's amulet, and she also had a list and description of what the old lords carried and a drawing of two of the carved pillars."

"What happened to the items?" Penhallow asked with more excitement in his voice than Connor had ever heard.

Lowrey looked away, suddenly tense, his eyes downcast with guilt. "Lady Alarian was a very old woman, and she took her role as guardian very seriously. The objects had passed from the wife of the old lord to his eldest son's wife down through all these years. They were to keep the items secret and guard them with their lives."

"So how did she decide to trust you?" Connor asked.

"Lady Alarian set great stock by dreams," Lowrey said. "She had been troubled by a dream in which the carved posts were talking to her, telling her that a 'glass-eyed messenger' would come and that she should share her secrets with him."

"Glass-eyed?" Connor asked, and then looked at the wire spectacles perched precariously on Lowrey's thin nose.

Lowrey shrugged. "When I finally tracked down the hints and clues to find Lady Alarian, she took one look at me and told me that the gods instructed her to confide in me. I was pleased, to say the least."

"Who else knew that you had the objects?" Penhallow asked. "Once their existence was known, it would be a death sentence to possess them."

Lowrey's face lost its joviality. "I pursued the stories of the first lords with a scholar's zeal. Even after the Great Fire, I never thought that my strange academic passion could have anything to do with the real world. I wanted to find a bit of history, to touch the past." His voice had a pleading quality, like a child begging to be forgiven for a yet-undiscovered transgression.

"What happened to Lady Alarian?" Connor asked quietly, though the tightness in his gut feared a response.

Lowrey crumpled in his chair, his expression miserable. "I never meant her any harm. It was all just a game, a puzzle to solve. No one ever pays attention to scholars. We're used to being ignored, or ridiculed. Some of the old houses had already died out. And as far as I could tell, the heirs of the remaining great Lords of the Blood were killed either in the war or in the

Great Fire. Hunting for the amulets seemed like a purely academic exercise. I never thought—"

"What happened, Treven?" Penhallow's voice was silky, reassuring, and Connor knew that it carried a nearly irresistible compulsion for those who were not linked by blood to the *talishte*.

Penhallow's voice helped Lowrey collect himself, though his face still showed pain and regret. "A day after I'd been to visit Lady Alarian, rough men came to her house. They demanded to know what she'd told me. But the dreams had warned her, and she brandished a sword at them, told them to get out of her house. Imagine that." He chuckled sadly. "An old lady thin as a reed, swinging a sword and cursing at them like a pirate."

Lowrey drew a deep breath. "They were Pollard's men, of course, probably sent by Reese. The men didn't leave, and they overpowered her and her servants." He swallowed hard. "Sweet Esthrane, Penhallow, they tortured her, an old lady, trying to make her tell them. She died," he said, swallowing again. "But she didn't tell them anything. Spat in their faces," he said, wiping a tear away.

"How do you know this?" Penhallow's voice was gentle, still satin smooth with compulsion.

"A few of the servants managed to escape. One of them remembered letting me in at the door and had obviously overheard a little of our conversation before Lady Alarian sent him away. He was frightened out of his wits, and he could only think to come find me, warn me."

"What happened to him?" Penhallow prompted.

"I took him to the abbey, where the silent scholars are, the ones who took a vow not to speak. I have friends there, and they hid him."

"Did you have any idea you were being followed?" Penhallow asked.

Lowrey shook his head miserably. "Not at the time. I was stupid. No, not stupid, just naïve. There were signs, warnings. I thought they were just strange coincidences. I wasn't thinking about my odd little obsession mattering to anyone but other scholars and mages. Never thought it would threaten anyone. I hadn't even heard of Vedran Pollard or Pentreath Reese." He looked at Penhallow as if pleading for absolution. "I wasn't even a prominent mage. I'd hoped that this study might get someone at one of the monastic archives to notice me."

"How long after all this were you kidnapped?" Penhallow asked gently.

"Just a day or two," Lowrey replied. "Traher Voss is the one who put the other pieces together, explained what was going on."

"What about your research? The things Lady Alarian gave you?" Connor asked, unable to wait any longer.

"I had hidden them, but not because I thought ruffians would want them. Professional jealousy among scholars can be quite vicious," Lowrey said, sniffing back tears. "I was afraid one of my colleagues might get wind of what I was working on and steal my notes. Once Voss told me what was actually going on, I realized that I didn't really have a choice about telling him. I was going to be in 'protective custody' by either Voss or Reese, and Voss seemed the better end of the deal."

He sighed. "Voss's men went out the night they abducted me—or saved me, depending on your point of view. Brought back everything. Good thing, too. Someone burned my house down the next night." Lowrey's bravado had disappeared. Without it, he looked older, defeated.

"You didn't realize the danger," Penhallow said in his most compelling tone. "You weren't to blame for what happened. You did the right thing to trust Voss, and now you can help stop Reese and Pollard."

To Connor's surprise, Lowrey sat up, his spine stiffened by sudden anger. "I don't need your damned compulsion to make me feel better, Penhallow. I'll keep my guilt, thank you very much. I need it to be angry enough to be brave. I'm no warrior, and I might be an old fool at times, but if I can do anything to bring down those bastards and hurt them like they hurt her, then I'm in." Lowrey's blue eyes crackled with anger, and his hard-angled face took on a look of determination.

Penhallow sat back. "Good. Because it's going to get interesting. But first, we've got to get out of here."

Connor shifted in his seat. From the time Lowrey had begun recounting his adventures, something nettled Connor in the back of his mind, although he couldn't quite put the feeling into words. Engrossed in Lowrey's tale, he'd tried to squelch the feeling, but it grew stronger until he felt it like an itch under his skin.

"Can I see what you collected?" Connor blurted. Penhallow and Lowrey looked at him strangely, and then Lowrey shrugged.

"Over here," he said, rising and beckoning Connor to follow.

The nettled feeling in Connor's mind grew stronger, as if a vital memory eluded his reach. Mystified at his own feelings, Connor knew that he could no more deny the urge than stop breathing.

He followed Lowrey to a small library off the sitting room. Books, scrolls, and iron-bound wooden trunks of every size and shape filled the floor-to-ceiling bookshelves to overflowing, and then were stacked around the sides of the room.

Penhallow was watching him with a puzzled expression, but said nothing. Connor was relieved; he could neither explain himself nor resist the compulsion flowing through him. The books on one side of the room seemed to draw him, and Connor let himself move closer. His right hand stretched out, as if on its own volition, seeking a book Connor was sure he had never seen before, but whose image was clear and sharp in his mind.

"Connor?" Penhallow said quietly. Connor ignored him, intent on the book. He began digging among the stacks of books and scrolls, tossing things aside in his urgency.

"Connor!" This time, Penhallow's voice carried compulsion, but for once, it had no effect. Connor kept digging. Penhallow took a step toward him, but Lowrey laid a hand on Penhallow's arm and shook his head, watching Connor with a thoughtful expression.

Just then, Connor's right hand touched the binding on a small leather journal. Its worn cover was unadorned, and it was of a size to fit easily into a pouch or beneath a vest without attracting attention. By comparison to the illuminated manuscripts and fancy scrolls around it, the journal was utterly unremarkable, easily overlooked.

Connor turned to the others, holding the journal aloft, brandishing it in triumph.

"Connor—" Penhallow ventured again. Lowrey hushed him, watching owlishly as Connor carried the journal to a table and opened it.

Inside, the pages were filled with a tight, neat script in symbols Connor had never seen before. He remembered opening the journal to its first page, and then everything went black.

"Connor?" Penhallow's voice was soothing. Connor found himself lying on the small sofa in the parlor, a cold cloth across his forehead. Both Lowrey and Penhallow were regarding him with a mixture of curiosity and concern.

"Oh, gods," Connor moaned, and closed his eyes. "I'm sorry. I'm so, so sorry."

"Connor—"

"I tried to tell Garnoc. I meant to. Then he sent me to the library to find the map and the Great Fire came, and he sent me away. Oh, gods. I never meant to betray anyone. I'm so sorry."

"Connor." This time, the voice sounded with compulsion, cutting through Connor's panic and the blinding headache that throbbed behind his temples. "What makes you think you've betrayed anyone?"

Connor did not open his eyes. Shame overwhelmed him, and he struggled to find his voice. "I kept blacking out. At least three times, either on my way back to Garnoc from seeing you, or when I was on an errand for Garnoc, I'd be on the road and then suddenly wake up in a ditch candlemarks later, with no memory of what happened. And I swear, I had nothing to drink. You've got to believe me," he said desperately. He opened his eyes and clutched at Penhallow's sleeve.

"No memory at all. I was so afraid that I'd been bewitched by someone who wanted to know Lord Garnoc's business. I knew I should tell him, but I was ashamed—and afraid."

"You were bewitched all right, by a master," Lowrey said, and to Connor's amazement, the mage chuckled. "I haven't seen a 'buried treasure' spell for a long time, and I'm betting this is a powerful one."

"Buried treasure?" Penhallow raised one eyebrow inquiringly.

"Oh, it has a fancy magical name, but that's what we called it. It's a memory charm wrapped in a forget spell. The good ones are quite complex, and this one would need to be if you never noticed anything amiss through the *kruvgaldur*."

"What in Raka are you talking about?" Connor tried to sit up, but Penhallow pressed him gently back into the cushions.

Lowrey grinned. "Do you remember anything about the passage you just read from that journal for us?"

"Read?" Connor looked from Lowrey to Penhallow as if he expected a bad joke. "I couldn't read a word of it. It was nothing but symbols and nonsense." Lowrey and Penhallow exchanged glances. "What?"

"I figured as much from the vacant look in your eyes when you were reading. Fact is, you scanned through that mage's book without a hitch, even though that script is only known to master mages. Then you read a portion out loud to us." Lowrey looked at Penhallow and grinned. "I've got a good idea who set this up."

Penhallow looked at him nonplussed. "If you don't stop teasing the boy, Treven, I shall be forced to extract your main point myself," he said, giving a flash of his eyeteeth.

Lowrey grimaced. "No need to be a bully. I thought it was plain. Vigus Quintrel left us a trail of bread crumbs to find him—and he hid the trail in here," he said, reaching over to tap Connor's forehead.

"Explain," Penhallow said, regarding Connor with a worried glance.

"Vigus obviously feared Meroven would make some kind of major magical strike. He planned his disappearance carefully. But he also knew that you and Garnoc would need a way to find him," Lowrey replied, warming to the topic. "And if he'd been paying attention, he'd have realized Conroy here was your courier."

"Connor," Connor corrected under his breath.

Lowrey dismissed his objection with a gesture. "It would have been easy for a mage like Quintrel to use magic on Connor, put him into a deep sleep, plant information in his head that wouldn't be remembered without a trigger, and then erase any memory of the event. Connor would have a 'blackout,' as he calls it. There would be nothing for your *kruvgaldur* to find, and no one would be the wiser until the triggers Quintrel set made Connor remember part of the message."

"Part of the message?" Penhallow looked sharply at Lowrey.

Lowrey nodded. "I'm quite sure that if there were multiple blackouts, Quintrel took the opportunity to hide all the information he thought we'd need where no one would find it—until it was time."

"So I didn't betray anyone?" Connor asked, feeling hopeful for the first time in months.

Lowrey chuckled. "Doubtful. You're the key Quintrel hid in plain sight." He looked at Penhallow. "Which makes him a pawn in a very dangerous game, Lanyon. If Reese ever suspected—"

Penhallow nodded solemnly. "I understand."

Connor's eyes widened. "Oh, no. I didn't ask for some mage to go mucking around in my mind, shifting my memories around. Reese will try to kill me, won't he?"

Lowrey shrugged. "Only if he finds out. And he won't kill you right away—he'll try to find out what you know, even if he has to cut your—"

Penhallow cleared his throat loudly. "That's quite enough, Treven. Connor's already had a fright. You're not helping." He looked at Connor, and Connor saw a flicker of worry in the *talishte*'s blue eyes. "I will protect you, Connor. I've bested Reese for several hundred years, and I'm not about to lose to him now. You have my word."

Lowrey snorted. "Did you forget we're bottled up under siege?"

"Safe for the moment," Penhallow muttered.

"What...what did I say? When I read from the book?" Connor asked. His headache was easing, and he managed to sit up.

"You said, 'A remnant remains. I have hidden hope. When the light returns, so will the lanterns and their keepers.'"

"That's it?" Connor said incredulously. "That's all I repeated, out of that whole journal? That bit of rubbish is what's had me scared out of my head these last few months?"

Lowrey grinned. "If there's one thing a mage likes better than a complicated spell, it's a riddle. Quintrel's hidden away mages with potential, spirited them out of the city before the Great Fire. That's his remnant. When the light—magic—comes back, there will be mages with the potential to wield great power—the lantern keepers—to use the magic. That's his 'hidden hope.'"

"So Quintrel thought that magic could return," Penhallow pressed.

Lowrey nodded. "Apparently so."

"You think there's more hidden in my head?" Connor asked. He was proud that his voice sounded reasonably calm, although his heart was still thudding.

"I'm sure of it. Probably triggered by some other item of Quintrel's he's left lying around. Like that journal. Meaningless to anyone else, but with the key," Lowrey said with a meaningful look at Connor, "everything is clear." He met Penhallow's gaze. "I suggest you hang on tight to that journal," he added. "There may be more you need later."

Connor frowned. "If Treven's right and it takes timing as well as the special objects to raise the magic, then we've got to tell Blaine. He could get to Mirdalur and have nothing happen."

"Or he could find Reese and Pollard waiting for him," Penhallow said grimly.

Lowrey sat up in alarm. "Blaine? Blaine McFadden is still alive? Is he still in Velant?"

Connor shook his head. "No. He came back to Donderath to see if he could raise the magic."

Lowrey looked distressed. "That's bad. He can't go to Mirdalur, not without the proper preparations."

"Why not?" Penhallow asked, concerned. "What's the risk? Without the other elements, nothing will happen."

Lowrey shook his head. "No, that was one of the pieces I discovered from the journals and notes Lady Alarian shared with me. The first lords set a trap. They were afraid that someone would try to undo what they had done. For those who aren't of the blood, Mirdalur is just a ruin. But if a Lord of the Blood returns without the proper elements, the energies will protect themselves."

"How?" Connor pressed.

"I'm not sure exactly, but the warning was unmistakable," Lowrey said. He looked from Connor to Penhallow. "Of course, that was when the tame magic, the *hasithara*, still worked. Without it, who knows? Mirdalur is a place of power— a place where the *visithara*, wild magic, is strong. That magic is feral now. It makes Mirdalur a very dangerous place. We've got to stop Blaine McFadden from going to Mirdalur until we know what Quintrel had in mind."

"Because if anything happens to Blaine, the ability to fix the magic may die with him," Connor murmured.

CHAPTER TWENTY-NINE

WHERE DID YOU GET THE HORSES?" BLAINE stared at Geir and the six horses that stood waiting for them.

"Since the Great Fire, finding a horse isn't really a problem," Geir replied. "So many of the manors were destroyed that some of the best horseflesh in the Ascendant Kingdoms is wandering around riderless—if you're fast enough to catch them," he said with a smile that showed the tips of his long eyeteeth.

"You stole them?" Piran asked incredulously.

Kestel elbowed him. "No king. No soldiers. Remember? We're not likely to hang as horse thieves."

"It's just a touchy subject with me," Piran said, misgiving clear in his face. "It was one of the things that landed me in Velant."

Blaine chuckled, knowing that brawling while on duty, disorderly conduct, and behavior unbecoming to an officer were likewise among the charges that got Piran a one-way ticket to Velant, but he did not mention it. "I think they're the most beautiful things I've seen since we landed," Blaine replied. "I was trying to figure out how long it would take to walk home, and I didn't like the answer."

The horses had no tack, promising an uncomfortable three-day ride to Glenreith. "If you were going to steal horses, couldn't you have managed a few saddles as well?" Piran grumbled good-naturedly.

Blaine and the others fell silent as they rode across the moon-lit landscape. They rode cross-country, avoiding the roads to elude Reese and the highwaymen Geir assured them lay in wait around nearly every bend. Their route also gave them their clearest view yet of just what Donderath's fall had cost. When they had landed in the ruined city of Castle Reach, Blaine had prepared himself for the devastation. This was worse.

Once-fertile farm fields were scorched black. Stone fences and cottages were nothing more than blackened heaps. Of the houses made from sod, wood, or thatch, nothing but charred posts remained. None of them spoke as they rode across untended farm fields grown high with weeds. Here and there, they spotted pigs and chickens, cows and mules, wandering free, mute survivors of the Cataclysm.

"The fire did so much damage," Dawe murmured.

"It was worse by harvest," Geir said. "Without their small magics, farmers were beset by locusts. They had relied on the magic for so long, many forgot the old ways to drive away pests. Magic helped them drain fields or redirect streams in ways that fought nature. Without the magic, the low places flooded. Rot and blight made for a slim harvest.

"Tradesmen who cut corners building fences and barns and who had used a flicker of magic to cover their lapses were caught out when their buildings and hedgerows collapsed," Geir went on. "And without the midwives' magic, animals and people alike suffered."

Blaine glanced at Geir, surprised at the sorrow in his voice and the pained expression on his face. "It was much worse than even the *talishte* could remember," Geir said quietly. "Even most of the old ones can't remember a time before magic. Many of us still have descendants living in Donderath, and while they may be distant relatives, we are aware of how they fare. So very many died," he murmured. "Most mortals no longer know the way things were done before the magic. There are few aside from the *talishte* to teach them, but most scorn our help."

The night was cold, and a thin dusting of fresh snow lay across the ground. Kestel shivered, pulling her cloak more tightly around her shoulders, but Blaine wondered whether it was due to the chill or to the awful realization of what had befallen their homeland. Finally Verran broke the silence. "There's naught left to steal," he said in a hushed voice. The others turned to him with a questioning look.

"On the way back aboard the ship, I had a picture in my mind what it might be like. I'd figured all the strange lights and such that Connor told us about would have scared off the locals and left a bounty to pick through." Verran sighed. "I'd fancied myself sifting through the leavings, gathering a small fortune in pilfered goods." His expression grew serious. "But there's nothing left, and nowhere to sell it, is there?" Grief was clear in his voice. "I guess I didn't want to understand what Connor was telling us. I can't believe that it's all gone."

Blaine listened numbly, fear growing as he wondered what they would find when they reached Glenreith. Growing up under the harsh discipline of his father, Blaine had often dreamed that lightning would strike the old manor, collapsing it around the old man. Now that the possibility appeared very real, grief and fear filled him. All the years in Velant, and after that, as a "free" man in Edgeland, Blaine had kept alive the hope that his sacrifice had enabled Mari, Carr, and Judith to live a better life. In dreams, he had seen himself reunited with his family, walking the familiar pathways on the manor's large grounds. Glenreith had always remained a constant. He did not want to come so far to find that only rubble remained.

At Geir's request, they rode with swords and crossbows at the ready, visibly armed. To Blaine's eye, they appeared to be the very highwaymen they sought to elude. They passed few other travelers on the rutted roads, and their group outnumbered all of the small clutches of wayfarers who were unlucky enough to be about by night. Blaine was relieved when the first night was uneventful.

They took shelter just before dawn in the ruins of an old stone barn. "If it hasn't fallen down by now, it's not likely to do so tonight," Geir said, offering scant comfort as Blaine eyed the rubble of the barn's old walls and lofts. "If it's still standing, we'll be safe enough for one day."

Dawe poked among the wreckage as the others found places to sleep. Blaine saw Dawe stoop and sift through the leaf-strewn rubble, pocketing items as he went. Curious, Blaine walked over. "I thought Verran was the thief in our bunch," Blaine said with as much lightness as he could manage.

Dawe stretched his lanky frame and ran a hand back through his hair. "Can't steal from the dead, Mick," he said with a lop-sided smile. "You know me. Always tinkering. I'm just gathering up bits of metal. Got an idea for a special kind of crossbow that could fire faster and get off more arrows than an archer can shoot. Might come in handy if Reese's *talishte* come at us, or if Pollard's men outnumber us."

Blaine eyed the collection of iron bits Dawe had gathered in a rag. "You think you can make something like that?"

Dawe's eyes sparked with the first enthusiasm Blaine had

seen in several days. "I'd sure like to give it a try. I'm guessing Glenreith had a blacksmith, didn't it? If so, I can get the forge going, see what I can do."

Blaine sighed. "It used to. Had to make repairs to the farm tools, shoe the horses, fix the wagons. That's assuming that there's anything standing at all," he added.

Dawe seemed to sense his mood, and he nodded. "So that's what's had you so quiet. Should have figured as much."

"I might drag everyone out here only to find that there's nothing left," Blaine replied, trying to keep his voice from giving away just how much he feared that outcome.

"Might be," Dawe allowed. "Then again, maybe it got off easy, on account of there not being a Lord of the Blood in residence. We might show up on the doorstep and have your aunt decide she doesn't want a bunch of criminals as houseguests."

Blaine pictured his aunt Judith, a thin, quiet woman who had withstood heartache and loss. She had married well as a young woman, to a man she had actually loved. First, there had been miscarriages, several of them. Finally, two treasured children were born, only to die before their tenth birthdays. Then her husband broke his neck in a riding accident. Grief-stricken and alone, Judith took on a new cause, doing her best to protect her sister by marriage from the brutality of Blaine's father. She had not succeeded, nor had she been able to protect Blaine, Mari, or Carr from Ian McFadden's wrath, although she did the best she could to offer comfort and healing. If anyone could have survived the Cataclysm, it would be Judith McFadden Ainsworth.

"In the old days, she might have been scandalized if a pack of ruffians showed up," Blaine said. "That was before she knew what a monster her brother was, and before I became a murderer," he added ruefully. "Aunt Judith is a survivor. If anyone's managed to keep a household together, it would be Judith, and if I know her, she's cared for the servants and the hired help as if they were family."

"Sounds like a formidable lady," Dawe said, bending to retrieve another bit of iron.

Blaine nodded. "She loved my brother and sister and I fiercely, and after our mother died, she did the best she could to protect us." He sighed. "What happened wasn't her fault. No one could control father." He paused. "What about you? We've been so busy running for our lives since we got back, I don't even know what the rest of you need to do now that we're home again."

"My wife ran off with another man not long after I was sent to Velant," Dawe said, kicking at stones to free a small iron bar. "That was the one letter I received." He gathered a few more rusted pieces, and then straightened. "Verran's sister died of the pox before we got our Tickets of Leave. We've been talking, Verran, Piran, Kestel, and me. None of us left anyone behind, not that would care. We came back to help you save the magic, and that's what we aim to do. Like it or not, Mick, you're stuck with us." *And with Geir*, Blaine thought.

Dawe and Blaine walked back to the rest of the group in silence. Dawe clapped him on the shoulder. "Get some sleep, Mick. I'll take first watch. It'll give me a chance to fiddle around with the metal I found and think about what I'll make of it." He grinned. "I've got the idea of the thing pretty well worked out in my head. By the time I can get a forge fired up, I ought to be able to get it built." He paused. "Geir's gone to ground in the storage bins, but he said we could count on him being ready to go just after sunset."

"I have the feeling we'll need your invention sooner than we think," Blaine said with a yawn, suddenly exhausted. "Wake me when it's my shift," he added, finding a spot near the others to stretch out. Aching in every muscle from the ride as well as from the fight with Reese's men, Blaine was asleep almost immediately.

It felt to Blaine as if he had just finished his shift at watch and gotten settled when a voice roused him.

"Get up!"

It was the alarm in Geir's voice as much as the command that roused Blaine. Anything that alarmed a *talishte* was worthy of attention. "What's wrong?" Blaine asked, getting to his feet and grabbing his sword. Piran and the others were also struggling to wake.

Blaine looked out over the ruined stone wall. Night had fallen. A full moon hung just above the horizon, but tonight it was blood red, with an eerie white ring. A swath of crimson light below it cast a bloody path to the horizon. Between the moon and the horizon, the sky seemed unnaturally dark.

"That darkness is a magic storm," Geir said. "You've got to get below, into the granary bins, until it passes over us. Go!"

A rush of adrenaline drove the last of sleep from Blaine's mind as he and the others gathered their few possessions and headed for the hole in the floor where Geir had taken his daytime rest. There was no ladder, so Blaine and Piran were the first to swing down, letting themselves drop a few feet to the packed ground below. Dawe and Verran lowered Kestel, then swung down themselves, followed by Geir, who appeared to levitate down effortlessly, drawing the warped wooden trapdoor into place overhead.

"What now?" Piran asked.

"We wait," Geir replied. "You're just lucky that the storm came when one of us was awake to spot it."

They fell silent, huddled in the farthest corner of the cramped bin. A distant rumbling, like the sound of an army approaching at full gallop, grew louder, then became deafening. The air in the bin was alive with energy, the way Blaine had felt once when he'd narrowly missed being struck by lightning. His skin prickled with warning, the fine hairs on his arms and on the back of his neck stood up, and the air had an odd tang that left a bitter taste in the back of his mouth.

Overhead, it sounded as if large rocks pummeled the barn floor, and Blaine wondered whether their ramshackle shelter could withstand the assault. Wind howled, and the air grew heavy around them. A sudden headache made Blaine reel, and he reached a hand out to steady himself against the side of the bin. His vision blurred with the pain, and his ears throbbed as if they might burst from pressure.

As Blaine watched, the air in the small chamber began to glow, glistening like snow crystals on a bitter winter's day. The air grew colder, then frigid. The glistening crystals cast a cold light that illuminated their hiding place. The light gradually changed from clear to a rainbow of shades, rippling and arcing like the Spirit Lights Blaine had seen in the far north of Edgeland. The mist began to swirl around them though the air in the bin had been stuffy and still.

Forms began to appear in the glistening, shifting air. At first, the images were abstract, difficult to make out. Gradually, they grew clearer. Glowing eyes in baleful faces took form amid shimmering particles. Bent and gnarled shapes with long, sharp claws growled as if to attack. Disembodied spirits loomed up from the mist, shadow people with long, grasping arms. Finally in the nightmare shapes, Blaine saw the face of his father. The face that appeared to him was not that of the older man that Blaine had killed. Instead it was the image of a younger Ian McFadden, disfigured with rage, the way he had looked to Blaine as a young boy.

Blaine had no idea whether others saw the same shapes he did, but by their expressions, they, too, saw horrors. He was willing to wager that whatever the nightmares the others saw, none but he was visited by the image of Ian McFadden.

Beside him, Kestel cried out in pain and collapsed. A moment later, Dawe groaned and fell to one side. Their bodies twitched and bucked as if possessed. Kestel's face twisted in pain, and Dawe's features grew tight and his breathing shallow. Verran said nothing, but he fell over as if poleaxed and lay very still.

Blaine fought the headache and the growing pressure that made it difficult to breathe, but in the end, he fell to his knees and then collapsed as consciousness faded. He had no idea how long he was out, but he came around slowly and heard voices nearby.

Blaine groaned and struggled to sit. Geir helped him up.

"Do you feel it?" Blaine asked, breathing slowly and deeply against the throbbing pain in his head.

"Yes," Geir replied. "In my blood."

"Blood?"

"It burned like fire in every vein," Geir said, his voice tight with pain. "The old magic of the Dark Gift fights the rogue power of the storm. If I weren't as old as I am, it could destroy me."

Slowly, Blaine's headache began to ease, retreating from his skull little by little and returning both vision and the ability to think clearly.

No one spoke for a while. Blaine had no idea how long the

storm had taken. He rested against the stone wall, afraid to move for fear of bringing back the awful pain. They waited in silence. The air in the bin had grown stuffy with their breath and sweat, despite how cold it was outside. Finally, Geir stood. He levitated up to the top of the bin and threw the wooden panel back. Sweet, fresh, cold air swept into the bin, chilling after the unnatural warmth of being huddled in such a small space.

Moonlight filtered into the bin. In the faint light, Blaine could see that Kestel lay near him, but her features had relaxed and her breathing was now regular.

Dawe blinked several times and sat up, with Piran's assistance. "I didn't feel this bad when Prokief had me stuffed in the Hole," he said in a strangled voice.

"Count yourself lucky that you survived," Geir replied. "Had we not been able to take shelter belowground, at least some—if not all—of us might have died."

Verran groaned and rolled over on his side, managing to sit up without help. He let out a potent curse. "Torven's horns! How can a storm leave me feeling as if I've been turned inside out?"

"Because these storms have the power to do just that," Geir replied.

Kestel was the last to rouse. It was rare for Kestel to show weakness, unless she feigned distress to gain the advantage of a mark. Now her skin was pale and pain glinted in her eyes.

"I don't need help," Kestel protested as both Blaine and Piran gently eased her to a sitting position, though the fact that she accepted their assistance gave the lie to her words.

"Are you all right?" Verran asked.

Kestel gave a weak nod. "By the stars and the gods, I've never felt anything like that, not even when I'd been poisoned."

"You were poisoned?" Piran asked, glancing at her sideways.

Kestel made a dismissive gesture. "It was a long time ago, at court. I survived."

"Obviously."

Geir held out his hand to Piran. "I'll get you up to the top," he said. "I'd like a fighter up first, just in case," he said. Piran nodded, taking his meaning.

Blaine was next. A few moments more, and Geir had retrieved the rest of the party from the bin. Geir kicked the door shut and walked over to where Blaine and Piran stood.

"Let's see what the storm made of our horses," Geir said tersely.

They had slept through the day in the safety of the barn before the storm struck just after sunset. Now they looked across the moonlit landscape at terrain that had changed dramatically since they sought shelter the day before. Balls of ice larger than a man's fist littered the ground, thick as fallen leaves. Trees had been uprooted, split down the middle, burned as if by lightning or just reduced to a scattering of wood chips. The far corner of the stone barn had also collapsed, and the remnants of its roof had torn away completely.

Piran wrapped a rag from the barn around a broken board and struck flint to steel to light the makeshift torch. He held it aloft, giving them a better look at the devastation. Verran made a second torch and lit it from the blazing rag.

"Dear gods above and below. Look there," Kestel said in a strangled voice, pointing to a bloody heap. Blaine ventured closer and found what was left of one of their horses. At first, Blaine thought the animal had been skinned alive, but when he dared venture closer, he saw that it had been mangled.

"What about the other horses?" Piran asked.

"Over here," Verran shouted, scouting around to the other

side of the barn. In a copse of trees outside of the circle of damage inflicted by the storm, the other five horses grazed peacefully, totally unscathed.

Scattered across the ruined landscape, Blaine saw grisly examples of the storm's effects on living creatures. Pieces of the ruined barn roof had been flung with such violence that they were impaled through the trunks of trees. Formerly level ground had buckled into a rippling obstacle course, and large rocks had been thrust up from below the ground's surface.

"Can you bring a torch over here?" Dawe called. Piran and Blaine walked to where Dawe bent to look at a small carcass. "That's interesting," he said, pointing to the dead bird. "It's a coteril, a bird that only lives in the high mountains in the north of Donderath. I heard a man, an adventurer, talk about them once. They don't migrate out of their area. But look," he said, sweeping his arm around the circle of devastation. "There are dozens of them."

Geir walked up behind them. "No one knows how the magic storms work, but what you're seeing isn't uncommon. Things disappear in the storms and are never seen again. People and animals, too. But it's just as common for the storm to set down the bodies of strange animals, people no one knows, and plants that grow nowhere in the vicinity. Once or twice, the person left behind by the storm has been alive."

"Could they say what happened to them?" Dawe asked.

Geir shook his head. "Nothing coherent. The most anyone could coax out of them was a name or a place and ramblings about the lights. It was enough to prove that they'd been taken by the storm a great distance from where they appeared. Unfortunately, the experience drove them mad, so there was very little useful information to be gained from them."

Blaine stared at the clear line between the storm-damaged

circle and the unaffected land just beyond it. "How often do the storms come?" he asked.

"There's no predicting them," Geir replied. "But I can tell you that they're happening more frequently with each month that passes."

"Is the magic trying to heal itself?" Dawe asked.

Geir shrugged. "Perhaps. Maybe, left to itself, the energies will balance themselves and the storms will cease. But with the storms happening more often and in growing strength, none of us may be alive to see that day."

"Is it safe to travel to Glenreith?" Blaine felt restless, impatient. Whether it was the aftereffects of nearly dying or just a wish to end the uncertainty about his home and family, he could not be sure. All he knew was that he was anxious to get moving.

Geir nodded. "As safe as anything is these days on the Continent. It's not impossible for more than one storm to pass through an area in a short time, but it is uncommon. We'd best get going. Storms aren't the only danger, and the longer we stay still, the more likely it is for another problem to find us."

"But we're short a horse," Dawe protested.

"I'll leave the horses for you," Geir said with a trace of a smile. "I can move as quickly as a horse, though it drains me and I'll need to feed more often." At Dawe's worried look, Geir's smile widened. "Don't worry. I can find suitable animal 'donors,' unless we run into a deserving brigand or two. And with all the farm animals running free, it shouldn't take long to find a replacement for the horse." He looked up at the sky. "I'm more concerned about making sure we've got shelter before dawn. Best we get going."

Blaine began to recognize landmarks, confirming that they were getting close to Glenreith. He grew quiet the closer they got to his old home, letting the others keep up the conversation. Doubts gnawed at him, making him question whether or not going to Glenreith was a good idea. Kestel said nothing, but she had let her horse drop back to ride beside him, and he suspected that she guessed the direction of his thoughts.

Twice they left the road at Geir's warning to circle cross-country to avoid small groups of armed men. Both times, they were able to dodge the patrols without incident, but after the second time, Geir led them off the main road to a wagon trail that was hardly more than a path. Doing so slowed their progress, but there were no further sightings, and the patrols appeared to have remained on the main highway.

"A few candlemarks' ride and we should be at Glenreith," Blaine said at last. He looked at Geir. "If it's all the same to you, I'd like to circle around to high ground before we ride up to the manor." Blaine pointed to a rise in the distance. "I'd rather know how much of it is standing, and whether brigands have taken over."

Geir nodded. "It would be good to know if it's inhabited, or even habitable." He met Blaine's gaze. "And even better if we can assure that its residents are who you believe them to be."

Although it broke Blaine's heart to admit, it was quite possible that his family was dead, and that the manor stood empty or was claimed by squatters. "We'll know soon enough," Blaine said tightly, mounting up.

Before long, they reached the crest of the hill. Clouds hid the moon, and Blaine was thankful that they would not be silhouetted against the sky atop the rise. He dismounted and walked with Geir up to the edge of the overlook, staying low so as not to be seen from below.

"It looks like some buildings survived while others didn't," Geir observed.

In the valley below them, Blaine saw the manor compound. Glenreith's original manor house, abandoned long before Blaine's birth but still standing when he left for Velant, was now a heap of rubble, as were the old outbuildings and the ancient fortifications. The "new" estate, which was farther from the river, had been built over one hundred years ago. It was still standing, along with the stables and dependencies and a high, solid wall that encircled them. The buildings that remained and the wall were several centuries newer than the original manor. The high wall around the perimeter of Glenreith's grounds was also standing—a good thing, since at that moment, there was a force of twenty armed men camped outside the manor's gates. "Damn." Blaine swore under his breath.

"Any idea whose men those are?" Blaine asked, an angry undercurrent in his voice.

"If I had to guess, I'd say Pollard's," Geir replied. "They're not wearing livery. We've seen more militia units since the Great Fire. Most of them are nothing but brigands." He paused, straining for a better view in the faint moonlight, and Blaine wondered just how much the *talishte*'s more acute vision and hearing could make out.

"It appears to be a small occupation," Geir said. "They don't look bent on attacking. There aren't any catapults or battering rams. Odd. They just seem to be waiting for something."

"Or someone?" Piran asked with a glance toward Blaine.

Blaine frowned. "Pollard thought he'd taken care of me back in Edgeland, remember? Unless he had a spy on the ship..." He paused, thinking. "One of the *talishte* we fought at Penhallow's crypt made a comment about how I 'should have stayed in Velant.'"

He shook his head. "If Pollard knows I'm back, it's not unlikely to assume I'd return to Glenreith."

"Whoever they are, they're not friends," Geir replied tersely. "And if we want into the manor, we're going to need to take care of the problem."

"There are twenty of them," Dawe protested.

Geir grinned, making his long eyeteeth plain. "Good odds for us, I'd say." He grew serious. "They don't seem to be worried about attacking; seems to me, they're focused on keeping everyone bottled up within the walls. We could be on them before they know we're even here."

Piran nodded. "We're fairly well armed. It's several candle-marks yet before dawn. I'm with Geir. I think we can take them."

Blaine considered the situation for a moment. "What if they've got *talishte*, too? I've had my fill of fighting vampires."

Geir looked back toward the encampment, his eyes narrowing as he thought. "If they were *talishte*, they would have already struck. It's nighttime. They have no reason to wait. They wouldn't have to break down the gate; they could fly over it. And there's precious little cover. *Talishte* wouldn't play a waiting game. They'd take a small force and strike quickly." His smile became predatory. "As we will do."

Within another candlemark, they were ready. The horses were tethered in a stand of trees well back from the crest of the hill, safely out of sight. Piran handed out weapons from the cache they had gathered. Through it all, Dawe sat to the side, fiddling with his crossbow, which Blaine noticed had been oddly altered.

"What'd you do to that thing?" he asked.

Dawe looked up. "It's not as good as it could be, but we haven't exactly had a forge for me to work with. Still, I've made a few modifications, changed the tension, added a few extras," he said with a hint of pride in his voice. "It won't shoot quite as far as before, but I can reload faster."

Blaine clapped him on the shoulder. "That's good enough for me."

Moving silently, they made their way down, with the hill between them and their quarry. A stand of tangled, dead weeds gave them cover as they circled the soldiers encamped at Glenreith's doorstep. Blaine and Piran went to the left of the camp. Dawe took his altered crossbow and found a sheltered spot from which to pick off soldiers along the back of the camp. Kestel and Verran followed, ready to provide a distraction to lure soldiers closer to Dawe's range. Geir took to the air, and within minutes had eliminated both sentries without making a sound.

Verran and Kestel slipped closer to the back row of tents, and Verran began to play a lively tune on his pennywhistle. Kestel let her cloak drop, revealing a mix of silk scarves and split skirts that showed more than they covered, the costume of a successful camp follower. She began to dance to the tune Verran played, and the soft jangle of bells at her wrists coupled with the strange music soon drew the men from their tents. Blaine shook his head in wonder at the outfit Kestel had managed to put together from the odds and ends in her small bag, but improvised as it was, the scandalous outfit quickly overcame the soldiers' suspicions, and soon a row of men in their nightshirts gathered, catcalling and whistling their admiration.

Kestel swayed a few steps closer, then sashayed back, beckoning with the graceful movement of her hands for her admirers to follow. Verran played, seemingly intent on his music. Blaine had watched both Verran and Kestel hide at least a dozen knives each beneath their garments, and the soldiers would soon be within striking distance.

With the attention drawn toward the rear of the camp, Geir touched down in shadows near the front, moving with *talishte* speed from one darkened tent to another, quickly dispatching those who had not roused to watch the show. Blaine and Piran waited for their part in the attack. Kestel had lured the soldiers several yards from their tents, and in a few steps, they would be within Dawe's range. Verran began a new tune, and Kestel's dance became even more suggestive, swaying her hips, revealing more than a flash of breast, and undulating with the rhythm of the music until Blaine feared that the cheering men might rush toward her. Kestel was moving steadily backward, closer to Dawe, and as the music reached its climax, she reached up languorously to loosen the knot of the silk scarves that covered her chest, letting the silk fall away to dance naked from the waist up. Eagerly the soldiers edged closer, and Kestel flashed them an enigmatic smile, their attention completely focused on her breasts, her narrow swaying hips, and the promise of paradise in her eyes.

They never had a chance.

Dawe got off three good shots before most of the soldiers even realized they were under attack. Blaine and Piran rushed from the shadows, attacking with swords and daggers. Before the besotted soldiers could react, Kestel had slipped her hands down her torso as if to loosen the ties on her skirts, but her hands snapped up and toward the soldiers, sending several small throwing knives with the practiced aim of an assassin. Verran had also unsheathed two of the knives hidden in his clothing, and rushed at the two nearest soldiers, striking one through the heart and slashing another across the throat before they had gathered their wits.

Belatedly, the camp's survivors roused in alarm. Geir easily held his own against three soldiers who had obviously just rolled from their cots and grabbed their swords, running out to meet the threat without full uniforms or armor. Blaine and

Piran each fought two soldiers, who battled fiercely as the odds against them became clear.

One of the soldiers rushed at Kestel, enraged, and grabbed her by the shoulder, wheeling her to face him. His look of rage shifted to shock and then fear as she used his momentum against him, tumbling him across her back and onto the ground, then ramming a knife between his ribs an instant later. Blood spattered her bare chest, and in the moonlight she looked like a savage, avenging goddess.

In moments, the battle was over. The bodies of half-dressed, bloody soldiers littered the ground. Verran and Kestel had already begun to loot the tents of the dead, and sometime amid the action, Kestel managed to retie her scarves into a semblance of propriety and to retrieve her cast-off cloak. Geir joined Blaine and Piran as they were cleaning their swords, and Dawe sauntered over, his altered crossbow slung over his shoulder.

"Pitiful excuses for mercenaries," Piran said, looking disdainfully at the bodies scattered around them. "Have none of them seen a woman before?"

Dawe chuckled. "Maybe they've never seen a woman like Kestel," he said. "Even if we've become familiar with her charms."

"In your dreams," Kestel snorted, rejoining them. She and Verran each carried an armful of stolen treasures: food, supplies, and weapons.

"Piran's right," Blaine said. "If these are Pollard's men, he's scraping the bottom of the barrel."

Geir shrugged. "Be thankful for small favors. Would you prefer another fight like the one at Penhallow's crypt?"

"That's not what I meant," Blaine replied quickly. "But you've got to admit, they were hardly crack troops. Makes you wonder what their real purpose was and why they were sent here. I'm beginning to doubt their presence had anything to do with us."

"Actually, if Pollard gambled that their presence alone would intimidate the people inside the walls, he was betting it would never come to a fight," Piran replied. "Why waste your best troops if all you really want to do is keep someone bottled up?"

Blaine sighed. The moment he had often dreamed about and most dreaded was now upon him. The group gathered up the last of the usable plunder and headed for the gates, dragging their stolen windfall behind them wrapped in tent canvas. The rest of the group waited at a distance as Blaine approached the gates.

We look like vagabonds, beggars, or worse, Blaine thought. *I left in disgrace, and I'm not exactly coming back in triumph.*

Blaine reached the locked gates and stood far enough back to afford any watcher on the walls a clear view. *And a clear shot*, he thought gloomily. With his hands well away from his weapons, Blaine looked up at the top of the wall.

"We're here to see Lady Judith," he shouted.

"She has no time for the likes of you," a voice called back. "Be gone."

Blaine glowered. "We just saved your asses. A little gratitude, please. I need to see Lady Judith."

"Saved us so you could loot the place yourselves, you mean," the voice shouted back. "Be gone."

Blaine struggled with his temper. "If I can't see Lady Judith, then let me see Edward."

"What need do you have to see the seneschal?"

"I have a message from Lord Penhallow," Blaine replied, his voice growing brittle with anger. "You don't want to be responsible for the message not being delivered."

The threat of angering one of the *talishte* seemed to move the obdurate guard to action. Blaine heard a mumble of voices and saw motion as a runner was sent from the gate. After what seemed like an eternity, there was motion again, and Blaine spotted a second shadow above the wall's crenellation.

"I am Edward. Say your piece."

Despite his earlier mood, Blaine could not stop from smiling at the sound of the familiar voice. "Edward, It's me, Blaine. I've come home." He stood where the moonlight gave the watchers on the wall the best view, and looked up so that his face would be easily identifiable. He heard a gasp.

"How can it be? No one returns from Velant."

"Long story. Velant fell when the magic died. A merchant ship made it to Edgeland, and some of us sailed it back home. I'll tell you all the details when someone comes to let me into my own damned house," Blaine replied.

"How do we know it's really him?" the guard argued. "He could be the one who sent the soldiers."

"Vedran Pollard sent the soldiers," Blaine shouted. "He's working with Pentreath Reese, and every moment my friends and I stand here like targets, he could pick us off with bowmen. Let us in, and I'll explain everything."

"Let him in." Edward's voice carried down to the waiting group below. "I'll take responsibility." There was a murmured conference. "Oh, all right. Have it your way. Just let them in."

A few moments later, Blaine heard the sound of the gate's massive bar sliding back, and one of the heavy iron-bound oak doors swung partway open. "Enter slowly, hands away from your weapons," an unseen guard shouted.

Swearing under his breath, Blaine nodded to his friends and then approached the gate warily, hands raised. On the other side of the wall, eight bowmen with crossbows stood with quarrels notched and ready, aiming at his heart. His companions filed inside the gate and stood silently behind him. They had abandoned the looted weapons outside the gate.

"Get a good enough look yet? It's only been six godsdamned years," Blaine snapped.

A thin, older man pushed past the guards, and Blaine recognized Edward. They stood in silence for a moment, and then Edward nodded.

"Lower your weapons. It's Lord McFadden, all right." Edward gave a tired smile, and stepped forward to embrace Blaine, thumping him on the shoulder. "Welcome home, m'lord."

Blaine stepped back and laid a hand on Edward's shoulder. "It's good to see you, Edward." His face tightened in concern. "Aunt Judith, is she well?"

To his relief, Edward nodded once more. "As well as any of us are these days," he said.

"Trapped by brigands, and now vagabonds at the gate— sure, I understand." Blaine's tone made the comment seem such an everyday occurrence that Edward chuckled.

"Good to see the past few years haven't changed your sense of humor, m'lord," the seneschal said. For the first time, he looked up to take in Blaine's companions. "I see that you have friends with you."

"Kin now as much as kith," Blaine replied. "In a place like Edgeland, you make your own family."

Edward met his gaze, and a flicker of comprehension for what Blaine hadn't said aloud gave Blaine to know that the seneschal did understand. "Your guests are always welcome, m'lord. Let's get out of the cold and inside, where you can refresh yourselves. You've had a long journey."

Blaine chuckled. "In other words, we're filthy, unshaven vagabonds, and it would be nice to look presentable before Aunt Judith sees us."

A smile twitched at the corners of Edward's mouth. "As you say, m'lord."

Piran cleared his throat. "What about the weapons we scavenged...m'lord," he added a breath too late with a light touch of sarcasm.

Blaine looked to the guard. "When we fought off the intruders, we liberated weapons whose owners didn't need them anymore. They're wrapped in a tarp just beyond the gates. I believe we can never have too many weapons. Please have your men retrieve them."

Doubt and duty warred in the man's face, but training took precedence over his skepticism. "As you wish, m'lord."

Blaine looked at Kestel and the others who were still hanging back. "I don't know about you, but a hot bath and a shave sounds like an acceptable price for dinner and a roof over our heads."

Kestel chuckled. "I'll pass on the shave."

He waved for them to follow Edward, who stood waiting for Blaine to catch up with him. "Come on. You'll be safe here. I killed the only thing worth fearing at Glenreith."

"If you say so...m'lord," Verran murmured, following Blaine with a wary glance at the soldiers, who had lowered their weapons but who still regarded the group with barely veiled suspicion.

Blaine was silent as they walked toward the manor house. He winced as they crossed the place in the long gravel carriage approach where he had killed Ian McFadden. *He more than deserved it. I don't regret it, not even with what it cost me. Or maybe I don't know yet just how much it cost me*, he thought, glancing up at the manor with a sense of foreboding.

Before his exile, Glenreith had been neatly kept. It lacked the opulence of the great manor houses, eschewing the gold leaf, elaborate statuary, and ornate grounds that graced the homes of the wealthiest lords. Yet Blaine had never thought that Glenreith looked plain or austere. Built originally as a fortification, the original manor house had a hulking presence. The newer manor, which had been Blaine's home, was less fortresslike and more gracious. What it did not have in ornamentation, it made up for with "good bones," as his aunt Judith would have said. The stone manor was well proportioned, amply large, and stately in its own way.

The last six years had not been kind to Glenreith. As Blaine had glimpsed from a distance, one wing had collapsed. Much of the grounds lay untended, and the gardens, even in late autumn, showed signs of obvious neglect. Several large, grand oaks had fallen, split by lightning or pulled up by the roots. *Magic storms?* he wondered, taking in the magnitude of the damage.

As they walked up the cracked stone steps, Blaine felt a wave of sadness. Now that he was up close, he could see broken windowpanes and damage to the manor's roof. *With father dead and me in exile, Judith and Edward would have had to rely on their wits to keep the lands going,* he thought with a pang of guilt. *Carr is just now old enough to really help. What a choice. Suffer the dragon, and at least have enough to eat. Slay the dragon and starve.*

At the top of the steps, Edward stopped in front of the manor's once-grand doors. Their paint was peeling and Blaine could see where the wood had been pitted in places by something that had slammed against it hard enough to mar the surface.

"I apologize for the condition of the house and grounds, m'lord," Edward said quietly, shame clear in his voice. "We've fallen on hard times, and the death of magic made even small improvements too difficult and expensive to undertake. I'm sorry you have to see it like this." He paused. "For whatever reason, we were spared the brunt of the attack, though the old manor and its buildings were almost completely destroyed."

If Meroven struck at the old lords' castles, maybe that's not as surprising as it seems, Blaine thought. *Technically, Meroven hit their target. Luckily, you weren't living there anymore.*

Blaine mustered a faint smile that he did not feel. In the pit of his stomach, the apprehension he had felt about his homecoming increased. "I had a hand in your hard luck too," he said with a sigh. "And to tell you the truth, since I never expected to see Glenreith again before I died, it still looks pretty damn good to me."

The doors opened before Edward could pull on the handle. Judith McFadden Ainsworth stood in the doorway, staring at Blaine as if he had risen from the dead. "Gods above and below, can it be?" she breathed.

This time, Blaine's smile was genuine, if tempered by sadness. "It's really me, Aunt Judith." He turned to indicate Kestel, Dawe, Geir, Verran, and Piran behind him. "And I brought some friends."

The last six years had aged Judith more than the mere passage of time. Her dark hair, still raven-colored when Blaine had been exiled, was now liberally salted with gray. Judith's naturally lean form seemed gaunt, and there was a new tightness around her eyes and mouth. Her eyes flickered from Blaine to the others, but if she had any misgivings, Judith kept them to herself. "Of course," she said graciously. "You're all more than welcome."

To Blaine's surprise, his usually reserved aunt stepped forward and embraced him. "I never thought I'd see you again, my dear boy," she murmured, her voice catching.

Blaine returned the embrace, though he was acutely aware of

how filthy he was and how rank they all must smell after their adventures on the road. "If you can come within ten paces of me without gagging, you must have missed me," he joked half-heartedly. "I stink like a tinker."

Judith sniffed back tears. "Perhaps that's why my eyes are watering," she said, blinking. "And here I blamed it on sentiment."

Edward cleared his throat. "I will be glad to see our guests to their quarters, but perhaps introductions might be in order?"

"Sorry," Blaine said, stepping back from Judith. "We came through Velant together," he said with a meaningful glance at Judith and Edward. "There, and afterward, we survived by banding together. They're as much kin to me as you are," he said, a warning edge in his voice in case anyone thought to argue. When neither Judith nor Edward moved to say anything, Blaine relaxed a bit.

He nodded to Piran. "This is Piran Rowse. A fine soldier of the king—back when we had a king." His gaze shifted. "Dawe Killick, silversmith extraordinaire. Which reminds me—tomorrow morning we need to fire up the forge, if it survived. Dawe's got an idea for some new weapons we're going to need."

"Weapons?" Judith asked.

Blaine held up a hand. "All in good time. First, introductions." Judith nodded her assent, though Blaine could see concern in her eyes, and saw the worried gaze she shared with Edward. *They're wondering how much more trouble I'll cause for them, and whether I'm going to disappear again and leave them to clean up the mess*, Blaine thought. *Can't blame them for thinking it, although with luck, they'll support what we came to do.*

"Verran Danning, an excellent musician and agile lock-smith," Blaine said, watching as Verran squelched a guffaw at the respectable turn of phrase to describe his thievery.

"Geir is one of Lord Penhallow's men," Blaine said, hoping his pointed gaze silently impressed upon Judith and Edward the importance of that relationship. "He's *talishte*, so he'll need...special quarters."

"Oh, my," Judith murmured.

Geir gave a smile that was charming in spite of his long eyeteeth. "My dear lady," he said with a deep bow. "I swear that I will cause you no trouble at all. I'm quite adept at hunting for my own provisions in the forest. I give you my word that none of the mortals loyal to Lord McFadden will come to any harm."

Blaine wondered if he was the only one to hear the nuance in Geir's vow. *Meaning that anyone who is disloyal had better watch out.*

Judith recovered her poise and managed a sociable smile worthy of court. "Of course, Sir Geir. Please forgive my surprise."

Geir's charm never wavered. "Nothing to forgive, m'lady. Completely understandable, given the circumstances."

Kestel ended the awkward moment by stepping forward. Blaine gave a silent sigh of relief. "And this is—"

"Mistress Kestel," Judith finished, her tone utterly neutral.

Kestel's expression was equally unreadable. "Lady Judith," she said with a fluid curtsy.

Blaine's gaze flickered between the two women, trying to discern the nature of their acquaintance. "You two...know each other?"

"We crossed paths in certain circles at court," Judith replied.

Kestel gave a quick glance in Blaine's direction. "Before you ask—or even think it—no, I was never a companion to your father."

Judith surprised Blaine with her knowing chuckle. "You were out of Ian's league. You drew a much better sort of suitor, and Ian's tastes were more savage than civilized," she said with more than a trace of bitterness.

Judith looked to Blaine. "Are the two of you—"

"No, not at all," Blaine replied quickly.

"No, no, no—just friends," Kestel said in the same breath.

Blaine met his aunt's gaze. "I took a wife in Edgeland. Her name was Selane. She died of fever."

Judith looked down. "I'm sorry, Blaine."

There were so many things Blaine longed to ask Judith, not the least of which centered around Carensa and what had become of her, but an awkward silence descended over the group, and Blaine became aware of just how badly they needed to make themselves presentable. Judith, too, seemed to struggle between playing the gracious hostess and her hunger for details. With a sigh, she brightened, and Blaine knew that for now, the hostess had won.

"You must all be tired and hungry," Judith said. "Edward will see you to your rooms, and I'll have someone draw baths for you." She blushed. "Our meals aren't quite the fare they once were, but no one's gone hungry yet. I'll see that food is ready for you when everyone's had a chance to be refreshed." She looked to Geir, and took a deep breath.

"Sir Geir," she said gingerly, "If you'll inform Edward of your requirements for safe quarters, he'll find you something suitable."

For the first time in their acquaintance, Blaine spied a hint of laughter in Geir's eyes at Judith's discomfort, but Geir's manner was charming as ever. "Please don't worry overmuch, m'lady. I'll be quite content with a wine cellar or other below-ground vault so long as it has no windows or outer door."

Edward nodded, as if hosting a *talishte* was an everyday

occurrence at Glenreith. "That won't be difficult. I'll see to it right away."

The others followed Edward up the long, sweeping stairway to the second floor. Blaine noted how marred the once-beautiful balustrade had become and how worn the treads were, details that would never have gone without maintenance in the old days.

"Your room is where it always was," Judith said quietly, jarring him out of his thoughts.

Blaine looked up, caught by surprise. "You didn't clean it out?" he said with halfhearted humor.

Judith linked her arm through his. "Don't be silly," she said quietly. "Even though we didn't think you would ever return, I couldn't bear to part with your things. You'll find it much as you left it, if a bit dustier."

"What about Carr and Mari?"

Judith sobered. "Carr went off to war with the king's troops and never returned. Like so many of the young men, he just disappeared."

Blaine caught his breath, stunned. "Mari?" he said, knowing Judith could hear the despair in his voice.

"Blaine!" Blaine looked up at the shout. A young woman came running down the corridor. Her dark hair was unbound, and it streamed behind her as she ran. She barely stopped when she reached him, and threw her arms around Blaine, clutching him to her so hard that he could scarcely breathe.

"Mari?"

Mari covered his cheeks with kisses. "I can't believe you're back! I didn't believe Edward when he told me. I'm so happy to see you again!"

Mari drew back, and Blaine got a good look at her. Just a half-grown girl when he left, Mari was now a pretty young woman. Her features were thinner than he remembered, due no doubt to the manor's circumstances, but her eyes were bright and the fear that had always darkened her gaze was gone. He took a second look and saw that Mari's face was more careworn than it should have been for a woman who was barely twenty-two years old. Mari continued to chatter on excitedly, not noticing his assessment.

"You have a nephew, Blaine! I can't wait to introduce you to him, but he's sleeping," Mari continued.

Blaine shot a look toward Judith, alarmed. Judith shook her head slightly. "I'm sorry that you missed Mari's handfasting," Judith said as Blaine gave a sigh of relief that the child was not his father's. "Her husband, Evaret, went to war with Carr and also did not return."

Mari's chatter abruptly stopped. Blaine took her hand. "I'm sorry, Mari. Of course I want to meet your son."

Mari swallowed hard and nodded. "You couldn't know. We had no idea whether or not you were still alive. We wrote letters for so long, but nothing ever came back to us."

Blaine felt a surge of anger at Prokief. "I never received them. I would have paid whatever the smugglers asked to have gotten any letters from you at all."

Mari gave him another fierce hug. "Crazy world, huh?"

"I'm beginning to realize just how crazy," Blaine replied ruefully. They reached the door to his room, and Judith touched Mari's arm.

"Perhaps we'd best let your brother get a bath and change his clothes. You'll have plenty of time to trade stories." She looked quickly to Blaine. "You are staying, aren't you?"

Blaine nodded. "If you'll have us. And we've got some important business to discuss, later."

Judith drew a deep breath and then managed a worried

smile. "Absolutely. But first, I'm certain that a hot bath and a fresh change of clothing will help. By Esthrane's stars! Here we are, keeping you talking, with no regard to how far you've traveled or how tired you must be."

You have no idea, Blaine thought.

Blaine walked into his room at Glenreith and let the door close behind him. He could hear shuffling in the attached parlor as servants brought in warm water and a tub for him to bathe. For the moment, he stood transfixed, feeling as if he had crossed into a netherworld where time had stood still in his absence.

His room was, as Judith said, much the way he had left it. Only a light film of dust covered the books on his desk and the surfaces of the furniture, testimony to the fact that someone had bothered to dust fairly often while he was away. *No one expected me to ever come back, but Judith and Mari kept the room for me, like a memorial*, Blaine thought. He realized that he was holding his breath, and willed himself to step farther into the room.

It was so like he remembered that for a moment he felt as if the last six years had never happened. He felt as if he had just come in from the hunt or from lending a hand in the fields, as it had always been. *Only back then, I'd have heard father thundering about, cursing me or Carr or the servants. It was never this quiet when he was alive.*

He moved slowly around the room, as if in a daze. His boots made prints in the dust on the carpet as he walked over to the bookshelves. Blaine's finger traced the leather spines of his favorite volumes, which were just where he had left them. Beside them on the shelf, a clever wooden puzzle lay next to a small silver statue of a dragon, a long-ago gift from his mother.

He smiled sadly as he looked across the shelf, at the clumsily carved wooden bird Carr had made for him as a young boy and at the carefully knotted token Mari had once given him, the day she was playing at being a princess and had named Blaine as her champion.

Neither of us ever thought it would be true in real life, Blaine thought. *And unlike Mari's games of pretend, it didn't end happily ever after.*

He moved farther into the room, still captured by the past. His writing desk had been cleaned off, evidence that someone, sometime, had made the room presentable after his departure. Blaine did not doubt that he would find everything as he left it in his wardrobe, and in the desk drawers.

I know all these things were mine, but they belong to another life, another person, he thought. *I've been "Mick" so long I barely recognize "Blaine." Gods forgive me, I once lived such a soft life and never even knew to be grateful.*

He had moved around the room to stop at his desk, and as he glanced down at the dusty quills and yellowed parchment, one item made him catch his breath. Blaine's hand shook as he reached out for a small silver frame. The delicate oil portrait of a young woman stared back at him, unchanged by the years. *Carensa*, Blaine thought, surprised that the stab of longing he felt was so strong after all this time.

For a few moments, he stood without moving, staring at the portrait, lost in thought. Quiet rapping at the door startled him.

"M'lord? Your bath is drawn," a servant's voice called from outside the door.

"Thank you," Blaine replied absently. "That will be all."

With a sigh, Blaine set the portrait back where it had been and turned away from the desk. He went to the wardrobe and rummaged through its contents until he found a tunic and trews that would be suitable to the weather. As he stripped off his old clothing, torn and filthy from travel and the fight outside the gate, his gaze lingered on the brand scar on his right forearm. "M" for murderer.

If I'd have had any inkling of the full consequences of what I did that day, would I have ever had the nerve to kill father? Blaine wondered. *I was willing to die. I thought that would be the end of it. Would it have changed anything if I'd still have been here when the magic died? Mari would have had more years of abuse. I probably couldn't have stopped Carr from going off to the war; I would have likely gone with him. I'd have married Carensa and probably left her a widow if the war took me like it took Carr. Perhaps it doesn't matter which road was taken. There seems to be sorrow and despair regardless of the choices.*

Wrapped in the old robe he found in his wardrobe, Blaine found himself alone in the sitting room. He felt chagrined that he had carried his sword with him, yet caution had been the foremost lesson of the years in Edgeland. The servants had left him to his bath and had poured a generous portion of whiskey into a glass on a small table beside the tub. In the candlelight, the room revealed little of the shabbiness that Blaine knew would be unmistakable come daylight. Resolutely pushing dark thoughts from his mind, Blaine dropped the robe and laid his sword aside, then slid into the hot water, which was gently scented with lavender.

Only then, when he had sunk chin-deep into the water, did he allow himself to relax. Blaine closed his eyes and took a sip of the whiskey, willing himself to dwell neither on the distant nor on the recent past, and to banish his worry about the future. Just for a few, precious moments, he focused on nothing

more urgent than the delectable experience of soaking clean of
the sweat, blood, and dirt from the journey home.

The water grew cold far too quickly, and with a sigh Blaine
climbed from the tub. He dried himself off and finished the
whiskey in his glass. On a side table, the servant had set out a
bowl and a razor. A large mirror hung on the wall with enough
light from the candles in the wall sconce that he stood a chance
of shaving without butchering himself.

He paused, regarding the reflection that looked back at him.
Mirrors had been scarce and expensive in Edgeland, and over
the years, he had caught only glimpses of himself in windows
or still water. *Who in Raka is that man?* Blaine wondered, meeting his gaze. He'd been just twenty when he was exiled; now
the man who stared back at him looked older, careworn. Fine
lines were etched around the corners of his eyes from squinting
against the harsh glare of the Edgeland sun. He did not remember the hard set to his mouth, nor the steel in his blue eyes.
With several days' growth of dark beard, he looked rough, and
much more wary. Pleased that he only cut himself once with
the straight razor, Blaine finished his shave and wiped off the
blade. He slipped a shirt from his wardrobe over his head, and
was surprised to find that it now fit too snugly across the arms
and chest. It took a few moments to find something that he
could wear. *All that time in the mines and on the herring boats
apparently put some muscle on my bones*, he thought. When he
had dressed, he tied his damp hair back at the nape of his neck,
disdaining a formal queue. *It's a little late to be putting on airs.*

Once again, the servant's tapping roused him from his
thoughts. "When you're done, m'lord, Lady Judith desires your
company in her parlor."

"I'll be there," Blaine replied. Bathed, shaved, and dressed, he looked almost respectable, and he headed for the door, wondering how it could be that he felt like a total stranger in his childhood home.

"I know you must be tired," Judith said as Blaine entered the room. His aunt's private parlor looked just as he remembered it. The walls were covered with expensive wallpaper in a delicate floral design, imported from the Far Shores. Judith's furniture had a fine-boned, feminine sense, far different from the dark woods and sturdy pieces in his own room. Candles glittered around the room in silver and crystal sconces, and over the porcelain-tiled fireplace hung an oil painting of Judith, her late husband, and their two children, along with two favorite hunting dogs.

The candlelight flattered both the room and its occupant. On second glance, Blaine could see where water had stained parts of the ceiling and wall, where the elegant wallpaper was coming loose, and where the imported rug had gone threadbare in places.

Judith smiled from her seat on a small couch and beckoned for him to take the chair across from her. Between them lay a small plate of tea biscuits, a decanter of brandy, and two glasses. Even by candlelight, Blaine could see that the fine crystal was chipped and that the silk upholstery of the seat cushion was rubbed thin in places. Judith had also taken advantage of the time since his arrival to change her gown. Her dress was much less elaborate than what Blaine remembered her favoring, and it was frayed along the hem.

"Please, have something to eat," Judith said, pouring drinks for both of them. "I know you've been up for a long time, but I've sent the servants to set supper for you and your friends.

The food will take a little while, and I thought you and I could talk for a bit, before we join the others."

"You never used to play coy with me, Aunt Judith," Blaine said, taking the proffered glass of brandy and leaning back in his chair. He crossed his legs, feigning a level of confidence that currently eluded him, and he wondered whether Judith's cool demeanor was likewise just a bluff. "What is it you want to ask me without the others around?"

Judith blushed and looked down. "You always preferred to come straight to the point, Blaine," she said, swirling the brandy in her glass. It occurred to Blaine that Judith usually chose sherry over brandy or whiskey, and wondered if the change in liquor was coincidental or a concession to harder times and bitter memories.

"Are we unwelcome here?" Blaine's voice was carefully neutral.

"Of course not!" The outrage in Judith's eyes seemed real. "Glenreith will always be your home."

"But we've upset things, showing up like this," Blaine supplied, guessing at the reason for her discomfort.

Judith shrugged. "We feared you were dead," Judith said quietly. "Having a ghost walk through the front door takes a bit of getting used to."

"A ghost with outlaw friends and a vampire bodyguard."

Judith managed a faint smile. "That, too."

Blaine found that the brandy did nothing to take the edge off his mood. "I really never thought I'd come back," Blaine said quietly. "Even after Velant fell, we guessed that whatever havoc the death of magic brought to Edgeland, it had worked more chaos here in Donderath." He paused, and the silence stretched out between them.

"Believe it or not," he finally continued, "I'd made a decent life for myself in Edgeland. I earned my Ticket of Leave, which meant I was a colonist instead of a convict. My mates and I pooled our earnings to buy a homestead and build a sturdy little house that kept the cold out. Had a right nice little farm going, and hard as it might be to picture it, Kestel was quite at home tending the chickens and the rabbits and the sheep."

Judith chuckled. "I'd have had to see that to believe it."

Blaine stared down into the amber liquid in his glass. "After I left Velant, I made a handfasting with Selane, a lass from Bodderton who'd been framed for a theft she didn't commit." He knew his voice was thick with bitterness. "Not exactly a hardened criminal," he added, then paused. "Until the fever took her, we were as happy as I guess anyone could be in Edgeland."

For a few minutes, both Blaine and Judith were silent. Finally, Blaine forced himself to ask the question that had haunted him since his exile. "After I left, what happened to Carensa?"

Judith looked down at her hands and then raised her head to meet his gaze. "She mourned you," Judith replied quietly. "In the weeks after your ship left, Carensa refused to eat, until she collapsed. She took to her bed, and we were afraid we might lose her." Judith paused. "Finally, she rallied. She asked her father to allow her to enter the women's university, to study astronomy and become a scholar."

Blaine frowned. "Did he allow it?"

Judith shook her head. "No. Instead, he brokered an arranged marriage with Oten Simmons and forced her to go through with it."

Blaine drew a deep breath, struggling with the sudden pang of loss that lanced through his chest. "I knew Oten. He was a decent sort, but much older."

Judith nodded. "Older, established, dependable, and just threadbare enough to barter his respectability for the Rhystorp fortune."

Blaine winced. "Respectability," he repeated bitterly. "I'd always wondered how badly my actions damaged Carensa's reputation. I guess that's my answer."

"Carensa changed after you left," Judith said quietly. "She shut everyone out. Despite her father's protests, she managed to get Oten to allow her to study with a tutor, and the studies seemed to be her only passion, even after her son was born."

"Son?" The word caught in Blaine's throat. He had resigned himself to the possibility that Carensa had become another man's wife, but the reality that she had borne someone else a child hurt like a fresh wound.

"I saw him once or twice, at a distance," Judith said. "He was a healthy lad, who took after his father."

"When the magic died, was Rhystorp spared?"

Judith met his gaze and slowly shook her head. "Rhystorp was completely destroyed. Oten and the boy are buried in the family cemetery, along with Carensa's father."

"And Carensa?"

"Her body was never found," Judith said. She reached out to touch his hand. "I'm sorry, Blaine."

Blaine swallowed hard and nodded. "Thank you for telling me. I shouldn't be surprised that she moved on; after all, I married Selane. All these years, I told myself it was likely that she'd married. I wanted her to be happy, to escape my shame. It's just different, knowing for certain."

Judith cleared her throat. "You never finished your story, about how you managed to return."

Blaine sighed, grateful for the change of topic, thankful for his aunt's perceptiveness. "When Velant fell, we found ourselves sovereign, for all practical purposes," he said. He gave a bitter chuckle. "Would you believe that I was named to the ruling Council?"

Judith shrugged. "You were, after all, a lord—by birth if no longer by law."

Blaine shook his head. "No one knew that except for Kestel. To everyone else, including my housemates until very recently, I was just Mick, a common murderer with a penchant for settling brawls."

Judith's lip quirked in an almost smile. "Mick," she repeated, and Blaine heard the amusement in her voice. "A solid street name." Her smile faded, and she met his gaze. "So who is the man who sits across from me? Blaine? Or Mick?"

Blaine took a sip from his glass and did not speak right away. "I'm not really sure," he said finally. "If it had been up to Mick, I'd have stayed in Edgeland. Life there is never easy, but I'd carved out something fairly comfortable, something thoroughly my own." He let out a long breath. "Mick had no reason to leave. Blaine had no right to stay."

Judith's brow furrowed as she looked at him quizzically. "How so?"

Judith listened patiently without interrupting as Blaine told his tale. "So, according to some ancient texts and some equally ancient *talishte*, I'm quite possibly the last surviving Lord of the Blood," Blaine ended his story. "And maybe the only one who can bring the magic back to Donderath."

He waited for her response, half expecting her to break out laughing at his implausible tale. Instead, she rose from her seat, set aside her glass, and walked to the bookshelves on the other side of the room, returning with a worn, leather-bound book filled with yellowed parchment pages.

"Lord of the Blood," she repeated quietly, untying the old

ribbon that bound the book together and carefully turning the fragile pages. "I haven't heard that term for a very long while."

"At first, I thought it was nonsense," Blaine said. "But Lanyon Penhallow sets stock by it." His hand went absently to the recent scars on his shoulder. "And apparently, Pentreath Reese is willing to kill me in order to stop me."

Judith ran a thin finger down the parchment page. "Lord of the Blood," she repeated softly, and then turned the book so that Blaine could see.

"This is a history of the McFadden family," Judith said. "This book is quite old, and the history was copied down from the tales and names passed from father to son for generations." She grimaced. "Aside from your father, the McFaddens had a distinguished and reputable line.

"I came across that phrase when I looked up some bit of family history to please Ian," she said. "And it stuck in my mind. Here it is," she added, noting a page near the very beginning of the book.

Blaine leaned over the book. The handwriting was small and the ink was faded, making him strain to make out the lettering. He frowned. "Lord Rogarth McFadden, liege man to Hougen, king of all Donderath," he read aloud. "One of the thirteen Lords of the Blood."

"Why did you come back?" Judith watched Blaine, waiting for an answer.

He leaned back from the book and sighed. "Crazy as it sounds, I came back to make the magic work again, if I can. I came back to go to Mirdalur and see if blood tells."

CHAPTER
THIRTY

B LAINE AWOKE JUST AS THE FIRST LIGHT OF DAWN
lit the horizon. He lay looking up at the familiar ceiling for
a few moments, luxuriating in the feel of a real bed and the
comfort of good linens. Waking in his old room at Glenreith
seemed like something out of a dream, yet he had the events of
the night before to convince him of its reality. And more importantly, he reminded himself, swinging his legs out of bed, there
was work to be done.

Blaine dressed and slipped silently downstairs, letting himself out of the manor house. He stood at the top of a small hill
as the sun came up, and looked out over the ruined fortress
that had been the old manor. The grand building was now
merely a pile of rubble. Blaine made his way through the brambles and overgrowth toward the burying grounds. A large oak
tree marked the spot where his mother was buried. He remembered how majestically the oak had risen high into the sky,
spreading its branches over a large area, standing watch over
more than a century of Glenreith's dead. Now a splintered
trunk, blackened by lightning and stripped of bark by insects,
was all that remained.

Although the old manor had not been the family's residence for a long time, Blaine had played in its deserted hallways as a child. Built to withstand a war, the old manor had been used to billet troops back in the day when a lord kept his own private army. *And with the way things are now, it might come to that again*, Blaine thought. But now the heavy stone walls of the old manor were rubble. He could see blackened places where the magic fire Connor had told them about had scorched the thick rocks of the old building. The walls of the old manor had been three feet thick, yet they had tumbled like a child's blocks. Blaine shivered. If that kind of power had struck at the other nobles' homes, it was indeed quite possible that he was the last surviving Lord of the Blood.

Blaine trampled down the dry, dead weeds around the tombstones. Lord Ian's grave was the most recent. Blaine avoided his father's grave and stood beside his mother's stone, then sank down on one knee next to the oak tree and covered his eyes with his hand. The tears that flowed were old tears, long denied. Grief pressed down on him as he mourned for Carensa, for possibilities lost forever, and for all that had been swept away by magic's fall. In his years in Edgeland, Blaine had never permitted himself to feel the full weight of grief for everything he had left behind, and now it choked him with its intensity.

When his sorrow was spent, Blaine made his way to a small reflecting pool and brushed aside the thin ice to splash his face with freezing-cold water. It braced him like a slap, making his eyes sting.

Blaine returned to the house and slipped into the kitchen entrance, removed his boots and cloak, and silently climbed the servants' stairs. His ruse enabled him to saunter down the main staircase as if he had just come from his room. Familiar voices rose in greeting from the great hall.

"Best of the morning to you," Verran called to him with an exaggerated cheeriness. All of his friends, except Geir, were seated at the long great-hall table. "We wondered how long it would be before you joined us." He made a show of stretching. "Personally, I slept better than I have in years, since I didn't have to listen to you and Piran thrash in your sleep."

"I don't thrash," Piran muttered.

Dawe gave him a look. "Trust us. You thrash. Wake up fighting your way out of the blankets, cursing and swinging. Mick's nearly as bad. Last night was the first good night's sleep I've had in years."

Kestel made a show of stretching sinuously. "I had a marvelous night's rest," she said with a mischievous grin. "Good morning, Mick. Or should we start calling you Blaine?"

Blaine grimaced as he pulled up a chair near his friends and sat down. A platter of sausages lay in front of them, as well as a bowl of pickled eggs and a loaf of crusty bread. A kettle, recently enough pulled from the hearth to still be steaming, sat next to a bowl of dried herbs and berries that Blaine recognized as a homemade substitute for more costly—and probably unavailable—tea.

"None of you have ever had trouble coming up with something to call me," Blaine replied. He took a sausage from the plate and wrapped it in a piece of bread, taking time for a bite while he considered his answer.

Piran chuckled. "True enough. And may I say, you earned every one of the names I've used for you over the years."

Kestel rolled her eyes. "Be serious," she admonished Piran. She looked at Blaine. "So what's it to be?"

Blaine sighed. "You knew Mick, so call me Mick. Aunt Judith and the others knew Blaine, and I figure that's what they'll call me, even if I tried to change it. We have much more important things to discuss than what name I go by."

Kestel met his eyes. "My grandmother was particular about names. She said that how you're called—and how you call yourself—matters. Before all's said and done, I think you'll need to decide who you really are," she added quietly.

"Maybe," he replied. "But not today."

Piran snorted. "We're already well into today, thank you very much," he said. "And while the lord of the manor was sleeping, some of us got a leg up on the day." He leaned back, hooking one arm over the back of the chair, and bit a chunk from the sausage he held. "I've already been out and done reconnaissance."

"And?" Blaine asked, pouring himself a cup of the substitute tea. Judith had always been quite particular about her tea, and he knew that the homemade substitute was another clue to just how far his family's fortunes had fallen.

"For one thing, I caught a spy."

Blaine's attention refocused immediately. "How do you know he was a spy?"

"Because he was spying—how do you think I know?" Piran replied. "I caught a man posted at the edge of the woods with a looking glass who seemed awfully interested in what was going on inside the manor."

"Please tell me you didn't just kill him." Blaine sighed.

"Of course not," Piran replied indignantly. "I figured we could at least interrogate him before we killed him."

"So where is he?"

Piran frowned. "Well, that's the funny thing. When I knocked him out, I searched him for weapons, and for some clue as to why he was there. Figured he must belong to someone, and that those Reese or Pollard fellows were the logical suspects. And what do you know? Turns out he's bitten up and down his arms like our friend Connor, which makes me think he's Reese's man."

Blaine looked at Piran. "What did you do with him?"

Piran shrugged. "Tied him up and threw him in the cellars. Figured Geir would want to be around to question him."

"If he's really Reese's man, you'd have done better to kill him," Kestel replied. "He's Reese's eyes and ears, through the *kruvgaldur.*"

Piran gave a slow, knowing smile. "Now that you mention it, I did remember that little trick. So I blindfolded him and stuffed a bit of rag in each ear, and put a hood on him when we brought him through the gates. Told the guard at the gate who took him to say nothing around him and to make sure he was in a place where no one would find him, locked up good. He'll have nothing to report to his master except darkness and silence."

"Good work," Blaine said, taking a sip of the tea and grimacing at the flavor. "Anything else?"

Piran shrugged. "Got a map of the roads and figured out our choices to get from here to Mirdalur. Wanted to know what our options were if we've got Reese and Pollard on our tail. If your aunt can spare the men, I think it would be a good idea to take a few guards with us, just in case."

Blaine nodded. "Sounds reasonable. I'll talk to Aunt Judith about it—I have no idea how the manor is staffed right now," he said with an apologetic shrug. "Frankly, I'm amazed there are any servants left at all."

Dawe stretched out his lanky frame. "I was up before the lot of you," he said, yawning. "Got a good look at the blacksmith's forge. It's still in use and actually in pretty good shape, so I talked to the smith and showed him the pieces I want to forge.

With luck, we'll work on it this afternoon, in exchange for my help shoeing some horses," he said with a grin. "Which means that in a day or two, we might have a couple of my altered crossbows ready for service."

Verran grinned. "I've actually been retained by the lady of the manor for a little job," he said, interlacing his fingers and then stretching his hands in front of him. "Seems there's a locked trunk in your father's room that she's been dying to break into, and lacked someone with the necessary skills."

"Count me in on that adventure," Blaine said. "If Aunt Judith thinks there's something hidden in the trunk, I'm betting it's something we'll find interesting. I told her what we're planning to do, and she wasn't as surprised as I expected."

"I'm worried that we haven't heard anything from Penhallow," Kestel said. "I thought he'd be waiting for us when we got here. Do you think he and Connor survived the ambush?"

Blaine shrugged. "I hope so. Although I can't say I completely trust either of them, Penhallow seemed like a good guy to have on our side—whatever his reasons. And Connor is a decent sort. It helps to have friends, especially if Reese and Pollard are against us."

"Maybe Geir knows something he's not telling us," Dawe said. "After all, Penhallow is his master. Maybe he's got the same kind of bond Connor has."

"We'll have to wait until sunset to find out anything from Geir." Blaine shook his head. "If Penhallow isn't here—and assuming he's not more dead than usual—he's got his reasons. Since Pollard's men were camped out here, perhaps Reese has Penhallow pinned down somewhere."

Kestel frowned. "Do we know for certain *why* Pollard's men were here? If he sent the assassin to Edgeland to kill Mick, why come after Glenreith?"

"I can answer that." They all looked toward the doorway. Judith stood in the entrance, looking surprisingly awake despite the late night before.

"Please, come join us," Blaine said, standing to pull back a chair for Judith. She smiled, and took a seat next to Blaine.

"Vedran Pollard has had his eye on Glenreith since you went to Velant," Judith said with a glance toward Blaine. "Even more so after the other manors were completely destroyed." She paused. "At first, he tried courting me, if you can believe that!"

Blaine smiled. "You're a fine-looking woman, Aunt Judith. I don't think it's so remarkable that a man might pay you court."

Judith dismissed his compliment with a shake of her head. "Anyone but Vedran Pollard, and I might have been flattered. But I've never liked that man, nor trusted his business dealings. And while my late, unlamented brother had his failings, his judgment of business partners wasn't one of them. He thought Pollard was a snake."

"And coming from him, that's saying something," Blaine muttered.

"Pollard wanted Glenreith's lands, and I'm certain he thought we had more coin hidden away than we did," Judith went on. "But I always thought there was more to it than what he was saying. And after our conversation last night," she said with a glance at Blaine, "I'm sure of it."

"Pollard's illegitimate," Kestel said. "That's why he's not a Lord of the Blood, even though his family is descended from the thirteen original lords. It wouldn't matter if he managed to buy, bully, or steal all of the old lords' manors and titles—that won't change blood."

"When I didn't fall for his flattery, Pollard got nasty," Judith continued. "He tried to blackmail me, but after what happened with Blaine and Ian, I told him that we had no reputation left to lose and that nothing he could say about us mattered a whit."

Blaine flinched. Judith patted his arm. "None of that. We've already been over it. Ian had to die."

"I like your aunt," Piran said with a grin. "Very practical."

Judith managed to look flattered. "I'm a survivor." She drew a deep breath. "Anyway, when flowers and blackmail failed, Pollard tried to buy off the guards, intimidate the servants, anything to ruin what little was left. Every time I'd rebuff one of his offers, we'd find a field of wheat burned, or horses in the pasture lamed, or fences broken down to let the livestock out." She shook her head. "After the Great Fire, it got so bad that I had to post guards, and even then we couldn't keep him completely at bay."

"So now he's taken to occupying the front yard?" Blaine asked.

Judith shrugged. "Apparently so. At first, Edward and I thought it was just harassment. A few of Pollard's men were watching the manor house, so I sent an armed guard with anyone who had to leave the walls. Then, two days ago, Pollard sent more men and made an actual encampment. The men were armed. We took it for the beginning of a siege, and no one has left since then." She shook her head. "Thank the gods we had the foresight to bring in what livestock we still have so they weren't stranded out in the fields." Judith sighed. "Our flocks and herds aren't nearly as sizable as before the Great Fire, and the magic storms took an additional toll. But with luck, we'll have enough to make it to spring."

"But you can't feed the livestock and the people forever without going out again," Blaine finished.

"Exactly." Judith paused and looked at Blaine worriedly. "What's this about an assassin?"

Blaine drew a deep breath. "That's a bit of a long story," he said uncomfortably. Judith listened silently as he recounted the attacks in Edgeland, ending with the death of the hired killer.

"Maybe the assassin wasn't Pollard's only man in Edgeland," Kestel said when Blaine finished. "Someone on the ship with us could have easily seen Blaine and carried the tale back to Pollard."

"We don't know that the soldiers out front have anything to do with me," Blaine argued. "Aunt Judith's account makes much more sense. It's just an accident that we blundered into the occupation."

Kestel met his gaze. "Maybe so, but the question is—how long until Pollard figures out you're still alive and decides to change that?"

"Well, for the moment, Pollard's men are gone, and we won't see any of Reese's *talishte* until nightfall," Piran said with more good cheer than Blaine felt.

"For now," Kestel added, leaning forward, intent on the conversation. She gave Judith an encouraging smile. "At least, despite everything, you've managed to keep quite a few of your retainers."

Judith nodded. "And for that, I'm grateful. The servants who stayed after the Great Fire had been with us for many years, or came from families that have been in our employ for a long time. And, in truth, there's nowhere else for most of them to go. The other noble homes, I hear, are in worse straits than we are. The countryside is lawless, and the city is worse. Here, they're protected and fed. When you've lost as much as Donderath has, survival is a simple equation."

"And I've brought you more mouths to feed," Blaine said, feeling a pang of guilt.

Judith made a dismissive gesture. "You routed Pollard's men, which gives our people a chance to forage and gather until he can post replacements. And you're our best bet for bringing back the magic." She favored him with a tired smile. "This is your home. It's where you belong."

"And we're more than willing to earn our keep," Verran spoke up, finishing his last mouthful of food. "Dawe does smithing. Kestel's a right good cook, don't let her fool you. Geir and Piran beat up people you don't like. And I fix those sticky locks that you just can't open," he said with a grin. "Speaking of which—"

Judith chuckled. "I saw your eyes light up the moment I mentioned Ian's trunk. I'm amazed you've lasted this long without bursting." She glanced up and down the table. "If you're finished, we can go see what he thought was so important that it needed to stay locked up all these years."

They followed Judith upstairs to Ian McFadden's bedroom. At the door, Blaine felt a twinge of the old fear. His father's room had always been strictly off-limits, and neither Blaine nor his siblings would have ever dared a beating to try to enter. The most he had ever seen was a glimpse from the hallway.

Blaine walked into the room, expecting it to look as he remembered. But unlike his own room, Ian McFadden's room had been completely emptied of personal items. The large, four-poster bed had been stripped of its linens and bed curtains, the writing desk had been cleaned of ink and parchment, and the wardrobe stood with its doors wide open, empty of clothing. No books or trinkets were on any of the shelves. All that remained was the furniture and a large, black iron-bound trunk.

Verran's face lit up at the sight of the trunk, and he gave a soft moan of anticipation. "Oh, you little beauty," he murmured, flexing his fingers. "Come to Papa."

The others watched in silence as Verran walked slowly around the chest. He knelt beside it and ran his hands lightly over the top and sides.

"You're supposed to open the bloody thing, not make love to it," Piran grumbled.

"Savage," Verran replied without taking his eyes off the chest. He touched the lock gently with his fingertips and bent to study it.

"It's Vellanese workmanship," he said. "Very old. Seen a bit of wear. From the dents on the bindings, I'd say someone tried to take an ax to it, and someone also tried to pry it open at the lips."

"The thought crossed my mind," Piran muttered.

"When Ian died, we looked for a key," Judith said. "When we didn't find one, I had the blacksmith try to break in as gently as possible. Since we didn't know what was inside, we were limited, because I didn't want to smash the contents getting it open."

Verran nodded, only half listening. "Whatever was in here mattered enough for someone to put holding spells on it," he said. "If you tried to open it before the magic died, that had as much to do with why you failed as the strength of the bindings. The magic is gone now, but I feel the residue. Whoever put the hocus on this box had power. Even now, it... tingles."

"Can you break in?" Judith asked.

Verran grinned. "Oh, yes. Without the hocus, it's just a pretty box." He reached into his pocket for the tools Dawe made for him, and selected the right piece with a surgeon's precision. Bending closer so that his ear was level with the lock, Verran delicately inserted the tool and began to coax the thin metal into the workings. A click broadened his smile. "That's one down," he said.

"One? How many locks are there?" Judith asked.

"At least three," Verran replied. "Possibly one underneath—I haven't looked yet. Someone really wanted whatever's in this trunk to stay safe."

The others waited in silence as Verran worked. Blaine found that he was holding his breath. Finally, after nearly a candlemark had passed, Verran tilted the chest up on one end and felt carefully beneath it. He nodded, muttering to himself.

"What did you find?" Kestel asked.

"The master lock is on the bottom," Verran said. "It's not only got multiple locks, but there's an order to how they're supposed to open, or the whole thing jams. It's called a Tollerby mechanism. I've heard about them, but I hadn't worked one before." He looked up. "Piran, be a good fellow and come hold this, will you?"

Piran glared at him, but came over and kept the chest tilted. "Why not just lay it on its side?"

Verran shook his head without looking at him. "Some of these Tollerby boxes have levels in them. Turn them over, rough them up, and there's a whole second internal locking mechanism that slides into place until the levels reset."

After another long silence, Verran let out a deep breath and straightened, indicating that Piran could set the chest back down. "I think I've gotten all the locks," Verran said, eyeing the trunk as if it might bite him. "But before I open it, I'd advise you all to move to the side of the room."

"Why?" Blaine asked.

Verran shrugged. "Old Victor, the man who taught me my craft, was the only person I knew who ever cracked one of these—or even saw one. He told me all about it; moment of glory and all. But he carried a nasty scar on his shoulder until his dying day, and he said it was because Tollerby boxes have a surprise inside. If you're directly in front of them when they're opened, they shoot out a small quarrel. Just in case the wrong person is doing the opening. He was lucky it caught him in the shoulder instead of square in the chest."

Blaine and the others needed no further urging, and moved to the sides of the room. Verran slipped around to the back of the trunk and put a hand on either side of its heavy lid. "Here we go," he murmured, gripping the lid with his fingertips and pulling it open.

As soon as Verran opened the box, a small metal spike launched with deadly speed from the lip of the trunk, speeding across the room and embedding itself with a thunk in the doorpost. Verran let out his breath and grinned broadly.

"We're in!"

Blaine and the others crowded around the trunk. "Aunt Judith? Do you want to do the honors?" Blaine asked.

"Go ahead," Judith said. "You may recognize things I wouldn't."

Blaine knelt next to the open trunk and realized that his heart was pounding. He bent closer, tensed for another potentially lethal surprise. When nothing happened, he relaxed and looked inside the box.

The trunk was mostly empty. Its interior was lined in old velvet, once red but now muted and discolored with time. Blaine could see that there were just a few small items within the chest, but they, too, were wrapped in velvet, tied with silken cords. Verran took out the first velvet-shrouded item and held it up for Blaine.

It was heavy in his hand, and Blaine unwrapped it gingerly, alert for traps. But the velvet fell back without incident, revealing a round crystal sphere.

"That's a focus crystal," Verran said in an awed voice. "Those with a bit of magic can use it, so they say, to strengthen their power. Some even claim to scry with it." He frowned. "Did your father have any magic?"

Blaine nodded distractedly. "Some. Battle magic, like mine." He handed the sphere to Judith, who laid it aside on a table.

Carefully, Blaine reached into the chest and withdrew a thin velvet pouch. He shook the contents out into his palm.

"Well, would you look at that," Kestel murmured. "Where have we seen one of those before?"

In his palm lay a pendant like the one Lanyon Penhallow had given to Connor.

"The design is different," Blaine said. "The slits to read the map are in different places."

Kestel nodded. "The markings on the pendant are different, too," she said, tracing the elaborate etchings on the new pendant with her finger.

"If Ian McFadden had a pendant, did each of the Lords of the Blood?" Piran asked. "Because we've only got two of them, if that's the case. How many do we need?"

Blaine shrugged. "Who knows? But we've only got one Lord of the Blood—me. So would it matter if we had all thirteen of the other pendants? There's no one to stand for them."

"Penhallow didn't say where he got that pendant, did he?" Verran asked. "As a thief, I know that where you got something makes it as valuable as what it's made of. So which of the lords did the first disk belong to?"

"Mick's got a point—if he's the only Lord of the Blood, maybe the other disks don't even matter," Dawe said.

"Or maybe Pollard wants what's his," Verran challenged. "Sure, *we* know he can't use it to bring back the magic because he's a bastard. But does *he* know that?"

"I'm pretty sure he knows he's a bastard," Piran grumbled, and Judith stifled a chuckle.

Verran glared at Piran. "I mean, does Pollard know that the disk won't work for him because he isn't a true Lord of the Blood? Maybe he's been chasing Penhallow, and us, because he wants to control the magic himself."

Blaine considered Verran's words and shrugged. "Could be. That would be just like the Pollard I remember. I saw him get into a row with my father once at a dinner party. I thought then that he was the only one I'd ever met who was as nasty a son of a bitch as my father. Only, where father wanted control over the people around him, I got the feeling Pollard had bigger plans."

"Vedran Pollard lusted after influence the way some men lust after women," Kestel said. "He was constantly trying to bully or ingratiate himself with people he believed could maneuver him into positions of power. Merrill didn't particularly care for Pollard, as I heard it, but it was whispered that even the king recognized the danger in Pollard's naked ambition, and as a result, Pollard did get several plum positions at court."

"The better for the king to keep an eye on him," Judith said.

"Court intrigue doesn't really matter, since there isn't a court anymore," Dawe said. "Question is—what's Pollard after now? We're making a pretty big guess that he's after the pendant, or even knows that there *is* a pendant. Maybe he's trying to grab Glenreith for the land, and his fight with Penhallow is completely separate. He might be after Blaine just because he thinks that will complicate him being able to grab Glenreith unopposed."

Blaine sighed. "There's no way of guessing what Pollard knows or doesn't know. I'm not sure it matters. Geir told me that he intends to check out the area to make sure Pollard doesn't have his men guarding the place," Blaine said. "I know what *I* need to do, and that means going to Mirdalur and seeing if I can raise the magic. And if I can't—for whatever reason—then Pollard's schemes may not matter much, because with the magic storms increasing, we won't be around to care."

"I'd like to see what your father's pendant makes of Ifrem's map," Dawe said. "And I wish Connor were here with his map and pendant. Maybe each pendant was designed to get a different part of a message from the words it revealed."

"We can check the pendant against the book Grimur gave us," Kestel said. "And at least we've still got Ifrem's map, and the drawing I made."

Blaine looked at Verran. "Is there anything else in the chest?"

"There's this," he said, holding up another velvet-wrapped item. "It feels like a scroll. It was rolled up tightly and tucked into a corner." Verran carefully felt along the bottom of the chest and unfolded the velvet to make sure that no small treasures had gone overlooked. "That's it."

Blaine slipped the contents from the velvet to reveal a piece of goatskin parchment, tightly rolled and tied with a yellowed bit of silk. He carried the parchment to the desk and gently unrolled it. On it was a drawing of what appeared to be two very uneven concentric circles.

"Thirteen points on the inner circle," Dawe observed. "Thirteen Lords of the Blood."

"There's a name beside each point," Blaine said, squinting at the small, cramped writing. "And something that looks like a symbol." He drew the parchment closer to see it better, and moved into the sunlight near the window. "There's the name 'McFadden.' And there's 'Pollard,'" he said, noting two of the points. "It's not much, but at least with this, I'll know where to stand when we get to Mirdalur."

"What about the symbol? Does it match what's on the pendant?" Verran asked.

Blaine squinted again at the parchment. "Not that I can tell. Maybe there's something at Mirdalur that will match it."

Kestel returned after a few moments, bearing Grimur's book and Ifrem's map. Bunched in one hand was the gossamer shawl on which she had traced the location of the places of power and the null spaces. "Got them!" she said brightly.

They gathered around the desk, positioning themselves to take advantage of the light that streamed in from the window. Kestel carefully laid out the map, and Blaine held up Ian's pendant.

"I don't know how long it took someone to create the writing on the maps and in that book so that each pendant deciphered something different," Blaine muttered.

"They had magic to help them," Verran reminded him. "That's the whole point of this."

"If I had to guess," Dawe said, "I'd say that Valtyr wanted to record the process but also wanted to make sure that no single lord had all of the information."

"For what purpose?" Kestel asked. "If the magic had already been created, what was Valtyr afraid of?"

Blaine frowned. "Maybe Valtyr knew that magic that was created could also be destroyed. Meroven managed to wipe out the magic by accident—we think. What if it wasn't a coincidence that they struck the noble houses first?" Another thought occurred to him. "Maybe there's more than one hand in this. If Pollard sent an assassin after me, did he and Reese also assassinate any of the Lords of the Blood that didn't die in the war or the Great Fire?"

Piran grimaced. "That makes no sense. What possible reason would Meroven have to do something like that? And if the magic was already dead, why would Reese and Pollard bother killing the remaining lords?"

"You're assuming the generals really understood what their mages were doing," Judith said quietly. "There had been talk, when the war started, that some in Meroven felt that the world had become too corrupt. They wanted to 'start over' free of the corruption." She paused. "We took it to mean that Meroven thought Donderath was corrupt. But what if Meroven's mages wanted something different from what the generals intended?"

"You mean, what if the mages lied to the generals about what the strike would accomplish?" Piran asked, staring at the map as he thought through the ramifications.

Judith nodded. "It would be a lie of omission, because the generals would see the nobles' manors as a worthy military target. But suppose the mages—or at least some of the mages—had a different agenda?"

"Why would mages want to destroy magic?" Kestel looked up, clearly troubled by the conversation.

Judith shrugged. "They wouldn't be the first men to be willing to burn down everything in the service of their cause. Maybe they were willing to give up their magic to 'purify' the world. Who knows? It might have only taken one or two mages to pull it off. The others might have never had any idea that they were destroying their own power."

Blaine nodded slowly. "Glenreith got lucky because you weren't living in the old manor—hadn't for a couple of generations. The other lords built onto the old houses instead of replacing them outright." He paused, thinking. "Connor told us that Pentreath Reese likes the situation as it is, without magic. Magic gave mortals a fighting chance against the vampires. That's one of the reasons Reese is fighting Penhallow—Penhallow would like to see the magic restored."

Blaine sighed. "I'm not sure there's any more we can do than go to Mirdalur and see what happens. At worst, we get the lay of the land and find out that one Lord of the Blood can't do a damned thing alone."

"Speaking of which," Dawe said, "I'm headed for the forge. With luck, I should be able to make the pieces I need to modify the crossbows. We could be ready to go to Mirdalur tomorrow night if all goes well." He headed out of the room, and Blaine turned back to the others.

"That gives Kestel and me the rest of the day to study the map and Grimur's book with the new pendant, in case there's a clue to what we need to do," Blaine said. "And it gives me tonight to talk with Geir."

He looked at his other companions. "Piran and Verran—I'd like you to work with Edward to gather what we need for the trip to Mirdalur. Horses, food, supplies, weapons—whatever he can spare. I wouldn't mind having a couple more guards if it doesn't weaken Glenreith's defenses."

"We can certainly spare a few guards," Judith replied. Blaine nodded. "Then it's set. We go to Mirdalur."

CHAPTER
THIRTY-ONE

ALL WE WANT TO KNOW IS, WHO SENT YOU?"
Piran's voice was reasonable, but there was a dangerous
edge. Their prisoner glowered, but said nothing.

"I'm telling you, he'd have more to say if you'd let me knock
him around," Piran grumbled. Blaine leaned against the far
wall, arms crossed, watching the interrogation.

Blaine looked at the spy Piran had brought back from the
edge of Glenreith's holdings. The man had a growing bruise on
his cheek, and one eye was partially swollen shut. From the way
he held himself, Blaine guessed the spy had at least one broken
rib, made more painful by the ropes binding his wrists behind
his back. "You roughed him up plenty just bringing him in,"
Blaine replied. "You go at him again and break his jaw, he's not
going to tell us anything."

Piran shrugged. "I guess it depends on what our 'guest'
would prefer. It's nearly sundown. After dark, I turn him over
to Geir." Piran leaned closer to the spy and gave an unpleasant
smile.

"I may not be your friend, but I'm mortal. Geir's a vampire.
Wakes up hungry. Real hungry," Piran said, taking his cue

from their prisoner's discomfort. "If you don't tell me something useful by the time I go off watch, I walk out of this room and leave you with Geir." He gave an exaggerated shrug and turned away. "Whatever secrets you're keeping, he can glamour them out of you. Make you sing like we put you to the rack. Or," he said with a deliberate touch of ennui, "I imagine he'll get what he needs from your thoughts when he drains you. No secrets in death, you know."

The prisoner paled but said nothing, although his eyes moved nervously between Piran and the door as the latch lifted. The door swung open, and Geir stood framed in the doorway. Blaine had no doubt that Geir had heard every word from the corridor. In fact, Geir seemed to be playing to Piran's threats. He wore a white shirt with no frock coat, heightening the pallor of his skin. His eyeteeth, usually discreetly hidden, were quite prominent. "I thought I smelled dinner," Geir remarked offhandedly as he walked into the chamber.

Piran spared a quick glance toward the spy. "Oh, well. Time's up." He turned to Geir. "Let me know when you're done." He looked to Blaine. "Just tell me where you want the body buried." With that, he walked out of the room, closing the door behind him.

Their prisoner looked as if he might faint. His bravado was gone, and he looked to Blaine imploringly. "You're just going to let the biter have me?"

Blaine shrugged. "Piran warned you." He gave a cold smile. "Don't worry—it's reasonably quick, though not... painless."

Geir moved toward the prisoner with a slow, gliding grace. The man was shaking, and a whiff told Blaine that the spy had soiled himself. "I was just sent to watch and report back. I don't know anything," the spy argued.

"I suspect you know more than you realize." Geir's voice was silky smooth. He was standing in front of the prisoner. The man turned his head, but Geir took his chin firmly in his hand and forced him to make eye contact. The spy closed his eyes tightly, but Geir squeezed his jaw and the man's eyes flew open as he yelped in pain. "Tell me."

All resistance drained from the man, and his features, tight with fear, relaxed. "What do you want to know?"

Geir chuckled. "That's a good man. Now, who sent you?"

"Pollard."

"And where is Pollard?"

"Don't know."

Geir frowned, and the spy twitched uncomfortably as Geir increased the level of compulsion. "Where was he when you received your orders?"

"A candlemark south of Glenreith, not far off the main road."

Geir shot a glance at Blaine, who nodded. Pollard was watching the main road between Glenreith and Castle Reach. "What about the other roads? Are there watchers?"

The fight had drained out of the captive, and he looked up at Geir with a pathetic eagerness to please. "Pollard has guards on every road around Glenreith. We were to watch for McFadden and report back if he left the manor walls."

Geir nodded. "Good. You're doing very well. How large is Pollard's force?"

The spy frowned, thinking. "Don't rightly know, because men have been coming in for several days. Several men on each road."

Blaine cursed silently. The stakes of going to Mirdalur had suddenly gotten much higher.

"Are there encampments, or just watchers?"

"Just watchers."

"Is Reese with Pollard?"

"I only saw Pollard."

Geir's expression shifted from unreadable into a warm smile that was mirrored by the look on the spy's face. "You've been very helpful," Geir said in a comforting voice. "You've done a very good job. In a moment, you're going to fall into a deep sleep. When you awaken, you won't remember this conversation. You won't remember being captured, or seeing any of us. You *will* remember being robbed by highwaymen, who took your wages and knocked you out. You'll return to Pollard and tell him that you saw no one. Do you understand?"

"Yes."

"Now, sleep." Geir's voice was honeyed with compulsion. Immediately, the prisoner slumped against his bonds, and his head drooped forward.

Geir and Blaine left the room and found Piran pacing the hallway. "Well?" Piran asked, looking up.

"We got what we wanted. Pollard's set traps for us on the main roads," Blaine reported.

Piran chuckled. "I had a feeling he'd fess up for Geir."

Geir grimaced. "Next time, you can play the monster in the dark."

"You didn't mind when we cooked this scheme up," Piran reminded him. "And you saved me some bruised knuckles. By the way, how did he taste?"

Geir glowered at him. "Like chicken. What do you mean, 'how did he taste'? Do you really think I'd feed on that pathetic creature if I had a choice in the matter?"

Piran glanced at Blaine. "You left him alive?"

Blaine shrugged. "His memory's been altered. I'll have the guards put him back where you found him, a little worse for the wear. He'll report that nothing happened except for a common robbery."

Piran sighed. "Better, I guess, not to tip our hand to Pollard. But it does raise the question: What does this mean for your plan to go to Mirdalur?"

Geir looked from Piran to Blaine. "I was going to propose that I make a quick trip out there to scout the area, even before you found our 'guest.' If I leave right away, I can be back before dawn the day after tomorrow."

Blaine gave a low whistle. "You'll be moving pretty fast. It's a three-day ride one way."

Geir smiled. "I can move more quickly, but only for short periods. Double speed will have to do."

"Then we sit tight until you come back," Blaine said with a shrug. "The rest of us could use the recovery time, and we can get our provisions together. With luck, your reconnaissance will give us an idea of the best way to get to Mirdalur and avoid problems on the way. I'd rather not take on Pollard if we don't have to, and I certainly don't want to go up against a large force."

"At least, not without a large force of our own," Piran said with a grin that suggested he relished the brawl.

Blaine shook his head. "And where are we going to get a private army? I've got no desire to take on Pollard, especially since we don't know that going to Mirdalur will even work. If it does, we've already scored a victory by bringing the magic back. If not, I'd like to get back to Glenreith in one piece to decide what happens next."

"I'm still troubled by the fact that Penhallow hasn't joined us," Geir said. "The connection through the *kruvgaldur* is damnably imperfect. I believe Penhallow's been detained against his will. I can sense warning and urgency. I have images of a fortress, but I don't recognize it. What that means, other than that Penhallow seems to think we're in danger, I'm not sure."

"And no idea whether or not Connor is with him," Blaine replied. He sighed. "Sounds like we're on our own until Penhallow can get free. And the longer we wait, the more likely that Pollard will decide to bottle us up here." He looked from Piran to Geir. "We go on with the plan to go to Mirdalur. It's better than sitting still waiting to be besieged."

The next morning, Blaine awoke with the sunrise from an unsettled sleep. The day had dawned fair and clear, though with a chill in the air that said winter was coming soon. On impulse, he dressed quickly and grabbed his cloak, then stepped out onto the balcony.

The sunlight carried little warmth. Without needing a marked candle, Blaine knew that the days were growing shorter. He smiled to himself. After Edgeland's white nights and long dark, Donderath's seasonal change seemed much gentler than he remembered. He looked out over the rolling hills and the gray blur of the forest's leafless trees. In the fields, just a few dry stalks remained from the harvest, with haystacks piled at intervals for the coming winter.

Glenreith's far pastures were empty. Even from his balcony, Blaine could see guards posted at intervals around the manor's lands, protecting both the workmen who labored to bring in the last of the root crops for winter and the animals that grazed on the near pastures, closer to the walls and easier to protect. To the west would be the ruins of Rhystorp, Carensa's family home. He swallowed hard and looked away, unwilling to think about that loss, not now, and perhaps not for a long time.

To the east, if they were still standing, would be the miller's home and mill, and toward the north, Aringarte, home to the family of Lars Theilsson, a prosperous farmer and wealthy landowner. Theilsson had risen far without the benefit of a title or any position at court.

"A copper for your thoughts."

Blaine startled at Judith's quiet approach. He gestured toward the rolling hills that spread out to the horizon. "Just wondering how Miller Storr and Lars Theilsson weathered the war."

"You knew Theilsson's son, didn't you?"

Blaine nodded. "Niklas. We were great mates before...well, before."

Judith gave a faint smile. "I seem to remember you two hunting together."

Blaine looked off into the distance. "Niklas was the rare friend who enjoyed books as much as hunting—and ale. Once he went into the army and got his officer's commission, I didn't see much of him, but when he did come home, it was always as if nothing had changed." He looked at Judith. "What became of him, with the war?"

Judith sighed. "Niklas was the commander of the unit Carr signed up with. I felt a little better entrusting Carr to Niklas, although I hadn't wanted Carr to go at all. Niklas promised he'd watch out for Carr," she said, and her voice caught. She shook her head to dispel the emotion and went on.

"Niklas led a battalion that was sent to the Vellanaj front. Neither he nor Carr returned, and none of Niklas's men have been seen or heard from since." Her expression tightened with pain. "It's been over half a year since the war ended. If they were going to come back, I imagine they would have by now."

Blaine looked down. "I'm sorry to hear that. He'd have been a good man to have on our side. I'd hoped to recruit him to give us a hand, or protect Glenreith while we see what can be done at Mirdalur."

Judith gave him a worried look. "You're still planning to go?"

Blaine shrugged and turned his hands palms up. "What else can I do? If there's any chance that I might be able to bring back the magic, it seems worth the risk."

"You've got a pocketful of old trinkets, some antique maps, and tall tales told by a vampire," Judith replied. "You have no idea what will happen when you get to Mirdalur, or whether there's even enough of it left to matter. You could put yourself, and your friends, at risk for nothing."

"Maybe. But what if Penhallow and Grimur are right? What if I really am the last Lord of the Blood, and what if I could bring back the magic?" Blaine asked. "Granted, I've never had a lot of magic myself, but what if that spark is enough? If I try and fail, at least we know that the magic is really dead, and we can move on."

"And if bringing the magic back kills you?" Judith asked, meeting his gaze levelly.

"Velant and almost seven years in Edgeland didn't do the job, I doubt Mirdalur will," Blaine replied, managing a wan smile. "But I have a responsibility to try, if there's any chance at all."

Judith's gaze did not waver. "Would you have come back if it weren't for Mirdalur?"

Blaine looked away. He was silent for a long time. "I'm not sure. I'd carved out a good life up there. I figured the rest of you had moved on without me. Maybe I'd have come back eventually, especially with the magic gone. That's going to make Edgeland even less hospitable than it was, and it was rough country."

Judith turned away. "And after you go to Mirdalur? What then?"

Blaine turned back toward the balcony rail. "Whether it works or whether it doesn't, I'm here to stay. One way or another, I want to get Glenreith back on its feet. Without a king, and with the countryside in ruins, I figure we'll need to make alliances, pool resources, see to the protection of our own."

Judith gave a wan smile. "You almost sound like a warlord."

Blaine chuckled. "Do I? A very unlikely one. But that's exactly what men like Pollard are trying to become, and if we don't have our own alliances, the next time, he'll do more than camp here; he'll lay siege."

Judith shivered and wrapped her arms around herself. "That thought has crossed my mind."

"When I get back from Mirdalur, I'll pay a call to the miller and to Lars. See who else is still alive and might be on our side. If we work together, we might be able to get through the winter." Blaine was surprised when Judith moved beside him and laid a hand on his arm.

"Whatever you decide, I'll support you, Blaine," she said. "Before you arrived, I was afraid for the future. It didn't look very likely that Edward and Mari and I could keep this place running, even with the servants who've stayed on. Now," she said and paused, "I've got some hope for the first time since the war began."

Blaine chuckled. "I'll try not to disappoint you—again."

"Mirdalur is a ruin," Geir reported when he returned from his reconnaissance. Despite the hour, a small group was gathered in Glenreith's parlor to hear the news. Judith sat on a small couch near the fireplace, sitting as straight and prim as if at court. Edward was behind her with a hand resting on the back of the couch, watchful and protective. Blaine wondered whether their relationship had become more than employer and retainer over the harsh years since his exile. Mari had stayed in her rooms to tend her son, but she had made Blaine promise to give her a recap at breakfast.

Piran leaned against the back wall, arms crossed. Verran was studying the selection of small trinkets that lay about the room, and Blaine could guess that Verran's past thieving had given him a good appreciation for their value. Dawe sat in a high-backed chair across from Judith. The lanky silversmith was bent forward with his elbows on his knees, playing with a bit of twisted wire.

Kestel perched on the arm of the couch, still dressed in the gown she had worn to dinner. It was one of Mari's old gowns, which Kestel had reworked. The dress was in a light-brown satin that might not have flattered Mari's coloring, but on Kestel, it played up her red hair and made her green eyes sparkle. Kestel shifted just a bit, and the light from the lamps caught a glint of metal in the folds of her skirt. Blaine smiled. He had no doubt that Kestel had more than one slim knife concealed in the folds of her gown.

Blaine realized that it was the first time he had ever seen Kestel dressed in anything better than Edgeland's homespun finery, and it struck him just what a beauty she was. A blush crept across Kestel's cheeks, and Blaine realized his appreciation had been more evident in his expression than he thought. He chuckled and looked away.

"We knew the keep was destroyed a long time ago," Dawe replied. "Is there anything left?"

"I'd expected to find nothing left," Geir said. "But I was

wrong. Sometime between the old war and the Meroven strike, someone had obviously tried to rebuild at least part of one wing. I'm guessing that was a while ago; even the new ruins seemed to have been deserted for quite a while."

"What was left? Enough to chance a trip?" Blaine asked.

Geir frowned, nodding. "Yes. I believe so. While the keep is a ruin and the walls are broken down in many places, there are several outbuildings that are still standing and in fairly good shape. What's more interesting is that, from the air, those outbuildings are laid out in the pattern of Esthrane's constellation," he added.

"One of the outbuildings housed a large cistern," Geir continued. "That building is at the fifth point, the 'child' in the constellation. The well house was solidly built; it looked as if it lasted until the Great Fire. Kept the cistern protected from the elements, and when the roof collapsed, it covered the cistern so it didn't get clogged with debris. It's quite a large, deep cistern; I'd guess it to be about four paces by three paces. I went down it to have a look. The cistern is functional, but about halfway down there's a ledge, and off the ledge is a small passageway that branches off from the wall, and at the end is a locked door. I didn't try to open it, and it didn't look as if it had been disturbed in a long time. I'm willing to lay bets that's where we need to go."

"Might be nothing but a secret hiding place for the old lord's treasures," Piran said, looking on skeptically from his spot against the wall.

"Was there anything special about the door?" Kestel asked, her eyes alight with interest. "Anything that might have been magical?"

Geir nodded. "There were runes carved on the lintel of the door, and some markings that looked like the ones on the obsidian disks. If the door leads to an area underground, there's a chance it survived both attacks."

"The hills around these parts are riddled with caves," Edward said. "It's not uncommon for the old manors to incorporate the caves as storage chambers beneath the house, or even as escape routes for the manors that were once fortresses."

Blaine looked thoughtful. "If there was another entrance through the keep, the building's collapse would have blocked it off long ago. No one except the *talishte* will have seen it from the air." He looked to Geir. "Any evidence that Reese has already been there?"

Geir shrugged. "No way to tell, really. If Reese has been there, he didn't leave any trace. And there's no reason why he would have seen it from the air. I just went up on a whim, not really expecting to find anything. There are no nearby cliffs, so no one is going to see the pattern by accident. From the ground, it's not noticeable."

"How about Pollard's men? Can we get there without a fight?" Piran asked.

Geir nodded. "Pollard seems to have thrown a wide net without anticipating that we'll go anywhere in particular. He had the largest force on the road to Castle Reach, like the spy said, so my bet is he expects us to go back to the city, maybe even to what's left of Quillarth Castle." He paused. "He's got groups of about a dozen men on all the main roads leading away from Glenreith. But there are too many side roads and farm lanes for him to watch them all."

"You think he expects us to travel the king's highway?" Blaine asked with a chuckle.

Kestel looked up. "Pollard's thinking like a lord, not a colonist. A group on horseback with guards would be easy to spot.

A covered farm wagon, a couple of tinkers, and a few vagrants all heading the same direction on farm lanes wouldn't be worth anyone's attention."

"Why do I have the feeling Piran and I get to be the vagrants?" Dawe asked, not really expecting an answer.

"I don't mind being a tinker," Verran spoke up without looking over his shoulder. "You'd be amazed how much a good tinker can steal by the time he leaves town, if he's careful."

"Would you two be serious?" Kestel chided. Her eyes were alight with the challenge. "We can hide several guards in the wagon. That way, if we find anything at Mirdalur, we can bring it back with us without attracting notice."

"Mirdalur is a three-days' ride from here," Judith warned. "Won't it be suspicious if such an odd group of strangers make camp together?"

Geir considered for a moment, then shook his head. "Not necessarily. With the brigands and the magic storms, I've seen some motley groups on the road. There's safety in numbers, and conditions nowadays don't favor the lone traveler. Few are willing to ride alone unless they're a skilled fighter or *talishte*, and even my kind are wary with raiders about."

"Knowing that even the undead don't feel safe on the road makes me feel so much better about this," Piran grumbled.

"Any other hazards on the way?" Blaine asked Geir, ignoring Piran.

"Interestingly enough, Pollard's men are something of a deterrent for the usual highwaymen," Geir said. "None of the roads are in good shape, and the farm trails even more so, but I mapped a route without missing bridges or downed trees. It's not without risk, but I think we stand a good chance of getting there and back with Pollard none the wiser."

Blaine looked to Dawe and Edward. "How much longer do you think it would take to pull together what we need: provisions, wagon, disguises, and a half-dozen guards for backup?"

"I've been helping your captain at arms repair the weapons in the armory," Dawe replied. "I've enjoyed being back in a forge again. Point is, both the guards who come with us and those who stay behind will be well armed. I believe the captain could have his men ready on a few candlemarks' notice."

Edward nodded. "Wagons we have aplenty, and we can spare the horses you need, both for your 'tinkers' and for your wagon team. As for the vagabonds, we've taken in some stray horses that wandered loose for a while after the Great Fire. They've regained their strength, but they look a little ragged. They'll do just fine."

Kestel and Judith were conferring in quiet tones. Kestel looked up with a broad grin. "Leave the disguises to Lady Judith and me. Give us a day, and we'll have what we need. We'll look the part—I promise."

"Give me an old nag or a mule and a small cart and a few odds and ends from the rubbish pile and I can put a tinker's buggy together," Verran said. "Won't take but a couple of candlemarks."

Geir cleared his throat. "There is one more thing to consider." His expression had grown even more serious than before, and Blaine thought he saw worry in Geir's eyes. "Penhallow has contacted me through the *kruvgaldur*."

"Do you know why he hasn't joined us?" Blaine asked.

"Did he get Connor to safety?" Kestel added.

Geir shrugged. "The connection was strained. At best, I receive images and impressions. This time, it was fragmentary. That could be because of distance or because of the presence of magic storms near either of us. I saw Connor's face, and a fortified castle. Penhallow's frustration was high. I believe he and Connor are either prisoners or perhaps under siege." He frowned. "I didn't get much more, but I did receive a clear sense of warning coupled with images of Mirdalur."

"Meaning what?" Blaine asked cautiously.

Geir grimaced. "That's where it's open to interpretation. Penhallow was alerting me to danger, but whether it was a caution to avoid Mirdalur or to tread carefully, I don't know."

"That's just great," Piran said, adding a potent curse. "We could be in danger if we go, or in more danger if we don't go— with no way to tell exactly what we're being warned about."

"The *kruvgaldur* is not precise at a distance," Geir replied. "I debated whether or not to share it with you and decided that I owed you full disclosure, even if the information isn't complete."

Blaine began to pace. "The longer we wait here, the more likely it is that either Pollard or Reese will return with more troops to bottle us up. Once that happens, we won't get to Mirdalur without a fight. Without more information from Penhallow, we have no way of knowing whether he's saying 'stop' or 'wait.' But I can't shake the feeling that standing still is a mistake."

"If we go to Mirdalur and you can unlock the magic, we gain a weapon against Reese and Pollard," Kestel said. "Once the magic works, if we can find Vigus Quintrel, he might even be able to help us go up against them and win."

"We'll need an army, not just a few mages for that," Piran muttered. "I don't like any of it. I don't really trust Penhallow, so getting a muddy message from him doesn't carry a lot of weight with me. I don't much like magic, but things were better when we had some, so anything with a chance of getting the magic back seems like a good idea to me. Sitting still waiting to be attacked, not so much."

Dawe made a face. "Much as it pains me to agree with Piran on anything," he said with a glance toward Piran, "I think he's right." Piran answered Dawe with an obscene gesture, and Dawe grinned.

"I rather like the idea of seeing if we can steal the magic back," Verran said. He had continued to peruse the library shelves as the others talked, and Blaine hadn't been sure Verran was even paying attention. He looked over at him to see Verran easily linking and undoing a complex puzzle of metal circles. "Hate to say it, but I agree with Piran too."

Blaine sighed. "I'm not discounting Geir's warning. It's good to know Penhallow and Connor made it out of the crypt, but if they haven't joined us by now, it stands to reason they'd been detained against their will. Whatever we do, we're on our own."

"We'll take every precaution," Blaine said, looking at Geir, who nodded. "We'll assume that we're being watched, and we'll take as many guards as Glenreith can spare. But staying here until we're attacked gains us nothing." He looked from face to face and saw them waiting for his decision.

"The longer we hesitate, the more likely it is that Pollard or Reese will get ahead of us. We leave for Mirdalur day after tomorrow."

CHAPTER
THIRTY-TWO

THEY RODE THROUGH THE NIGHT, ALERT FOR spies. Geir ranged ahead of them while Piran lagged behind, watching for any signs of ambush. Next to him on the seat of the wagon, Dawe had his altered crossbow at the ready. In their time at Glenreith, he had managed to alter half a dozen bows, so that the guards who rode with them or hid in the wagons also carried the enhanced weapons. Beneath their cloaks, they were all well armed. Piran and Blaine preferred their swords to crossbows, as did Geir. Kestel wore a bandolier of throwing knives over her plain tunic and trews, and had a short sword in a scabbard at her hip. Clad like tinkers and peddlers, they drew little attention from those few travelers they passed on the moonlit roads.

"I'm still not sure this is a good idea," Kestel murmured.

Blaine shot her a weak grin. "Neither am I. Did you come up with an alternative we hadn't thought of?"

Kestel chewed her lip and shook her head. "No."

"Me neither."

They rode for a while in silence, and Blaine found his thoughts wandering. It was almost Twelfth Month, and even in Donderath, the days were growing short and the night stretched long. Edgeland's long dark and white nights had given him a completely different perspective on the season's change.

"A copper for your thoughts," Kestel said after a long pause.

Blaine shrugged and smiled. "Just thinking about how we celebrated the coming and going of the long dark and white nights in Edgeland. The solstice is coming up. Despite father's many faults, he did keep Vessa Night on the solstice eve and the Feast of Torven on the day itself, and he kept them with style." He sighed. "Just wondering if I could persuade Edward and Judith to make an effort to keep the holidays."

Kestel chuckled. "I used to love the bonfires at court on Vessa Night, and the red banners and music to the goddess. King Merrill also had his faults, but he knew how to hold a feast that was the talk of the castle for months afterward. And the food! I'll remember the roast goose with honeyed parsnips for the rest of my life."

Blaine's smile was sad. "Given the circumstances, I suspect anything we could manage at Glenreith would be a pale reflection of the feasts you're used to."

Kestel's smile faded and her expression became pensive. "There were parts of those times that are pleasant to remember, but much of it wasn't. I don't miss those days. I enjoyed the feasts we kept at the homestead in Edgeland much more than those at court, largely because at the homestead, there was none of the posturing and politics."

"Things here are such a mess, it may feel like homesteading to put Glenreith back on its feet," Blaine admitted. "We've been so focused on going to Mirdalur that I haven't had much time to think about afterward, assuming there is an afterward," he said with a dour look.

"Let's hope so," Kestel said. She shivered and drew her cloak more tightly around herself.

"I'm just hoping that once we get the magic settled, you and the others will consider staying on at Glenreith. There's plenty of room, more than we had at the homestead. That is, if you don't have somewhere else you'd rather be."

Kestel smiled and was quiet for a few breaths. "One thing at a time, huh? Let's see how things work out." There was a sadness in her voice Blaine couldn't place, and she looked away when he tried to meet her gaze.

"Personally, I'm game to stay." Verran had ridden up behind them. He was still linking and unlinking the metal puzzle, which Blaine knew from personal experience was much more complex than Verran made it look. "I daresay I could assist Edward in procurement."

Blaine chuckled. "You mean looting the countryside?"

Verran gave a lopsided grin. "Doesn't sound as good when you put it that way, but yes. There's a small fortune in livestock wandering free since the Great Fire, and I'm betting that there are still valuables buried in the rubble of the buildings that have been abandoned. I'd see it as my duty to forage on your behalf and bring back the spoils to share with the household."

They were all joking to relieve the tension, but Blaine had to admit that the idea of continuing the homestead at Glenreith held great appeal. Postwar Donderath was an unforgiving, forbidding place. Keeping people he trusted close to him seemed like more than just friendship; it could be the basis for survival, as it had been in Edgeland. "I'd like that," he said.

"Stay sharp; there's a ruin up ahead." Geir seemed to appear out of nowhere. "I can't sense anyone inside, but some *talishte* can cloak themselves from others. Keep your eyes open."

Around the next bend, Blaine saw the ruin. The foundation

stones were very old, and even in disrepair, the structure was impressive. The remains of a large tower still stretched high into the sky, despite the fact that its top lay in rubble in a wide swath of tumbled stones around the base. The thick stone wall was breached in several places, and behind the wall, Blaine glimpsed a roofless façade. He could see straight through the empty windows to the dark sky beyond, reminding him of the eye sockets of a skull.

They rode on high alert, weapons at the ready. In the distance, Blaine heard the hoot of an owl and a faraway howl of a wolf, but in the ruins themselves, nothing stirred. When they were well past the ruined tower, he and Kestel drew up alongside Geir. "Is it true what they said about the tower, that it was a citadel of the Knights of Esthrane?"

"Is that what's said?" Geir replied. "Do you know who the Knights were?"

Blaine frowned. "I've only heard legends. As a child, I was told the tower was destroyed because the Knights betrayed King Merrill's grandfather. There was talk that they dealt in the dark arts."

Geir chuckled. "Oh, they're dark enough, that's certain. They were *talishte* and mages whose job was to hunt down rogues of both kinds and bring them to the king's justice. As the king's agents, they had immunity from prosecution and nearly limitless power. At their best, they did the kingdom a great service by eliminating true monsters. At their worst..." Geir paused and gave an eloquent shrug. "At their worst, they *were* the monsters."

"What happened to them?" Kestel asked. "That tower looked as if it fell long before the Great Fire."

Geir nodded, but Blaine thought he looked uncomfortable with the subject. "King Merrill's father began to fear that the

Knights of Esthrane might someday turn against him. He was wise to fear what he had created, though to my knowledge the Knights' loyalty was never suspect. He rescinded their letter of immunity and had their leaders watched. There were some incidents that led him to decide the Knights were too dangerous to keep around. He disbanded the order and imprisoned those he could find until he could assure their loyalty."

"And how, pray, could he do that?" Kestel's voice was skeptical.

Geir gave a cold half smile. "The king gave the captured Knights over to the royal mages for questioning. But the royal mages had always feared and envied the power of the Knights. Few were surprised when the mages declared the Knights to be traitors. All but a handful of the leaders were destroyed on orders of the king."

Blaine let out a low whistle. "So, from the Knights' point of view, the king used them until they became inconvenient, and then betrayed them."

Geir nodded, tight-lipped. "Exactly."

"What became of the ones who escaped?" Blaine asked.

Geir looked away. "Merrill's father didn't find all of the Knights, and a few of their leaders slipped the net as well. Some among the *talishte* recognized the service that the Knights did in bringing down rogues and felt that the king had been faithless. It was rumored that the Knights survived, with the aid of their fellow *talishte*, in the high country, or in the southern desert. I haven't heard anything about them in a very long time, so I suspect the survivors eventually died off and the *talishte* members moved on." He shrugged. "Too bad. They might have been helpful in our current task."

They rode on, taking shelter just before dawn in the ruins of an abandoned mill. Though Blaine and the others took turns at watch, the day passed without incident. By the time Geir rose for the night, Piran and Dawe had caught a brace of rabbits and captured a wandering goat, which they cooked over a concealed fire, careful to save the blood for Geir.

"I have to admit, you've brought us on some roads I've never even seen before," Blaine said as they ate the roasted meat along with hard bread from Glenreith. Almost from the time they left the manor, they had traveled along rutted side roads and trails that were long disused and barely passable.

Geir shrugged. "A necessary inconvenience. Pollard could put men on the main roads and some of the byways, but he couldn't possibly scout every farm path." He gave a cold smile. "Some of these trails have not been well traveled for several lifetimes. I have the benefit of a long memory."

The wind shifted, and Blaine pulled his cloak around him. "Too bad we can't risk more of a fire," he said. "It's damn cold out here."

Geir nodded. "We've been fortunate that there hasn't been snow. The trails can be treacherous when they drift closed."

"I'm just glad there haven't been more of those magic storms," Piran said over a mouthful of rabbit.

Dawe made a gesture of warding. "Don't even mention the storms," he said.

Piran rolled his eyes. "Warding won't do any good—magic doesn't work, remember?"

"It's the thought that counts," Dawe rejoined. "And the gesture is meant to ask the gods for safety, not the magic."

"Not sure that the gods are real, either," Piran replied, stuffing a piece of bread into his mouth and washing it down with a drink from his wineskin.

"Personally, I'll take all the help we can get," Blaine said, anxious to avoid another foray into the long-running argument between Dawe and Piran. He turned back to Geir. "How long until we get to Mirdalur?"

Geir consulted the sky, reckoning their position by the stars. The night was clear and cold. "We'll be to the ruins by daybreak," he said. "I'd hoped for better, but the roads haven't been in any shape for us to make better time."

"I don't imagine it matters," Dawe said. "The magic will be just as broken when we get there."

"Do you think Pollard will have scouts at Mirdalur?" Blaine asked.

Geir frowned. "He'd have to suspect that we had some reason to go there. Since we don't know what Pollard knows, there's no way to tell. I figured I'd check out the road ahead when the sun goes down tomorrow. There were no intruders when I did my initial reconnaissance, but it would be wise to be certain."

Blaine slept restlessly, finally rising a candlemark before his shift at watch. He found Piran moving from window to window, watching the approach to the mill, his crossbow at the ready.

"See anything?" Blaine asked, still groggy.

Piran shook his head. "No. That's a good thing." He gestured toward a pot of *fet* that still sat on the warm embers of last night's fire. "There's still some in the pot. You look like you could use a cup." He grinned. "It's black as night and thick as tar; just the thing to wake you up."

Blaine mumbled a curse and poured himself a cup. Without sugar and milk to cut the bitter taste, it was barely palatable, and Blaine grimaced as he swallowed it. Within minutes, however, the *fet* had begun to wake him up, and he felt clearheaded.

"Horrid stuff," he said, spitting to get the taste out of his mouth.

Piran chuckled. "We've had worse in Velant."

"I try not to think about that." Blaine leaned against the mill wall. "You don't like this whole Mirdalur thing, do you?"

Piran shrugged. "Hey, I'm a soldier. Soldiers take orders. We don't plan the campaigns." He gave Blaine a skeptical look. "And we trust that the generals have a good idea of what they're doing."

Blaine grimaced. "I'm hardly a general. And I've got my doubts about the whole idea, too. But if it's really possible to bring back the magic, if it does somehow depend on me, how can I not try?"

Piran cursed. "You can't. And maybe Grimur—and Penhallow—knew that. Geir's all right, for a biter, but the *talishte* think different than we do. They're older, and they've had to live by their wits, lie to survive. How do we know that what happens at Mirdalur is what we think is happening? You might trigger something, but it might not be what they've led us to believe."

"Now, there's a comforting thought," Blaine replied. Much as he hated to admit it, the same thing had occurred to him, more than once, since they had set out from Edgeland. "I'll grant you that, but where does it leave us? I don't entirely trust Penhallow's word, but I don't have a better option, except to do nothing." He sighed. "And if we do nothing, I don't know how we'll protect Glenreith from Pollard and Reese if they really decide to make an effort to take it."

Piran made a face. "I don't have any better ideas, that's why I'm happy to just take orders, most of the time. I hope Penhallow's really on our side, and I hope the magic comes back. I'm just saying, be careful and watch your back."

"That's your job, remember?" Blaine said with a weak attempt at humor. He sobered. "Don't worry. I'll be as careful as possible. I'm just not sure what that means in this situation."

Piran grinned. "Hey, any battlefield you leave alive is a good battle. I'd start with that."

"Let's hope we get that lucky," Blaine replied. He stared out the window toward the horizon where the sun was setting. "Geir should be up soon. We'll know what Mirdalur holds for us soon enough."

CHAPTER THIRTY-THREE

"FOR A PLACE THAT'S SUPPOSED TO BE SO DAMNED important, it looks like a dump," Piran said as they rode into sight of Mirdalur.

The ruins looked as Geir had described them. In places, remains of the shattered walls lay in an overgrown heap, and the keep itself was a mound of rubble. Fresh scorch marks were silent testimony that the Great Fire had not left Mirdalur unscathed. Parts of the wall still stood above the brambles and tall brown grass, and as Geir had said, five stone outbuildings marked the edges of the compound. Over the centuries, trees and scrub had filled in most of the open spaces, while the remaining buildings were vine covered and weed shrouded.

"Maybe that's a good thing," Blaine replied absently, scanning the area for hidden attackers. He spotted no one, but that did not enable him to relax. The night's work ahead of them offered plenty of danger.

A shattered fountain was the centerpiece of what had been a large bailey. The fountain was filled with leaves and foul-smelling water. A few ornamental statues, broken and overgrown, remained along the edge of its basin. Blaine startled as Geir came up beside him, moving silently.

"There's a faint tingle about the fountain, enough to tell me that it was probably once enchanted," Geir said. "Not uncommon at the time it was built, if a family had a good mage on retainer."

"Do you think it's part of whatever Grimur was talking about?"

Geir shook his head. "No. There's no real power in the fountain, just a shadow of what was once there. Anything that still exists here is down below. And the only way to get to it is through the cistern."

"Do you think it leads under the manor?" Blaine asked.

"Hard to tell until we get there," Geir replied. "After the first war, long ago, the descendants rebuilt the keep," Geir said. "It fell into disuse and stood abandoned for a long time. I've heard it said the keep is haunted; the locals appear to have believed that. They left it alone, didn't even steal stones for their fences. The Meroven strike knocked down whatever was still standing, and you can see that the Great Fire left its mark." He paused, and then nodded toward a ruined building toward the lower end of the compound. "What we need is down there."

They picked their way over the tumbled stone that had once been the cistern house's walls. That the building's roof had survived until the Great Fire was evidence that magic had protected the keep and its buildings until very recently. Geir had thrown aside many of the burned timbers of its roof, a task that would have taken the strength of many mortal men. Beneath the wreckage was a large cistern.

Blaine could tell at a glance that the cistern was old; when he moved closer, it was obvious from the age of the stone that the cistern had been in use for many lifetimes. He peered down, but could see nothing.

"Down about twenty feet, there's a ledge about a foot wide around the inside," Geir said. "I imagine when this was in use, the ledge didn't keep anyone from using the cistern."

"Why would anyone build a secret room off the side of a cistern?" Piran asked, holding tight to the edge and leaning down so far that Kestel grabbed him by the belt to keep him from falling.

"The cistern is old and very deep. I suspect it taps into an underground river. Such places are a potent focus for magic," Geir said. "I also would guess that the cistern entrance wasn't intended as the front door. There was probably a connection through caves or tunnels into the lowest floor of the manor, but it's likely those were sealed off when the house collapsed."

"Are you sure about this?" Kestel asked. The torchlight heightened the red-gold color of her hair. She looked uncertain, but determined.

"We're not totally 'sure' about any of this," Geir replied. "But from the clues we have, it looks like our best option—unless we dig out the manor."

"I guess we're as ready as we'll ever be," Blaine said when they looked at him, awaiting his signal. "Let's go."

Blaine quietly gave orders to four of the guards to fan out along the perimeter, while the remaining two stood near the cistern. Piran unfolded a long rope ladder he had carried in his saddlebags and Dawe helped him fasten it to the cistern's side. Kestel readied a torch and lanterns for the descent.

Geir descended first, levitating down without need of the ladder. Verran came second to work the formidable lock on the door. Piran and Dawe remained above, waiting to see if Verran could get the lock open. Kestel was next, dropping lightly down to the ledge.

Blaine made a point of not looking at the water below him as he climbed down the rope ladder. The cistern was made from blocks of hand-hewn stone that fit tightly together even after centuries of use. Moss clung to the stone in places, and the farther down the cistern Blaine descended, the colder it became.

He carefully stepped onto the narrow ledge. Blaine could hear the distant sound of flowing water, and cast an uneasy glance toward the depths below. He looked toward where the others stood in the passageway leading to the door. It was recessed several feet into the rock, with a doorframe of intricately carved stone. From where Blaine stood, he could not make out the carvings in the torchlight, but saw Verran run a hand tentatively just above the stone and heard him let out a low whistle.

"I don't think this is a door to the root cellar," Verran said quietly, his voice echoing in the confined space. "Someone went to a lot of trouble to carve runes of protection on the lintel and doorposts."

"Do you pick up any magic?" Kestel asked, holding the torch closer so that Verran could see better.

Verran shook his head. "Not anything active. But there's still a residue of power, so whatever warded the door must have been quite strong, or there'd be no trace left at all. I'm glad we're tackling it now, instead of when it was at full strength."

"What's the lock like?" Blaine asked.

Verran crouched close to the handle and its large, ornately wrought iron lock. "Offhand, I'd say it's a lot like the box in your father's room, a Tollerby mechanism. Watch yourselves: It'll be nasty in a small space like this when it sends out its spike."

"Can you work the lock without getting hit?" Kestel asked.

Verran gave a nervous smile. "We'll see, won't we?" He hesitated. "Perhaps the rest of you should move out of the passageway and over to the side, just in case this lock has a surprise."

Blaine looked down as the others spread out along the ledge. Geir had levitated silently down below the ledge, his blond hair barely visible in the torchlight. After a few moments, as Verran was deep in concentration working the lock, Geir rejoined them.

"Well?" Blaine asked in a hushed voice, with a glance toward Verran to make sure he had not disturbed anything.

Geir shrugged. "Just being careful. The cistern is even deeper than I thought, but there are no other ledges or doors that I can see. The deeper I went, the louder the sound of running water, so I think the guess about an underground river was correct. Such 'deep places' are believed to have substantial natural magic, and they would be an ideal source of power for a ritual chamber, especially if someone intended to access natural magic and mold it to their will."

Geir hesitated and closed his eyes. He swayed, and Blaine reached out a hand to steady him. When Geir opened his eyes, he looked at Blaine with concern. "A sending from Penhallow, through the *kruvgaldur*. It's a warning. We're in danger. No other details, except a strong sense that we should leave." He met Blaine's gaze. "I don't think he wants us to enter the chamber."

Blaine swore under his breath. "With Pollard and his men around, there's no telling when we'll get another chance. I'm as leery about this as anyone else, but we need to know if there's anything to the maps and the disks. If I go in there and nothing happens, then we go looking for Quintrel. But at least we'll know where we stand." He shook his head. "I'm going in."

Verran gave a muted cry of triumph. "I've almost got it.

Watch out; the dart's coming." With that, the lock mechanism gave a resounding click and a thin iron spike flashed across the well at deadly speed, sinking into the stone wall. The heavy wooden door swung open. "We're in."

Geir signaled for Piran and Dawe to descend, and two of the Glenreith guards took their place at the cistern's mouth. Verran was happy to hand off the torch to Piran. Geir, who needed no extra light, led the way down the corridor that opened from the doorway. Blaine followed, with the rest filing in behind him. They walked for a long while in silence. The passageway sloped slightly up from the opening in the cistern and turned several sharp corners.

"Where do you think this takes us?" Kestel whispered.

Blaine shrugged. "I'm guessing that we'll end up somewhere underneath the keep. I don't think the cistern door was ever meant to be the main way in and out; whoever built this corridor probably meant it as an escape tunnel."

A new door stopped their progress. Verran moved forward, with Piran holding the torch so he could see.

"Same type of runes and lock as the first door," Verran mused aloud. "Better get against the wall, in case there's another dart."

They waited in silence as Verran worked the lock. The Tollerby mechanism gave with a click, propelling a dart with enough force to send it down the corridor beyond the glow of the torch. A rush of stale air reached them as Verran cautiously opened the door and stood aside.

Kestel and Dawe found torches in sconces near the door and lit them, illuminating the large underground room. Part of its ceiling was hewn from solid rock, and Blaine wondered if it was a natural cave. The rest had been reinforced with stone in high barrel vaults.

From the antechamber, they passed into an even larger ceremonial hall. On the far side of this room, the walls were damaged, and rubble was piled in front of what might have been another doorway. The walls of the ceremonial hall and its floor had been chiseled smooth, and the walls bore detailed paintings of thirteen constellations at intervals around the room. Set into the floor were pavers in an elaborate labyrinth pattern.

"Thirteen constellations, thirteen Lords of the Blood," Kestel said in a hushed voice.

Blaine felt beneath his tunic for the obsidian disk from his father's room. It seemed to tingle at the touch of his fingers, and he wondered if he was imagining the sensation. "Either something big is going to happen, or we've all wasted our time," Blaine said, stepping forward. "I'm going to walk the path. The rest of you, stay by the wall."

Blaine gingerly placed one foot on the labyrinth pathway, alert for danger. When nothing happened, he took a tentative step, and then another. He had reread the cryptic notes in Grimur's book and examined the disk in great detail, but he still felt completely unprepared. *I have no magic of any significance,* he thought. *I'm qualified to be here only because I'm still alive. And I have absolutely no idea what I'm supposed to do except show up with the damned disk.*

The closer he got to the center of the labyrinth, the more the room's layout became clear. The thirteen constellations corresponded with thirteen circles on the floor, circles that reminded Blaine of the obsidian disks and their odd patterns of markings and slits. He knew from the paper in his father's trunk that each of the original thirteen Lords of the Blood had their place in the ritual circle, and that the carvings in the stone might well match those in the missing disks. He'd memorized the drawing on the paper, and now he headed toward the place in the labyrinth that had been marked with his family's symbol. Stones carved with runes were set alongside the labyrinth pathway.

As he neared the center of the labyrinth, he felt as if he were moving against an invisible force. Yet just beyond the maze's center, he could see the circle on the floor that looked to be the best match to the disk he wore. The last few steps to the heart of the labyrinth seemed to require all of his strength, but with effort, he stepped onto the red stone nexus.

Light flashed, and a white-hot bolt of wild energy caught Blaine full in the chest, furious as the magic storms they had survived aboveground. Uncontrolled, rogue power crackled in the air. A scream tore from Blaine's throat as the light seemed to boil through his veins.

I've triggered something, Blaine thought as he fell to his knees. *Was it meant to be a trap? Maybe this is what Penhallow was trying to warn us about. Or did the death of magic make the ritual power go wild, like the storms?*

Kestel's scream echoed from the rock walls, followed by a cry of pain. She fell to her knees clutching her head. Verran and Dawe also fell, anguish clear in their faces. Piran stood longer and then cried out and toppled backward. Geir was the last to go down, and Blaine could see determination warring with pain in the *talishte*'s face.

"Blaine—get out of there!" Geir shouted, his voice hoarse. He crumpled against the stone wall and lay still.

The light flared, making it impossible for Blaine to see. Excruciating pain radiated from where the bolt pinned him, and Blaine could hear his blood thundering in his ears. His body convulsed, shuddering uncontrollably, and Blaine could not draw breath. His vision blurred, reduced to dancing pinpoints of light as he gasped for air, and consciousness slipped away, leaving nothing but darkness and pain.

*　　　*　　　*

Gradually, the pain receded. He had no idea how long he lay on the stone floor of the vault. Blaine groaned and opened his eyes, managing to turn his head slightly to one side.

He could see the bodies of his friends around him, motionless on the floor. Blaine felt panic rise in his chest. *Sweet Charrot, don't let them all be dead because of me.*

Blaine drifted in and out of awareness, unable to tell whether it was sleep or unconsciousness that took him. The air around them had grown bitterly cold, and all but one of the torches had guttered out. The attack had left him numb, unable to move, and the immobility coupled with the darkness triggered suffocating fear.

Faint light came from the doorway, and in it, the figures of men appeared. Blaine tried to hail them, but only a rasp escaped his lips.

"Over here!" Boots crunched on the stone floor as their guards entered the room. This time, no wild magic flared.

"Can you stand?" The captain of the guards bent over Blaine. "We've got a situation topside."

"What kind of situation?" Blaine asked, using all of his willpower to pull himself up.

"There's a sizable force headed this direction. Toley and Danner took the wagons and horses back the way we came so they wouldn't give us away, and threw the rope ladder down to us. Said they saw armed men, at least thirty strong. We didn't think a fight would go in our favor, so I'm hoping there's another way out, or we're stuck down here for a while," the captain replied.

To Blaine's relief, the others were stirring, helped to stand by the guards. Blaine pointed to the rubble at the other side of the room. "There might be a door under there, but no telling where it leads."

The captain grinned. "Anywhere away from here is good," he said. He turned to the guards. "Let's get to it, men."

Verran and Kestel locked the door to the cistern passageway while the others made slow progress clearing the ruined doorway. Geir insisted on being at the forefront, protected more than once from falling stone by his *talishte* reflexes. They worked as quietly as possible, unable to tell whether the armed troops had stopped in the ruins above them.

The doorway opened into a tunnel, but the first several feet of the passageway had collapsed. Gradually, they cleared the rocks away until an opening was big enough to pass through.

"Where do you think it goes?" Blaine said to Geir.

"Back under the old fort, would be my guess," Geir replied. "Of course, given the damage the fort has taken over the years—and in the Great Fire—there's no guarantee that we can get through at the other end."

Blaine shrugged. "Unless you want to take your chances with a small army up top, I don't see that we've got a choice."

Armed with torches, they filed carefully through the doorway and into the dark tunnel. Geir went on ahead, not needing the torchlight. He returned a few minutes later.

"There's some blockage down the way a bit, but I think we can clear it. From what I can tell, the ceiling looks sturdy. And I found this," he said, holding out a small leather book.

"What is it?" Blaine asked.

"I couldn't see much, but what I saw looked like mage symbols. And several of the pages are signed with a 'V.' "

Blaine looked up sharply. "Vigus Quintrel?"

"That would be my guess. Why the book is here, I don't know, but I don't think it's been down here for very long, which means someone else passed this way fairly recently." Geir paused. "I don't think the passageway collapsed. I think it was intentionally blocked."

"To prevent anyone from using the ritual chamber?"

"Maybe. Or to protect it. No way to know."

Blaine took the book and slipped it into his shirt for safekeeping. They soon reached the next place where the tunnel was blocked, and worked in shifts to clear away the fallen rock, passing the stones back along a human chain to clear the way. Once again, Geir scouted on ahead, and this time, he returned with a smile.

"We can get into the cellars of the old fort. I didn't go farther than that, but at least it gets us out of the tunnels," he reported.

Tired, hungry, and covered with dirt, the group climbed through a narrow opening into a large room. Blocks of hewn stone formed the walls of a cellar large enough to hold them all with room to spare.

"The question is—are we trapped in here?" Piran muttered.

A large slab of stone blocked the cellar's entrance. Without Geir's *talishte* strength, Blaine wasn't sure they would have been able to move the stone, but together, they forced it back far enough for everyone to squeeze through, and then put it back to conceal their escape route.

They found themselves in what remained of a storage room. The ceiling, like the floors that once were above the room, was long gone. Ruined walls remained, open to the elements. By the position of the moon, Blaine could see that the night was far spent.

Wordlessly, the captain tapped Blaine on the shoulder, indicating with a gesture toward the courtyard near the cistern's entrance. Soldiers armed with broadswords roamed the area, but none of them seemed to focus on the cistern itself. Nor was their attention at the moment focused on the ruined fortress.

Two by two, they stole away, moving silently in the darkness. To Blaine's relief, they found the guards and their horses waiting safely a short distance from Mirdalur. Only then did they feel comfortable speaking, and only after Geir had scouted the area and confirmed that they were alone.

"Do you think those were Pollard's men?" Kestel asked in a near whisper.

"Hard to tell, m'lady," the captain replied. "I didn't see any insignia. Since the Fire, there've been armed bands springing up everywhere. No telling whose they are."

They mounted up and rode single file, anxious to put distance between themselves and Mirdalur before dawn. When they had traveled several miles without incident, Kestel rode up alongside Blaine.

"What now?"

Blaine thought about the failed attempt in the chamber beneath Mirdalur, and the leather-bound book inside his shirt. "Pollard and Reese apparently think that one Lord of the Blood might bring back the magic. So do I."

"Mirdalur didn't work," Kestel said.

"We don't know what Penhallow's found out, or what's in this book." Blaine tapped the journal beneath his shirt. He met her gaze. "Pollard's not going to quit coming after me until one of us is dead," he replied. "I've got other plans. First, we'll figure out what happened to Penhallow and Connor. Then, I'm going after Vigus Quintrel. Magic or no magic, I'm going to get this settled, once and for all."

extras

orbit

meet the author

Donna Jernigan

GAIL Z. MARTIN discovered her passion for SF, fantasy, and ghost stories in elementary school. The first story she wrote—at age five—was about a vampire. Her favorite TV show as a preschooler was *Dark Shadows*. At age fourteen she decided to become a writer. She enjoys attending SF/Fantasy conventions, Renaissance fairs, and living-history sites. She is married and has three children, a Himalayan cat, and a golden retriever. For book updates, tour information, and contact details, visit www.AscendantKingdoms.com. Gail is the host of the Ghost in the Machine Fantasy Podcast, and you can find her on Facebook (The Winter Kingdoms), Goodreads, Shelfari, and Twitter (@GailZMartin). She blogs at www.DisquietingVisions.com.

interview

Your previous five novels, including the Chronicles of the Necromancer books and the Fallen Kings Cycle, were all set in the same world and featured many of the same characters. Ice Forged *marks the beginning of a new series. How much of a departure are we in for? How did the new series come about?*

This is a whole new enchilada! Brand-new world, completely new characters, totally new magic system and gods.

I love my Fallen Kings Cycle and Chronicles of the Necromancer series characters (and do plan to come back to tell more stories about them at some point), but let's be honest— after everything I've put them through, in what for the characters is a little over two years, the survivors really deserve to put their feet up and have a few beers for a while.

So I'd been playing with the idea of what if magic broke (as it nearly did in the Chronicles books), and what if we had a postapocalyptic medieval world, and what if a world sent its convicts to the northern rim (instead of, in our world, Australia)...and I was off and running.

One element Ice Forged *shares with your previous series is vampires. What about them fascinates you? How do they enhance the way you build your worlds?*

extras

I watched *Dark Shadows* when I was in preschool (what *was* my mom thinking?), and the first story I "wrote," at age five (I had to have my grandmother write it down because I couldn't spell yet) was about a vampire. I've been hooked ever since. In my world of the Winter Kingdoms, you saw vampires as a paranormal minority, treated as ethnic minorities have been in our world—accepted in some places, persecuted or tolerated in others. In the new Ascendant Kingdoms Saga, the vampires (*talishte*) are more rare, although not the only immortals. I enjoy looking at the world through the eyes of a character who has lived several lifetimes and wonder what would keep you wanting to stick around? Would it be power? Wealth? Family? Nostalgia? The answer, I believe, is highly personal to the specific *talishte*. I think they represent both the ultimate outsider and a melancholy creative force. For those few who do choose to remain among mortals for hundreds of years, there has to be a good story. I want to tell that story.

In your novels, magic appears as a kind of vast natural force. In Ice Forged *particularly, magic is taken for granted and incompletely understood by the people wielding it. Does anything from our reality guide how you present magic in your fiction?*

I've always been intrigued by the idea of magic as a force of nature. Those with a talent for magic have an inborn ability to sense and use the power. In the world of the Ascendant Kingdoms, magic is much more prevalent than in the Winter Kingdoms books—until the magic disappears, and the civilization that utilized it crumbles. In that sense, magic becomes a natural resource, like water or fertile ground, and when any civilization takes its resources for granted, problems ensue.

History is full of vanished civilizations that thrived and then disappeared because a river changed course, land was over-farmed, or other natural catastrophes made the resources unusable. Modern-day postapocalyptic fiction doesn't intrigue me (a long story, but it has to do with my upbringing, which expected the end of the world at any moment by various means), but I was interested in how it might play out under these circumstances in a medieval setting. So here we are!

Despite some pretty harsh conditions, your characters manage to sit down to some delicious-sounding meals on occasion. Where do you get your menu ideas?

I'm constantly amazed at the ingenuity of our ancestors when it came to putting a good meal on the table despite rudimentary tools. When you realize all the cakes, breads, roasts, and other goodies that were cooked over an open fire or in an oven with no temperature control, you just have to stand in awe. Fortunately, many of the recipes have survived, or at least been approximated thanks to historians and the Society for Creative Anachronism, and have been posted online. So when I'm at a loss for a menu, I go Web-surfing and always find mouthwatering, historically correct options!

In the rare moments when you're not writing, what do you do for fun?

I like hanging out with my husband, three teenage children, my dog, and some friends. So that includes movies (yes, usually SF/F), reading, going to Renaissance festivals when I'm not signing books, and hanging out at Disney World (so shoot me, I'm a Mickey fan—I think Walt Disney was the ultimate creative genius). I don't read as much epic stuff as I used to, not wanting to be influenced, but I do read a lot of urban fantasy, paranormal mystery, and plain-old mystery (I usually post the books I've read in any given month on my Twitter account @GailZMartin and on Shelfari). With all the travel I do, I read a *lot*—around a hundred books a year! Fortunately, I really do enjoy going to conventions as a fan as well as an author, so when I'm not on panels, I like hanging out and getting my geek on. I love to go to Myrtle Beach and veg with a book in hand, and I also love to spend time with extended family in Pennsylvania. Lots to do!

introducing

If you enjoyed
ICE FORGED,
look out for

THE DRAGON'S PATH

The Dagger and the Coin 1

by Daniel Abraham

All paths lead to war...

Marcus's hero days are behind him. He knows too well that even the smallest war still means somebody's death. When his men are impressed into a doomed army, staying out of a battle he wants no part of requires some unorthodox steps.

Cithrin is an orphan, ward of a banking house. Her job is to smuggle a nation's wealth across a war zone, hiding the gold from both sides. She knows the secret life of commerce like a second language, but the strategies of trade will not defend her from swords.

Geder, sole scion of a noble house, has more interest in philosophy than in swordplay. A poor excuse for a soldier, he is a pawn in these games. No one can predict what he will become.

extras

Falling pebbles can start a landslide. A spat between the Free Cities and the Severed Throne is spiraling out of control. A new player rises from the depths of history, fanning the flames that will sweep the entire region onto The Dragon's Path—the path to war.

The apostate pressed himself into the shadows of the rock and prayed to nothing in particular that the things riding mules in the pass below him would not look up. His hands ached, the muscles of his legs and back shuddered with exhaustion. The thin cloth of his ceremonial robes fluttered against him in the cold, dust-scented wind. He took the risk of looking down toward the trail.

The five mules had stopped, but the priests hadn't dismounted. Their robes were heavier, warmer. The ancient swords strapped across their backs caught the morning light and glittered a venomous green. Dragon-forged, those blades. They meant death to anyone whose skin they broke. In time, the poison would kill even the men who wielded them. All the more reason, the apostate thought, that his former brothers would kill him quickly and go home. No one wanted to carry those blades for long; they came out only in dire emergency or deadly anger.

Well. At least it was flattering to be taken seriously.

The priest leading the hunting party rose up in his saddle, squinting into the light. The apostate recognized the voice.

"Come out, my son," the high priest shouted. "There is no escape."

The apostate's belly sank. He shifted his weight, preparing to walk down. He stopped himself.

Probably, he told himself. *There is* probably *no escape. But perhaps there is.*

On the trail, the dark-robed figures shifted, turned, consulted among themselves. He couldn't hear their words. He waited, his body growing stiffer and colder. Like a corpse that hadn't had the grace to die. Half a day seemed to pass while the hunters below him conferred, though the sun barely changed its angle in the bare blue sky. And then, between one breath and the next, the mules moved forward again.

He didn't dare move for fear of setting a pebble rolling down the steep cliffs. He tried not to grin. Slowly, the things that had once been men rode their mules down the trail to the end of the valley, and then followed the wide bend to the south. When the last of them slipped out of sight, he stood, hands on his hips, and marveled. He still lived. They had not known where to find him after all.

Despite everything he'd been taught, everything he had until recently believed, the gifts of the spider goddess did not show the truth. It gave her servants something, yes, but not *truth*. More and more, it seemed his whole life had sprung from a webwork of plausible lies. He should have felt lost. Devastated. Instead, it was like he'd walked from a tomb into the free air. He found himself grinning.

The climb up the remaining western slope bruised him. His sandals slipped. He struggled for finger- and toeholds. But as the sun reached its height, he reached the ridge. To the west, mountain followed mountain, and great billowing clouds towered above them, thunderstorms a soft veil of grey. But in the farthest passes, he saw the land level. Flatten. Distance made the plains grey-blue, and the wind on the mountain's peak cut at his skin like claws. Lightning flashed on the horizon. As if in answer, a hawk shrieked.

It would take weeks alone and on foot. He had no food, and worse, no water. He'd slept the last five nights in caves and under bushes. His former brothers and friends—the men he had known and loved his whole life—were combing the trails and villages, intent on his death. Mountain lions and dire wolves hunted in the heights.

He ran a hand through his thick, wiry hair, sighed, and began the downward climb. He would probably die before he reached the Keshet and a city large enough to lose himself in.

But only *probably*.

In the last light of the falling sun, he found a stony overhang near a thin, muddy stream. He sacrificed a length of the strap from his right sandal to fashion a crude fire bow, and as the cruel chill came down from the sky, he squatted next to the high ring of stones that hid his small fire. The dry scrub burned hot and with little smoke, but quickly. He fell into a rhythm of feeding small twig after small twig into the flame, never letting it grow large enough to illuminate his shelter to those hunting and never letting it die. The warmth didn't seem to reach past his elbows.

Far off, something shrieked. He tried to ignore it. His body ached with exhaustion and spent effort, but his mind, freed now from the constant distraction of his journey, gained a dangerous speed. In the darkness, his memory sharpened. The sense of freedom and possibility gave way to loss, loneliness, and dislocation. Those, he believed, were more likely to kill him than a hunting cat.

He had been born in hills much like these. Passed his youth playing games of sword and whip using branches and woven bark. Had he ever felt the ambition to join the ranks of the monks in their great hidden temple? He must have, though from the biting cold of his poor stone shelter, it was hard to imagine it. He could remember looking up with awe at the high wall of stone. At the rock-carved sentries from all the thirteen races of humanity worn by wind and rain until all of them—Cinnae and Tralgu, Southling and Firstblood, Timzinae and Yemmu and Drowned—wore the same blank faces and clubbed fists. Indistinguishable. Only the wide wings and dagger teeth of the dragon arching above them all were still clear. And worked into the huge iron gate, black letters spelled out words in a language no one in the village knew.

When he became a novice, he learned what it said. BOUND IS NOT BROKEN. He had believed once that he knew what it meant.

The breeze shifted, raising the embers like fireflies. A bit of ash stung his eye, and he rubbed at it with the back of his hand. His blood shifted, currents in his body responding to something that was not him. The goddess, he'd thought. He had gone to the great gate with the other boys of his village. He had offered himself up—life and body—and in return...

In return the mysteries had been revealed. First, it had only been knowledge: letters enough to read the holy books, numbers enough to keep the temple's records. He had read the stories of the Dragon Empire and its fall. Of the spider goddess coming to bring justice to the world.

Deception, they said, had no power over her.

He'd tested it, of course. He believed them, and still he had tested. He would lie to the priests, just to see whether it could be done. He'd chosen things that only he could know: his father's clan name, his sister's favorite meals, his own dreams. The priests had whipped him when he spoke false, they had spared him when he was truthful, and they were never, *never* wrong. His certainty had grown. His faith. When the high priest had chosen him to rise to novice, he'd been certain that great things awaited him, because the priests had told him that they did.

After the nightmare of his initiation was over, he'd felt the power of the spider goddess in his own blood. The first time he'd felt someone lie, it had been like discovering a new sense. The first time he had spoken with the voice of the goddess, he'd felt his words commanding belief as if they had been made from fire.

And now he had fallen from grace, and none of it might be true. There might be no such place as the Keshet. He believed there was, so much so that he had risked his life on flight to it. But he had never been there. The marks on the maps could be lies. For that matter, there might have been no dragons, no empire, no great war. He had never seen the ocean; there might be no such thing. He knew only what he himself had seen and heard and felt.

He knew *nothing*.

On violent impulse, he sank his teeth into the flesh of his palm. His blood welled up, and he cupped it. In the faint firelight, it looked nearly black. Black, with small, darker knots. One of the knots unfurled tiny legs. The spider crawled mindlessly around the cup of his hand. Another one joined it. He watched them: the agents of the goddess in whom he no longer believed. Carefully, slowly, he tipped his hand over the small flame. One of the spiders fell into it, hair-thin legs shriveling instantly.

"Well," he said. "You can die. I know *that*."

The mountains seemed to go on forever, each crest a new threat, each valley thick with danger. He skirted the small villages, venturing close only to steal a drink from the stone cisterns. He ate lizards and the tiny flesh-colored nuts of scrub pine. He avoided the places where wide, clawed paws marked paths in the dirt. One night, he found a circle of standing pillars with a small chamber beneath them that seemed to offer shelter and a place to recover his strength, but his sleep there had been troubled by dreams so violent and alien that he pushed on instead.

He lost weight, the woven leather of his belt hanging low around his waist. His sandals' soles thinned, and his fire bow wore out quickly. Time lost its meaning. Day followed day followed day. Every morning he thought, *This will probably be the last day of my life. Only probably.*

The *probably* was always enough. And then, late one morning, he pulled himself to the top of a boulder-strewn hill, and there wasn't another to follow it. The wide western plains spread out before him, a river shining in its cloak of green grass and trees. The view was deceptive. He guessed it would still be two days on foot before he reached it. Still, he sat on a wide, rough stone, looked out over the world, and let himself weep until almost midday.

As he came nearer to the river, he felt a new anxiety start to gnaw at his belly. On the day, weeks ago, when he had slipped over the temple's wall and fled, the idea of disappearing into a city had been a distant concern. Now he saw the smoke of a hundred cookfires rising from the trees. The marks of wild animals were scarce. Twice, he saw men riding huge horses in the distance. The dusty rags of his robe, the ruins of his sandals, and the reek of his own unwashed skin reminded him that this was as difficult and as dangerous as anything he'd done to now. How would the men and women of the Keshet greet a wild man from the mountains? Would they cut him down out of hand?

He circled the city by the river, astounded at the sheer size of the place. He had never seen anything so large. The long wooden buildings with their thatched roofs could have held a thousand people. The roads were paved in stone. He kept to the underbrush like a thief, watching.

It was the sight of a Yemmu woman that gave him courage. That and his hunger. At the fringe of the city, where the last of the houses sat between road and river, she labored in her garden. She was half again as tall as he was, and broad as a bull across the shoulders. Her tusks rose from her jaw until she seemed in danger of piercing her own cheeks if she laughed. Her breasts hung high above a peasant girdle not so different from the ones his own mother and sister had worn, only with three times the cloth and leather.

She was the first person he had ever seen who wasn't a Firstblood. The first real evidence that the thirteen races of humanity truly existed. Hiding behind the bushes, peeking at her as she leaned in the soft earth and plucked weeds between gigantic fingers, he felt something like wonder.

He stepped forward before he could talk himself back into cowardice. Her wide head rose sharply, her nostrils flaring. He raised a hand, almost in apology.

"Forgive me," he said. "I'm ... I'm in trouble. And I was hoping you might help me."

The woman's eyes narrowed to slits. She lowered her stance like a hunting cat preparing for battle. It occurred to him that it might have been wiser to discover if she spoke his language before he'd approached her.

"I've come from the mountains," he said, hearing the desperation in his own voice. And hearing something else besides. The inaudible thrumming of his blood. The gift of the spider goddess commanding the woman to believe him.

"We don't trade with Firstbloods," the Yemmu woman growled. "Not from those twice-shat mountains anyway. Get away from here, and take your men with you."

"I don't have any men," he said. The things in his blood roused themselves, excited to be used. The woman shifted her head as his stolen magic convinced her. "I'm alone. And unarmed. I've been walking for…weeks. I can work if you'd like. For a little food and a warm place to sleep. Just for the night."

"Alone and unarmed. Through the mountains?"

"Yes."

She snorted, and he had the sense he was being evaluated. Judged.

"You're an idiot," she said.

"Yes," he said. "I am. Friendly, though. Harmless."

It was a very long moment before she laughed.

She set him to hauling river water to her cistern while she finished her gardening. The bucket was fashioned for Yemmu hands, and he could only fill it half full before it became too heavy to lift. But he struggled manfully from the little house to the rough wooden platform and then back again. He was careful not to scrape himself, or at least not so badly as to draw blood. His welcome was uncertain enough without the spiders to explain.

At sunset, she made a place for him at her table. The fire in the pit seemed extravagant, and he had to remind himself that the things that had been his brothers weren't here, scanning for signs of him. She scooped a bowl of stew from the pot above the fire. It had the rich, deep, complex flavor of a constant pot; the stewpot never leaving the fire, and new hanks of meat and vegetables thrown in as they came to hand. Some of the bits of dark flesh swimming in the greasy broth might have been cooking since before he'd left the temple. It was the best meal he'd ever had.

"My man's at the caravanserai," she said. "One of the princes s'posed to be coming in, and they'll be hungry. Took all the pigs with. Sell 'em all if we're lucky. Get enough silver to see us through storm season."

581

He listened to her voice and also the stirring in his blood. The last part had been a lie. She *didn't* believe that the silver would last. He wondered if it worried her, and if there was some way he could see she had what she needed. He would try, at least. Before he left.

"What about you, you poor shit?" she asked, her voice soft and warm. "Whose sheep did you fuck that you're begging work from me?"

The apostate chuckled. The warm food in his belly, the fire at his side, and the knowledge that a pallet of straw and a thin wool blanket were waiting for him outside conspired to relax his shoulders and his belly. The Yemmu woman's huge gold-flecked eyes stayed on him. He shrugged.

"I discovered that believing something doesn't make it true," he said carefully. "There were things I'd accepted, that I believed to my bones, and I was...wrong."

"Misled?" she asked.

"Misled," he agreed, and then paused. "Or perhaps not. Not intentionally. No matter how wrong you are, it's not a lie if you believe it."

The Yemmu woman whistled—an impressive feat, considering her tusks—and flapped her hands in mock admiration.

"High philosophy from the water grunt," she said. "Next you'll be preaching and asking tithes."

"Not me," he said, laughing with her.

She took a long slurp from her own bowl. The fire crackled. Something—rats, perhaps, or insects—rattled in the thatch overhead.

"Fell out with a woman, did you?" she asked.

"A goddess," he said.

"Yeah. Always seems like that, dunit?" she said, staring into the fire. "Some new love comes on like there's something different about 'em. Like God himself talks whenever their lips flap. And then..."

She snorted again, part amusement, part bitterness.

"And what all went wrong with your goddess?" she asked.

The apostate lifted a scrap of something that might have been a potato to his mouth, chewed the soft flesh, the gritty skin. He struggled to put words to thoughts that had never been spoken aloud. His voice trembled.

"She is going to eat the world."